private
peaceful

KT-143-438

With my thanks to Piet Chielens of
In Flanders Field Museum in Ypres

michael morpurgo

private peaceful

HarperCollins *Children's Books*

Although the title was inspired by the name on a gravestone in Ypres, this novel is a work of fiction. Any references to real people (living or dead), actual locales and historical events are used solely to lend the fiction an appropriate cultural and historical setting. All other names, characters, places and incidents portrayed in this book are the product of the author's imagination, and any resemblance to actual persons, living or dead, is entirely coincidental.

First published in hardback in Great Britain by HarperCollins*Children's Books* 2003
First published in paperback in Great Britain by HarperCollins*Children's Books* 2004
HarperCollins*Children's Books* is a division of HarperCollins*Publishers* Ltd,
77-85 Fulham Palace Road, Hammersmith, London W6 8JB

The HarperCollins website address is
www.harpercollins.co.uk

45

Text copyright © Michael Morpurgo 2003

Michael Morpurgo asserts the moral right to be identified
as the author of this work.

ISBN-13   978 0 00 7150076

Printed and bound in England by
Clays Ltd, St Ives plc

Conditions of Sale
This book is sold subject to the condition that it shall not, by way of trade
or otherwise, be lent, re-sold, hired out or otherwise circulated without the
publisher's prior written consent in any form of binding or cover other than
that in which it is published and without a similar condition including this
condition being imposed on the subsequent purchaser.

Mixed Sources
Product group from well-managed
forests and other controlled sources
www.fsc.org Cert no. SW-COC-1806
© 1996 Forest Stewardship Council

FSC is a non-profit international organisation established to promote the
responsible management of the world's forests. Products carrying the FSC
label are independently certified to assure consumers that they come
from forests that are managed to meet the social, economic and
ecological needs of present and future generations.

Find out more about HarperCollins and the environment at
www.harpercollins.co.uk/green

For my dear godmother,
Mary Niven

FIVE PAST TEN

They've gone now, and I'm alone at last. I have the whole night ahead of me, and I won't waste a single moment of it. I shan't sleep it away. I won't dream it away either. I mustn't, because every moment of it will be far too precious.

I want to try to remember everything, just as it was, just as it happened. I've had nearly eighteen years of yesterdays and tomorrows, and tonight I must remember as many of them as I can. I want tonight to be long, as long as my life, not filled with fleeting dreams that rush me on towards dawn.

Tonight, more than any other night of my life, I want to feel alive.

Charlie is taking me by the hand, leading me because he knows I don't want to go. I've never worn a collar before and it's choking me. My boots are strange and heavy on my feet. My heart is heavy too, because I dread what I am going to. Charlie has told me often how terrible this school-place is: about Mr Munnings and his raging tempers and the long whipping cane he hangs on the wall above his desk.

Big Joe doesn't have to go to school and I don't think that's fair at all. He's much older than me. He's even older than Charlie and he's never been to school. He stays at home with Mother, and sits up in his tree singing *Oranges and Lemons*, and laughing. Big Joe is always happy, always laughing. I wish I could be happy like him. I wish I could be at home like him. I don't want to go with Charlie. I don't want to go to school.

I look back, over my shoulder, hoping for a reprieve, hoping that Mother will come running after me and take me home. But she doesn't come and she doesn't come, and school and Mr Munnings and his cane are getting closer with every step.

"Piggyback?" says Charlie. He sees my eyes full of tears and knows how it is. Charlie always knows how it is. He's three years older than me, so he's done everything and knows everything. He's strong, too, and very good at piggybacks. So I hop up and cling on tight, crying behind my closed eyes, trying not to whimper out loud. But I cannot hold back my sobbing for long because I know that this morning is not the beginning of anything – not new and exciting as Mother says it is – but rather the end of my beginning. Clinging on round Charlie's neck I know that I am living the last moments of my carefree time, that I will not be the same person when I come home this afternoon.

I open my eyes and see a dead crow hanging from the

fence, his beak open. Was he shot, shot in mid-scream, as he began to sing, his raucous tune scarcely begun? He sways, his feathers still catching the wind even in death, his family and friends cawing in their grief and anger from the high elm trees above us. I am not sorry for him. It could be him that drove away my robin and emptied her nest of her eggs. My eggs. Five of them there had been, live and warm under my fingers. I remember I took them out one by one and laid them in the palm of my hand. I wanted them for my tin, to blow them like Charlie did and lay them in cotton wool with my blackbird's eggs and my pigeon's eggs. I would have taken them. But something made me draw back, made me hesitate. The robin was watching me from Father's rose bush, her black and beady eyes unblinking, begging me.

Father was in that bird's eyes. Under the rose bush, deep down, buried in the damp and wormy earth were all his precious things. Mother had put his pipe in first. Then Charlie laid his hobnail boots side by side, curled into each other, sleeping. Big Joe knelt down and covered the boots in Father's old scarf.

"Your turn, Tommo," Mother said. But I couldn't bring myself to do it. I was holding the gloves he'd worn the morning he died. I remembered picking one of them up. I knew what they did not know, what I could never tell them.

Mother helped me to do it in the end, so that Father's gloves lay there on top of his scarf, palms uppermost, thumbs touching. I felt those hands willing me not to do it, willing me to think again, not to take the eggs, not to take what was not mine. So I didn't do it. Instead I watched them grow, saw the first scrawny skeletal stirrings, the nest of gaping, begging beaks, the frenzied screeching at feeding time; witnessed too late from my bedroom window the last of the early-morning massacre, the parent robins watching like me, distraught and helpless, while the marauding crows made off skywards cackling, their murderous deed done. I don't like crows. I've never liked crows. That crow hanging there on the fence got what he deserved. That's what I think.

Charlie is finding the hill up into the village hard going. I can see the church tower and below it the roof of the school. My mouth is dry with fear. I cling on tighter.

"First day's the worst, Tommo," Charlie's saying, breathing hard. "It's not so bad. Honest." Whenever Charlie says "honest", I know it's not true. "Anyway I'll look after you."

That I do believe, because he always has. He does look after me too, setting me down, and walking me through all the boisterous banter of the school yard, his hand on my shoulder, comforting me, protecting me.

The school bell rings and we line up in two silent rows, about twenty children in each. I recognise some of them from Sunday school. I look around and realise that Charlie is no longer beside me. He's in the other line, and he's winking at me. I blink back and he laughs. I can't wink with one eye, not yet. Charlie always thinks that's very funny. Then I see Mr Munnings standing on the school steps cracking his knuckles in the suddenly silent school yard. He has tufty cheeks and a big belly under his waistcoat. He has a gold watch open in his hand. It's his eyes that are frightening and I know they are searching me out.

"Aha!" he cries, pointing right at me. Everyone has turned to look. "A new boy, a new boy to add to my trials and tribulations. Was not one Peaceful enough? What have I done to deserve another one? First a Charlie Peaceful, and now a Thomas Peaceful. Is there no end to my woes? Understand this, Thomas Peaceful, that here I am your lord and master. You do what I say when I say it. You do not cheat, you do not lie, you do not blaspheme. You do not come to school in bare feet. And your hands will be clean. These are my commandments. Do I make myself absolutely clear?"

"Yes sir," I whisper, surprised I can find my voice at all.

We file in past him, hands behind our backs. Charlie smiles across at me as the two lines part: "Tiddlers" into my classroom, "Bigguns" into his. I'm the littlest of the Tiddlers. Most of the Bigguns are even bigger than Charlie, fourteen years old some of them. I watch him until the door closes behind him and he's gone. Until this moment I have never known what it is to feel truly alone.

My bootlaces are undone. I can't tie laces. Charlie can,

11

but he's not here. I hear Mr Munnings' thunderous voice next door calling the roll and I am so glad we have Miss McAllister. She may speak with a strange accent, but at least she smiles, and at least she's not Mr Munnings.

"Thomas," she tells me, "you will be sitting there, next to Molly. And your laces are undone."

Everyone seems to be tittering at me as I take my place. All I want to do is to escape, to run, but I don't dare do it. All I can do is cry. I hang my head so they can't see my tears coming.

"Crying won't do your laces up, you know," Miss McAllister says.

"I can't, Miss," I tell her.

"Can't is not a word we use in my class, Thomas Peaceful," she says. "We shall just have to teach you to tie your bootlaces. That's what we're all here for, Thomas, to learn. That's why we come to school, don't we? You show him, Molly. Molly's the oldest girl in my class, Thomas, and my best pupil. She'll help you."

So while she calls the roll Molly kneels down in front of me and does up my laces. She ties laces very differently from Charlie, delicately, more slowly, in a great loopy double knot. She doesn't look up at me while she's doing it, not once, and I wish she would. She has hair the same colour as Billyboy, Father's old horse – chestnut brown and shining – and I want to reach out and touch it. Then she looks up at me at last and smiles. It's all I need. Suddenly I no longer want to run home. I want to stay here with Molly. I know I have a friend.

In playtime, in the school yard, I want to go over and talk to her, but I can't because she's always surrounded by a gaggle of giggling girls. They keep looking at me over their shoulders and laughing. I look for Charlie, but Charlie's splitting conkers open with his friends, all of them Bigguns. I go to sit on an old tree stump. I undo my bootlaces and try to do them up again remembering how Molly did it. I try again and again. After only a short while I find I can do it. It's untidy, and it's loose, but I can do it. Best of all, from across the school yard Molly sees I can do it, and smiles at me.

At home we don't wear boots, except for church. Mother does of course, and Father always wore his great hobnail boots, the boots he died in. When the tree came down I was there in the wood with him, just the two of us. Before I ever went to school he'd often take me off to work with him, to keep me out of mischief, he said. I'd ride up behind him on Billyboy and hang on round his waist, my face pressed into his back. Whenever Billyboy broke into a gallop I'd love it. We galloped all the way that morning, up the hill, up through Ford's Cleave Wood. I was still giggling when he lifted me down.

"Off you go, you scallywag, you," he said. "Enjoy yourself."

I hardly needed to be told. There were badger holes and fox holes to peer into, deer prints to follow perhaps, flowers to pick, or butterflies to chase. But that morning I found a mouse, a dead mouse. I buried it under a pile of leaves. I was making a wooden cross for it. Father was chopping away rhythmically nearby, grunting and groaning at every stroke as he always did. It sounded at first as if Father was just groaning a bit louder. That's what I thought it was. But then, strangely, the sound seemed to be coming not from where he was, but from somewhere high up in the branches.

I looked up to see the great tree above me swaying when all the other trees were standing still. It was creaking while all the other trees were silent. Only slowly did I realise it was coming down, and that when it fell it would fall right on top of me, that I was going to die and there was nothing I could do about it. I stood and stared, mesmerised at the gradual fall of it, my legs frozen under me, quite incapable of movement.

I hear Father shouting: "Tommo! Tommo! Run, Tommo!" But I can't. I see Father running towards me through the trees, his shirt flailing. I feel him catch me up and toss me aside in one movement, like a wheat sheaf. There is a roaring thunder in my ears and then no more.

When I wake I see Father at once, see the soles of his boots with their worn nails. I crawl over to where he is lying, pinned to the ground under the leafy crown of the great tree. He is on his back, his face turned away from me as if he doesn't want me to see. One arm is outstretched towards me, his glove fallen off, his finger pointing at me. There is blood coming from his nose, dropping on the leaves. His eyes are open, but I know at once they are not seeing me. He is not breathing. When I shout at him, when I shake him, he does not wake up. I pick up his glove.

In the church we're sitting side by side in the front row, Mother, Big Joe, Charlie and me. We've never in our lives sat in the front row before. It's where the Colonel and his family always sit. The coffin rests on trestles, my father inside in his Sunday suit. A swallow swoops over our heads all through the prayers, all through the hymns, flitting from window to window, from the belfry to the altar, looking for some way out. And I know for certain it is Father trying to escape. I know it because he told us more than once that in his next life he'd like to be a bird, so he could fly free wherever he wanted.

Big Joe keeps pointing up at the swallow. Then without any warning he gets up and walks to the back of the church where he opens the door. When he gets back he explains to Mother what he's done in his loud voice, and Grandma Wolf, sitting beside us in her black bonnet, scowls at him, at all of us. I know then what I never understood before, that she is ashamed to be one of us. I didn't really understand why until later, until I was older.

The swallow sits perched on a rafter high above the coffin. It lifts off and swoops up and down the aisle until at last it finds the open door and is gone. And I know that Father is happy now in his next life. Big Joe laughs out loud and Mother takes his hand in hers. Charlie catches my eye. At that moment all four of us are thinking the very same thing.

The Colonel gets up into the pulpit to speak, his hand clutching the lapel of his jacket. He declares that James Peaceful was a good man, one of the best workers he has ever known, the salt of the earth, always cheerful as he went about his work, that the Peaceful family had been employed in one capacity or another, by his family, for five generations. In all his thirty years as a forester on the estate James Peaceful had never once been late for work and was a credit to his family and his village. All the while as the Colonel drones on I'm thinking of the rude things Father used to say about him – "silly old fart", "mad old duffer" and much worse – and how Mother had always told us that he might well be a "silly old fart" or "mad old duffer", but how it was the Colonel who paid Father's wages and owned the roof over our heads, how we children should show respect when we met him, smile and touch our forelocks, and we should look as if we meant it too, if we knew what was good for us.

Afterwards we all gather round the grave and Father's lowered down, and the vicar won't stop talking. I want

Father to hear the birds for the last time before the earth closes in on top of him and he has nothing left but silence. Father loves larks, loves watching them rising, rising so high you can only see their song. I look up hoping for a lark, and there is a blackbird singing from the yew tree. A blackbird will have to do... I hear Mother whispering to Big Joe that Father is not really in his coffin any more, but in heaven up there – she's pointing up into the sky beyond the church tower – and that he's happy, happy as the birds.

The earth thuds and thumps down on the coffin behind us as we drift away, leaving him. We walk home together along the deep lanes, Big Joe plucking at the foxgloves and the honeysuckle, filling Mother's hands with flowers, and none of us has any tears to cry or words to say. Me least of all. For I have inside me a secret so horrible, a secret I can never tell anyone, not even Charlie. Father needn't have died that morning in Ford's Cleave Wood. He was trying to save me. If only I had tried to save myself, if I had run, he would not now be lying dead in his coffin. As Mother smooths my hair and Big Joe offers her yet another foxglove, all I can think is that I have caused this.

I have killed my own father.

TWENTY TO ELEVEN

I don't want to eat. Stew, potatoes and biscuits. I usually like stew, but I've no appetite for it. I nibble at a biscuit, but I don't want that either. Not now. It's a good thing Grandma Wolf is not here. She always hated us leaving food on our plates. "Waste not, want not," she'd say. I'm wasting this, Wolfwoman, whether you like it or not.

Big Joe ate more than all the rest of us put together. Everything was his favourite – bread and butter pudding with raisins, potato pie, cheese and pickle, stew and dumplings – whatever Mother cooked, he'd stuff it in and scoff it down. Anything Charlie and I didn't like we'd shuffle on to his plate when Mother wasn't looking. Big Joe always loved the conspiracy of that, and he loved the extra food too. There was nothing he wouldn't eat. When we were little, before we knew better, Charlie once bet me an owl's skull I'd found that Big Joe would even eat rabbit droppings. I couldn't believe he would, because I thought Big Joe must know what they were. So I took the bet. Charlie put a handful of them in a paper bag and told him they were sweets. Big Joe took them out of the bag and popped them into his mouth, savouring every one of them. And when we laughed, he laughed too and offered us one each. But Charlie said they were especially for him, a present. I thought Big Joe might get ill after that, but he never did.

Mother told us when we were older that Big Joe had nearly died just a few days after he was born. Meningitis, they told her at the hospital. The doctor said Joe had brain damage, that he'd be no use to anyone, even if he lived. But Big Joe did live, and he did get better, though never completely. As we were growing up, all we knew was that he was different. It didn't matter to us that he couldn't speak very well, that he couldn't read or write at all, that he didn't think like we did, like other people did. To us he was just Big Joe. He did frighten us sometimes. He seemed to drift off to live in a dream world of his own, often a world of nightmares I thought because he could become very agitated and upset. But sooner or later he always came back to us and would be himself again, the Big Joe we all knew, the Big Joe who loved everything and everyone, especially animals and birds and flowers, totally trusting, always forgiving – even when he found out that his sweets were rabbit droppings.

Charlie and I got into real trouble over that. Big Joe would never have found out, not by himself. But, always generous, he went and offered one of the rabbit droppings to Mother. She was so angry with us I thought she'd burst. She put a finger in Big Joe's mouth, scooped out what was still in there and made him wash it out. Then she made Charlie and me eat one rabbit dropping each so that we'd know what it was like.

"Horrible, isn't it?" she said. "Horrible food for horrible children. Don't you treat Big Joe like that ever again."

We felt very ashamed of ourselves – for a while anyway. Ever since then someone has only had to mention rabbits, for Charlie and me to smile at one another and remember. It's making me smile again now, even just thinking of it. It shouldn't, but it does.

In a way our lives at home always revolved around Big Joe. How we thought about people depended largely on how they behaved with our big brother. It was quite simple really: if people didn't like him or were offhand or treated him as if he was stupid, then we didn't like them. Most people around us were used to him, but some would look the other way, or worse still, just pretend he wasn't there. We hated that more than anything. Big Joe never seemed to mind, but we did on his behalf – like the day we blew raspberries at the Colonel.

No one at home ever spoke well of the Colonel, except Grandma Wolf of course. Whenever she came for her visits she wouldn't hear a word against him. She and Father would have dreadful rows about him. We grew up thinking of him mostly as just a "silly old fart". But the first time I saw for myself what the Colonel was really like, was because of Big Joe.

One evening Charlie and Big Joe and I were coming back home up the lane. We'd been fishing for brown trout in the brook. Big Joe had caught three, tickled them to sleep in the shallows and then scooped them out on to the bank before they knew what had happened. He was clever like that. It was almost as if he knew what the fish were thinking. He never liked killing them though, and nor did I. Charlie had to do that.

Big Joe always said hello, loudly, to everyone. It's how he was. So when the Colonel rode by that evening, Big Joe called out hello, and proudly held up his trout to show him. The Colonel trotted by as if he hadn't even seen us. When he'd passed Charlie blew a noisy raspberry after him, and Big Joe did the same because he liked rude noises. But the trouble was that Big Joe was enjoying himself so much blowing raspberries that he didn't stop. The Colonel reined in his horse and gave us a very nasty look. For a moment I thought he was going to come after us. Luckily he didn't, but he did crack his whip. "I'll teach you, you young ruffians!" he roared. "I'll teach you!"

I've always thought that was the moment the Colonel began to hate us, that from then on he was always determined one way or another to get his own back. We ran for it all the way home. Whenever anyone farts or blows raspberries I always think of that meeting in the lane, of how Big Joe always laughs at rude noises, laughs like he'll never stop. I think too of the menacing look in the Colonel's eye and the crack of his whip, and how Big Joe blowing raspberries at him that evening may well have changed our lives for ever.

It was Big Joe, too, who got me into my first fight. There was a lot of fighting at school, but I was never much good at it and always seemed to end up getting a swollen lip or a bleeding ear. I learned soon enough that if you don't want to get hurt you keep your head down and you don't answer back, particularly if the other fellow is bigger. But one day I discovered that sometimes you've got to stand up for yourself and fight for what's right, even when you don't want to.

It was at playtime. Big Joe came up to school to see Charlie and me. He just stood and watched us from outside the school gate. He did that often when Charlie and I first went off to school together – I think he was finding it lonely at home without us. I ran over to him. He was breathless, bright-eyed with excitement. He had something to show me. He opened his cupped hands just enough for me to be able to see. There was a slowworm curled up inside. I knew where he'd got it from – the churchyard, his favourite hunting ground. Whenever we went up to put flowers on Father's grave, Big

Joe would go off on his own, hunting for more creatures to add to his collection; that's when he wasn't just standing there gazing up at the tower and singing *Oranges and Lemons* at the top of his voice and watching the swifts screaming around the church tower. Nothing seemed to make him happier than that.

I knew Big Joe would put his slowworm in with all his other creatures. He kept them in boxes at the back of the woodshed at home – lizards, hedgehogs, all sorts. I stroked his slowworm with my finger, and said it was lovely, which it was. Then he wandered off, walking down the lane humming his *Oranges and Lemons* as he went, gazing down in wonder at his beloved slowworm.

I am watching him go when someone taps me hard on my shoulder, hard enough to hurt. It is big Jimmy Parsons. Charlie has often warned me about him, told me to keep out of his way. "Who's got a loony for a brother?" says Jimmy Parsons, sneering at me.

I cannot believe what he's said, not at first. "What did you say?"

"Your brother's a loony, off his head, off his rocker, nuts, barmy."

I go for him then, fists flailing, screaming at him, but I don't manage to land a single punch. He hits me full in the face and sends me sprawling. I find myself suddenly sitting on the ground, wiping my bleeding nose and looking at the blood on the back of my hand. Then he puts the boot in, hard. I curl up in a ball like a hedgehog to protect myself, but it doesn't seem to do me much good. He just goes on kicking me on my back, on my legs, anywhere he can. When he finally stops I wonder why.

I look up to see Charlie grabbing him round the neck and pulling him to the ground. They're rolling over and over, punching each other and swearing. The whole school has gathered round to watch now, egging them on. That's when Mr Munnings comes running out of the school, roaring like a raging bull. He pulls them apart, takes them by their collars and drags them off inside the school. Luckily for me Mr Munnings never even notices me sitting there, bleeding. Charlie gets the cane, and so does Jimmy Parsons – six strokes each. So Charlie saves me twice that day. The rest of us stand there in the school yard in silence, listening to the strokes and counting them. Big Jimmy Parsons gets it first, and he keeps crying out: "Ow, sir! Ow, sir! Ow, sir!" But when it's Charlie's turn, all we hear are the whacks, and then the silences in between. I am so proud of him for that. I have the bravest brother in the world.

Molly comes over and, taking me by the hand, leads me towards the pump. She soaks her handkerchief under it and dabs my nose and my hands and my knee – the blood seems to be everywhere. The water is wonderfully cold and soothing, and her hands are soft. She doesn't say anything for a while. She's dabbing me very gently, very carefully so as not to hurt me. Then all of a sudden she says: "I like Big Joe. He's kind. I like people who are kind."

Molly likes Big Joe. Now I know for sure that I will love her till the day I die.

After a while Charlie came out into the school yard hitching up his trousers and grinning in the sunshine. Everyone was crowding around him.

"Did it hurt, Charlie?"

"Was it on the back of the knees, Charlie, or on your bum?"

Charlie never said a word to them. He just walked right through everyone, and came straight over to me and Molly. "He won't do it again, Tommo," he said. "I hit him where it hurts, in the goolies." He lifted my chin and peered at my nose. "Are you all right, Tommo?"

"Hurts a bit," I told him.

"So does my bum," said Charlie.

Molly laughed then, and so did I. So did Charlie, and so did the whole school.

From that moment on Molly became one of us. It was as if she had suddenly joined our family and become our sister. When Molly came home with us that afternoon Big Joe gave her some flowers he'd picked, and Mother treated her like the daughter she'd never had. After that, Molly came home with us almost every afternoon. She seemed to want to be with us all the time. We didn't discover the reason for this until a lot later. I remember Mother used to brush Molly's hair. She loved doing it and we loved watching.

Mother. I think of her so often. And when I think of her I think of high hedges and deep lanes and our walks down to the river together in the evenings. I think of meadowsweet and honeysuckle and vetch and foxgloves and red campion and dog roses. There wasn't a wild flower or a butterfly she couldn't name. I loved the sound of their names when she spoke them: red admiral, peacock, cabbage white, adonis blue. It's her voice I'm hearing in my head now. I don't know why, but I can hear her better than I can picture her. I suppose it was because of Big Joe that she was always talking, always explaining the world about us. She was his guide, his interpreter, his teacher.

They wouldn't have Big Joe at school. Mr Munnings said he was backward. He wasn't backward at all. He was different, "special" Mother used to call him, but he was not backward. He needed help, that's all, and Mother was his help. It was as if Big Joe was blind in some way. He could see perfectly well, but very often he didn't seem to understand what he was seeing. And he wanted to understand so badly. So Mother would be forever telling him how and why things were as they were. And she would sing to him often, too, because it always made him happy and soothed him whenever he had one of his turns and became anxious or troubled. She'd sing to Charlie and me as well, more out of habit, I think. But we loved it, loved the sound of her voice. Her voice was the music of our childhood.

After Father died the music stopped. There was a stillness and a quietness in Mother now, and a sadness about the house. I had my terrible secret, a secret I could scarcely ever put out of my mind. So in my guilt I kept more and more to myself. Even Big Joe hardly ever laughed. At meals the kitchen seemed especially empty without Father, without his bulk and his voice filling the room. His dirty work coat didn't hang in the porch any more, and the smell of his pipe lingered only faintly now. He was gone and we were all quietly mourning him in our way.

Mother still talked to Big Joe, but not as much as before. She had to talk to him, because she was the only one who truly understood the meaning of all the grunts and squawks Big Joe used for language. Charlie and I understood some of it, some of the time, but she seemed to understand all he wanted to say, sometimes even before he said it. There was a shadow hanging over her, Charlie and I could see that, and not only the shadow of Father's death. We were sure there was something else she wouldn't talk about, something she was hiding from us. We found out what it was only too soon.

We were back home after school having our tea – Molly was there too – when there was a knock on the door. Mother seemed at once to know who it was. She took time to gather herself, smoothing down her apron and arranging her hair before she opened the door. It was the Colonel. "I wanted a word, Mrs Peaceful," he said. "I think you know what I've come for."

Mother told us to finish our tea, closed the door and went out into the garden with him. Charlie and I left Molly and Big Joe at the table and dashed out of the back door. We hurdled the vegetables, ran along the hedge, crouched down behind the woodshed and listened. We were close enough to hear every word that was said.

"It may seem a little indelicate to broach the subject so soon after your late husband's sad and untimely death," the Colonel was saying. He wasn't looking at Mother as he spoke, but down at his top hat which he was smoothing with his sleeve. "But it's a question of the cottage. Strictly speaking, of course, Mrs Peaceful, you have no right to live here any more. You know well enough I think that this is a tied cottage, tied to your late husband's job on the estate. Now of course with him gone..."

"I know what you're saying, Colonel," Mother said. "You want us out."

"Well, I wouldn't put it quite like that. It's not that I want you out, Mrs Peaceful, not if we can come to some other arrangement."

"Arrangement? What arrangement?" Mother asked.

"Well," the Colonel went on, "as it happens there's a position up at the house that might suit you. My wife's lady's maid has just given notice. As you know my wife is not a well woman. These days she spends most of her life in a wheelchair. She needs constant care and attention seven days a week."

"But I have my children," Mother protested. "Who would look after my children?"

It was a while before the Colonel spoke. "The two boys are old enough now to fend for themselves, I should have thought. And as for the other one, there is the lunatic asylum in Exeter. I'm sure I could see to it that a place be found for—"

Mother interrupted, her fury only barely suppressed, her voice cold but still calm. "I could never do that, Colonel. Never. But if I want to keep a roof over our heads, then I have to find some way I can come to work for you as your wife's maid. That is what you're telling me, isn't it."

"I'd say you understand the position perfectly, Mrs Peaceful. I couldn't have put it better myself. I shall need your agreement within the week. Good day Mrs Peaceful. And once again my condolences."

We watched him go, leaving Mother standing there. I had never in my life seen her cry before, but she cried now. She fell on her knees in the long grass holding her face in her hands. That was when Big Joe and Molly came out of the cottage. When Big Joe saw Mother he ran and knelt down beside her, hugging and rocking her gently in his arms, singing *Oranges and Lemons* until she began to smile through her tears and join in. Then we were all singing together, and loudly in our defiance so that the Colonel could not help but hear us.

Later, after Molly had gone home, Charlie and I sat in silence in the orchard. I almost told him my secret then. I wanted to so badly. But I just couldn't bring myself to do it. I thought he might never speak to me again if I did. The moment passed. "I hate that man," said Charlie under his breath. "I'll do him, Tommo. One day I'll really do him."

Of course Mother had no choice. She had to take the job, and we only had one relative to turn to for help, Grandma Wolf. She moved in the next week to look after us. She wasn't our grandmother at all, not really – both our grandmothers were dead. She was Mother's aunt, but always insisted we called her "Grandma" because she thought Great Aunt made her sound old and crotchety, which she always was. We hadn't liked her before she moved in – as much on account of her moustache as anything else – and we liked her even less now that she had. We all knew her story; how she'd worked up at the Big House for the Colonel for years as housekeeper, and how, for some reason, the Colonel's wife couldn't stand her. They'd had a big falling out, and in the end she'd had to leave and go to live in the village. That was why she was free to come and look after us.

But between ourselves Charlie and I had never called her either Great Aunt or Grandma. We had our own name for her. When we were younger Mother had often read us *Little Red Riding Hood*. There was a picture in it Charlie and I knew well, of the wolf in bed pretending to be Little Red Riding Hood's grandma. She had a black bonnet on her head, like our "Grandma" always used to wear, and she had big teeth with gaps in between, just like our "Grandma" too. So ever since I could remember we had called her "Grandma Wolf" – never to her face, of course. Mother said it wasn't respectful, but secretly I think she always quite liked it.

Soon it wasn't only because of the book that we thought of her as Grandma Wolf. She very quickly showed us who was in charge now that Mother was not there. Everything had to be just so: hands washed, hair done, no talking with your mouth full, no leaving anything on your plate. Waste not, want not, she'd say. That wasn't so bad. We got used to it. But what we could not forgive was that she was nasty to Big Joe. She talked to him, and about him, as if he were stupid or mad. She'd treat him as if he were a baby. She was forever wiping his mouth for him, or telling him not to sing at the table. When Molly protested once, she smacked her and sent her home. She smacked Big Joe too, whenever he didn't do what she said, which was often. He would start to rock then and talk to himself, which is what he always did whenever he was upset. But now Mother wasn't there to sing to him, to calm him. Molly talked to him, and we tried too, but it was not the same.

From the day Grandma Wolf moved in, our whole world changed. Mother would go to work up at the Big House at dawn, before we went off to school, and she still wouldn't be back when we got home for our tea. Instead Grandma Wolf would be there, at the door of what seemed to us now to be her lair. And Big Joe, who she wouldn't allow to go off on his wanders as he'd always loved to do, would come rushing up to us as if he hadn't seen us in weeks. He'd do the same to Mother when she came home, but she was often so exhausted she could hardly talk to him. She could see what was going on but was powerless to do anything about it. It seemed to all of us as if we were losing her, as if she was being replaced and pushed aside.

It was Grandma Wolf who did all the talking now, even telling Mother what to do in her own house. She was forever saying how Mother hadn't brought us up properly, that our manners were terrible, that we didn't know right from wrong – and that Mother had married beneath her. "I told her then and I've told her since," she ranted on, "she could have done far better for herself. But did she listen? Oh no. She had to marry the first man to turn her head, and him nothing but a forester. She was meant for better things, a better class of person. We were shopkeepers – we ran a proper shop, I can tell you – made a tidy profit, too. In a big way of business, I'll have you know. But oh no, she wouldn't have it. Broke your grandfather's heart, she did. And now look what she's come to: a lady's maid, at her age. Trouble. Your mother's always been nothing but trouble from the day she was born."

We longed for Mother to stand up to her, but each time she just gave in meekly, too worn out to do anything else. To Charlie and me she seemed almost to have become a different person. There was no laughter in her voice, no light in her eyes. And all along I knew full well whose fault it was that this had all happened, that Father was dead, that Mother had to go to work up at the Big House, and that Grandma Wolf had moved in and taken her place.

At night we could sometimes hear Grandma Wolf snoring in bed, and Charlie and I would make up this story about the Colonel and Grandma Wolf; how one day we'd go up to the Big House and push the Colonel's wife into the lake and drown her, and then Mother could come home and be with us and Big Joe and Molly, and everything could be like it had been before. Then the Colonel and Grandma Wolf could marry one another and live unhappily ever after, and because they were so old they could have lots of little monster children born already old and wrinkly with gappy teeth: the girls with moustaches like Grandma Wolf, the boys with whiskers like the Colonel.

I remember I used to have nightmares filled with those monster children, but whatever my nightmare it would always end the same way. I would be out in the woods with Father and the tree would be falling, and I'd wake up screaming. Then Charlie would be there beside me, and everything would be all right again. Charlie always made things all right again.

NEARLY QUARTER PAST ELEVEN

There's a mouse in here with me. He's sitting there in the light of the lamp, looking up at me. He seems as surprised to see me as I am to see him. There he goes. I can hear him still, scurrying about somewhere under the hayrack. I think he's gone now. I hope he comes back. I miss him already.

Grandma Wolf hated mice. She had a deep fear of them that she could not hide. So Charlie and I had lots to smile about in the autumn when the rain and the cold came and the mice decided it was warmer inside and came to live with us in the cottage. Big Joe loved the mice – he'd even put out food for them. Grandma Wolf would shout at him for that and smack him. But Big Joe could never understand why he was being smacked, so he went on feeding the mice just as he had before. Grandma Wolf put traps down, but Charlie and I would find them and spring them. All that autumn she only ever managed to catch one.

That mouse had the best funeral any mouse ever had. Big Joe was chief mourner and he cried enough for all of us. Molly, Charlie and I dug the grave, and when we'd laid him to rest Molly piled the grave high with flowers and sang *What a friend we have in Jesus*. We did all this at the bottom of the orchard hidden behind the apple trees where Grandma Wolf could not see or hear us. Afterwards we sat in a circle round the grave and had a funeral feast of blackberries. Big Joe stopped crying to eat the blackberries, and then with blackened mouths we all sang *Oranges and Lemons* over the mouse's grave.

Grandma Wolf tried everything to get rid of the mice. She put poison down under the sink in the larder. We swept it up. She asked Bob James, the wart charmer from the village with the crooked nose, to come and charm the mice away. He tried, but it didn't work. So in the end, in desperation, she had to resort to chasing them out of the house with a broom. But they just kept coming back in again. All this made her nastier than ever towards us. But for Charlie and me, just to see her frightened silly and screeching like a witch was worth every smack she gave us.

In bed at night our Grandma Wolf story was changing every time we told it. Now the Colonel and Grandma Wolf didn't have human children at all. Instead she gave birth to giant mice-children, all of them with great long tails and twitchy whiskers. But after what she did next, we decided that even that horrible fate was too good for her.

Although Grandma Wolf did smack Molly from time to time, it soon became obvious that she liked her a great deal better than the rest of us. There were good reasons for this. Girls were nice, Grandma Wolf would often tell us, not coarse and vulgar like boys. Besides she was good friends with Molly's mother and father. They lived as we did in a cottage on the Colonel's estate – Molly's father was groom up at the Big House. They were *proper* people, Grandma Wolf told us; good, God-fearing people who had brought their child up well – which meant strictly. And from what Molly told us, they *were* strict too. She was forever being sent to her room, or strapped by her father for the least little thing. She was an only child of older parents and, as Molly often said, they wanted her to be perfect. Anyway, it was a good thing for us that Grandma approved of her family, otherwise I'm sure she would have forbidden Molly to come and see us. As it was, Grandma Wolf said Molly was a good influence, that she could teach us some manners, and make us a little less coarse and vulgar. So, thank goodness, Molly kept coming home with us for tea every day after school.

Not long after the mouse's funeral, it was Big Joe's birthday. Charlie and I had got him some humbugs from Mrs Bright's shop in the village – which he always loved – and Molly brought him a present in a little brown box with air holes in it and elastic bands round it. While we were in school she kept it hidden in the shrubs at the bottom of the school yard. It was only because we pestered her that she showed us what it was as we were walking home. It was a harvest mouse,

37

the sweetest little mouse I ever saw, with oversized ears and bewildered eyes. She stroked him with the back of her finger and he sat up for her in the box and twitched his whiskers at us. She gave him to Big Joe after tea, down in the orchard out of sight of the cottage, well hidden from Grandma Wolf's ever watchful gaze. Big Joe hugged Molly as if he'd never let her go. He kept the birthday mouse in his own box and hid him away in a drawer in his bedroom cupboard – he said it would be too cold for him outside in the woodshed with all his other creatures. The mouse became his instant favourite. All of us tried to make Big Joe understand that he mustn't ever tell Grandma Wolf, that if she ever knew, she'd take his mouse away and kill it.

I don't know how she found out, but when we came home from school a few days later Big Joe was sitting on the floor of his room, sobbing his heart out, his drawer empty beside him. Grandma Wolf came storming in saying she wasn't going to have any nasty dirty animals in *her* house. Worse still, so that he'd never bring any of his other animals into the house, she'd got rid of them all: the slowworm, the two lizards, the hedgehog. Big Joe's family of animals were gone, and he was heartbroken. Molly screamed at her that she was a cruel, cruel woman and that she'd go to Hell when she was dead, and then ran off home in tears.

That night Charlie and I made up a story about how we'd put rat poison in Grandma Wolf's tea the next day and kill her. We did get rid of her in the end too, but thankfully without the use of rat poison. Instead, a miracle happened, a wonderful miracle.

First, the Colonel's wife died in her wheelchair, so we didn't have to push her into the lake after all. She choked on a scone at teatime, and despite everything Mother did to try to save her, she just stopped breathing. There was a big funeral which we all had to go to. She had a shining coffin with silver handles, piled high with flowers. The vicar said how loved she was in the parish, and how she'd devoted her life to caring for everyone on the estate – all of which was news to us.

Afterwards they opened up the church floor and lowered her into the family vault while we all sang *Abide with me*. And I was thinking that I'd rather be in Father's simple coffin and buried outside where the sun shines and the wind blows, not down in some gloomy hole with a crowd of dead relatives. Mother had to take Big Joe out in the middle of the hymn because he started singing *Oranges and Lemons* again very loudly and would not stop. Grandma Wolf bared her teeth at us – as wolves do – and furrowed her brow in disapproval. We didn't know it then, but very soon she would disappear almost totally from our lives, taking all her anger, all her threats and disapproval with her.

So suddenly, joy of joys, Mother was back home with us again, and we hoped it was only a question of time before

Grandma Wolf moved back up to the village. There was no job for Mother any more up at the Big House, no lady to be a maid to. She was home, and day by day she was becoming her old self again. There were wonderful blazing arguments between her and Grandma Wolf, mostly about how Grandma Wolf treated Big Joe. Mother said that now she was home she wouldn't stand for it any more. We listened to every word, and loved every moment of it. But there was one big shadow over all this new joy. We could see that with Mother out of work and no money coming in, things were becoming desperate. There was no money in the mug on the mantelpiece, and every day there was less food on the table. For a while we had little to eat but potatoes, and we all knew perfectly well that sooner or later the Colonel would put us out of the cottage. We were just waiting for the knock on the door. Meanwhile we were becoming very hungry.

It was Charlie's idea to go poaching: salmon, sea trout, rabbits, even deer if we were lucky, he said. Father had done a bit of poaching, so Charlie knew what to do. Molly and I would be on lookout. He could do the trapping or the fishing. So, at dusk, or dawn, whenever we could get away together, we went off poaching on the Colonel's land: in the Colonel's forests or in the Colonel's river where there were plenty of sea trout and plenty of salmon. We couldn't take Big Joe because he could start his singing at any time and give us away. Besides he'd tell Mother. He told Mother everything.

We did well. We brought back lots of rabbits, a few trout and, once, a fourteen-pound salmon. So now we had something to eat with our potatoes. We didn't tell Mother we'd been on the Colonel's land. She wouldn't have approved of that sort of thing at all, and we definitely didn't want Grandma Wolf knowing because she'd certainly have gone and reported us to the Colonel at once. "My friend, the Colonel," she called him. She was always full of his praises, so we knew we had to be careful. We said we'd caught our rabbits in the orchard and the fish from the village brook. The trout you could catch there were only small, but they didn't know that. Charlie told them that the salmon must have come up the brook to spawn, which they did do of course. Charlie always lied well, and they believed him. Thank God.

Molly and I would keep watch while Charlie set the traps or put out his nets. Lambert, the Colonel's bailiff, may have been old, but he was clever, and we knew he'd let his dog loose on us if he ever caught us at it. Late one evening, sitting by the bridge with Charlie busy at his nets downstream, Molly took my hand in hers and held it tight. "I don't like the dark," she whispered. I had never been so happy.

When the Colonel turned up at the house the next day, we thought it must be either because we'd been found out somehow or because he was going to evict us. It was neither. Grandma Wolf seemed to be expecting him, and that was strange. She went to the door and invited him in. He nodded at Mother and then frowned at us. Grandma Wolf waved us outside as she asked the Colonel to sit down. We tried eavesdropping but Big Joe was no good at keeping quiet, so we had to wait until later to hear the worst. As it turned out, the worst was not the worst at all, but the best.

After the Colonel had gone, Grandma Wolf called us in. I could see she was puffed up with self-importance, aglow with it. "Your mother will explain," she declared grandly, putting on her bonnet. "I have to get up to the Big House right away. I've work to do."

Mother waited until she'd gone and could not help smiling as she told us. "Well," she began, "you know some time ago your great aunt used to work as housekeeper up at the Big House?"

"And then she got kicked out by the Colonel's wife," said Charlie.

"She lost her job, yes," Mother went on. "Well, now the Colonel's wife has passed away it seems the Colonel wants her back as live-in housekeeper. She'll be moving up to the Big House as soon as possible."

I didn't cheer, but I certainly felt like it.

"What about the cottage?" Charlie asked. "Is the old duffer putting us out then?"

"No, dear. We're staying put," Mother replied. "He said his wife had liked me and made him promise to look after me if ever anything happened to her. So he's keeping that promise. Say what you like about the Colonel, he's a man of his word. I've agreed I'll do all his linen for him and his sewing work. Most of it I can bring home. So we'll have some money coming in. We'll manage. Well, are you happy? We're staying put!"

Then we did cheer and Big Joe cheered too, louder than any of us. So we stayed on in our cottage and Grandma Wolf moved out. We were liberated, and all was right with the world again. For a while at least.

Both of them being older than me, Molly by two years, Charlie by three, they always ran faster than I did. I seem to have spent much of my life watching them racing ahead of me, leaping the high meadow grass, Molly's plaits whirling about her head, their laughter mingling. When they got too far ahead I sometimes felt they wanted to be without me. I would whine at them then to let them know I was feeling all miserable and abandoned, and they'd wait for me to catch up. Best of all Molly would sometimes come running back and take my hand.

When we weren't poaching the Colonel's fish or scrumping his apples – more than anything we all loved the danger of it, I think – we would be roaming wild in the

43

countryside. Molly could shin up a tree like a cat, faster than either of us. Sometimes we'd go down to the river bank and watch the kingfishers flash by, or we'd go swimming in Okement Pool hung all around by willows, where the water was dark and deep and mysterious, and where no one ever came.

I remember the day Molly dared Charlie to take off all his clothes, and to my amazement he did. Then she did, and they ran shrieking and bare-bottomed into the water. When they called me in after them, I wouldn't do it, not in front of Molly. So I sat and sulked on the bank and watched them splashing and giggling, and all the while I was wishing I had the courage to do what Charlie had done, wishing I was with them. Molly got dressed afterwards behind a bush and told us not to watch. But we did. That was the first time I ever saw a girl with no clothes on. She was very thin and white, and she wrung her plaits out like a wet cloth.

It was several days before they managed to entice me in. Molly stood waist-deep in the river and put her hands over her eyes. "Come on, Tommo," she cried. "I won't watch. Promise." And not wanting to be left out yet again, I stripped off and made a dash for the river, covering myself as I went just in case Molly was watching through her fingers. After I'd done it that first time, it never seemed to bother me again.

Sometimes when we tired of all the frolicking we'd lie and talk in the shallows, letting the river ripple over us. How we talked. Molly told us once that she wanted to die right there and then, that she never wanted tomorrow to come because no tomorrow could ever be as good as today. "I know," she said, and she sat up in the river then and collected a handful of small pebbles. "I'm going to tell our future. I've seen the gypsies do it." She shook the pebbles around in her cupped hands, closed her eyes and then scattered them out on to the muddy shore. Kneeling over them she spoke very seriously and slowly as if she were reading them. "They say we'll always be together, the three of us, for ever and ever. They say that as long as we stick together we'll be lucky and happy." Then she smiled at us. "And the stones never lie," she said. "So you're stuck with me."

For a year or two Molly's stones proved right. But then Molly got ill. She wasn't at school one day. It was the scarlet fever, Mr Munnings told us, and very serious. Charlie and I went up to her cottage that evening after tea with some sweetpeas Mother had picked for her – because they smell sweeter than any flower she knew, she said. We knew we wouldn't be allowed in to see her because scarlet fever was very catching, but Molly's mother did not look at all pleased to see us. She always looked grey and grim, but that day she was angry as well. She took the flowers with scarcely a glance at them, and told us it would be better if we didn't come again. Then Molly's father appeared from behind her, looking gruff and unkempt, and told us to be off, that we were disturbing Molly's sleep. As I walked away, all I could think of was how unhappy Molly must be living in that dingy little cottage with a mother and father like that, and how trees fall on the wrong fathers. We stopped at the end of the path and looked up at Molly's window, hoping she would come and wave at us. When she didn't we knew she must be really ill.

Charlie and I never said our prayers at all any more, not since Sunday school, but we did now. Kneeling side by side with Big Joe we prayed each night that Molly would not die. Joe sang *Oranges and Lemons* and we said *Amen* afterwards. We had our fingers crossed too, just for good measure.

TEN TO MIDNIGHT

I'm not sure I ever really believed in God, even in Sunday school. In church I'd gaze up at Jesus hanging on the cross in the stained-glass window, and feel sorry for him because I could see how cruel it was and how much it must be hurting him. I knew he was a good and kind man. But I never really understood why God, who was supposed to be his father, and almighty and powerful, would let them do that to him, would let him suffer so much. I believed then, as I believe now, that crossed fingers and Molly's stones are every bit as reliable or unreliable as praying to God. I shouldn't think like that because if there's no God, then there can be no heaven. Tonight I want very much to believe there's a heaven, that, as Father said, there is a new life after death, that death is not a full stop, and that we will all see one another again.

It was while Molly was ill in bed with the scarlet fever that Charlie and I discovered that although in one way Molly's stones had let us down, in another way they had indeed spoken the truth: with her, with the three of us together, we *were* lucky, and without her we weren't. Up until now, whenever the three of us had gone out together poaching the Colonel's fish, we had never been caught. We'd had a few close shaves with old Lambert and his dog, but our lookout system had always worked. Somehow we'd always heard them coming and managed to make ourselves scarce. But the very first time Charlie and I went out poaching without Molly, things went wrong, badly wrong, and it was my fault.

We had chosen a perfect poaching night, not a breath of wind so we could hear anyone coming. With Molly beside me on lookout I'd never felt sleepy, and we'd always heard old Lambert and his dog in plenty of time for Charlie to get out of the river, for us all to make good our escape. But on this particular night my concentration failed me. I'd made myself comfortable, probably too comfortable, in our usual place by the bridge with Charlie netting downstream. But after sitting there for a while I just fell asleep. I don't drop off all that easily, but when I do sleep I sleep deeply.

The first I knew of anything was a dog snuffling at my neck. Then he was barking in my face, and old Lambert was dragging me to my feet. And there was Charlie way out in the middle of the moonlit river hauling at the nets.

"Peaceful boys! You young rascals," Lambert growled. "Caught you red-handed. You're for it now, make no mistake."

Charlie could have left me there. He could have made a run for it and got clean away, but Charlie's not like that. He never has been.

At the point of a shotgun Lambert marched us back along the river and up to the Big House, his dog snarling at our heels from time to time just to remind us he was still there, and that he'd eat us alive if we made a run for it. Lambert locked us in the stables and left us. We waited in the darkness, the horses shifting and munching and snorting around us. All too soon we saw the approaching light of a lamp, and heard footsteps and voices. Then the Colonel was there in his slippers and his dressing gown, and he had Grandma Wolf with him in her nightcap looking every bit as fierce as Lambert's dog.

The Colonel looked from one to the other of us, shaking his head in disgust. But Grandma Wolf had the first word. "I've never in all my life been so ashamed," she said. "My own family. You're nothing but a downright disgrace. And after all the Colonel's done for us. Common thieves, that's what you are. Nothing but common thieves."

When she'd finished it was the Colonel's turn. "Only one way to deal with young ruffians like you," he said. "I could have you up before the magistrate, but since I'm the magistrate anyway there's no need to go to all that trouble, is there? I'll sentence you right now. You will come up here tomorrow morning at ten o'clock sharp, and I'll give each of you the hiding you so richly deserve. Then you can stay and clean out the hunt kennels till I say you can go. That should teach you not to come poaching on my land."

When we got home we had to tell Mother everything we'd done, everything the Colonel had said. Charlie did most of the talking. Mother sat listening in silence, her face stony. When she spoke, she spoke in little more than a whisper. "I can tell you one thing," she said. "There'll be no hiding. Over my dead body." Then she looked up at us, her eyes full of tears. "Why? You said you'd been fishing in the brook. You told me. Oh Charlie, Tommo." Big Joe stroked her hair. He was anxious and bewildered. She patted his arm. "It's all right, Joe. I'll go up there with them tomorrow. Cleaning out the kennels I don't mind – you deserve that. But it stops there. I won't let that man lay a finger on you, not one finger, no matter what."

Mother was as good as her word. How she did it and what was said we never knew, but the next day after Mother and the Colonel had had a meeting in his study, she made us stand in front of him and apologise. Then after a long lecture about trespassing on private property, the Colonel said that he'd changed his mind, that instead of the hiding we would be set to cleaning out the Colonel's kennels every Saturday and Sunday until Christmas.

As it turned out we didn't mind at all because, although the smell could be disgusting, the hounds were all around us as we worked, their tails high and waving and happy. So we often stopped work to pet them, after we'd made quite sure no one was looking. We had a particular favourite called Bertha. She was almost pure white with one brown foot and had the most beautiful eyes. She would always stand near us as we scraped and swept, gazing up at us in open adoration. Every time I looked into her eyes I thought of Molly. Like Bertha, she too had eyes the colour of heather honey.

We had to be careful, because Grandma Wolf, now more full of herself than ever, would frequently come out into the stable yard to make sure we were doing our work properly. She'd always have something nasty to say: "Serves you right," or "That'll teach you," or "You should be ashamed of yourselves," always delivered with a tut and a pained sigh. To finish there'd be some nasty quip about Mother. "Still, with a mother like that, I suppose you're not entirely to blame, are you?"

Then Christmas Eve came and our punishment was over at last. We said fond farewells to Bertha and ran off home down the Colonel's drive for the last time, blowing very loud raspberries as we went. Back in the cottage we found waiting for us the best Christmas present we could ever have hoped for. Molly was sitting there smiling at us as we came in through the door. She was pale, but she was back with us. We were together again. Her hair was cut shorter. The plaits were gone, and somehow that changed the whole look of her. She wasn't a girl any more. She had a different beauty now, a beauty that at once stirred in me a new and deeper love.

I think, without knowing it, I had always charted my own growing up by constant comparison to Molly and Charlie. Day by day I was becoming ever more painfully aware of how far behind them I was. I wasn't just smaller and slower than they were – I had never liked that, but I was used to it by now. The trouble was that it was becoming evident to me that the gap between us was more serious, and that it was widening. It really began when Molly was moved up into the Bigguns' class. I was stuck being a Tiddler and they were growing away from me. But whilst we were still at the village school together I didn't mind all that much because at least I was always near them. We walked to school together, ate our lunch together as we always had – up in the pantry in the vicarage, where the vicar's wife would bring us lemonade – and then we'd come home together.

I looked forward all day to that long walk home, the school day done, their other friends not with us, with the fearsome Mr Munnings out of sight and out of mind for another day. We'd hare down the hill to the brook, pull off our great heavy boots and release our aching feet and toes at long last. We'd sit there on the bank wiggling our toes in the blessed cool of the water. We'd lie amongst the grass and buttercups of the water meadows and look up at the clouds scudding across the sky, at the wind-whipped crows chasing a mewing buzzard. Then we'd follow the brook home, feet squelching in the mud, our toes oozing with it. Strange when I think of it now, but there was a time when I loved mud, the smell of it, the feel of it, the larking about in it. Not any more.

Then quite suddenly, just after my twelfth birthday, the last of the larking was all over. Charlie and Molly left school and I was alone. I was a Biggun, in Mr Munnings' class and hating him now even more than I feared him. I woke up dreading every day. Both Charlie and Molly had found work up in the Big House – almost everyone in the village worked up there or on the estate. Molly was under-parlour maid, and Charlie worked in the hunt kennels and in the stables looking after the dogs and the horses, which he loved. Molly didn't come round to see us nearly so often as before – like Charlie, she worked six days a week. So I hardly saw her.

Charlie would come home late in the evenings as Father had before him, and he'd hang his coat up on Father's peg and put his boots outside in the porch where Father's boots had always been. He warmed his feet in the bottom oven when he came in out of the cold of a winter's day, just as Father had done. That was the first time in my life I was ever really jealous of Charlie. I wanted to put *my* feet in the oven, and to come home from proper work, to earn money like

Charlie did, to have a voice that didn't pipe like the little children in Miss McAllister's class. Most of all though I wanted to be with Molly again. I wanted us to be a threesome again, for everything to be just as it had been. But nothing stays the same. I learnt that then. I know that now.

At nights as Charlie and I lay in bed together Charlie just slept. We never made up our stories any more. When I did see Molly, and it was only on Sundays now, she was as kind to me as she always had been, but too kind almost, too protective, more like a little mother to me than a friend. I could see that she and Charlie lived in another world now. They talked endlessly about the goings on and scandals up at the Big House, about the prowling Wolfwoman – it was around this time they dropped the "Grandma Wolf" altogether and began to call her "Wolfwoman". That was when I first heard the gossip about the Colonel and the Wolfwoman. Charlie said they'd had a thing going for years – common knowledge. That was why the late "Mrs Colonel" had kicked her out all those years before. And now they were like husband and wife up there, only she wore the trousers. There was talk of the Colonel's dark moods, how he'd shut himself up in his study all day sometimes, and of Cook's tantrums whenever things were not done just so. It was a world I could not be part of, a world I did not belong in.

I tried all I could to interest them in my life at school. I told them about how we'd all heard Miss McAllister and Mr

Munnings having a blazing argument because he refused to light the school stove, how she'd called him a wicked, wicked man. She was right too. Mr Munnings would never light the stove unless the puddles were iced over in the school yard, unless our fingers were so cold we couldn't write. He shouted back at her that he would light the stove when he thought fit, and that anyway suffering was part of life and good for a child's soul. Charlie and Molly made out they were interested, but I could tell they weren't. Then one day down by the brook, I turned and saw them walking away from me through the water meadows holding hands. We'd all held hands before, often, but then it had been the three of us. I knew at once that this was different. As I watched them I felt a sudden ache in my heart. I don't think it was anger or jealousy, more a pang of loss, of deep grief.

We did have some moments when we became a threesome again, but they were becoming all too few and far between. I remember the day of the yellow aeroplane. It was the first aeroplane any of us had ever seen. We'd heard about them, seen pictures of them, but until that day I don't think I ever really believed they were real, that they actually flew. You had to see one to believe it. Molly and Charlie and I were fishing down in the brook, just for tiddlers, or brown trout if we were lucky – we'd done no more salmon poaching, Mother had made us promise.

It was late on a summer evening and we were just about

to set off home when we heard the distant sound of an engine. At first we thought it was the Colonel's car – his Rolls Royce was the only car for miles around – but then we all realised at the same moment that this was a different kind of engine altogether. It was a sound of intermittent droning, like a thousand stuttering bees. What's more, it wasn't coming from the road at all; it was coming from high above us. There was a flurry of squawking and splashing further upstream as a flight of ducks took off in a panic. We ran out from under the trees to get a better look. An aeroplane! We watched, spellbound, as it circled above us like some ungainly yellow bird, its great wide wings wobbling precariously. We could see the goggled pilot looking down at us out of the cockpit. We waved frantically up at him and he waved back. Then he was coming in lower, lower. The cows in the water meadow scattered. The aeroplane was coming in to land, bouncing, then bumping along and coming to a stop some fifty yards away from us.

The pilot didn't get out, but beckoned us over. We didn't hesitate. "Better not switch off!" he shouted over the roar of the engine. He was laughing as he lifted up his goggles. "Might never get the damn thing started again. Listen, the truth is I reckon I'm a bit lost. That church up there on the hill, is that Lapford church?"

"No," Charlie shouted back. "That's Iddesleigh. St. James."

The pilot looked down at his map. "Iddesleigh? You sure?"

"Yes," we shouted.

"Whoops! Then I really was lost. Jolly good thing I stopped, wasn't it? Thanks for your help. Better be off." He lowered his goggles and smiled at us. "Here. You like humbugs?" And he reached out and handed Charlie a bag of sweets. "Cheerio then," he said. "Stand well back. Here we go."

And with that, off he went bouncing along towards the hedge, his engine spluttering. I thought he couldn't possibly lift off in time. He managed it, but only just, his wheels clipping the top of the hedge, before he was up and away. He did one steep turn, then flew straight at us. There was no time to run. All we could do was throw ourselves face down in the long grass. We felt the sudden blast of the wind as he passed above us. By the time we rolled over he was climbing up over the trees and away. We could see him laughing and waving. We watched him soaring over Iddesleigh church tower and then away into the distance. He was gone, leaving us lying there breathless in the silence he'd left behind.

For some time afterwards we lay there in the long grass watching a single skylark rising above us, and sucking on our humbugs. When Charlie came to share them out we had five each, and five for Big Joe, too.

"Was that real?" Molly breathed. "Did it really happen?"

"We've got our humbugs," said Charlie, "so it must have been real, mustn't it?"

"Every time I eat humbugs from now on," Molly said, "every time I look at skylarks, I'm going to think of that yellow aeroplane, and the three of us, and how we are right now."

"Me too," I said.

"Me too," said Charlie.

Most people in the village had seen the aeroplane, but only we three had been there when it landed, only we had talked to the pilot. I was so proud of that – too proud as it turned out. I told the story, several embellished versions of it, again and again at school, showing everyone my humbugs just to prove all I'd said was true. But someone must have snitched on me, because Mr Munnings came straight over to me in class and, for no reason at all, told me to empty out my pockets. I had three of my precious humbugs left and he confiscated them all. Then he took me by the ear to the front of the class where he gave me six strokes of the ruler in his own very special way, sharp edge down on to my knuckles. As he did it I looked him in the eye and stared him out. It didn't dull the pain, nor I'm sure did it make him feel bad about what he was doing, but my sullen defiance of him made me feel a lot better as I walked back to my desk.

As I lay in bed that night, my knuckles still throbbing, I was longing to tell Charlie about what had happened at school, but I knew that everything about school bored him now, so I said nothing. But the longer I lay there thinking about my knuckles and my humbugs the more I was bursting to talk to him. I could hear from his breathing that he was still awake. For just a moment it occurred to me this might be the time to tell him about Father, and how I'd killed him in the forest all those years before. That at least would interest him. I did try, but I still could not summon up the courage to tell him. In the end all I told him was that Mr Munnings had confiscated my humbugs. "I hate him," I said. "I hope he chokes on them." Even as I was speaking I could tell he wasn't listening.

"Tommo," he whispered, "I'm in trouble."

"What've you done?" I asked him.

"I'm in real trouble, but I had to do it. You remember Bertha, that whitey-looking foxhound up at the Big House, the one we liked?"

"Course," I said.

"Well, she's always been my favourite ever since. And then this afternoon the Colonel comes by the kennels and tells me... he tells me he's going to have to shoot Bertha. So I ask him why. Because she's getting a bit old, a bit slow, he says. Because whenever they go out hunting she's always going off on her own and getting herself lost. She's no use for hunting any more, he says, no use to anyone. I asked him not to, Tommo. I told him she was my favourite. 'Favourite!' he says, laughing at me. 'Favourite? How can you have a favourite? Lot of sentimental claptrap. She's just one of a pack of dumb beasts, boy, and don't you forget it.' I begged him, Tommo. I told him he shouldn't do it. That's when he got really angry. He said they're his foxhounds and he'd shoot them as and when he felt like it, and he didn't want any more lip from me about it. So you know what I did, Tommo? I stole her. I ran off with her after dark, through the trees so no one would see us."

"Where is she now?" I asked. "What've you done with her?"

"Remember that old forester's shack Father used, up in Ford's Cleave Wood? I've put her in there for the night. I gave her some food. Molly pinched some meat for me from the kitchen. She'll be all right up there. No one'll hear her, with a bit of luck anyway."

"But what'll you do with her tomorrow? What if the Colonel finds out?"

"I don't know, Tommo," Charlie said. "I don't know."

We hardly slept a wink that night. I lay there listening out for Bertha all the while. When I did drop off, I kept waking up suddenly thinking I had heard Bertha barking. But always it turned out to be a screeching fox. And once it was an owl hooting, right outside our window.

TWENTY-FOUR MINUTES PAST TWELVE

I haven't seen a fox while I've been out here. It's hardly surprising, I suppose. But I have heard owls. How any bird can survive in all this I'll never know. I've even seen larks over no-man's-land. I always found hope in that.

"He'll know," Charlie whispered to me in bed at dawn. "As soon as they find Bertha gone, the Colonel will know it was me. I won't tell him where she is. I don't care what he does, I won't tell him."

Charlie and I ate our breakfast in silence, hoping the inevitable storm wouldn't break, but knowing that sooner or later it must. Big Joe sensed something was wrong – he could always feel anxiety in the air. He was rocking back and forth and wouldn't touch his breakfast. So then Mother knew something was up as well. Once she was suspicious Mother was a difficult person to hide things from, and we weren't very good at it, not that morning.

"Is Molly coming over?" she asked, beginning to probe.

There was a loud and insistent knocking on the door. She could tell at once it wouldn't be Molly. It was too early for

Molly, and anyway she didn't knock like that. Besides, I think she could already see from our faces that Charlie and I were expecting an unwelcome visitor. As we feared, it was the Colonel.

Mother invited him in. He stood there glaring at us, thin-lipped and pale with fury. "I think you know why I've come, Mrs Peaceful," he began.

"No, Colonel, I don't," said Mother.

"So the young devil hasn't told you." He was shouting now, shaking his stick at Charlie. Big Joe began to whimper and clutched Mother's hand as the Colonel ranted on.

"That boy of yours is a despicable thief. First of all he steals the salmon out of my river. And now, in my employ, in a position of trust, he steals one of my foxhounds. Don't deny it, boy. I know it was you. Where is she? Is she here? Is she?"

Mother looked to Charlie for an explanation.

"He was going to shoot her, Mother," he said quickly. "I had to do it."

"You see!" roared the Colonel. "He admits it! He admits it!"

Big Joe was beginning to wail now and Mother was smoothing his hair, trying to reassure and comfort him as she spoke. "So you took her in order to save her, Charlie, is that right?"

"Yes, Mother."

"Well, you shouldn't have done that, Charlie, should you?"

"No, Mother."

"Will you tell the Colonel where you've hidden her?"

"No, Mother."

Mother thought for a moment or two. "I didn't think so," she said. She looked the Colonel full in the face. "Colonel, am I right in thinking that if you were going to shoot this dog, presumably it was because she's no use to you any more – as a foxhound I mean?"

"Yes," the Colonel replied, "but what I do with my own animals, or why I do it, is no business of yours, Mrs Peaceful. I don't have to explain myself to you."

"Of course not, Colonel," Mother spoke softly, sweetly almost, "but if you were going to shoot her anyway, then you wouldn't mind if I were to take her off your hands and look after her, would you?"

"You can do what you like with the damned dog," the Colonel snapped. "You can bloody well eat her for all I care. But your son stole her from me and I will not let that go unpunished."

Mother asked Big Joe to fetch the money mug from the mantelpiece. "Here, Colonel," she said, calmly offering him a coin from the money mug. "Sixpence. I'm buying the dog off you for sixpence, not a bad price for a useless dog. So now it's not stolen, is it?"

The Colonel was utterly dumbfounded. He looked from the coin in his hand to Mother, to Charlie. He was breathing hard. Then, regaining his composure, he pocketed the sixpence in his waistcoat and pointed his stick at Charlie. "Very well, but you can consider yourself no longer in my employ." With that he turned on his heel and went out, slamming the door behind him. We listened to his footsteps going down the path, heard the front gate squeaking.

Charlie and I went mad, mostly out of sheer relief, but also quite overwhelmed with gratitude and admiration. What a mother we had! We whooped and yahooed. Big Joe was happy again, and sang *Oranges and Lemons* as he gambolled wildly round the kitchen.

"I don't know what you've got to be so almightily pleased about," said Mother when we had all calmed down. "You do know you've just lost your job, Charlie?"

"I don't care," said Charlie. "He can stuff his stinking job. I'll find another. You put the silly old fart in his place good and proper. And we've got Bertha."

"Where is that dog anyway?" Mother asked.

"I'll show you," Charlie said.

We waited for Molly to come and then we all went off up to Ford's Cleave Wood together. As we neared the shack, we could hear Bertha yowling. Charlie ran on ahead and opened the door. Out she came, bounding up to us, squeaking with delight, her tail swiping at our legs. She jumped up at all of us, licking everything she could, but right away she seemed to attach herself particularly to Big

Joe. She followed him everywhere after that. She even slept on his bed at nights – Big Joe insisted on that no matter how much Mother protested. She'd sit under his apple tree howling up at him while he sang to her from high up in the branches. He only had to start singing and she'd join in, so from now on he never sang his *Oranges and Lemons* unaccompanied. He never did anything unaccompanied. They were always together. He fed her, brushed her and cleared up her frequent puddles (which were more like lakes). Big Joe had found a new friend and he was in seventh heaven.

After a few weeks going round all the farms in the parish looking for work, Charlie found a job as dairyman and shepherd at Farmer Cox's place on the other side of the village. He would go off before dawn on his bicycle to do the milking and was back home late, so I saw even less of him than before. He should have been much happier up there. He liked the cows and the sheep, though he said that the sheep were a bit stupid. Best of all, he said, he didn't have the Colonel or the Wolfwoman breathing down his neck all day.

But Charlie, like me, was very far from happy, because Molly had suddenly stopped coming. Mother said she was sure there could only be one reason. Someone must have put it about – and she thought it could only be the Colonel or the Wolfwoman or both – that Charlie Peaceful was a thieving rascal, and that therefore the Peaceful family were no longer considered fit folk for Molly to visit. She said Charlie should just let things cool down for a while, that Molly would be back. But Charlie wouldn't listen. Time after time he went to Molly's cottage. They wouldn't even answer the door. In the end, because he thought I'd have a better chance of getting to see Molly, he sent me over with a letter. Somehow, he said, I had to deliver it to her. I had to.

Molly's mother met me at the door with a face like thunder. "Go away," she yelled at me. "Just go away. Don't you understand? We don't want your kind here. We don't want you bothering our Molly. She doesn't want to see you." And with that she slammed the door in my face. I was walking away, Charlie's letter still in my pocket, when I happened to glance back and saw Molly waving at me frantically through her window. She was mouthing something I couldn't understand at all at first, gesticulating at me, pointing down the hill towards the brook. I knew then exactly what she meant me to do.

I ran down to the brook and waited under the trees where we'd always done our fishing together. I didn't have long to wait before she came. She took my hand without a word, and led me down under the bank where we couldn't possibly be seen. She was crying as she told me everything: how the Colonel had come to the cottage – she'd overheard it all – how he'd told her father that Charlie Peaceful was a thief; how he'd heard Charlie Peaceful had been seeing much more of Molly than was good for her, and that if he had any sense Molly's father should put a stop to it. "So my father won't let me see Charlie any more. He won't let me see any of you," Molly told me, brushing away her tears. "I'm so miserable without you, Tommo. I hate it up at the Big House without Charlie, and I hate it at home too. Father'll strap me if I see Charlie. And he said he'll take a gun to Charlie if he ever comes near me. I think he means it too."

"Why?" I asked. "Why's he like that?"

"He's always been like that," she said. "He says I'm wicked. Born in sin. Mother says he's only trying to save me from myself, so I won't go to Hell. He's always talking about Hell. I won't got to Hell, will I, Tommo?"

I did what I did next without thinking. I leant over and kissed her on the cheek. She threw her arms around my neck, sobbing as if her heart would break. "I so want to see Charlie," she cried. "I miss him so much." That was when I remembered to give her the letter. She tore it open and read it at once. It can't have been long because she read it so quickly. "Tell him yes. Yes, I will," she said, her eyes suddenly bright again.

"Just yes?" I asked, intrigued, puzzled and jealous all at the same time.

"Yes. Same time, same place, tomorrow. I'll write a letter back and you can give it to Charlie. All right?" She got up and pulled me to my feet. "I love you, Tommo. I love you both. And Big Joe, and Bertha." She kissed me quickly and was gone.

That was the first of dozens of letters I delivered from Charlie to Molly and from Molly to Charlie over the weeks and months that followed. All through my last year at school I was their go-between postman. I didn't mind that much, because it meant I got to see Molly often, which was all that really mattered to me. It was all done in great secrecy – Charlie insisted on that. He made me swear on the Holy Bible to tell no one, not even Mother. He made me cross my heart and hope to die.

Molly and I would meet most evenings and exchange letters in the same place, down by the brook, both of us having made quite sure we were not followed. We'd sit and talk there for a few precious minutes, often with the rain dripping through the trees, and once I remember with the wind roaring about us so violently that I thought the trees might come down on us. Fearing for our lives, we ran out across the meadow and burrowed our way into the bottom of a haystack and sat there shivering like a couple of frightened rabbits.

It was in the shelter of this haystack that I first heard news of the war. When Molly talked it was often, if not always, about Charlie – she'd forever be asking news of him. I never showed her I minded, but I did. So I was quite pleased that day when she started telling me about how all the talk up at the Big House these days was of war with Germany, how everyone now thought it would happen sooner rather than later. She'd read about it herself in the newspaper, so she knew it had to be true.

It was Molly's job every morning, she told me, to iron the Colonel's *Times* newspaper before she took it to him in his study. Apparently he insisted his newspaper should be crisp and dry, so that the ink should not come off on his fingers while he was reading it. She didn't really understand what the war was all about, she admitted, only that some archduke – whatever that was – had been shot in a place called Sarajevo – wherever that was – and Germany and France were very angry with each other about it. They were gathering their armies to fight with each other and, if they did, then we'd be in it soon because we'd have to fight on the French side against the Germans. She didn't know why. It made about as much sense to me as it did to her. She said the Colonel was in a terrible mood about it all, and that everyone up at the Big House was much more frightened of his moods than they were about the war.

But apparently the Colonel was gentle as a lamb compared to the Wolfwoman these days (everyone called her that now, not just us). It seemed that someone had put salt in her tea instead of sugar and she swore it was on purpose – which it probably was, Molly said. She'd been ranting and raving about it ever since, telling everyone how she'd find out who it was. Meanwhile she was treating all of them as if they were guilty.

"Was it you?" I asked Molly.

"Maybe," she said, smiling, "and maybe not." I wanted to kiss her again then, but I didn't dare. That has always been my trouble. I've never dared enough.

Mother had it all arranged before I left school. I was to go and work with Charlie up at Mr Cox's farm. Farmer Cox was getting on in years and, with no sons of his own, was in need of more help on the farm. He was a bit keen on the drink too, Charlie said. It was true. He was in the pub most evenings. He liked his beer and his skittles, and he liked to sing, too. He knew all the old songs. He kept them in his head, but he'd only sing if he'd had a couple of beers. So he never sang on the farm. He was always rather dour on the farm, but fair, always fair.

I went up there mostly to look after the horses at first. For me it couldn't have been better. I was with Charlie again, working alongside him on the farm. I'd put on a spurt and was almost as tall as him by now, but still not as fast, nor as strong. He was a bit bossy with me sometimes, but that didn't bother me – that was his job after all. Things were changing between us. Charlie didn't treat me like a boy any more, and I liked that, I liked that a lot.

The newspapers were full of the war that had now begun, but aside from the army coming to the village and buying up lots of the local farm horses for cavalry horses, it had hardly touched us at all. Not yet. I was still Charlie's postman, still Molly's postman. So I saw Molly often, though not as often as before. For some reason the letters between them seemed less frequent. But at least with me now working with Charlie for six days a week we were all three together again in a kind of way, linked by the letters. Then that link was cruelly broken, and what followed broke my heart, broke all our hearts.

I remember Charlie and I had been haymaking with Farmer Cox, young buzzards wheeling above us all day, swallows skimming the mown grass all about us as the shadows lengthened and the evening darkened. We arrived home later than usual, dusty and exhausted, and hungry, too. Inside we found Mother sitting upright in her chair doing her sewing and opposite her Molly and, to our surprise, her mother. Everyone in the room looked as grim-faced as Molly's mother, even Big Joe, even Molly whose eyes I could see were red from crying. Bertha was howling ominously from outside in the woodshed.

"Charlie," said Mother, setting her sewing aside. "Molly's mother has been waiting for you. She has something she wants to say to you."

"Yours, I believe," said Molly's mother, her voice as hard as stone. She handed Charlie a packet of letters tied up with a blue ribbon. "I found them. I've read them, every one of

71

them. So has Molly's father. So we know, we know everything. Don't bother to deny it, Charlie Peaceful. The evidence is here, in these letters. Molly has been punished already, her father has seen to that. I've never read anything so wicked in all my life. Never. All that love talk. Disgusting. But you've been meeting as well, haven't you?"

Charlie looked across at Molly. The look between them said it all, and I knew then that I had been betrayed.

"Yes," said Charlie.

I couldn't believe what he was saying. They hadn't told me. They'd been meeting in secret and neither of them had told me.

"There. Didn't I tell you, Mrs Peaceful?" Molly's mother went on, her voice quivering with rage.

"I'm sorry," said Mother. "But you'll still have to tell me why it is they shouldn't be meeting. Charlie's seventeen now, and Molly sixteen. Old enough, I'd say. I'm sure we both had our little rendezvous here and there when we were their age."

"You speak for yourself, Mrs Peaceful," Molly's mother replied with a supercilious sneer. "Molly's father and I made it quite plain to both of them. We forbade them to have anything to do with each other. It's wickedness, Mrs Peaceful, pure wickedness. The Colonel has warned us, you know, about your son's wicked thieving ways. Oh yes, we know all about him."

"Really?" said Mother. "Tell me, do you always do what the Colonel says? Do you always think what the Colonel thinks? If he said the earth was flat, would you believe him? Or did he just threaten you? He's good at that."

Molly's mother stood up, full of righteous indignation. "I haven't come here to argue the toss. I have come to tell of your son's misdemeanours, to say that I won't have him leading our Molly into the ways of wickedness and sin. He must never see her again, do you hear? If he does, then the Colonel will know about it. I'm telling you the Colonel will know about it. I have no more to say. Come along, Molly." And taking Molly's hand firmly in hers she swept out, leaving us all looking at one another and listening to Bertha still howling.

"Well," said Mother after a while. "I'll get your supper, boys, shall I?"

That night I lay there beside Charlie not speaking. I was so filled with anger and resentment towards him that I never wanted to speak to him again, nor to Molly come to that. Then out of our silence he said: "All right, I should've told you, Tommo. Molly said I should tell you. But I didn't want to. I couldn't, that's all."

"Why not?" I asked. For several moments he did not reply.

"Because I know, and she does too. That's why she wouldn't tell you herself," Charlie said.

"Know what?"

"When it was just letters, it didn't seem to matter so much. But later, after we began seeing each other... we didn't want to hide it from you, Tommo, honest. But we didn't want to hurt you either. You love her, don't you?" I didn't answer. There was no need. "Well, so do I, Tommo. So you'll understand why I'm going to go on seeing her. I'll find a way no matter what that old cow says." He turned to me. "Still friends?" he said.

"Friends," I mumbled, but I did not mean it.

After that no more was ever said between us about Molly. I never asked because I didn't want to know. I didn't want even to think about it, but I did. I thought about nothing else.

No one could understand why, but shortly after this Bertha began to go missing from time to time. She hadn't wandered off at all until now; she'd always stuck close to Big Joe. Wherever Big Joe was, that's where you'd be sure to find Bertha. Big Joe was frantic with worry every time she went off. She'd come back home in the end of course, when she felt like it, either that or Mother and Joe would find her somewhere all muddied and wet and lost, and they'd bring her home. But the great worry was that she'd start chasing after sheep or cows, that some farmer or landowner would shoot her, as they'd shoot any dog they found trespassing on their land that could be molesting their animals. Fortunately

Bertha didn't seem to go chasing sheep, and anyway up until now she had never been gone that long, nor strayed too far.

We did our very best to keep her from wandering. Mother tried shutting her in the woodshed, but Big Joe couldn't stand her howling and would let her out. She tried tying her up, but Bertha would chew at the rope and whine incessantly so that in the end Big Joe would always take pity and go and untie her.

Then, one afternoon, Bertha went missing again. This time she did not come back. This time we could not find her. Charlie wasn't about. Mother and Big Joe went one way looking for her, down towards the river, and I went up into the woods, whistling for her, calling for her. There were deer to be found up in Ford's Cleave Wood, and badgers and foxes. It would be just the sort of place she'd go. I'd been an hour or more searching in the woods with not a sign of her. I was about to give up and go back – perhaps she'd gone home anyway by now, I thought – when I heard a shot ringing out across the valley. It came from somewhere higher in the woods. I ran up the track, ducking the low slung branches, leaping the badger holes, dreading, but already knowing what I would find.

As I came up the rise I could see ahead of me the chimney of Father's old shack, and then the shack itself at the side of the clearing. Outside lay Bertha, her tongue lolling, the grass beside her soaked with blood. The Colonel stood looking down at her, his shotgun in his hands. The door of the shack opened and Charlie and Molly were standing there frozen in disbelief and horror. Then Molly ran over to where Bertha lay and fell to her knees.

"Why?" she cried, looking up at the Colonel. "Why?"

There's a sliver of a moon out there, a new moon. I wonder if they're looking at it back home. Bertha used to howl at the moon, I remember. If I had a coin in my pocket, I'd turn it over and make a wish. When I was young I really believed in all those old tales. I wish I still could believe in them.

But I mustn't think like that. It's no good wishing for the moon, no good wishing for the impossible. Don't wish, Tommo. Remember. Remembrances are real.

We buried Bertha the same day, where Big Joe always buried his creatures, where the mouse had been buried, at the bottom of the orchard. But this time we said no prayers. We laid no flowers. We sang no hymns. Somehow none of us had the heart for it. Perhaps we were all too angry to grieve. Walking back through the trees afterwards, Big Joe was pointing upwards and asking Mother if Bertha was up in Heaven now with Father. Mother said that she was. Then Big Joe asked if we all go up to Heaven after we die.

"Not the Colonel," Charlie muttered. "He'll go

downstairs where he belongs, where he'll burn." Mother darted a reproving glance at him for that.

"Yes, Joe," she went on, her arm around him. "Bertha's up in Heaven. She's happy now."

That evening Big Joe went missing. None of us was that worried, not at first, not while it was still light. Big Joe would often go wandering off on his own from time to time – he'd always done that – but never at night, because Big Joe was frightened of the dark. Our first thought was to look down in the orchard by Bertha's grave, but he wasn't there. We called, but he didn't come. So, as darkness fell and he still had not come home, we knew there was something wrong. Mother sent Charlie and me out in different directions. I went down the lane calling for him all the way. I went as far as the brook where I stood and listened for him, for his heavy stomping tread, for his singing. He sang differently when he was frightened, no tunes or songs, but instead a continuous wailing drone. But there was no drone to be heard, only the running of the brook, which always sounded louder at night. I knew Big Joe must be very frightened for it was by now quite dark. I made my way home, hoping against hope that either Charlie or Mother might have found him.

As I came into the house I could see neither of them had. They looked up hopefully at me as I came in. I shook my head. Out of the silence that followed Mother made up her mind what had to be done. We didn't have any choice, she said. All that mattered was finding Big Joe, and for that we needed more people. She would go up to the Big House right away to ask for the Colonel's help. She sent Charlie and me up to the village to raise the alarm. We knew the best place to go was the pub, that half the village would be in The Duke in the evening. They were singing when we got there, Farmer Cox in full voice. The hubbub and the singing took a while to die down as Charlie told them. By the time he had finished they were all listening in absolute silence. Afterwards, not one of them hesitated. They were putting on hats, shrugging on coats and heading homewards to search their farms, gardens and sheds. The vicar said he'd gather everyone he could in the village hall to organise a search around the village itself, and it was agreed the sounding of the church bell would be the signal that Big Joe had been found.

As everyone dispersed into the darkness outside The Duke, Molly came running up. She had just heard the news about Big Joe. It was her idea that he could be somewhere in the churchyard. I don't know why we hadn't thought of it before – it was always one of his favourite places. So the three of us made for the churchyard. We called for him. We looked behind every gravestone, up every tree. He was nowhere. All we heard was the wind sighing in the yew trees. All we saw were lights dancing through the village, down along the valley. Beyond, and as far as the dark horizon, the countryside was filled with pinpricks of moving lights. We knew then that Mother must have persuaded the Colonel to mobilise everyone on the estate to join in the search.

By dawn there was still no word of Big Joe, still no sign of him. The Colonel had called in the police, and as time passed everything was pointing towards the same dreadful conclusion. We saw the police searching the ponds and river banks with long poles – everyone knew Big Joe could not swim. That was when I first began to believe that the worst could really have happened. No one dared to voice this fear, but all of us were beginning to feel it, and we felt it in each other too. We were searching over ground we had already searched several times. All other explanations for Big Joe's disappearance were being discounted one by one. If he had fallen asleep somewhere, surely he must have woken up by now. If he'd gone and got himself lost, surely, with all the hundreds of people out looking, someone would have found him by now. Everyone I met was grey and grim-faced. All tried their best to raise a smile, but no one could look me in the eye. I could see it wasn't just fear any more. It was worse. There was desperation in those faces, a feeling of complete hopelessness that they could not disguise however hard they tried.

Round about noon, thinking it was just possible Big Joe might somehow have found his way home on his own, we went back to check. We found Mother sitting there alone, clutching the arms of her chair and staring ahead of her. Charlie and I tried to raise her spirits, tried to reassure her as best we could. I don't think we were at all convincing. Charlie made her a cup of tea but Mother would not touch it. Molly sat at her feet and laid her head in her lap. A ghost of a smile came to Mother's face then. Molly could give comfort where we could give none.

Charlie and I left them there together and went outside into the garden. Clinging to what little hope we had left we tried to go back in time, to work out what might have been in Big Joe's mind to make him go off like that. Perhaps it could help us to discover where he had gone if we understood why he had gone. Was he looking for something perhaps, something he'd lost? But what? Had he gone off to see someone? If so, who? There was little doubt in our minds that his sudden disappearance was in some way connected to Bertha's death. The day before, both Charlie and I had felt like going up to the Big House and killing the Colonel for what he had done. Maybe, we thought, maybe Big Joe was feeling the same. Perhaps he had gone out to avenge Bertha's death. Perhaps he was skulking up at the Big House, in the attics, in the cellars, just waiting for his opportunity to strike. But we realised, even as we voiced them, that all such ideas were nothing but ridiculous nonsense. Big Joe didn't have it in him even to think of doing such a thing. He had never in his life been angry at anyone, not even the Wolfwoman – and after all, she'd given him reason enough and plenty. He could be hurt very easily, but he was never angry, and certainly never violent. Time and again Charlie and I would come up with a new scenario, and a different reason for Big Joe's disappearance. But in the end we had to dismiss every one of them as fanciful.

Then we saw Molly come down the garden towards us. "I was just wondering," she said, "I was wondering where Big Joe would most want to be."

"What d'you mean?" Charlie asked.

"Well, I think he'd want to be wherever Bertha is. So he'd want to be in Heaven, wouldn't he? I mean, he thinks Bertha's up in Heaven, doesn't he? I heard your mother telling him. So if he wanted to be with Bertha, then he'd have to go up to Heaven, wouldn't he?"

I thought for one terrible moment that Molly was suggesting that Big Joe had killed himself so that he could go up to Heaven and be with Bertha. I didn't want to believe it, but it made a kind of dreadful sense. Then she explained.

"He told me once," Molly went on, "that your father was up in Heaven and could still see us easily from where he was. He was pointing upwards, I remember, and I didn't understand exactly what he was trying to tell me, not at first. I thought he was just pointing up at the sky in a general sort of a way, or at the birds maybe. But then he took my hand and made me point with him, to show me. We were pointing up at the church, at the top of the church tower. It sounds silly, but I think Big Joe believes that Heaven is at the top of the church tower. Has anyone looked up there?"

Even as she was speaking I remembered how Big Joe had pointed up the church tower the day we had buried Father, how he'd looked back up at it over his shoulder as he walked away.

"You coming, Tommo?" said Charlie. "Moll, will you stay with Mother? We'll ring the bell if it's good news." We ran down through the orchard, scrambled through a hole in the hedge and set off across the fields towards the brook – it would be the quickest way up to the village. We splashed through the brook and raced across the water meadows and up the hill towards the church. Trying to keep up with Charlie was difficult. I kept looking up at the church tower as I ran, all the while urging my legs to keep going, to take me faster, all the while praying that Big Joe would be up there in his heaven.

Charlie reached the village before I did and was haring up the church path ahead of me when he slipped on the cobbles and fell heavily. He sat there cursing and clutching his leg until I caught up with him. Then he called, and I called, "Joe! Joe! Are you up there?" There was no reply.

"You go, Tommo," said Charlie, grimacing in agony. "I

think I've done my ankle in." I opened the church door and walked into the silent dark of the church. I brushed past the bell ropes, and eased open the little belfry door. I could hear Charlie shouting, "Is he up there? Is he there?" I didn't answer. I began to climb the winding stairs. I'd been up into the belfry before, a while ago, when I was in Sunday school. I'd even sung up there in the choir one Ascension Day dawn, when I was little.

I dreaded those steps then and I hated them again now. The slit windows let in only occasional light. The walls were slimy about me, and the stairs uneven and slippery. The cold and the damp and the dark closed in on me and chilled me as I felt my way onwards and upwards. As I passed the silent hanging bells I hoped with all my heart that one of them would be ringing soon. Ninety-five steps I knew there were. With every step I was longing to reach the top, to breathe the bright air again, longing to find Big Joe.

The door to the tower was stiff and would not open. I pushed it hard, too hard, and it flew open, the wind catching it suddenly. I stepped out into the welcome warmth of day, dazzled by the light. At first glance I could see nothing. But then there he was. Big Joe was lying curled up under the shade of the parapet. He seemed fast asleep, his thumb in his mouth as usual. I didn't want to wake him too suddenly. When I touched his hand he did not wake. When I shook him gently by the shoulder he did not move. He was cold to my touch, and pale, deathly pale. I couldn't tell if he was breathing or not, and Charlie was calling up at me from below. I shook him again, hard this time, and screamed at him in my fear and panic. "Wake up, Joe. For God's sake, wake up!" I knew then that he wouldn't, that he'd come up here to die. He knew you had to die to go to Heaven, and Heaven was where he wanted to be, to be with Bertha again, with Father too.

When he stirred a moment later, I could hardly believe it. He opened his eyes. He smiled. "Ha, Tommo," he said. "Ungwee. Ungwee." They were the most beautiful words I'd ever heard. I sprang to my feet and leaned out over the parapet. Charlie was down there on the church path looking up at me.

"We've found him, Charlie," I called down. "We've got him. He's up here. He's all right."

Charlie punched the air and yahooed again and again. He yahooed even louder when he saw Big Joe standing beside me and waving. "Charie!" he cried. "Charie!"

Charlie hopped and limped into the church, and only moments later the great tenor bell rang out over the village, scattering the roosting pigeons from the tower, and sending them wheeling out over the houses, over the fields. Like the pigeons, Big Joe and I were shocked at the violence of the sound. It blasted our ears, sent a tremor through the tower that we felt through the soles of our feet. Alarmed at all this thunderous clanging, Big Joe looked suddenly anxious, his hands clapped over his ears. But when he saw me laughing, he did the same. Then he hugged me, hugged me so tight I thought he was squeezing me half to death. And when he began singing his *Oranges and Lemons*, I joined in, crying and singing at the same time.

I wanted him to come down with me, but Big Joe wanted to stay. He wanted to wave at everyone from the parapet. People were coming from all over: Mr Munnings, Miss McAllister and all the children were streaming out through the school yard and up towards the church. We saw the Colonel, coming down the road in his car, and could just make out the Wolfwoman's bonnet beside him. Best of all we saw Mother and Molly on bicycles racing up the hill, waving at us. Still Charlie rang the bell and I could hear him yahooing down below between each dong, and imagined him hanging on to the rope and riding with it up in the air. Still Big Joe sang his song. And the swifts soared and swooped and screamed all around us, in the sheer joy of being alive, and celebrating, it seemed to me, that Big Joe was alive too.

TWENTY-EIGHT MINUTES PAST ONE

I was once told in Sunday school that a church tower reaches up skywards because it is a promise of Heaven. Church towers are different in France. It was the first thing I noticed when I came here, when I changed my world of home for my world of war. In comparison the church towers at home seem almost squat, hiding themselves away in the folds of the fields. Here there are no folds in the fields, only wide open plains, scarcely a hill in sight. And instead of church towers they have spires that thrust themselves skywards like a child putting his hand up in class, longing to be noticed. But God, if there is one, notices nothing here. He has long since abandoned this place and all of us who live in it. There are not many steeples left now. I have seen the one in Albert, hanging down like a broken promise.

Now I come to think of it, it was a broken promise that brought me here, to France, and now to this barn. The mouse is back again. That's good.

There was a brief time just after we'd found Big Joe when all old hurts and grudges seemed suddenly to be forgiven and forgotten. Forgotten too was all talk of the war in France. No one spoke of anything that day except our search for Big Joe and its happy outcome. Even the Colonel and the Wolfwoman were celebrating with the rest of us up in The Duke. Molly's mother and father were there too, celebrating with everyone else, and smiling – though being strict chapel people, they didn't touch a drop of drink. I'd never seen Molly's mother smile before that. And then the Colonel announced that he was paying for all the drinks. It wasn't long – it only took a couple of pints – before Farmer Cox began singing. He was still singing when we left; some of the songs were getting a bit rude by then. I was there outside The Duke when Mother went up and thanked the Colonel for his help. He offered us all a lift home in his Rolls Royce! The Peacefuls in the back of the Colonel's car, and the Wolfwoman in the front, being friendly! We couldn't believe it, not after all the bad blood between us over the years.

The Colonel broke the spell on the way home, talking about the war, and how the army should be using more cavalry over in France.

"Horses and guns," he said, "in that order. That's how we beat the Boers in South Africa. That's what they should be doing. If I were younger, I'd go myself. They'll soon be needing every horse they can find, Mrs Peaceful, and every man, too. It's not going at all well out there."

Mother thanked him again as he helped us out of the car outside our gate. The Colonel touched his hat and smiled. "Don't you go running off again, young man," he said to Big Joe. "You gave us all a terrible fright." And even the Wolfwoman waved at us almost cheerily as they drove off.

That night Big Joe began coughing. He'd caught a chill and it had gone to his lungs. He was in bed with a fever for weeks afterwards, and Mother hardly left his side, she was so worried.

By the time he was better, the whole episode of his disappearance had been forgotten, overtaken by news in the papers of a great and terrible battle on the Marne, where our armies were fighting the Germans to a standstill, trying desperately to halt their advance through France.

One evening, Charlie and I arrived home from work a little late, having stopped on the way for a drink at The Duke as we often did. In those days, I remember, I had to pretend I liked the beer. The truth was I hated the stuff, but I loved the company. Charlie might have bossed me about on the farm, but after work, up at The Duke, he never treated me like the fifteen-year-old I was, though some of the others did. I couldn't have them knowing that I hated beer. So I'd force down a couple of pints with Charlie, and often left The Duke a little befuddled in the head. That was why I was woozy when we came home that evening. When I opened the door and saw Molly, sitting there on the floor with her head on Mother's lap, it seemed I was suddenly back to the day Big Joe had gone missing. Molly looked up at us, and I could see that she had been crying, and that this time it was Mother doing the comforting.

"What is it?" Charlie asked. "What's happened?"

"You may well ask, Charlie Peaceful," Mother said. She didn't sound at all pleased to see us. I wondered at first if she had seen we'd been drinking. Then I noticed a leather suitcase under the windowsill, and Molly's coat over the back of Father's fireside chair.

"Molly's come to stay," Mother went on. "They've thrown her out, Charlie. Her mother and father have thrown her out, and it's your fault."

"No!" Molly cried. "Don't say that. It isn't his fault. It's no one's fault." She ran over to Charlie and threw herself into his arms.

"What's happened, Moll?" asked Charlie. "What's going on?"

Molly was shaking her head as she wept uncontrollably now on his shoulder. He looked at Mother.

"What's going on, Charlie, is that she's going to have your baby," she said. "They packed her case, put her out of the door and told her never to come back. They never want to see her again. She had nowhere else to go, Charlie. I said she was family, that she belongs with us now, that she can stay as long as she likes."

It seemed an age before Charlie said anything. I saw his face go through all manner of emotions: incomprehension, bewilderment, outrage, through all these at once, and then at last to resolve. He held Molly away from him now and brushed away her tears with his thumb as he looked steadily into her eyes. When he spoke at last, it wasn't to Molly, but to Mother. "You shouldn't have said that to Moll, Mother," he spoke slowly, almost sternly. Then he began to smile. "That was for me to say. It's our baby, my baby, and Moll's my girl. So I should have said it. But I'm glad you said it all the same."

After that Molly became even more one of us than she had been before. I was both overjoyed and miserable at the same time. Molly and Charlie knew how I must have felt, I think, but they never spoke of it and neither did I.

They were married up in the church a short time later. It was a very empty church. There was no one there except the vicar and the four of us, and the vicar's wife sitting at the back. Everyone knew about Molly's baby by now, and because of that the vicar had agreed to marry them only on certain conditions: that no bells were to be rung and no hymns to be sung. He rushed through the marriage service as if he wanted to be somewhere else. There was no wedding feast afterwards, only a cup of tea and some fruit cake when we got home.

Shortly afterwards, Mother received a letter from the Wolfwoman saying it had been a marriage of shame; how she had thought of dismissing Molly and only decided against it because, whilst Molly was clearly a weak and immoral girl, she felt she could not in all conscience punish Molly for something that she was sure was much more Charlie's fault than hers, and that anyway Molly had already been punished enough for her wickedness. Mother read the letter out loud to all of us, then scrunched it up and threw it into the fire – where it belonged, she said.

I moved into Big Joe's room and slept with him in his bed, which wasn't easy because he was big and the bed very narrow. He muttered to himself loudly in his dreams, and tossed and turned almost constantly. But, as I lay awake at nights, that was not what troubled me most. In the next room slept the two people I most loved in all the world who, in finding each other, had deserted me. Sometimes, in the dead of night, I thought of them lying in each other's arms and I wanted to hate them. But I couldn't. All I knew was that I had no place at home any more, that I would be better off away, and away from them in particular.

I tried never to be alone with Molly for I did not know what to say to her any more. I didn't stop to drink with Charlie any more at The Duke, for the same reason. On the farm, I took every opportunity that came my way to work on my own, so as to be nowhere near him. I volunteered for any fetching and carrying that had to be done away from the farm. Farmer Cox seemed more than happy for me to do that. He was always sending me off with the horse and cart on some errand or other: bringing back feed from the merchants maybe, fetching the seed potatoes, or perhaps taking a pig to market to sell for him. Whatever it was, I took my time about it and Farmer Cox never seemed to notice. But Charlie did. He said I was skiving off work, but he knew that all I was doing was avoiding him. We knew each other so well. We never argued, not really; perhaps it was because neither of us wanted to hurt the other. We both knew enough hurt had been done already, that more would only widen the rift between us and neither of us wanted that.

It was while I was off "skiving" in Hatherleigh market one morning that I came face to face with the war for the first time, a war that until now had seemed unreal and distant to all of us, a war only in newspapers and on posters. I'd just sold Farmer Cox's two old rams, and got a good price for them too, when I heard the sound of a band coming down the High Street, drums pounding, bugles blaring. Everyone in the market went running, and so did I.

As I came round the corner I saw them. Behind the band there must have been a couple of dozen soldiers, splendid in their scarlet uniforms. They marched past me, arms swinging in perfect time, buttons and boots shining, the sun glinting on their bayonets. They were singing along with the band: *It's a long way to Tipperary, it's a long way to go.* And I remember thinking it was a good thing Big Joe wasn't there, because he'd have been bound to join in with his *Oranges and Lemons*. Children were stomping alongside them, some in paper hats, some with wooden sticks over their shoulders. And there were women throwing flowers, roses mostly, that were falling at the soldiers' feet. But one of them landed on a soldier's tunic and somehow stuck there. I saw him smile at that.

Like everyone else, I followed them round the town and up into the square. The band played *God Save the King* and then, with the Union Jack fluttering behind him, the first sergeant major I'd ever set eyes on got up on to the steps of the cross, slipped his stick smartly under his arm, and spoke to us, his voice unlike any voice I'd heard before: rasping, commanding.

"I shan't beat about the bush, ladies and gentlemen," he began. "I shan't tell you it's all tickety-boo out there in France – there's been too much of that nonsense already in my view. I've been there. I've seen it for myself. So I'll tell you straight. It's no picnic. It's hard slog, that's what it is, hard slog. Only one question to ask yourself about this war. Who would you rather see marching through your streets? Us lot or the Hun? Make up your minds. Because, mark my words, ladies and gentlemen, if we don't stop them out in France the Germans will be here, right here in Hatherleigh, right here on your doorstep."

I could feel the silence all around.

"They'll come marching through here burning your houses, killing your children, and yes, violating your women. They've beaten brave little Belgium, swallowed her up in one gulp. And now they've taken a fair slice of France too. I'm here to tell you that unless we beat them at their own game, they'll gobble us up as well." His eyes raked over us. "Well? Do you want the Hun here? Do you?"

"No!" came the shout, and I was shouting along with them.

"Shall we knock the stuffing out of them then?"

"Yes!" we roared in unison.

The sergeant major nodded. "Good. Very good. Then we shall need you." He was pointing his stick now into the crowd, picking out the men. "You, and you and you." He was looking straight at me now, into my eyes. "And you too, my lad!"

Until that very moment it had honestly never occurred to me that what he was saying had anything to do with me. I had been an onlooker. No longer.

"Your king needs you. Your country needs you. And all the brave lads out in France need you too." His face broke into a smile as he fingered his immaculate moustache. "And remember one thing, lads – and I can vouch for this – all the girls love a soldier."

The ladies in the crowd all laughed and giggled at that. Then the sergeant major returned the stick under his arm.

"So, who'll be the first brave lad to come up and take the king's shilling?"

No one moved. No one spoke up. "Who'll lead the way? Come along now. Don't let me down, lads. I'm looking for boys with hearts of oak, lads who love their King and their country, brave boys who hate the lousy Hun."

That was the moment the first one stepped forward, flourishing his hat as he pushed his way through the cheering crowd. I knew him at once from school. It was big Jimmy Parsons. I hadn't seen him for a while, not since his family had moved away from the village. He was even bigger than I remembered, fuller in the face and neck, and redder too. He was showing off now just like he always had done in the school yard. Egged on by the crowd, others soon followed.

Suddenly someone prodded me hard in the small of my back. It was a toothless old lady pointing at me with her crooked finger. "Go on, son," she croaked. "You go and fight. It's every man's duty to fight when his country calls, that's what I say. Go on. Y'ain't a coward, are you?"

Everyone seemed to be looking at me then, urging me on, their eyes accusing me as I hesitated. The toothless old lady jabbed me again, and then she was pushing me forward. "Y'ain't a coward, are you? Y'ain't a coward?" I didn't run, not at first. I sidled away from her slowly, and then backed out of the crowd hoping no one would notice me. But she did. "Chicken!" she screamed after me. "Chicken!" Then I did run. I ran helter-skelter down the deserted High Street, her words still ringing in my ears.

As I drove the cart out of the market, I heard the band strike up again in the square, heard the echoing thump thump of the big bass drum calling me back to the flag. Filled with shame, I kept on going. All the way back to the farm I thought about the toothless old lady, about what she had said, what the sergeant major had said. I thought about how fine and manly the men looked in their bright uniforms, how Molly would admire me, might even love me, if I joined up and came home in my scarlet uniform, how proud Mother would be, and Big Joe. By the time I was unhitching the horse back at the farm, I was quite determined that I would do it. I would be a soldier. I would go to France and, like the sergeant major said, kick the stuffing out of the lousy Germans. I made up my mind I would break the news to everyone at supper. I couldn't wait to tell them, to see the look on their faces.

We'd barely sat down before I began. "I was in Hatherleigh this morning," I said. "Mr Cox sent me to market."

"Skiving as usual," Charlie muttered into his soup.

I ignored him and went on. "The army was there, Mother. Recruiting, they were. Jimmy Parsons joined up. Lots of others too."

"More fool them," Charlie said. "I'm not going, not ever. I'll shoot a rat because it might bite me. I'll shoot a rabbit because I can eat it. Why would I ever want to shoot a German? Never even met a German."

Mother picked up my spoon and handed it to me. "Eat," she said, and she patted my arm. "And don't worry about it, Tommo, they can't make you go. You're too young anyway."

"I'm nearly sixteen," I said.

"You've got to be seventeen," said Charlie. "They won't let you join unless you are. They don't want boys."

So I ate my soup and said no more about it. I was disappointed at first that I hadn't had my big moment, but as I lay in bed that night I was secretly more than a little relieved that I wouldn't be going off to the war, and that by the time I was seventeen it would all be over anyway, as like as not.

A few weeks later the Colonel paid Mother a surprise visit, whilst Charlie and I were out at work. We didn't hear about it until we got home in the evening and Molly told us. I thought something strange was going on as Mother was unusually preoccupied and quiet at supper. She wouldn't even answer Big Joe's questions. Then when Molly got up saying she felt like a walk, and suggested both Charlie and I came with her, I knew for sure something was up. It was a very long time since we'd been out together, just the three of us. If Charlie had asked me, I'd have said no for sure.

But it was always more difficult for me to refuse Molly.

We went down to the brook, just like we'd done in the old days whenever we'd wanted to be alone together, where Molly and I had met up so often when I'd been their go-between postman. Molly didn't tell us until we were sitting either side of her on the river bank, until she had taken each of us by the hand.

"I'm breaking a promise I made to your mother," she began. "I so much don't want to tell you this, but I must. You have to know what's going on. It's the Colonel. He came in and told her this morning. He said he was only doing what he called his 'patriotic duty'. He told us that the war was going badly for us, that the country was crying out for men. So he's decided that now is the time for every able-bodied man who lives or works on his estate, everyone who can be spared, to volunteer, to go off to the war and do his bit for King and country. The estate will just have to manage without them for a while." I felt Molly's grip tighten on my hand, and a tremor come into her voice. "He said you've got to go, Charlie, or else he won't let us stay on in the cottage. Your mother protested all she could, but he wouldn't listen. He just lost his temper. He'll put us out, Charlie, and he won't go on employing your mother or me unless you go."

"He wouldn't do that, Moll. It's just a threat," Charlie said. "He can't do it. He just can't."

"He would," Molly replied, "and he can. You know he

can. And when the Colonel gets it into his head to do something, and he's in the mood to do it, he will. Look what he did to Bertha. He means it, Charlie."

"But the Colonel promised," I said. "And his wife did too before she died. She said she wanted Mother looked after. And the Colonel said we could stay on in the cottage. Mother told us."

"Your mother reminded him of that," Molly replied. "And d'you know what he said? He said it had never been a promise as such, only his wife's wish, and that anyway the war had changed everything. He was making no exceptions. Charlie has to join up or we'll be out of the cottage at the end of the month."

We sat there holding hands, Molly's head on Charlie's shoulder, as evening fell around us. Molly was sobbing quietly from time to time but none of us spoke. We didn't need to. We all knew there was no way out of this, that the war was breaking us apart, and that all our lives would be changed for ever. But at that moment, I treasured Molly's hand in mine, treasured this last time together.

Suddenly, Charlie broke the silence. "I'll be honest, Moll," he said. "It's been bothering me a lot just lately. Don't get me wrong. I don't want to go. But I've seen the lists in the papers – y'know, all the killed and the wounded. Poor beggars. Pages of them. It hardly seems right, does it, me being here, enjoying life, while they're over there. It's not all bad, Moll. I saw Benny Copplestone yesterday. He was sporting his uniform up at the pub. He's back on leave. He's been a year or more out in Belgium. He says it's all right. 'Cushy,' he called it. He says we've got the Germans on the run now. One big push, he reckons, and they'll all be running back to Berlin with their tails between their legs, and then all our boys can come home."

He paused, and kissed Molly on her forehead. "Anyway, it looks like I haven't got much choice, have I, Moll?"

"Oh Charlie," Molly whispered. "I don't want you to go."

"Don't worry, girl," Charlie said. "With a bit of luck I'll be back to wet the baby's head. And Tommo will look after you. He'll be the man about the place, won't you, Tommo? And if that silly old fart of a Colonel sticks his lousy head in our front door again when I'm gone, shoot the bastard, Tommo, like he shot Bertha." And I knew he was only half-joking, too.

I don't believe I even thought about what I said next. "I'm not staying," I told them. "I'm coming with you, Charlie."

They both tried all they could to dissuade me. They argued, they bullied, but I would not be put off, not this time. I was too young, Charlie said. I said I was sixteen in a couple of weeks and as tall as he was, that all I had to do was shave and talk deeper and I could easily be taken for seventeen. Mother wouldn't let me go, Molly said. I said I'd run away, that she couldn't lock me up.

"And who'll be there to look after us if you both go?" Molly was pleading with me now.

"Who would you rather I look after, Molly," I replied. "All of you at home who can perfectly well look after yourselves? Or Charlie, who's always getting himself into nasty scrapes, even at home?" When they had no answer to this, they knew I'd won, and I knew it too. I was going to fight in the war with Charlie. Nothing and no one could stop me now.

I've had two long years to think on why I decided like that, on the spur of the moment, to go with Charlie. In the end I suppose it was because I couldn't bear the thought of being apart from him. We'd lived our lives always together, shared everything, even our love for Molly. Maybe I just didn't want him to have this adventure without me. And then there was that spark in me newly kindled by those scarlet soldiers marching bravely up the High Street in Hatherleigh, the steady march of their feet, the drums and bugles resounding through the town, the sergeant major's stirring call to arms. Perhaps he had awoken in me feelings I never realised I'd had before, and that I had certainly never talked about. It was true that I did love all that was familiar to me. I loved what I knew, and what I knew was my family, and Molly, and the countryside I'd grown up in. I did not want any enemy soldier ever setting foot on our soil, on my place. I would do all I could to stop him and to protect the people I loved. And I would be doing it with Charlie. Deep down though, I knew that, more than Charlie, more than my country or the band or the sergeant major, it was that toothless old woman taunting me in the square. "Y'ain't a coward, are you? Y'ain't a coward?"

The truth was that I wasn't sure I wasn't, and I needed to find out.

I had to prove myself. I had to prove myself to myself.

Two days later, two days of parrying Mother's many attempts to keep me from going, we all went off together to Eggesford Junction Station where Charlie and I were to catch the train to Exeter. Big Joe had not been told anything about us going off to war. We were going away for a while, and we'd be back soon. We didn't tell him the truth, but we told him no lies either. Mother and Molly tried not to cry because of him. So did we.

"Look after Charlie for me, Tommo," Molly said. "And look after yourself too." I could feel the swell of her belly against me as we hugged.

Mother told me to promise to keep clean, to be good, to write home and to come home. Then Charlie and I were on the train – the first train we'd ever been on in our lives, and we were leaning out of the window and waving, only pulling back spluttering and coughing when we were engulfed suddenly in a cloud of sooty smoke. When it cleared and we looked out again, the station was already out of sight. We sat down opposite each other.

"Thanks, Tommo," said Charlie.

"For what?" I said.

"You know," he replied, and we both looked out of the window. There was no more to say about it. A heron lifted off the river and accompanied us for a while before veering away from us and landing high in the trees. A startled herd of Ruby Red cows scattered as we passed by, tails high as they ran. Then we were in a tunnel, a long dark tunnel filled with din and smoke and blackness. It seems like I've been in that tunnel every day since. So Charlie and I went rattling off to war. It all seems a very long time ago now, a lifetime.

FOURTEEN MINUTES PAST

I keep checking the time. I promised myself I wouldn't, but I can't seem to help myself. Each time I do it, I put the watch to my ear and listen for the tick. It's still there, softly slicing away the seconds, then the minutes, then the hours. It tells me there are three hours and forty-six minutes left. Charlie told me once this watch would never stop, never let me down, unless I forgot to wind it. The best watch in the world, he said, a wonderful watch. But it isn't. If it was such a wonderful watch it would do more than simply keep the time – any old watch can do that. A truly wonderful watch would *make* the time. Then, if it stopped, time itself would have to stand still, then this night would never have to end and morning could never come. Charlie often told me we were living on borrowed time out here. I don't want to borrow any more time. I want time to stop so that tomorrow never comes, so that dawn will never happen.

I listen to my watch again, to Charlie's watch. Still ticking. Don't listen, Tommo. Don't look. Don't think. Only remember.

"Stand still! Look to your front, Peaceful, you horrible little man!" ... "Stomach in, chest out, Peaceful." ... "Down in that mud, Peaceful, where you belong, you nasty little worm. Down!" ... "God, Peaceful, is that the best they can send us these days? Vermin, that's what you are. Lousy vermin, and I've got to make a soldier of you."

Of all the names Sergeant "Horrible" Hanley bellowed out across the parade ground at Etaples when we first came to France, Peaceful was by far the most frequent. There were two Peacefuls in the company of course, and that made a difference, but it wasn't the main reason. Right from the very start Sergeant Hanley had it in for Charlie. And that was because Charlie just wouldn't jump through hoops like the rest of us, and that was because Charlie wasn't frightened of him, like the rest of us were.

Before we ever came to Etaples, all of us, including Charlie and me, had had an easy ride, a gentle enough baptism into the life of soldiering. In fact we'd had several weeks of little else but larks and laughter. On the train to Exeter, Charlie said we could easily pass for twins, that I'd have to watch my step, drop my voice, and behave like a seventeen-year-old from now on. When the time came, in front of the recruiting sergeant at the regimental depot, I stood as tall as I could and Charlie spoke up for me, so my voice wouldn't betray me. "I'm Charlie Peaceful, and he's Thomas Peaceful. We're twins and we're volunteering."

"Date of birth?"

"5th October," said Charlie.

"Both of you?" asked the recruiting sergeant, eyeing me a little I thought.

"Course," Charlie replied, lying easily, "only I'm older than him by one hour." And that was that. Easy. We were in.

The boots they gave us were stiff and far too big – they hadn't got any smaller sizes. So Charlie and I and the others clomped about like clowns, clowns in tin hats and khaki. The uniforms didn't fit either, so we swapped about until they did. There were some faces from home we recognised in amongst the hundreds of strangers. Nipper Martin, a little fellow with sticking-out ears, who grew turnips on his father's farm in Dolton, and who played a wicked game of skittles up at The Duke. There was Pete Bovey, thatcher and cider drinker from Dolton too, red-faced and with hands like spades, who we'd often seen around the village in Iddesleigh, thumping away at the thatch, high up on someone's roof. With us too was little Les James from school, son of Bob James, village rat catcher and wart charmer. He had inherited his father's gifts with rats and warts and he always claimed to be able to know whether it was going to rain or not the next day. He was usually right too. He always had a nervous tick in one eye that I could never stop looking at when we were in class together.

At training camp on Salisbury Plain, living cheek by jowl,

we all got to know each other fast, though not necessarily to like one another – that came later. And we got to know our parts, too, how to make believe we were soldiers. We learnt how to wear our khaki costumes – I never did get to wear the scarlet uniform I'd been hoping for – how to iron creases in and iron wrinkles out, how to patch and mend our socks, how to polish our buttons and badges and boots. We learnt how to march up and down in time, how to about-turn without bumping into one another, how to flick our heads right and salute whenever we saw an officer. Whatever we did, we did together, in time – all except for little Les James who could never swing his arms in time with the rest of us, no matter how much the sergeants and corporals bellowed at him. His legs and arms stepped and swung in time with each other, and with no one else, and that was all there was to it. He didn't seem to mind how often they shouted at him that he had two left feet. It gave us all something to laugh about. We did a lot of laughing in those early days.

They gave us rifles and packs and trenching shovels. We learnt to run up hills with heavy packs, and how to shoot straight. Charlie didn't have to be taught. On the rifle range he proved to be far and away the best shot in the company. When they gave him his red marksman's badge I was so proud of him. He was pretty pleased himself, too. Even with the bayonets it was still a game of make-believe. We'd have to charge forward screaming whatever obscenities we knew

– and I didn't know many, not then – at the straw-filled dummies. We'd plunge our bayonets in up to the hilt, swearing and cursing the filthy Hun as we stabbed him, twisting the blade and pulling it out as we'd been taught. "Go for the stomach, Peaceful. Nothing to get hung up on in there. Jab. Twist. Out."

Everything in the army had to be done in lines or rows. We slept in long lines of tents, sat on privies in rows. Not even the privy was private, I learnt that very quickly. In fact nowhere was private any more. We lived every moment of every day together, and usually in lines. We lined up together for shaves, for food, for inspections. Even when we dug trenches, they had to be in lines, straight trenches with straight edges, and we had to dig fast, too, one company in competition with another. We poured sweat, our backs ached, our hands were permanently raw with blisters. "Faster!" the corporals shouted. "Deeper! You want to get your head blowed off, Peaceful?"

"No, Corporal."

"You want to get your arse blowed off, Peaceful?"

"No, Corporal."

"You want to get your nuts blowed off, Peaceful?"

"No, Corporal."

"Then dig, you lazy beggars, dig, 'cos when you get out there, that's all you've got to hide in, God's good earth. And when they whizzbangs come over I'm telling you you'll always wish you'd dug deeper. The deeper you dig the longer you'll live. I know, I've been there."

No matter what the officers and NCOs told us of the hardships and dangers of trench warfare, we still all believed we were simply in some kind of rehearsal, actors in costume. We had to play our part, dress our part, but in the end it would only be a play. That was what we tried to believe – if ever we spoke about it, that is. But the truth was that we didn't speak of it much. I think we didn't dare because deep down we all knew and we all trembled, and were trying to deny it or disguise it or both.

I remember we were on exercise in the hills, lying there on our backs in the sunshine one morning when Pete sat up suddenly. "Hear that?" he said. "It's guns, from over in France, real guns." We sat up and listened. We heard it. Some said it was distant thunder. But we heard it all right. We saw the sudden fear in each other's eyes and knew it for what it was.

But that same afternoon we were back to play-acting, war games in full pack, attacking some distant "enemy" copse. When the whistles blew we climbed out of our trenches and walked forward, bayonets fixed. Then on a bellowed command we threw ourselves face down and crawled on through the long grass. The ground under us was still warm with summer, and there were buttercups. I thought of Molly then and Charlie and the buttercups in the water meadows back home. A bee, heavy with pollen and still greedy for more, clover-hopped in front of me as I crawled. I remember I spoke to him. "We're much alike, bee, you and me," I said. "You may carry your pack underneath you and your rifle may stick out of your bottom. But you and me, bee, are much alike." The bee must have taken offence at this, because he took off and flew away. I lay where I was, propped up on my elbows, and watched him go, until my thoughts were rudely interrupted by the corporal.

"What d'you think you're on, Peaceful, a bloody picnic? On your feet!"

In those first few weeks in uniform I hardly had time to miss anyone, not even Molly, though I thought of her often, and Mother and Big Joe. But they were only ever fleeting thoughts. Charlie and I rarely talked of home – we were hardly ever alone together anyway. We'd even stopped cursing the Colonel by now. There didn't seem any point, not any more. It was a hateful thing he'd done, but it was a done thing. We were soldiers now, and it wasn't bad, so far. In fact, despite all the lining up and the bellowing, it was turning out to be a lark, a real lark. Charlie and I wrote cheery letters home – most of his were to Molly, all of mine to Mother and Big Joe. We read them aloud to each other, those bits we wanted to share anyway. We weren't allowed to say where we were or anything about the training, but we always found plenty to tell them, plenty to brag about, plenty to ask about. We told them the truth, that we were having a good time – eating well and being good – mostly. But the moment we got on the ship for France the good times ended. Little Les James said he smelled a storm in the air, and as usual he was right.

There wasn't a man on board that ship that didn't want to die before he ever got to France. Most of us, Charlie and me included, had never seen the sea before, much less the heaving grey waves of the English Channel, and we lurched about the deck like drunken ghosts longing only to be released from our agony. Charlie and I were vomiting over the side when a seaman came up to us, clapped us heartily on the back and told us that if we were going to die we'd feel much better doing it down below in the hold with the horses. So Charlie and I staggered down the gangways until we found ourselves deep in the bowels of the ship and in amongst the terrified horses, who seemed happy to have someone for company as we crawled in and curled up in their straw, too close to their hooves for safety, but feeling too ill to care. The seaman was right. Down here the ship seemed to roll much less, and despite the stifling stench of oil and horse dung we began to feel better almost at once.

When at long last the engines finally stopped we went up on deck and looked out at France for the first time. The

French gull that hovered overhead eyeing me with deep suspicion looked much like every gull I'd seen following the plough back at home. Every voice I heard on the quayside below was English. Every uniform and every helmet was like our own. Then, as we came down the gangplank into the fresh morning air, we saw them, the lines of walking wounded shuffling along the quay towards us, some with their eyes bandaged, holding on to the shoulder of the one in front. Others lay on stretchers. One of them, puffing on a cigarette between pale parched lips, looked up at me out of sunken yellow eyes. "G'luck lads," he cried as we passed. "Give 'em what for." The rest stayed silent and their staring silence spoke to each of us as we formed up and marched out of town. We all knew then that the larking and the play-acting were over. From that moment none of us doubted the seriousness of what this would be about. It was our lives we would be acting out over here, and for many of us, our deaths.

If any of us had any last lingering delusions then they were very soon dispelled by our first sight of the vast training camp at Etaples. The camp stretched away as far as the eye could see, a tented city, and everywhere I looked there were soldiers drilling – marching, doubling, crawling, wheeling, saluting, presenting arms. I had never in my life seen such a bustle of people, never heard such a racket of humanity. The air echoed with the din of barked orders and shrieked obscenities. That was when we first came across

Sergeant Horrible Hanley, our chief scourge and tormentor over the coming weeks, who was to do his utmost to make all our lives a misery.

From the moment we saw him most of us lived in dread of him. He was not a big man, but he had eyes of steel that bore into us, and a lashing snarl in his voice that terrified us. We just buckled under and did what he wanted us to. It was the only way to survive. However much he doubled us up hills with stones in our packs, however much he made us throw ourselves down in the freezing mud and crawl through it, we did it, and with a will, too. We knew that anything less – to protest, to complain, to talk back, even to look him in the eye – would be to draw down upon us even more fury, even more pain, even more punishment. We knew because we saw what happened to Charlie. Charlie wouldn't even go along with his little jokes. It was this that got him into trouble in the first place.

It was a Sunday morning and we were being inspected before a church parade when Sergeant Hanley found fault with Charlie's cap badge. He said it was crooked. Nose to nose, Hanley bellowed into Charlie's face. I was in the rank behind Charlie, but even there I could feel the spray from Hanley's spittle. "You know what you are? You're a blot on Creation, Peaceful. What are you?"

Charlie thought for a moment and then replied in a clear, firm voice, and utterly without fear: "Happy to be here, Sergeant."

Hanley looked taken aback. We all knew the answer Hanley was looking for. He asked again. "You're a blot on Creation. What are you?"

"Like I said, Sergeant, happy to be here." Charlie just would not give Hanley the satisfaction of playing his game, no matter how often Hanley asked, nor how loud he shouted. For that Charlie was put on extra sentry duty, so that night after night Charlie hardly got any sleep. Hanley never let up after that, never missed an opportunity to pick on Charlie and punish him.

There were some in the company who didn't at all like what Charlie was doing, Pete amongst them. He said Charlie was stirring Hanley up unnecessarily, and was making things difficult for the rest of us. I've got to say I half agreed with them – though I didn't tell them that, and I certainly didn't tell Charlie. It was quite true that Hanley was giving our company in particular a lot of grief, and it was obvious this was because he had a vendetta against Charlie. Charlie was swiping at the wasp, and the wasp wasn't just stinging him, he was stinging all of us. Charlie was beginning to be thought of as a bit of a liability in the company, a bit of a Jonah. No one said as much to him – they all liked and respected Charlie too much – but Pete and Little Les and Nipper Martin did come to me on the quiet, and asked me to talk to him. I tried as best I could to warn Charlie. "He's like Mr Munnings back at school, Charlie. Our lord and master, remember? Hanley's our lord and master out here. You can't fight him."

"But that doesn't mean I have to lie down and let him walk all over me," he said. "I'll be all right, you'll see. You look after yourself. You watch your back. He's got his eye on you, Tommo, I've seen him." That was typical Charlie. I was trying to warn him, and he just turned the whole thing around and ended up warning me.

It was a little enough thing that sparked it off, a dirty rifle barrel. Thinking back now I know for sure Hanley must have done it quite deliberately, to provoke Charlie. Everyone knew by now that I was Charlie's younger brother, and a year too young to enlist. We'd long ago given up the pretence of being twins. After we'd first met up with Pete and Little Les and Nipper from home, we'd had to come clean about it, and by then it didn't much matter. There were dozens of others underage in the regiment and everyone knew it. After all, they needed all the men they could get. The other lads teased me about it, about having a chin like a baby's bottom and about my not needing to shave, which wasn't true, and about my squeaky voice, too. But they all knew that Charlie was looking out for me. If ever the teasing got a bit out of hand, Charlie would give them a little look and it would stop. He never nannied me, but everyone knew he'd stick by me no matter what.

Hanley was nasty but he wasn't stupid. He must have sensed it too, and that was why he began picking on me as well. I'd had plenty of practice at putting up with this kind of thing back at school with Mr Munnings, but Horrible Hanley was a tormentor in a class of his own. He found excuse after excuse to pick on me and punish me. Worn down by extra drills and sentry duty, I was very soon exhausted. The more exhausted I became the more mistakes I made, and the more mistakes I made, the more Hanley punished me.

We'd been drilling one morning, and were stood to attention in three ranks, when he grabbed my rifle. Looking down the barrel, Hanley pronounced it "dirty". I knew the punishment, we all did: five times doubling around the parade ground holding your rifle above your head. After only two circuits I just could not keep my rifle up there any more. My arms buckled at the elbows, and Hanley bellowed at me: "Every time you let that rifle fall, Peaceful, you begin the punishment again. Five more, Peaceful."

My head was swimming. I was staggering now, not running, and barely able to keep upright. My back was on fire with pain. I simply hadn't the strength to lift the rifle above my head at all. I remember hearing a shout, knowing it was Charlie, and wondering why he was shouting. Then I passed out. When I woke in my tent they told me what had happened. Charlie had broken ranks and run at Hanley, screaming at him. He hadn't actually hit him, but he had stood there nose to nose with Hanley telling him exactly what he thought of him. They said it was magnificent, that everyone cheered when he'd finished. But Charlie had been marched off to the guardroom under arrest.

The next day, in heavy rain, the whole battalion was paraded to witness Charlie's punishment. He was brought out and lashed to a gun wheel. Field Punishment Number One, they called it. The brigadier in command sat high on his horse and said that this should be a warning to all of us, that Private Peaceful had got off lightly, that insubordination in time of war could be seen as mutiny and that mutiny was punishable by death, by the firing squad. All day long Charlie was lashed there in the rain, legs apart, arms spread-eagled. As we marched past him, Charlie smiled at me. I tried to smile back, but no smile came, only tears. He seemed to me like Jesus hanging on the cross in the church back home in Iddesleigh. And I thought then of the hymn we used to sing in Sunday school, *What a friend we have in Jesus*, and sang it to myself only to banish my tears as I marched. I remembered Molly singing it down in the orchard when we buried Big Joe's mouse, and as I remembered I found myself involuntarily changing the words, changing Jesus into Charlie. I sang it to myself under my breath as we were marched away. "What a friend I have in Charlie."

A MINUTE PAST THREE

I dropped off to sleep. I've lost precious minutes – I don't know
how many, but they are minutes I can never have back. I should
be able by now to fight off sleep. I've done it often enough on
lookout in the trenches, but then I had cold or fear or both as
my wakeful companions. I long for that moment of surrender
to sleep, just to drift away into the warmth of nothingness.
Resist it, Tommo, resist it. After this night is over, then you can
drift away, then you can sleep for ever, for nothing will ever
matter again. Sing *Oranges and Lemons*. Go on. Sing it. Sing it
like Big Joe does, over and over again. That'll keep you awake.

Oranges and Lemons, say the bells of St. Clements,
You owe me five farthings, say the bells of St. Martins.
When will you pay me? say the bells of Old Bailey.
When I grow rich, say the bells of Shoreditch.
When will that be? say the bells of Stepney.
I'm sure I don't know, says the great bell at Bow.
Here comes a candle to light you to bed,
And here comes a chopper to chop off your head.

They tell us we're going up to the front, and we're all relieved. We are leaving Etaples and Sergeant Hanley for ever, we hope. We're leaving France and marching into Belgium, singing as we go. Captain Wilkes likes us to sing. Good for morale, he says, and he's right too. The more we sing the more cheery we become, and that's in spite of all we see – the shell-shattered villages we march through, the field hospitals we pass, the empty coffins waiting. The captain was a choirmaster and a teacher back home in Salisbury, so he knows what he's doing. We hope he'll know what he's doing when we get to the trenches. It's difficult to believe he and Sergeant Horrible Hanley are in the same army, on the same side. We have never come across anyone who treats us with such kindness and consideration. As Charlie says, "he treats us right". So we treat him right too, except that is for Nipper Martin who ribs him whenever he can. Nipper can be like that, a bit mean sometimes. He's the only one who still keeps on about my squeaky voice.

"Are we downhearted? No! Then let your voices ring and altogether sing: are we downhearted? No." We sing out and march with a new spring in our step. And when that finishes and there's just the sound of marching feet Charlie starts up with *Oranges and Lemons*, which makes us all laugh, the captain too. I join in and soon they're all singing along. No one knows why we sing it of course. It's a secret between Charlie and me, and I know as we sing that he's thinking of Big Joe and home as I am.

The captain has told us we're going to a sector that's been quiet for a while now, that things shouldn't be too bad. We're happy about that of course, but we honestly don't care that much. Nothing could be worse than what we've just left. We pass a battery of heavy guns, the gunners sitting round a table playing cards. The guns are silent now, their barrels gaping at the enemy. I look where they point but can see no enemy. All I have seen of our enemy so far is a huddle of ragged prisoners sheltering from the rain under a tree as we marched past, their grey uniforms caked in mud. Some of them were smiling. One of them even waved and called out: "Hello, Tommy."

"He's talking to you," said Charlie laughing. So I waved back. They seemed much like us, only dirtier.

Two aeroplanes circle like buzzards in the distance. As they come closer I see they are not circling at all, but chasing one another. They are still too far away for us to see which of them is ours. We make up our minds it is the smaller one and cheer for him madly, and I'm wondering suddenly if the pilot from the yellow plane that landed in the water meadows that day might be up there in our plane. I can almost taste the humbugs he gave us as I watch them. I lose them in the sun, and then the smaller one spirals earthwards and our cheering is instantly silenced.

At rest camp they give us our first letters. Charlie and I lie in our tent and read them over and over again, till we know them almost by heart. We've both had letters from Mother and Molly, and Big Joe's put his mark at the bottom of each one, his smudged thumbprint in ink with "Joe" written large beside it in heavily indented pencil. That makes us smile. I can see him writing it, nose to the paper, tongue between his teeth. Mother writes that they're turning most of the Big House into a hospital for officers, and the Wolfwoman rules the roost up there more than ever. Molly says the Wolfwoman now wears a lady's wide-brimmed straw hat with a big white ostrich feather instead of her old black bonnet, and that she smiles all the time "like Lady Muck". Molly writes, too, that she's missing me, and that she is well, except that she feels a little sick sometimes. She hopes the war will be over quickly and then we can all be together again. I can't read the rest, or her name, because Joe's finger has blotted everything else out.

They let us out of camp for an evening and we go into the nearest village, Poperinghe, "Pop" everyone seems to call it. Captain Wilkes tells us there's an *estaminet* there – that's a sort of pub he says, where you can drink the best beer outside England and eat the best egg and chips in the entire world. He's right. Pete, and Nipper, Little Les, Charlie and me stuff ourselves on egg and chips and beer. We're like camels filling up at an oasis that we've discovered by accident and may never find again.

There's a girl in the restaurant who smiles at me when she

clears the plates away. She's the daughter of the owner who is always very smartly dressed and very round and very merry, like a Father Christmas without the beard. It's difficult to believe she's his daughter, for in every way she's the opposite, wonderfully elf-like and delicate. Nipper notices her smiling at me and makes something dirty of it. She knows it and moves away. But I don't forget her smile, nor the egg and chips and the beer. Charlie and me drink to the Colonel and the Wolfwoman again and again, wishing them all the misfortune and misery and all the little monster children they so richly deserve, and then we stagger back to camp. I'm properly drunk for the first time in my life, and feel very proud of myself, until I lie down and my head swirls and threatens to drag me down into some black abyss where I fear to go. I struggle to think straight, to picture the girl in the *estaminet* in Pop. But the more I think of her the more I see Molly.

The big guns bring me to my senses. We crawl out of our tent into the night. The sky is lit up all along the horizon. Whoever is underneath all that, friend or foe, is taking a terrible pounding. "That's Ypres," says the captain beside me in the darkness.

"Poor beggars," says someone else. "Glad we're not in Wipers tonight."

We go back to our tent, huddle under our blankets and thank God it's not us, but every one of us knows our time must come, and soon.

The next evening we go up into the line. There are no big guns tonight, but rifle fire and machine-gun fire crackle and rattle ahead of us, and flares go up, intermittently lighting the darkness. We know we are close now. It seems as if the road is taking us down into the earth itself, until it is a road no more but rather a tunnel without a roof, a communications trench. We have to be silent now. Not a whisper, not a word. If the German machine gunners or mortars spot us, and there are places they can, then we're done for. So we stifle our curses as we slither and slide in the mud, holding on to one another to stop ourselves falling. A line of soldiers passes us coming the other way, dark-eyed men, sullen and weary. No need for questions. No need for answers. The haunted, hunted look in their eyes tells it all.

We find our dugout at last, every one of us yearning only for sleep now. It has been a long, cold march. A mug of hot sweet tea and to lie down, it's all I want. But with Charlie, I'm posted to sentry duty. For the first time I look out through the wire over no-man's-land and towards the enemy trenches, less than two hundred yards from our front line, they tell us, but we can't see them, only the wire. The night is still now. A machine gun stutters and instantly I duck down. I needn't have bothered. It's one of ours. I'm overwhelmed by fear, numbed by it, and for the moment that fear banishes the wretched discomfort of my wet feet and frozen hands. I feel Charlie there beside me. "Fine night for poaching, Tommo," he whispers. I can see his smile in the dark and my fear is gone at once.

It's just as the captain said it would be, quiet. Every day I wait for the Germans to shell us, and they don't. It seems they're too busy shelling Wipers further up the line to bother about us, and I can't say I'm sorry. I even begin to hope that they might have run out of shells. Every time I look through the periscope I expect to see the grey hordes coming at us across no-man's-land, but no one comes. I am almost disappointed. We hear occasional sniper fire, so there is no smoking in the trenches at night, "unless you want your head shot off," the captain says. Our artillery lobs a shell or two over into their trenches once in a while, and they do the same. Each one, theirs or ours – and ours sometimes drop short – comes as a surprise and terrifies me at first, terrifies all of us, but in time we become used to it and pay less attention.

Our trench and our dugouts have been left in a mess by the previous occupants, a company of Jocks from the Seaforths, so when we're not on stand-to at dawn, brewing up or sleeping, we're set to clearing up their mess. Captain Wilkes – or "Wilkie" as we call him now – is meticulous about tidiness and cleanliness, "because of the rats," he says. We find out soon enough he's right again. I am the first to find them. I am detailed to begin shoring up a dilapidated trench wall. I plunge my shovel in and open up an entire nest of them. They come pouring out, skittering away over my boots. I recoil in horror for a moment and then set about stamping them to death in the mud. I don't kill a single one, and we see them everywhere after that. Fortunately we have Little Les, our own professional rat-catcher, who is now called upon whenever a rat is spotted, whatever the time, day or night, he doesn't mind. He jokes that it makes him feel at home. He knows the ways of rats, and kills with a will each time, tossing their corpses up into no-man's-land with a flourish of triumph. After a while the rats seem to know they have met their match in Little Les and leave us be.

But our other daily curse, lice, we all have to deal with ourselves. Each of us has to burn off his own with a lighted cigarette end. They inhabit us wherever they can, the folds of our skin, the creases of our clothes. We long for a bath to drown the lot of them, but above all we long to be warm again and dry.

Our greatest scourge is neither rats nor fleas but the unending drenching rain, which runs like a stream along the bottom of our trench, turning it into nothing but a mud-filled ditch, a stinking gooey mud that seems to want to hold us and then suck us down and drown us. I have not had dry feet since I got here. I go to sleep wet. I wake up wet, and the cold soaks through my sodden clothes and into my aching bones. Only sleep brings any real relief, sleep and food. God, how we long for both. Wilkie moves among us at dawn on the firestep, a word here, a smile there. He keeps us going, keeps us up to the mark. If he has fear he never shows it, and if that is courage then we're beginning to catch it.

But we couldn't do without Charlie either. It's Charlie who keeps us together, breaks up our squabbles (which are many and frequent now that we are so closely confined together) and jollies each of us along when we get downhearted. He's become like a big brother to everyone. After Sergeant Hanley and the field punishment, and the way Charlie managed to smile through it all, there isn't a man in the company who doesn't look up to him. Being his real brother I could feel I live in his shadow, but I never have and I do not now. I live in his glow.

We have a few more miserable days in the line, all of us longing for the comforts of rest camp. But when we get there they keep us endlessly busy. We clean our kit, march up and down, turn out for inspections again and again, do our gas mask drill again, and then there are always more ditches and drains to dig to take away the incessant rain. But we do have letters from home, from Molly and Mother, and they have knitted woollen scarves and gloves and socks for us both. We have communal baths in great steaming vats in a barn down the road and, best of all, eggs and chips and beer at the *estaminet* in Pop. The beautiful girl with the doe eyes is there, but she does not always notice me, and when she doesn't I drink even more, to drown my sorrows.

The first snow of winter sees us back in the trenches. It freezes as it falls, hardening the mud – and that certainly is a blessing. Providing there is no wind we are no colder than we were before and can at least keep our feet dry. The guns have stayed relatively silent in our sector and we have had few casualties so far: one wounded by a sniper, two in hospital with pneumonia, and one with chronic trench foot – which affects us all. From what we hear and read we are in just about the luckiest sector we could be.

Word has come down from Headquarters, Wilkie says, that we must send out patrols to find out what regiments have come into the line opposite us and in what strength – though why we have to do that we do not know. There are spotter planes doing that almost every day. So most nights now, four or five of us are picked, and a patrol goes out into no-man's-land to find out what they can. More often than not they find out nothing. No one likes going, of course, but nobody's been hurt so far, and you get a double rum ration before you go and everyone wants that.

My turn soon comes up as it was bound to. I'm not particularly worried. Charlie's going with me, and Nipper Martin, Little Les and Pete – "the whole skittle team", Charlie calls us. Wilkie's heading the patrol and we're glad of that. He tells us we have to achieve what the other patrols have not. We have to bring back one prisoner for questioning. They give us each a double rum ration, and

I'm warmed instantly to the roots of my hair, to the toes of my feet.

"Stay close, Tommo," Charlie whispers, and then we are climbing out over the top, crawling on our bellies through the wire. We snake our way forward. We slither into a shell hole and lie doggo there for a while in case we've been heard. We can hear Fritz talking now, and laughing. There's the sound of a gramophone playing – I've heard all this before on lookout, but distantly. We're close now, very close, and I should be scared witless. Strangely, I find I'm not so much frightened as excited. Maybe it's the rum. I'm out poaching again, that's what it feels like. I'm tensed for danger. I'm ready for it, but not frightened.

It takes an eternity to cross no-man's-land. I begin to wonder if we'll ever find their trenches at all. Then we see their wire up ahead. We wriggle through a gap, and still undetected we drop down into their trench. It looks deserted, but we know it can't be. We can still hear the voices and the music. I notice the trench is much deeper than ours, wider too and altogether more solidly constructed. I grip my rifle tighter and follow Charlie along the trench, bent double like everyone else. We're trying not to, but we're making too much noise. I can't understand why no one has heard us. Where are their sentries, for God's sake? Up ahead I can see Wilkie waving us on with his revolver. There is a flickering of light now coming from a dugout ahead, where the voices are, where the music is. From the sound of it there could be half a dozen men in there at least. We only need one prisoner. How are we going to manage half a dozen of them?

At that moment the light floods into the trench as the dugout curtain opens. A soldier comes out shrugging on his coat, the curtain closing behind him. He is alone, just what we are after. He doesn't seem to see us right away. Then he does. For a split second the Hun does nothing and neither do we. We just stand and look at one another. He could so easily have done what he should have done, just put up his hands and come with us. Instead he lets out a shriek and turns, blundering through the curtain back into the dugout. I don't know who threw the grenade in after him, but there is a blast that throws me back against the trench wall. I sit there stunned. There is screaming and firing from inside the dugout, then silence. The music has stopped.

By the time I get in there Little Les is lying on his side shot through the head, his eyes staring at me. He looks so surprised. Several Germans are sprawled across their dugout, all still, all dead – except one. He stands there naked, blood spattered and shaking. I too am shaking. He has his hands in the air and is whimpering. Wilkie throws a coat over him and Pete bundles him out of the dugout. Frantic now to get back we scrabble our way up out of the trench, the Hun still whimpering. He is beside himself with terror. Pete is shouting at him to stop, but he's only making it worse. We follow the captain through the German wire and run.

For a while I think we have got away with it, but then a flare goes up and we are caught suddenly in broad daylight. I hurl myself to the ground and bury my face in the snow. Their flares last so much longer than ours, shine so much brighter. I know we're for it. I press myself into the ground, eyes closed. I'm praying and thinking of Molly. If I'm going to die I want her to be my last thought. But she's not. Instead I'm saying sorry to Father for what I did, that I didn't mean to do it. A machine gun opens up behind us and then rifles fire. There is nowhere to hide, so we pretend to be dead. We wait till the light dies and the night is suddenly black again. Wilkie gets us to our feet and we go on, running, stumbling, until more lights go up, and the machine gunners start up again. We dive into a crater and roll down crashing through the ice into the watery bottom. Then the shelling starts. It seems as if we have woken up the entire German army. I cower in the stinking water with the German and Charlie, the three of us clinging together, heads buried in one another as the shells fall all about us. Our own guns are answering now but it is little comfort to us. Charlie and I drag the Hun prisoner out of the water. Either he is talking to himself or he's saying a prayer, it's difficult to tell.

Then we see Wilkie lying higher up the slope, too close to the lip of the crater. When Charlie calls out to him he doesn't reply. Charlie goes to him and turns him over. "It's my legs," I hear the captain whisper. "I can't seem to move my legs." He's too exposed up there, so Charlie drags him back down as gently as he can. We try to make him comfortable. The Hun keeps praying out loud. I'm quite sure he's praying now. "*Du lieber Gott*," I hear. They call God by the same name. Pete and Nipper are crawling over towards us from the far side of the crater. We are together at least. The ground shudders, and with every impact we are bombarded by showers of mud and stone and snow. But the sound I hate and fear most is not the sound of the explosion – by then it's done and over with, and you're either dead or not. No, it's the whistle and whine and shriek of the shells as they come over. It's the not knowing where they will land, whether this one is for you.

Then, as suddenly as the barrage begins, it stops. There is silence. Darkness hides us again. Smoke drifts over us and down into our hole, filling our nostrils with the stench of cordite. We stifle our coughing. The Hun has stopped his praying, and is lying curled up in his overcoat, his hands over his ears. He's rocking like a child, like Big Joe.

"I won't make it," Wilkie says to Charlie. "I'm leaving it to you to get them all back, Peaceful, and the prisoner. Go on now."

"No sir," Charlie replies. "If one goes we all go. Isn't that right, lads?"

That's how it happened. Under cover of an early-morning mist we made it back to our trenches, Charlie carrying Wilkie on his back the whole way, until the stretcher bearers came for him in the trench. As they lifted him, Wilkie caught Charlie by the hand and held it. "Come and see me in hospital, Peaceful," he said. "That's an order." And Charlie promised he would.

We had a brew up with our prisoner in the dugout before they came for him. He smoked a cigarette Pete had given him. He'd stopped shaking now, but his eyes still held their fear. We had nothing to say to one another until the moment he got up to leave. "*Danke*," he said. "*Danke sehr.*"

"Funny that," Nipper said when he'd gone. "Seeing him standing there with not a stitch on. Take off our uniforms and you can hardly tell the difference, can you? Not a bad bloke, for a Fritz that is."

That night I didn't think, as I should have done, of Little Les lying out there in the German dugout, with a hole in his head. I thought of the Hun prisoner we'd brought back. I didn't even know his name, yet, after that night cowering in the shell hole with him, I felt somehow I knew him better than I'd ever known Little Les.

We are back at last at rest camp, most of us anyway. We soon find out which hospital Wilkie is in, and we go to see him as Charlie had promised. It's a big chateau of a place, with ambulances coming and going, and crisp-looking nurses bustling everywhere. "Who are you?" asks the orderly at the desk.

"Peaceful," says Charlie smiling – he loves playing this joke. "Both of us are Peaceful."

The orderly does not look amused, but he seems to have been expecting us. "Which of you is Charlie Peaceful?"

"I am," says Charlie.

"Captain Wilkes said you would come." The orderly is reaching into the desk drawer. He takes out a watch. "He left this for you," he says, and Charlie takes the watch.

"Where is he?" Charlie asks. "Can we see him?"

"Back in Blighty by now. Left yesterday. In a bad way. Nothing more we could do for him here, I'm afraid."

As we walk down the steps of the hospital Charlie is putting the watch on his wrist.

"Does it work?" I ask.

"Course it does," he says. He shows it to me on his wrist. "What d'you think?"

"Nice," I reply.

"It's not just nice, Tommo," Charlie says. "It's wonderful, that's what it is. Ruddy wonderful. Tell you what – if anything happens to me it's yours, all right?"

TWENTY-FIVE PAST THREE

The mouse is here again. He keeps stopping and looking up at me. He's wondering if he should run away, whether I'm friend or foe. "*Wee, sleekit, caw'rin tim'rous beastie.*" I don't know what half the words mean, but I still know the poem. Back at school Miss McAllister made us stand up and recite it on Burns Day. She said it was good for us to have at least one great Scottish poem in our heads for ever. This wee beastie is tim'rous all right, but he's not Scottish, he's a Belgian mouse. I recite the poem to him all the same. He seems to understand because he listens politely. I do it in Miss McAllister's Scottish accent. I'm almost word perfect. I think Miss McAllister would have been proud of me. But the moment I finish he's gone, and I'm alone once more.

Earlier they came and asked if I wanted someone to stay with me through the night, and I said no. I even sent the padre away. They asked if there was anything I wanted, anything they could do to help, and I said there was nothing. Now I long to have them all here, the padre too. We could have had singsongs. They could have brought me egg and chips. We could have drunk ourselves silly and I could be numb with it by now. But all I've had for company is a mouse, a vanishing Belgian mouse.

The next time they sent us up into the line it wasn't back to our "quiet" sector, it was into the Wipers salient itself. For months now Fritz had been pounding away at Wipers, trying everything he could to batter it into submission. Time and again he'd almost broken through into the town and had only been driven back at the last moment. But the salient around the town was shrinking all the time. From the talk in the *estaminet* in Pop and from the almost constant bombardment a few miles to the east of us we all knew how bad it must be in there. Everyone knew they had us surrounded and overlooked on three sides, so that they could chuck all they wanted into our trenches and there was nothing much we could do about it, except grin and bear it.

Our new company commander, Lieutenant Buckland, told us how things were, how if we gave way then Wipers would be lost, and that Wipers must not be lost. He didn't say why it mustn't be lost, but then he wasn't Wilkie. We all felt the loss of Wilkie very keenly. Without him we were like sheep without a shepherd. Lieutenant Buckland was doing his best, but he was straight out from England. He might have been very properly spoken, but he knew even less about fighting this war than we did. Nipper said he was just a young pipsqueak, and that he belonged back at school. And it was true, he seemed younger than any of us, even me.

As we marched through Wipers that evening I wondered why it was worth fighting for at all. So far as I could see there was no town left, nothing you could call a town anyway. Rubble and ruin, that's all the place was, more dogs and cats than townspeople. We saw two horses lying dead and mangled in the street, as we passed by what was left of the town hall; and everywhere there were soldiers and guns and ambulances on the move, and hurrying. They were not shelling the town as we came through, but I was as terrified then as I ever had been. I could not get those horses and their terrible wounds out of my head. The sight of them haunted me, haunted all of us, I think. None of us sang. None of us talked. I longed only to reach the sanctuary of our new trenches, to crawl into the deepest dugout I could find and hide.

But when we got there the trenches were a bitter disappointment to us. Wilkie would have been appalled at the state of them. In places they were little more than shallow dilapidated ditches affording us precious little protection, and the mud here was even deeper than before. There was a sickly-sweet stench about the place that had to be more than stagnant mud and water. I knew well enough what it was, we all did, but no one dared speak of it. Word came back that from now on we should keep our heads down because here was where we could be most easily spotted by their snipers. But there was at least some consolation when we reached the dugout. It was the best we'd ever had, deep and warm and dry. I could not sleep though. I lay there that night, knowing how a hunted fox must feel lying low in his lair with the hounds waiting for him outside.

I am on stand-to the next morning, locked inside my gas mask in a world of my own, listening to myself breathing. The mist rises over no-man's-land. I see in front of me a blasted wasteland. No vestige of fields or trees here, not a blade of grass – simply a land of mud and craters. I see unnatural humps scattered over there beyond our wire. They are the unburied, some in field-grey uniforms and some in khaki. There is one lying in the wire with his arm stretched heavenwards, his hand pointing. He is one of ours, or was. I look up where he is pointing. There are birds up there, and they are singing. I see a beady-eyed blackbird singing to the world from his barbed-wire perch. He has no tree to sing from.

The pipsqueak of a lieutenant says, "Keep your eyes peeled, lads. Keep your wits about you." He's always doing that, always telling us to do things we're already doing. But nothing moves out there in no-man's-land but the crows. It is a dead man's land.

We're back down in the dugout after stand-to, brewing up when the bombardment starts. It doesn't stop for two whole days. They are the longest two days of my life. I cower there, we all do, each of us alone in our own private misery. We cannot talk for the din. There can be little sleep. When I do sleep I see the hand pointing skywards, and it is Father's hand, and I wake shaking. Nipper Martin has got the shakes, too, and Pete tries to calm him but he can't. I cry like a baby sometimes and not even Charlie can comfort me. We want nothing more than for it to stop, for the earth to be still again, for there to be quiet. I know that when it's over they'll be coming for us, that I'll have to be ready for them, for the gas maybe, or the flame-thrower, or the grenades, or the bayonets. But I don't mind how they come. Let them come. I just want this to stop. I just want it to be over.

When at last it does we are ordered out on to the firestep, gas masks on, bayonets fixed, eyes straining through the smoke that drifts across in front of us. Then out of the smoke we see them come, their bayonets glinting, one or two at first, but then hundreds, thousands. Charlie's there beside me.

"You'll be all right, Tommo," he says. "You'll be fine."

He knows my thoughts. He sees my terror. He knows I want to run.

"Just do what I do, right? And stay by me."

I stay and I do not run, only because of Charlie. The firing starts all along the line, machine guns and rifle fire, shelling, and I'm firing too. I'm not aiming, just firing, firing, loading and firing again. And still they do not stop. For a few moments it seems as if bullets do not touch them. They come on towards us unscathed, an army of invincible grey ghosts. Only when they begin to crumple and cry out and fall do I begin to believe they are mortal. And they are brave, too. They do not falter. No matter how many are cut down, those that are left keep coming. I can see their wild eyes as they reach our wire. It is the wire that stops them. Somehow enough of it has survived the bombardment. Only a few of them find the gaps, and they are shot down before they ever reach our trenches. Those that are left, and there are not many now, have turned and are stumbling back, some throwing away their rifles. I feel a surge of triumph welling inside me, not because we have won, but because I have stood with the others. I have not run.

"Y'ain't a coward, are you?"

No, old woman, I am not, I am not.

Then the whistle goes, and I am up with the others and after them. We pour through the gap in the wire. They lie here so thick on the ground it is hard not to step on them. I have no pity for them, but no hatred either. They came to kill us, and we killed them. I look up. They are running from us as we go forward. We fire at will now, picking them off. We are across no-man's-land before we know it. We find a way through their wire and leap down into their frontline trenches. I am a hunter seeking out my quarry, a quarry I will kill, but my quarry has gone. The trench is deserted.

Lieutenant Buckland is up on the parapet above us, screaming at us to follow him, that we've got them on the run. I follow. We all follow. He is not so much of a pipsqueak as we all thought. Everywhere I look, to my right, to my left, as far as I can see, we are advancing and I am a part of it and I feel suddenly exhilarated. But in front of us the enemy seems to have vanished. I am unsure what to do now. I look all around for Charlie, and cannot see him anywhere. That's when the first shell comes screaming over. I throw myself down, flatten myself into the mud, as it explodes close behind me, deafening me instantly. After a while I force myself to lift up my head and look. Ahead of me I see us advancing still, and everywhere in front of us the flash of rifle fire, the spitting flame of machine guns. For a moment I think I am dead already. All is soundless, all is unreal. A silent storm of shelling rages about me. Before my eyes we are scythed down, blown apart, obliterated. I see men crying out but I hear nothing. It is as if I am not there, as if this horror cannot touch me.

They are stumbling back towards me now. I can't see Charlie among them. The lieutenant grabs me and hauls me to my feet. He's shouting at me, then turning me and pushing me back towards our trenches. I am trying to run with the others, trying to keep with them. But my legs are leaden and will not let me run. The lieutenant stays with me, urging me on, urging us all on. He is a good man. He's right there alongside me when he's hit. He drops to his knees and dies looking up at me. I see the light fade in his eyes. I watch him fall forward on his face. I do not know how I manage to get back after that, but I do. I find myself curled up in the dugout, and the dugout is half-empty. Charlie is not there. He has not come back.

At least I can hear again now, even if it is mostly the ringing in my head. Pete has news of Charlie. He says he's sure he saw him on the way back from the German trenches, hobbling, using his rifle as a stick, but all right. That gives me some fragile hope, but it is hope that ebbs away as the hours pass. As I lie there I relive each and every horror. I see the puzzled look on the lieutenant's face as he kneels there, trying to speak to me. I see a thousand silent screams. To drive these visions away I tell myself all manner of reassuring tales about Charlie: how Charlie must be out there in some crater, only waiting for the clouds to cover the moon before he crawls back; how he's got himself lost and has landed up somewhere down the line with another regiment and will find his way back to us in the morning – it happens all the time. My mind races and will not let me rest. There is no shelling to interrupt my thoughts. Outside the world has fallen silent. Both armies lie exhausted in their trenches and bleeding to death.

By stand-to the next morning I knew for sure that Charlie would not be coming back, that all my stories had been just that, stories. Pete and Nipper and the others had tried to convince me that he might still be alive. But I knew he was not. I was not grieving. I was numb inside, as void of all feeling as the hands that clutched my rifle. I looked out over no-man's-land where Charlie had died. They lay as if they'd been heaped against the wire by the wind, and Charlie, I knew, was one of them. I wondered what I would write to Molly and Mother. I could hear Mother's voice in my head, hear her telling Big Joe how Charlie would not be coming back, how he had gone to Heaven to be with Father and Bertha. Big Joe would be sad. He would rock. He would hum *Oranges and Lemons* mournfully up his tree. But after a few days his faith would comfort him. He would believe absolutely that Charlie was up there in the blue of Heaven, high above the church tower somewhere. I envied him that. I could no longer even pretend to myself that I believed in a merciful god, nor in a heaven, not any more, not after I had seen what men could do to one another. I could believe only in the hell I was living in, a hell on earth, and it was man-made, not God-made.

That night, like a man sleepwalking, I got up to take my turn on sentry duty. The sky was filled with stars. Molly knew the stars well – the Plough, the Milky Way, the Pole Star – she'd often tried to teach me them all when we were out poaching. I tried to remember, tried to identify them in amongst the millions, and failed. As I was looking up in wonder at the immensity and beauty of it all, I found myself almost believing in Heaven again. I picked one bright star in the west to be Charlie and another next to him. That was Father. They were together looking down on me. I wished then I had told Charlie about how Father had died, for there would be no secrets between us now. I shouldn't have kept it from him. So, unspeaking, I told him then, saw him glisten and wink at me, and knew he had understood and did not blame me. Then I heard Charlie's voice in my head. "Don't go all dreamy on lookout, Tommo," he was saying. "You'll fall asleep. You can get shot for that." I widened my eyes, blinked them hard, and took in a deep gulp of cold air to wake me up.

Only moments later I saw something move out beyond the wire. I listened. There was still a ringing in my ears, so I couldn't be sure of it, but I thought I could hear someone, a voice, and a voice that was not inside my head. It was a whisper. "Hey! Anyone there? It's me, Charlie Peaceful. D Company. I'm coming in. Don't shoot." Perhaps I was already asleep and deep in a wonderful dream I wanted to be true. But the voice came again, louder this time. "What's the matter with you lot? Are you all fast asleep or what? It's Charlie, Charlie Peaceful."

From under the wire a dark shape shifted and moved towards me. Not a dream, not one of my make-believe stories. It was Charlie. I could see his face now and he could see mine. "Tommo, you dozy beggar, you. Give us a hand, will you?" I grabbed him and tumbled him down into the trench. "Am I glad to see you!" he said. We hugged one another then. I don't think we ever had before. I cried, and tried unsuccessfully to hide it, until I felt him crying too.

"What happened?" I asked.

"They shot me in the foot, can you believe it? Shot right through my boot. I bled like a pig. I was on my way back and I passed out in some shell hole. Then by the time I woke up all you lot had gone off and left me. I had to stay put till nightfall. Seems like I've been crawling all bloody night."

"Does it hurt?"

"I can't feel a thing," Charlie said. "But then, I can't feel the other foot either – I'm frozen stiff. Don't you worry, Tommo. I'll be right as rain."

They stretchered him to hospital that night, and I did not see him again until they pulled us out of the line a few days later. Pete and I went to see him as soon as we could. He was sitting up in his bed and grinning all over his face. "It's good in here," he said. "You want to try it sometime. Three decent meals a day, nurses, no mud, and a nice long way from Mister Fritz."

"How's the foot?" I asked him.

"Foot? What foot?" He patted his leg. "That's not a foot, Tommo. That's my ticket home. Some nice, kind Mister Fritz gave me the best present he could, a ticket home to Blighty.

They're sending me to a hospital back home. It's a bit infected. Lots of bones broken, they said. It'll mend, but it'll take an operation, and then I've got to rest it up. So they're packing me off tomorrow."

I knew I should be pleased for him, and I wanted to be, but I just could not bring myself to think that way. All I could think was that we'd come to this war together. We'd stuck together through thick and thin, and now he was breaking the bond between us, and deserting me. Worst of all he was going home without me, and he was so unashamedly happy about it.

"I'll give them your best, Tommo," he said. "Pete'll keep an eye on you for me. You'll look after him, won't you Pete?"

"I don't need looking after," I snapped.

But Charlie either hadn't heard me or he ignored me. "And you make sure he behaves, Pete. That girl in the *estaminet* in Pop, she's got her eye on him. She'll eat him alive." They laughed at my embarrassment, and I could not disguise my hurt and discomfort. "Hey, Tommo." Charlie put his hand on my arm. "I'll be back before you know it." And he was serious now, for the first time. "Promise," he said.

"You'll be seeing Molly, then, and Mother?" I asked.

"Just let them try and stop me," he said. "I'll wangle a bit of leave. Or maybe they'll come and see me in hospital. With a bit of luck I could get to see the baby. Less than a month to go now, Tommo, and I'll be a father. You'll be an uncle too. Think of that."

But the evening after Charlie had left for Blighty I wasn't thinking of that at all. I was in the *estaminet* in Pop drowning my anger in beer. And it *was* anger I was drowning, not just sorrows: anger at Charlie for abandoning me, anger that he was to see Molly and home, and that I was not. In my befuddled state I even thought of deserting, of going after him. I'd make my way to the Channel and find a boat. I'd get home somehow.

I looked around me. There must have been a hundred or more soldiers in the place that evening, Pete and Nipper Martin, and some of the others among them, but I felt completely alone. They were laughing and I could not laugh. They were singing and I could not sing. I couldn't even eat my egg and chips. It was stiflingly hot in there and the air was thick with cigarette smoke. I could hardly breathe. I went outside to get some air. That brought me very quickly to my senses, and I gave up at once all idea of deserting. I would go back to camp instead. It was the easier choice – you can get shot for desertion.

"Tommy?"

It was her, the girl from the *estaminet*. She was carrying out a crate of wine bottles.

"You are ill?" she asked me.

Tongue-tied, I shook my head. We stood for some moments

listening to the thunder of the guns as a heavy barrage opened up over Wipers, the sky lit up over the town like an angry sunset. Flares rose and hovered and fell over the front line.

"It is beautiful," she said. "How can it be beautiful?"

I wanted to speak, but I did not trust myself to do so. I felt suddenly overwhelmed by tears, by longing for home and for Molly.

"How old?" she asked.

"Sixteen," I muttered.

"Like me," she said. I found her looking at me more closely. "I have seen you before, I think?" I nodded. "I will see you again perhaps?"

"Yes," I said. Then she was gone and I was alone again in the night. I was calmer now, more at peace with myself and stronger, too. Walking back to camp I made up my mind. We were being sent away for training the next day, but as soon as I came back, I would go straight to Pop, to the *estaminet*, and when the girl brought me my egg and chips I would be brave – I would ask her her name.

Two weeks later I was back, and that's just what I did. "Anna," she told me. And she tinkled with laughter when I told her my name was Tommo. "It's true then," she said. "Every English soldier is called Tommy."

"I'm not Tommy, I'm Tommo," I replied.

"It's the same," she laughed. "But you are different, different from the others, I think."

When she heard I had worked on a farm, and with horses, she took me into the stable and showed me her father's carthorse. He was massive and magnificent. Our hands met as we patted him. She kissed me then, brushed my cheek with her lips. I left her and walked back along the gusty road to camp under the high riding moon, singing *Oranges and Lemons* at the top of my voice.

Pete greeted me in the tent with a scowl. "You won't be so ruddy happy, Tommo, when you hear what I've got to tell you."

"What?" I asked.

"Our new sergeant. It's only Horrible-bleeding-Hanley from Etaples."

From then on, every waking hour of every day, Hanley was at us. We'd been mollycoddled, he said. We were sloppy soldiers and he was going to lick us back into shape. And we weren't allowed out of camp until he was satisfied. And of course he was never satisfied. So I couldn't get out of camp to see Anna again. By the time we went back up into the line, Hanley snapping at our heels, his voice had become a vicious bark inside each of our heads. Every one of us hated him like poison, a great deal more than we had ever hated Fritz.

NEARLY FOUR O'CLOCK

There is the beginning of day in the night sky, not yet the pale light of dawn, but night is certainly losing its darkness. A cockerel sounds his morning call, and tells me what I already know but do not want to believe, that morning will break and soon.

Morning at home used to be walking with Charlie to school, wading through piles of autumn leaves and stamping the ice in the puddles, or the three of us coming up through the woods after a night's poaching on the Colonel's river, and crouching down to watch a badger that didn't know we were there. Morning here has always been to wake with the same dread in the pit of my stomach, knowing that I will have to look death in the face again, that up to now it may have been someone else's death, but that today it could be mine, that this may be my last sunrise, my last day on earth.

All that is different about this morning is that I know whose death it will be and how it will happen.

Looking at it that way it seems not so bad. Look at it that way, Tommo. Look at it that way.

I always imagined I'd be lost without Charlie at my side, and the truth is that I might have been had it not been for the new batch of recruits that joined us straight from home. And how we needed them. Almost half of us were missing by this time, killed or wounded or sick. Those of us that were left were to them battle-hardened soldiers, old lags who had seen it all, and therefore to be admired, respected, and even a little feared, it seemed. Young though I still felt, I don't think I looked it, not any more. Pete and Nipper Martin and I were old soldiers now, and we behaved like it, alternately reassuring the new recruits or terrifying them with our stories, befriending them or teasing them. I think we rather played up to the role they gave us and we revelled in it, too, particularly Pete, who was more inventive with his stories than Nipper and me. All this gave me less time to dwell on my own fears. I was far too busy pretending I was someone else.

For some time, life was about as quiet as it could get in the front line. We and Fritz did little more than irritate each other with occasional whizzbangs and night patrols, and in the close confinement of the dugout and the trenches even Sergeant Hanley could do little to make our lives any more of a misery than they already were, though he still did his very best, with an endless succession of inspections and consequent punishments. But for days on end the guns stayed silent, the spring sun shone, warming our backs and drying out the mud. And best of all, we went to bed dry – a rare treat, a miraculous treat. Yes, the rats were still there and the lice loved us as much as ever, but this was a picnic compared to all we'd been through before.

By now I think the new recruits were all beginning to think that we old lags had been exaggerating with some of our harsher tales of trench warfare. Boredom and Sergeant Hanley seemed to them to be the worst they had had to endure so far. And it was certainly true, particularly in Pete's case, that we had laid it on a bit thick. But Pete, like the rest of us, had, for the most part anyway, told them stories that had at least some connection with the truth. None of us, not even Pete, could have imagined or invented what would happen to us on the quietest of May mornings, when we were least expecting it.

Stand-to on the firestep at dawn had been normal, by now a mere routine, and an annoying one too. Attacks came mostly at dawn, we knew that, but after all this time we expected nothing to happen, and nothing had happened, not for a long while now. We were lulled by the blue skies perhaps, or by sheer boredom. Fritz seemed to have gone to sleep on us and as far as we were concerned that suited us fine. We thought we could go to sleep too. The awakening came suddenly. I was in the dugout, and I was just beginning a letter home.

•

I am writing to Mother – I haven't written for a while and am feeling guilty about it. My pencil keeps breaking and I am sharpening it again. Everyone else is lying asleep in the sun or is sitting about smoking and chatting. Nipper Martin is cleaning his rifle again. He's always very particular about that.

"Gas! Gas!"

The cry goes up and is echoed all along the trench. For a moment we are frozen with panic. We have trained for this time and again, but nonetheless we fumble clumsily, feverishly with our gas masks.

"Fix bayonets!" Hanley's yelling while we're still trying frantically to pull on our gas masks. We grab our rifles and fix bayonets. We're on the firestep looking out into no-man's-land, and we see it rolling towards us, this dreaded killer cloud we have heard so much about but have never seen for ourselves until now. Its deadly tendrils are searching ahead, feeling their way forward in long yellow wisps, scenting me, searching for me. Then finding me out, the gas turns and drifts straight for me. I'm shouting inside my gas mask. "Christ! Christ!" Still the gas comes on, wafting over our wire, through our wire, swallowing everything in its path.

I hear again in my head the instructor's voice, see him shouting at me through his mask when we went out on our last exercise. "You're panicking in there, Peaceful. A gas mask is like God, son. It'll work bloody miracles for you, but you've got to believe in it." But I don't believe in it! I don't believe in miracles.

The gas is only feet away now. In a moment it will be on me, around me, in me. I crouch down hiding my face between my knees, hands over my helmet, praying it will float over my head, over the top of the trench and seek out someone else. But it does not. It's all around me. I tell myself I will not breathe, I must not breathe. Through a yellow mist I see the trench filling up with it. It drifts into the dugouts, snaking into every nook and cranny, looking for me. It wants to seek us all out, to kill us all, every one of us. Still I do not breathe. I see men running, staggering, falling. I hear Pete shouting out for me. Then he's grabbing me and we run. I have to breathe now. I can't run without breathing. Half-blinded by my mask I trip and fall, crashing my head against the trench wall, knocking myself half-senseless. My gas mask has come off. I pull it down, but I have breathed in and know already it's too late. My eyes are stinging. My lungs are burning. I am coughing, retching, choking. I don't care where I'm running so long as it is away from the gas. At last I'm in the reserve trench and it is clear of gas. I'm out of it. I wrench off my mask, gasping for good air. Then I am on my hands and knees, vomiting violently. When at last the worst is over I look up through blurred and weeping eyes. A Hun in a gas mask is standing over me, his rifle aimed at my head. I have no rifle. It is the end. I brace myself, but he does not fire. He lowers his rifle slowly. "Go boy," he says, waving me away with his rifle. "Go. Tommy, go."

So by the whim of some kind and unknown Fritz I survived and escaped. Later, back at our field hospital I heard that we had counterattacked, and had driven the Germans back and retaken our frontline trenches but, from what I could see all around me, it was at a terrible cost. I lined up with the rest of the walking wounded to see the doctor. He washed out my eyes, examined them, and listened to my chest. Despite all my coughing he pronounced me fit. "You're lucky. You can only have got a whiff of it," he said.

As I walked away I passed the others, those that had not been as lucky. They were lying stretched out in the sun, many of them faces I knew, and would never see again; friends I had lived with, joked with, played cards with, fought with. I looked for Pete amongst them. He was not there. But Nipper Martin was, the last body I came to. He lay so still. There was a green grasshopper on his trousers. When I got back to rest camp that evening I found Pete alone in the tent. He looked up at me, wide-eyed, as if he had seen a ghost. When I told him about Nipper Martin he was as near to tears as I'd ever seen him. We exchanged our escape stories over a mug of hot sweet tea.

When the gas attack came, Pete had run like me, like most of us, but with some of the others he had then regrouped in the reserve trench, had been part of the counterattack. "We're still here, Tommo, we're alive," he said. "And that's all that matters I suppose. Unfortunately, so is Horrible-bloody-Hanley. But at least I've got some good news for you." He waved a couple of letters at me. "You've got two of them, you lucky devil. No one back home writes to me. Hardly surprising I suppose, because they can't write, can they? Well, my sister can, but we don't speak, not any more. Tell you what, Tommo, you can read yours out to me and then I can pretend they're written to me as well, can't I? Go on, Tommo. I'm listening." He lay back, put his hands under his head and closed his eyes. He didn't leave me much choice.

I have them with me now, my very last letters from home. I tried to keep all the others, but some got lost and others were so often soaked through that they became unreadable and I threw them away. But these I've looked after with the greatest of care because everyone I love is in them. I keep them in waxed paper in my pocket, close to my heart. I've read them over and over again, and each time I can hear their voices in the words, see their faces in the writing. I'll read them aloud again now, just as I read them to Pete that first time in the tent. I'll read Mother's letter first because I read it first then.

My dear Son,

I hope this letter finds you in good health. I have such good news to tell you. Last Monday, in the early morning, Molly gave birth to a little boy. As you can imagine we are all delighted at the happy event. You can imagine also our surprise and joy when I answered a knock on the door less than a week later to find your brother Charlie standing in the porch. He looks thinner than I remember him and much older too. I do not think he has been eating enough and have told him he must do so in future. He says that in spite of everything we read in the papers here you have been having a fine time together over in Belgium. Everyone I meet in the village asks how you are, even your great-aunt. She was the first to come to see the baby. She said that although he was handsome she thought he had rather pointed ears, which is untrue of course, and upset Molly greatly. Why does she always say such hurtful things? As for the Colonel, if we are to believe all he says, he could win this war all by himself. Your father was so right about him.

Much has changed in the village, and none of it for the better. More of our young men go to join up all the time. There are scarcely enough men left to work the land. Hedges go untrimmed and many fields lie fallow. Sad to say Fred and Margaret Parsons had news only last month that Jimmy will not be coming home. It seems he died of his wounds in France.

But Charlie's short visit and the birth of the baby have cheered us all. Charlie tells us that very soon there will be another big push and then the war will be won and over with. We pray he is right. Dear Son, even with Charlie home, with Big Joe and Molly and the new baby, this little house seems empty because you are not with us. Come home safe and soon.

Your loving mother.

And Big Joe's inky thumbprint was smeared along the bottom of the page as usual, with his name beside it in huge spidery lettering.

"So that's what we're having, is it?" said Pete suddenly and angrily. "A fine time. Why does he tell them that? Why doesn't he say what it's really like out here, what a hopeless bloody mess it all is, how there's good men, thousands of them, dying for nothing – for nothing! I'll tell them. Give me half a chance and I'll tell them. Saying things like that, Charlie should be ashamed of himself. Those men who died today, were they having a fine time? Were they?" I'd never seen Pete this angry before. He was always the joker, the wag, always playing the fool. He rolled over on his side with his back to me and didn't speak again.

So I read the next letter to myself. It was from Charlie, mostly anyway. Unlike Mother he'd made lots of mistakes and crossings out, so his letter was much harder to read.

Dear Private Peaceful,

I am home again as you can see, Tommo. Better late than never as they say. I am the proud father, and you are the proud uncle, of the finest looking little fellow you ever saw. I wish you could see him. But you will, and soon I hope. Molly tells me he is even more handsome than his father, which I'm very sure is not true. Big Joe sits over him while he sleeps, like he used to do with Bertha. He worries I shall go off again soon, which of course I shall. He does not understand — how could he! — where we have been or what we have been doing. And I'd rather not tell him. I'd rather not tell anyone.

After I came out of hospital I managed to wangle only three days' leave, of which I now have only one day left. I shall make the best use of it. Lastly, you should know that we have all decided the little fellow will be called Tommo. Each time we say his name it makes me think you are here with us, as we all wish you were. Molly has said that she wants to write a few words also, so I shall end now. Chin up.

Your brother Charlie, or the other Private Peaceful.

Dear Tommo,

I write to say that I have told little Tommo all about his brave uncle, about how one day when this dreadful war is over, we shall all be together again. He has your blue eyes, Charlie's dark hair and Big Joe's great grin. Because of all this I love him more than I can say.

Your Molly.

These two letters I kept by me and read and re-read till I knew them almost by heart. They kept me going during the days ahead. I took from them the hope of Charlie's return, and the strength I needed to stop myself from going mad.

We might have thought, we certainly hoped, that Sergeant Hanley would let up on us now and let us rest before going back up into the line. But we were to discover what we should have known already, that this wasn't in his nature. He said we had shamed the regiment, that we had behaved like a bunch of cowards when the gas attack came, that if it was the last thing he did he would put backbone into us. So Hanley kept us at it morning, noon and night, day in, day out. Inspections, training, drilling, exercising, more inspections. He drove us mercilessly, drove us all to despair and exhaustion. Caught sleeping one night at his post, Ben Guy, the innkeeper's son from Exbourne, one of the new recruits, was subjected, as Charlie had been before him, to Field Punishment Number One. For day after day he was strapped there on the gun wheel in all weathers. As with Charlie at Etaples, we were forbidden even to speak to him or take him water.

These were the darkest days we had ever lived through. Sergeant Hanley had done what all the bloody attrition in the trenches had never done. He had taken away our spirit, and drained the last of our strength, destroyed our hope. More than once as I lay there in my tent at night I thought of deserting, or running to Anna in Pop and asking her to hide me, to help me find a way back to England. But when morning came, even my courage to be a coward had evaporated. I stayed each time because I was too cowardly to go, because I couldn't abandon Pete and the others, and not be there when Charlie got back. And I stayed, too, because Molly had said I was brave and had named little Tommo after me. I couldn't shame her. I couldn't shame him.

Much to our surprise we were granted one night of freedom before we were to be sent off up into the line again, and we all headed straight into Pop, to the *estaminet*. Most of us were going for the beer and food, and I longed for all that as well, but as we walked into town I realised I had Anna on my mind a lot more than eggs and chips. But Anna did not bring us our beers. Another girl did, a girl none of us had seen before. I looked around me, but I could not see Anna serving at any of the other tables either. When the girl brought us our egg and chips I asked her where Anna was. She just shrugged as if she didn't understand, but there was something about her that told me she did understand, that she did know but would not tell me. Thanks to Pete and Charlie, my liking for Anna had not been a secret in the company for some time now, and now everyone was teasing me mercilessly as I looked around for her. Tiring of it, I left their mocking laughter behind me and went outside to look for her.

I looked first in the stable, where she'd taken me before, but it was empty. I walked down the darkening farm track past the henhouses to see if the horse might be out in the field, and Anna there with him. There were a couple of bleating tethered goats, but I could see no horse, and no Anna. Only then did I think of going back and knocking on the back door. I screwed my courage up. I had to knock loudly to be heard because of all the noise coming from the *estaminet*. The door opened slowly, and there was her father, not dapper and smiling as I'd always known him, but in his braces and shirt, unshaven and dishevelled. He had a bottle in his hand and his face was heavy with drink. He was not pleased to see me.

"Anna?" I said. "Is Anna in?"

"No," he replied. "Anna isn't in. Anna will never be in again. Anna is dead. You hear this, Tommy? You come here and you fight your war in my place. Why? Tell me this. Why?"

"What happened?" I asked him.

"What happened? I tell you what happened. Two days ago I send Anna to fetch the eggs. She is driving the cart home along the road and a shell comes, a big Boche shell. Only one, but one is enough. I bury her today. So if you want to see my Anna, Tommy, then go to the graveyard. Then you can go to Hell all of you, British, German, French, you think I care? And you can take your war to Hell with you, they will like it there. Leave me alone, Tommy, leave me alone."

The door was slammed shut in my face.

There were several recently dug graves in the churchyard, but I found only one that was freshly dug and covered with fresh flowers. I had known Anna only from a few laughing words, from the light in her eyes, a touch of hands and a fleeting kiss, but I felt an ache inside me such as I had not felt since I was a child, since my father's death. I looked up at the church steeple, a dark arrow pointing at the moon and beyond, and tried with all my heart and mind to believe she was up there somewhere in that vast expanse of infinity, up there in Sunday-school Heaven, in Big Joe's happy Heaven. I couldn't bring myself to think it. I knew she was lying in the cold earth at my feet. I knelt down and kissed the earth, then left her there. The moon sailed above me, following behind me, through the trees, lighting my way back to camp. By the time I got there I had no more tears left to cry.

The next night we were marching up into the trenches

again along with hundreds of others, to stiffen the line they told us. That could only mean one thing: an attack was expected and we would be in for a packet of trouble. As it turned out, Fritz was to give us a couple of days' grace – no attack came, not yet.

Charlie came instead, just strolled into our dugout as if he'd been gone five minutes. "Afternoon, Tommo. Afternoon, all," he said, grinning from ear to ear. His arrival gave us all new heart. With Sergeant Hanley still on our backs, always on the prowl, we had our champion back, the only one of us who had ever faced him down. As for me, I had my guardian back, my brother and my best friend. Like everyone else I felt suddenly safer.

I was there when Sergeant Hanley and Charlie came face to face in the trench. "What a nice surprise, Sergeant," Charlie chirped. "I heard you'd joined us."

"And I heard you'd been malingering, Peaceful," Hanley snarled. "I don't like malingerers. I've got my eye on you, Peaceful. You're a troublemaker, always have been. I'm warning you, one step out of line. . ."

"Don't you worry yourself, Sergeant," said Charlie. "I'll be good as gold. Cross my heart and hope to die."

The sergeant looked first nonplussed, then explosive.

"Nice weather we're having, Sergeant," Charlie went on. "It's raining in Blighty, you know. Cats and dogs." Hanley pushed past him, muttering to himself as he went. It was a

164

little enough victory, but it cheered all of us who witnessed it to the bottom of our hearts.

That evening Charlie and I sat drinking our tea over a guttering lamp and talked quietly together for the first time. I was full of questions about everyone at home, but he seemed unwilling to say much about them. I was taken aback by this, hurt even, until he saw I was and explained why.

"It's like we're living two separate lives in two separate worlds, Tommo, and I want to keep it that way. I never want the one to touch on the other. I didn't want to bring horrible Hanley and whizzbangs back home, did I? And for me it's the same the other way round. Home's home. Here's here. It's difficult to explain, but little Tommo and Molly, Mother and Big Joe, they don't belong in this hell hole of a place, do they? By talking about them I bring them here, and I don't want to do that. You understand, Tommo?"

And I did.

We hear the shell coming and know from the shriek of it that it will be close, and it is. The blast of it throws us all to the ground, putting out lamps and plunging us into pungent darkness. It is the first shell of thousands. Our guns answer almost at once, and from then on the titanic duel is almost constant as the world above us erupts, the roar and thunder pounding us remorselessly all day, all night. When the guns do let up it is all the more cruel, for it gives us some fragile hope it might at last be over, only to snatch that hope away again minutes later.

To begin with we huddle together in the dugout and try to pretend to ourselves it isn't happening, and even if it is, that our dugout is deep enough to see us through. We all know in our heart of hearts that a direct hit will be the end of all of us. We know it and accept it. We just prefer not to think about it, and certainly not to talk about it. We drink our tea, smoke our Woodbines, eat when food comes – which isn't often – and go on living as best we can, as normally as we can.

It doesn't seem possible, but on the second day the bombardment intensifies. Every heavy gun the Germans have seems to be aimed at our sector. There is a moment when the last fragile vestiges of controlled fear give way to terror, a terror that can be hidden no longer. I find myself curled into a ball on the ground and screaming for it to stop. Then I feel Charlie lying beside me, folding himself around me to protect me, to comfort me. He begins to sing *Oranges and Lemons* softly in my ear, and soon I am singing with him, and loudly too, singing instead of screaming. Before we know it the whole dugout is singing along with us. But the barrage goes on and on and on, until in the end neither Charlie nor *Oranges and Lemons* can drive away the terror that is engulfing me and invading me, destroying any last glimmer of courage and composure I may have left. All I have now is my fear.

When their attack comes, in the pearly light of dawn, it falters before it even gets near our wire. Our machine gunners see to that, knocking them down like thousands of grey skittles, never to rise again. My hands are shaking so much I can hardly reload my rifle. When they recoil and turn and run we wait for the whistle and then go out over the top. I go because the others go, moving forward as if in a trance, as if outside myself altogether. I find myself suddenly on my knees and I don't know why. There is blood pouring down my face, and my head is wracked with a sudden burning pain so terrible that I feel it must burst. I feel myself falling out of my dream down into a world of swirling darkness. I am being beckoned into a world I have never been to before where it is warm and comforting and all-enveloping. I know I am dying my own death, and I welcome it.

FIVE TO FIVE

Sixty-five minutes to go. How shall I live them? Shall I try to sleep? It would be useless to try. Should I eat a hearty breakfast? I don't want it. Shall I scream and shout? What would be the point? Shall I pray? Why? What for? Who to?

No. They will do what they will do. Field Marshal Haig is God out here, and Haig has signed. Haig has confirmed the sentence. He has decreed that Private Peaceful will die, will be shot for cowardice in the face of the enemy at six o'clock on the morning of the twenty-fifth of June 1916.

The firing squad will be having their breakfast by now, sipping their tea, hating what they will have to do. No one has told me where exactly it will happen. I don't want it to be in some dark prison yard with grey walls all around. I want it to be where there is sky and clouds and trees, and birds. It will be easier if there are birds. And let it be quickly over. Please let it be quickly over.

I wake to the muffled sound of machine-gun fire, to the distant shriek of the shells. The earth quivers and trembles about me, but I am strangely relieved, for all this must mean that I'm not dead. Nor am I all that alarmed at first when I find that all I can see is darkness, because I remember at once that I have been wounded – I can still feel the throbbing in my head. It must be night and I am lying wounded somewhere in no-man's-land, looking up into the black of the sky. But then I try to move my head a little and the blackness begins to crumble and fall in on me, filling my mouth, my eyes, my ears. It is not the sky I am looking at, but earth. I feel the weight of it now, pressing down on my chest. My legs cannot move, nor my arms. Only my fingers. How slowly I come to know and understand that I am buried, buried alive, but then how fast I panic. They must have thought I was dead, and buried me, but I am not. I am not! I scream then, and the earth fills my mouth and at once chokes off my breathing. My fingers scrabble, clawing frantically at the earth, but I am suffocating and they cannot help me. I try to think, to calm my raging panic, to try to lie still, to force myself to try to breathe through my nose. But there is no air to breathe. I think of Molly then and commit myself to holding her in my head until the moment I die.

I feel a hand on my leg. One foot is gripped, then the other. From far away I think I hear a voice, and I know it is Charlie's voice. He is calling for me to hang on. They are digging for me, pulling at me, dragging me out into blessed daylight, out into blessed air. I gulp the air like water, choking on it, coughing on it, and then at last I can breathe it in.

The next thing I know I am sitting deep down in what looks like the remains of a concrete dugout, full of exhausted men, all faces I know. Pete is coming down the steps. He is gasping for breath like me. Charlie is still pouring the last dribbles from his water bottle on to my face, trying to clean me up. "Thought we'd lost you, Tommo," Charlie is saying. "The same shell that buried you killed half a dozen of us. You were lucky. Your head's a bit of a mess. You lie still, Tommo. You've lost a lot of blood." I'm shaking now. I'm cold all over and weak as a kitten.

Pete is crouching beside us now, his forehead pressed against his rifle. "All hell's broken loose out there," he says. "We're going down like flies, Charlie. They've got us pinned down, machine guns on three sides. Stick your head out of there and you're a dead man."

"Where are we?" I ask.

"Middle of bloody no-man's-land, that's where, some old German dugout," Pete replies. "Can't go forward, can't go back."

"Then we'd best stay put for a while, hadn't we?" Charlie says.

I look up and see Sergeant Hanley standing over us, rifle in hand and shouting at us. "Stay put? Stay put? You listen to me, Peaceful. I give the orders round here. When I say we go, we go. Do I make myself clear?"

Charlie looks him straight in the eye in open defiance and does not look away, just as he used to do with Mr Munnings at school when he was being ticked off.

"Soon as I give the word," the sergeant goes on, to everyone in the dugout now, "we make a dash for it, and I mean all of us. No stragglers, no malingerers – that means you, Peaceful. Our orders are to press home the attack and then hold our ground. Only fifty yards or so to the German trenches. We'll get there easy."

I wait till the sergeant moves away, until he can't hear. "Charlie," I whisper, "I don't think I can make it. I don't think I can stand up."

"It's all right," he says, and his face breaks into a sudden smile. "You look a right mess, Tommo. All blood and mud, with a couple of little white eyes looking out. Don't you worry, we'll stay together, no matter what. We always have, haven't we?"

The sergeant waits a minute or two by the opening of the dugout until there is a lull in the firing outside. "Right," he says. "This is it. We're going out. Make sure you've all got a full magazine and one up the spout. Everyone ready? On your feet. Let's go." No one moves. The men are looking at one another, hesitating. "What in Hell's name is the matter with you? On your feet, damn you! On your feet!"

Then Charlie speaks up, very quietly. "I think they're thinking what I'm thinking, Sergeant. You take us out there now and their machine guns'll just mow us down. They've seen us go in here, and they'll be waiting for us to come out. They're not stupid. Maybe we should stay here and then go back after dark. No point in going out there and getting ourselves killed for nothing, is there, Sergeant?"

"Are you disobeying my order, Peaceful?" The sergeant is ranting like a man demented now.

"No, I'm just letting you know what I think," Charlie replies. "What we all think."

"And I'm telling you, Peaceful, that if you don't come with us when we go, it won't just be field punishment again. It'll be a court martial for you. It'll be the firing squad. Do you hear me, Peaceful? Do you hear me?"

"Yes, Sergeant," says Charlie. "I hear you. But the thing is, Sergeant, even if I wanted to, I can't go with you because I'd have to leave Tommo behind, and I can't do that. As you can see, Sergeant, he's been wounded. He can hardly walk, let alone run. I'm not leaving him. I'll be staying with him. Don't you worry about us, Sergeant, we'll make our way back later when it gets dark. We'll be all right."

"You miserable little worm, Peaceful." The sergeant is threatening Charlie with his rifle now, the bayonet inches from Charlie's nose and trembling with fury. "I should shoot you right where you are and save the firing squad the trouble." For just a moment it looks as if the sergeant really will do it, but then he remembers himself, and turns away. "You lot, on your feet. On my word, I want you men out there. Make no mistake, it's a court martial for anyone who stays."

One by one the men get unwillingly to their feet, each one preparing himself in his own way, a last drag on a cigarette, a silent prayer, eyes closed.

"Go! Go! Go!" The sergeant is screaming, and they do go, leaping up the steps of the dugout and dashing out into the open. I hear the German machine guns opening up again. Pete is the last to leave the dugout. He pauses on the step and looks back down at us. "You should come, Charlie," he says. "He means it. The bastard means what he says, I promise you."

"I know he does," says Charlie. "So do I. G'luck, Pete. Keep your head down."

Then Pete is gone and we're alone together in the dugout. We don't need to imagine what is going on out there. We can hear it, the screams cut short, the death rattle of machine guns, the staccato of rifle fire picking them off one by one. Then it goes quiet and we wait. I look across at Charlie. I see there are tears in his eyes. "Poor beggars," he says. "Poor beggars." And then: "I think I've cooked my goose good and proper this time, Tommo."

"Maybe the sergeant won't come back," I tell him.

"Let's hope," says Charlie. "Let's hope."

I must have drifted in and out of consciousness after that. Each time I woke I saw that another one or two had made it back to the dugout, but still no Sergeant Hanley. Still I hoped. Then I woke to find myself lying with Charlie's arm around me, my head resting on his shoulder.

"Tommo? Tommo?" he said. "You awake?"

"Yes," I said.

"Listen Tommo, I've been thinking. If the worst happens—"

"It's not going to happen," I interrupted.

"Just listen, Tommo, will you? I want you to promise me you'll look after things for me. You understand what I'm saying? You promise?"

"Yes," I said.

Then after a long silence he went on: "You still love her, don't you? You still love Moll?" My silence was enough. He knew already. "Good," said Charlie. "And there's something else I want you to look after too." He lifted his arm away from behind me, took off his watch, and strapped it on my wrist. "There you are, Tommo. It's a wonderful watch, this. Never stopped, not once. Don't lose it." I didn't know what to say. "Now you can go back to sleep again," he said.

And in my sleep I dreamt again my childhood nightmare, Father's finger pointing at me, and I promised myself even as I dreamt that when I woke this time I would at last tell Charlie what I did in that forest all those years ago.

I opened my eyes. Sergeant Hanley was sitting across the dugout from us, looking at us darkly from under his helmet. As we waited for any others to come in and for darkness to fall, the sergeant sat there not saying another word to Charlie or to anyone, just glaring unwaveringly at Charlie. There was cold hate in his eyes.

By nightfall there was still no sign of Pete, nor of a dozen others who'd gone out with the sergeant to join that futile charge. The sergeant decided it was time to go. So in the dark of the night, by twos and threes, the remnants of the company crawled back to our trenches across no-man's-land, Charlie half dragging me, half lifting me all the way. From my stretcher in the bottom of the trench I looked up and saw Charlie being taken away under close arrest. It all happened so fast after that. There was no time for goodbyes. Only when he'd gone did I remember again my dream and the promise I'd made in it, and had not kept.

They did not let me see him again for another six weeks, and by then the court martial was all over, the death sentence passed and then confirmed. That was all I knew, all anyone knew. I knew nothing whatever of how it had all happened until yesterday, when at last I was allowed to see him. They were holding him at Walker Camp. The guard outside said he was sorry, but I had only twenty minutes. Orders, he said.

It is a stable – and it still smells like it – with a table and two chairs, a bucket in the corner, and a bed along one wall. Charlie is lying on his back, hands under his head, legs crossed. He sits up as soon as he sees me, and smiles broadly. "I hoped you'd come, Tommo," he says. "I didn't think they'd let you. How's your head? All mended?"

"Good as new," I tell him, trying to respond in kind to his cheeriness. And then we're standing there hugging one another, and I can't help myself.

"I want no tears, Tommo," he whispers in my ear. "This is going to be difficult enough without tears." He holds me at arm's length. "Understand?"

I can do no more than nod.

He has had a letter from home, from Molly, which he must read out to me, he says, because it makes him laugh and he needs to laugh. It's mostly about little Tommo. Molly writes that he's already learning to blow raspberries and they're every bit as loud and rude as ours when we were young. And she says Big Joe sings him to sleep at night, *Oranges and Lemons* of course. She ends by sending her love and hoping we're both well.

"Doesn't she know?" I ask.

"No," Charlie says. "And they won't know, not until afterwards. They'll send them a telegram. They didn't let me write home until today." As we sit down at the table he lowers his voice and we talk in half-whispers now. "You'll tell them how it really was, won't you, Tommo? It's all I care about now. I don't want them thinking I was a coward. I don't want that. I want them to know the truth."

"Didn't you tell the court martial?" I ask him.

"Course I did. I tried, I tried my very best, but there's none so deaf as them that don't want to hear. They had their one witness, Sergeant Hanley, and he was all they needed. It wasn't a trial, Tommo. They'd made up their minds I was guilty before they even sat down. I had three of them, a brigadier and two captains looking down their noses at me as if I was some sort of dirt. I told them everything, Tommo, just like it happened. I had nothing to be ashamed of, did I? I wasn't going to hide anything. So I told them that, yes, I did disobey the sergeant's order because the order was stupid, suicidal – we all knew it was – and that anyway I had to stay behind to look after you. They knew a dozen or more got wiped out in the attack, that no one even got as far as the German wire. They knew I was right, but it made no difference."

"What about witnesses?" I ask him. "You should have had witnesses. I could have said. I could have told them."

"I asked for you, Tommo, but they wouldn't accept you because you were my brother. I asked for Pete, but then they told me that Pete was missing. And as for the rest of the company, I was told they'd been moved into another sector, and were up in the line and not available. So they heard it all from Sergeant Hanley, and they swallowed everything he told them, like it was gospel truth. I think there's a big push coming, and they wanted to make an example of someone, Tommo. And I was the Charlie." He laughed at that. "A right Charlie. Then of course there was my record as a troublemaker, 'a mutinous troublemaker' Hanley called me. Remember Etaples? Had up on a charge of gross insubordination? Field Punishment Number One? It was all there on my record. So was my foot."

"Your foot?"

"That time I was shot in the foot. All foot wounds are suspicious, they said. It could have been self-inflicted – it goes on all the time, they said. I could have done it myself just to get myself out of the trenches and back to Blighty."

"But it wasn't like that," I say.

"Course it wasn't. They believed what they wanted to believe."

"Didn't you have anyone to speak up for you?" I ask him. "Like an officer or someone?"

"I didn't think I needed one," Charlie tells me. "Just tell them the truth, Charlie, and you'll be all right. That's what I thought. How wrong could I be? I thought maybe a letter of good character from Wilkie would help. I was sure they'd listen to him, him being an officer and one of them. I told them where I thought he was. The last I'd heard he was up in a hospital in Scotland somewhere. They told me they'd written to the hospital, but that he'd died of his wounds six months before. The whole court martial took less than an hour, Tommo. That's all they gave me. An hour for a man's life. Not a lot, is it? And do you know what the brigadier said, Tommo? He said I was a worthless man. Worthless. I've been called a lot of things in my life, Tommo, but none of them ever upset me, except that one. I didn't show it, mind. I wouldn't have given them the satisfaction. And then he passed sentence. I was expecting it by then. Didn't upset me nearly as much as I thought it would."

I hang my head, because I cannot stop my eyes filling.

"Tommo," he says, lifting my chin. "Look on the bright side. It's no more than we were facing every day in the trenches. It'll be over very quick. And the boys are looking after me all right here. They don't like it any more than I do. Three hot meals a day. A man can't grumble. It's all over and done with, or it will be soon anyway. You want some tea, Tommo? They brought me some just before you came."

So we sit either side of the table and share a mug of sweet strong tea, and speak of everything Charlie wants to talk about: home, bread and butter pudding with the raisins in and the crunchy crust on top, moonlit nights fishing for sea trout on the Colonel's river, Bertha, beer at The Duke, the yellow aeroplane and the humbugs.

"We won't talk of Big Joe or Mother or Moll," Charlie says, "because I'll cry if I do, and I promised myself I wouldn't." He leans forward suddenly in great earnest, clutching my hand. "Talking of promises, that promise you made me back in the dugout, Tommo. You won't forget it, will you? You will look after them?"

"I promise," I tell him, and I've never meant anything so much in all my life.

"You've still got the watch then," he says, pulling back my sleeve. "Keep it ticking for me, and then when the time comes, give it to Little Tommo, so he'll have something from me. I'd like that. You'll make him a good father, like Father was to us."

It is the moment. I have to do it now. It is my last chance. I tell him about how Father had died, about how it had happened, what I had done, how I should have told him years ago, but had never dared to. He smiles. "I always knew that, Tommo. So did Mother. You'd talk in your sleep. Always having nightmares, always keeping me awake about it, you were. All nonsense. Not your fault. It was the tree that killed Father, Tommo, not you."

"You sure?" I ask him.

"I'm sure," he says. "Quite sure."

We look at one another and know that time is getting short now. I see a flicker of panic in his eyes. He pulls some letters out of his pocket and pushes them across the table. "You'll see they get these, Tommo?"

We grip hands across the table, put our foreheads together and close our eyes. I manage to say what I've been wanting to say.

"You're not worthless, Charlie. They're the worthless bastards. You're the best friend I've ever had, the best person I've ever known."

I hear Charlie starting to hum softly. It is *Oranges and Lemons*, slightly out of tune. I hum with him, our hands clasping tighter, our humming stronger now. Then we are singing, singing it out loud so that the whole world can hear us, and we are laughing as we sing. And there are tears, but it does not matter because these are not tears of sadness, they are tears of celebration. When we've finished, Charlie says: "It's what I'll be singing in the morning. It won't be God Save the ruddy King or All Things bleeding Bright and Beautiful. It'll be *Oranges and Lemons* for Big Joe, for all of us."

The guard comes in and tells us our time is up. We shake hands then as strangers do. There are no words left to say. I hold our last look and want to hold it forever. Then I turn away and leave him.

When I got back to camp yesterday afternoon I expected the sympathy and the long faces and all those averted eyes I'd been used to for days before. Instead I was greeted by smiles and with the news that Sergeant Hanley was dead. He had been killed, they told me, in a freak accident, blown up by a grenade out on the ranges. So there was some justice, of a sort, but it had come too late for Charlie. I hoped someone at Walker Camp had heard about it and would tell Charlie. It would be small consolation for him, but it would be something. Any jubilation I felt, or any of us felt, turned very soon to grim satisfaction, and then evaporated completely. It seemed as if the entire regiment was subdued, like me quite unable to think of anything else but Charlie, of the injustice he was suffering, and the inevitability of what must happen to him in the morning.

We have been billeted this last week or so around an empty farmhouse, less than a mile down the road from where they're keeping Charlie at Walker Camp. We've been waiting to go up into the trenches further down the line on the Somme. We live in bell tents, and the officers are billeted in the house. The others have been doing their very best to make it as easy as they can for me. I know from their every look how much they feel for me, NCOs and officers too. But kind though they are I do not want or need their sympathy or their help. I do not even want the distraction of their company. I want simply to be alone. Late in the evening I take a lamp with me and move out of the tent into this barn, or what is left of it. They bring me blankets and food, and then leave me to myself. They understand. The padre comes to do what he can. He can do nothing. I send him away. So here I am now with the night gone so fast and the clock ticking towards six o'clock. When the time comes, I will go outside, and I will look up at the sky because I know Charlie will be doing the same as they take him out. We'll be seeing the same clouds, feeling the same breeze on our faces. At least that way we'll be together.

ONE MINUTE TO SIX

I try to close my mind to what is happening this minute to Charlie. I try just to think of Charlie as he was at home, as we all were. But all I can see in my mind are the soldiers leading Charlie out into the field. He is not stumbling. He is not struggling. He is not crying out. He is walking with his head held high, just as he was after Mr Munnings caned him at school that day. Maybe there's a lark rising, or a great crow wheeling into the wind above him. The firing squad stands at ease, waiting. Six men, their rifles loaded and ready, each one wanting only to get it over with. They will be shooting one of their own and it feels to them like murder. They try not to look at Charlie's face.

Charlie is tied to the post. The padre says a prayer, makes the sign of the cross on his forehead and moves away. It is cold now but Charlie does not shiver. The officer, his revolver drawn, is looking at his watch. They try to put a hood over Charlie's head, but he will not have it. He looks up to the sky and sends his last living thoughts back home.

"Present! Ready! Aim!"

He closes his eyes and as he waits he sings softly. "*Oranges and Lemons, say the bells of St. Clements.*" Under my breath I sing it with him. I hear the echoing volley. It is done. It is over. With that volley a part of me has died with him. I turn back to go to the solitude of my hay barn, and I find I am far from alone in my grieving. All over the camp I see them standing to attention outside their tents. And the birds are singing.

I am not alone that afternoon either when I go to Walker Camp to collect his belongings, and to see where they have buried him. He would like the place. He looks out over a water meadow down to where a brook runs softly under the trees. They tell me he walked out with a smile on his face as if he were going for an early-morning stroll. They tell me that he refused the hood, and that they thought he was singing when he died. Six of us who were in the dugout that day stand vigil over his grave until sundown. Each of us says the same thing when we leave.

"Bye Charlie."

The next day the regiment is marching up the road towards the Somme. It is late June, and they say there's soon going to be an almighty push and we're going to be part of it. We'll push them all the way to Berlin. I've heard that before. All I know is that I must survive. I have promises to keep.

POSTSCRIPT

In the First World War, between 1914 and 1918, over 290 soldiers of the British and Commonwealth armies were executed by firing squad, some for desertion and cowardice, two for simply sleeping at their posts.

Many of these men we now know were traumatised by shell shock. Court martials were brief, the accused often unrepresented.

It was only in 2006 that the authorities recognised the injustice these soldiers suffered. A conditional pardon was granted in November 2006.

FROM THE AUTHOR
OF THE AWARD-WINNING
PRIVATE PEACEFUL
AND THE INTERNATIONAL PHENOMENON
WAR HORSE
COMES A NEW WW1 MASTERPIECE

Out in hardback October 2014

MAY, 1915.

On an uninhabited island in the Scillies, Alfie and his father find an
injured girl – alone, and with no memory of who she is or how she
came to be there. Is she a mermaid, a ghost? Or could she even be,
as some islanders suggest, a German spy...?

*A major new story of family, forgiveness and memory,
this is a landmark Michael Morpurgo novel.*

AUTHOR'S NOTE

I was on my way to Ypres with Clare, my wife, on a research trip, already intent on writing a novel about one of the soldiers in the British Army who had been executed for cowardice or desertion during the First World War.

But I still had no name for my fictional soldier. We stopped by chance at the Bedford Cemetery a few miles outside Ypres, simply because we always made a point of paying our respects at one of the many Commonwealth War Grave Cemeteries in or around Ypres.

Walking down the line of Portland-stone headstones, Clare bent down to look more closely at one of them. "I think maybe I've found your soldier's name," she said. The stone read: 'Private T. S. H. Peaceful Royal Fusiliers 4th June 1915'.

PHOTOGRAPH COURTESY OF MAXINE KEEBLE

I knew at once that Peaceful had to be the name of my soldier, that it was absolutely the right name for this young farm boy brought up in the peace and tranquillity of the Devon countryside, who finds himself alongside his brother marching off to war in 1914, and living through the horrors of trench warfare.

Years later, through the kindness of his great niece, Maxine Keeble, I was to discover much more about the family of the real Private Peacefull (his name was misspelled on the headstone). Where he came from, how he had been a van boy in London, joined up at the outbreak of war, and died of his wounds in 1915; how Henry James Percy Peacefull, a brother of his, had been killed on July 1st 1916, the first day of The Battle of The Somme, when the British Army suffered over 60,000 casualties in one day; how another brother, William Arthur Peacefull, had been caught on barbed wire and taken prisoner of war; and how yet another brother, Lewis Percy Peacefull, had survived the war and served in the RAF in the Second World War. This was a family, like so many others in towns and villages all over the land, who had suffered terrible and irreplaceable loss.

Years later, after the book of *Private Peaceful* had been published, I found myself in another cemetery near Ypres. We were almost entirely on our own there, until a bus drew up, and dozens of teenagers – from a school in Epsom, as I later discovered – came into the graveyard, their natural boisterousness silenced almost at once by the sense of overwhelming sorrow we all feel in such places. I got talking to their teacher, who told me they were on a school trip around the battlefields of WW1, as part of their history studies, and had just visited the Bedford Cemetery where they had found the grave they had all been looking for, the grave of Private Peaceful. They had been studying the book at school prior to the visit, and in a way had chosen him as their 'Unknown Soldier'. They had made a wreath for him, written him messages and left them by his stone.

Going that way later that day we went to look. There lay the wreath and the letters, each in a rain-spattered plastic envelope, messages of gratitude and of sadness. And very recently, on my last visit, I found several poppies on his grave. I hope both he and his family do not mind me borrowing his name, and take some comfort from the fact that for so many young people, the Private Peaceful in the Bedford Cemetery has become not their Unknown Soldier any more, but a soldier they know, and care about.

Michael Morpurgo

MICHAEL MORPURGO OBE is one of Britain's best-loved writers for children. He has written over 100 books and won many prizes, including the Smarties Prize, the Blue Peter Book Award and the Whitbread Award. His recent bestselling novels include *Shadow, An Elephant in the Garden* and *Born to Run*.

Michael's stories have been adapted numerous times for stage and screen, and he was Children's Laureate from 2003 to 2005, a role which took him all over the country to inspire children with the joy of reading stories.

Other titles by Michael Morpurgo include:
Outlaw – the story of Robin Hood
Little Manfred
Shadow
An Elephant in the Garden
Running Wild
Kaspar
Born to Run
The Amazing Story of Adolphus Tips
Farm Boy
The Butterfly Lion
Sparrow - the story of Joan of Arc
Alone on a Wide, Wide Sea

Social
Policy
and
Social
Justice

The IPPR Reader

KEIGHLEY CAMPUS LIBRARY
LEEDS CITY COLLEGE

KC04611

Social Policy and Social Justice

The IPPR Reader

Edited by
Jane Franklin

Polity Press

PUBLISHED IN ASSOCIATION WITH THE
INSTITUTE FOR PUBLIC POLICY RESEARCH

© this collection Polity Press 1998
© Introduction and part introductions Jane Franklin/IPPR 1998
© Chapters 1, 2, 3, 4, 6, 7, 8, 9, 10, 11, 12, 13, 14, 15, 16 IPPR 1998
© Chapter 5 Dryden Press 1998

First published in 1998 by Polity Press in association with Blackwell Publishers Ltd.

Editorial office:
Polity Press
65 Bridge Street
Cambridge CB2 1UR, UK

Marketing and production:
Blackwell Publishers Ltd
108 Cowley Road
Oxford OX4 1JF, UK

Published in the USA by
Blackwell Publishers Inc.
Commerce Place
350 Main Street
Malden, MA 02148, USA

KEIGHLEY COLLEGE
LIBRARY

04611 50758

-1 DEC 2004

All rights reserved. Except for the quotation of short passages for the purposes of criticism and review, no part of this publication may be reproduced, stored in a retrieval system, or transmitted, in any form or by any means, electronic, mechanical, photocopying, recording or otherwise, without the prior permission of the publisher.

Except in the United States of America, this book is sold subject to the condition that it shall not, by way of trade or otherwise, be lent, re-sold, hired out, or otherwise circulated without the publisher's prior consent in any form of binding or cover other than that in which it is published and without a similar condition including this condition being imposed on the subsequent purchaser.

ISBN 0–7456–1939–8
ISBN 0–7456–1940–1 (pbk)

A catalogue record for this book is available from the British Library.

Library of Congress Cataloging-in-Publication Data
Social policy and social justice : the IPPR reader / edited by Jane
 Franklin.
      p. cm.
   Includes bibliographical references.
   ISBN 0–7456–1939–8 (hardcover). — ISBN 0–7456–1940–1 (pbk.)
   1. Great Britain—Social policy—1979– 2. Social justice—Great
Britain. I. Franklin, Jane. II. Institute for Public Policy
Research (London, England)
HN383.5.S6 1998
361.6′1′0941—dc21   97–44979
                                                                       CIP

Typeset in 10 on 12pt Sabon
by Graphicraft Typesetters Ltd., Hong Kong
Printed in Great Britain by TJ International, Padstow, Cornwall

This book is printed on acid-free paper.

Contents

Contributors

Adrienne Burgess is a Research Fellow at the Institute for Public Policy Research and has been writing and broadcasting on family structure and relationships for almost twenty years in the UK, the USA and Australia. She is the author of *Fatherhood Reclaimed* (Vermilion, 1997) and co-author with Sandy Ruxton of *Men and their Children* (IPPR, 1996).

Ian Bynoe is a part-time Research Fellow at the Institute for Public Policy Research specializing in social and human rights. A solicitor who has worked in law centres and in private practice, he was Legal Director of MIND from 1990 to 1994. He is the co-author of *Equal Rights for Disabled People* (IPPR, 1991) and author of *Beyond the Citizen's Charter* (IPPR, 1996) and *Rights to Fair Treatment* (IPPR, 1997). He also provides legal and practice training to local authorities and NHS Trusts on disability, health and social services law.

Anna Coote is Deputy Director of the Institute for Public Policy Research, where she initiated and now directs the Institute's work on Health and Social Policy, Media and Communications, and Citizens' Juries. Her recent publications include *New Agenda for Health* with D.J. Hunter (IPPR, 1996), *Converging Communications* with C. Murroni and R. Collins (IPPR, 1996) and *Citizens' Juries: Theory into Practice* with Jo Lenaghan (IPPR, 1997).

Dan Corry is Special Advisor to the Rt Hon. Margaret Beckett MP, President of the Board of Trade. He was formerly Senior Economist at the Institute for Public Policy Research and founding editor of its journal *New*

Economy. Recent publications, written during his time at IPPR, include *Restating the Case for EMU* (IPPR, 1995) and *Public Expenditure* (Dryden Press, 1997).

David Donnison is Professor Emeritus at the University of Glasgow and a Visiting Professor at the Local Government Centre, Warwick University. His recent publications include *Policies for a Just Society* (Macmillan, 1997), *The Politics of Poverty* (Martin Robertson, 1982) and *A Radical Agenda* (Rivers Oram Press, 1991).

Jane Franklin is a Research Fellow at South Bank University and an Associate of the Institute for Public Policy Research. Previously a Research Fellow at IPPR from 1994–1997, her recent publications include *Equality* (IPPR, 1997) and *The Politics of Risk Society* (Polity Press, 1998).

Ian Gough is Professor of Social Policy and Director of European Research Institute at the University of Bath. Recent publications include *A Theory of Human Need* (Macmillan, 1991) with Len Doyle, awarded the Deutscher and Myrdal prizes, and *Social Assistance in OECD Countries* (HMSO, 1996).

Harriet Harman was appointed Secretary of State for Social Security on 3 May 1997. In 1978–82 she was Legal Officer for the National Council of Civil Liberties. Elected MP for Peckham in 1982, she was the Shadow Minister for Social Services in 1984 and 1985–7 and the spokesperson for health in 1987–92. In 1992–4 she was the Shadow Chief Secretary to the Treasury, in 1994–5 Shadow Employment Secretary and in 1995–6 Shadow Health Secretary. Ms Harman was previously Shadow Social Security Secretary from 1996 to 1997.

Patricia Hewitt is the MP for Leicester West and a Trustee of the Institute for Public Policy Research. Previously, she was Director of Research at Anderson Consulting and prior to that Deputy Director of IPPR. She has written many books and reports, including *About Time: Revolution in Work and Family Life* (IPPR, 1993).

David J. Hunter has been Director of the Nuffield Institute for Health, University of Leeds, since 1989. He was appointed to a chair in 1991 and is Professor of Health Policy and Management at the University of Leeds. Recent publications include a series of three articles on managed care and disease management for the *British Medical Journal* (May 1997), and *Desperately Seeking Solutions: Rationing Health Care* (Longman, 1997).

Jo Lenaghan is a Researcher in Health Policy at the Institute for Public Policy Research, where she has worked since January 1995. She was formerly a Clinical Audit Co-ordinator at King's College Hospital and a Research Officer for a charity for people suffering from asbestos-related diseases. She graduated in 1992 from Glasgow University. She is author of *Rationing and Rights in Health Care* (IPPR, 1996), editor of *Hard Choices in Health Care* (BMJ Books, 1997) and co-author with Anna Coote of *Citizens' Juries: Theory into Practice* (IPPR, 1997).

Tariq Modood was a Lecturer in Political Theory before entering racial equality policy work, including work at the Commission for Racial Equality. Subsequently he has been a Research Fellow at Nuffield College, Oxford, and the University of Manchester, and is now a Programme Director at the Policy Studies Institute. His many publications include (as co-author) *Ethnic Minorities in Britain: Diversity and Disadvantage* (PSI, 1997), and (as editor) *Church, State and Religious Minorities* (PSI, 1997) and *The Politics of Multiculturalism in the New Europe* (Zed Books, 1997).

Raymond Plant, Master of St Catherine's College, Oxford, previously Professor of Politics at the University of Southampton, sits as a Labour member of the House of Lords. His recent publications include *Political Philosophy and Social Welfare*, with H. Lesser and P. Taylor-Gooby (Routledge/Humanities Press, 1981), *Philosophy, Politics and Citizenship*, with A. Vincent (Blackwell, 1983), *Conservative Capitalism in Britain and the United States*, with K. Hoover (Routledge/Humanities Press, 1988) and *Politics, Theology and History* (Cambridge University Press, forthcoming).

Sandy Ruxton is a freelance researcher and policy analyst. He worked for ten years with young men in education, community work and the penal system. He has written extensively on issues concerning children and young people, especially in the field of youth justice, and is a regular contributor to the magazine *Working with Men*. His current research interest is the development of children's issues within the European Union. His publications include *Children in Europe* (NCH Action for Children, 1996) and *What's He Doing at the Family Centre?* (NCH Action for Children, 1992).

Mai Wann is an experienced practitioner and leading analyst in the field of self-help and mutual aid. She set up the Self Help Centre at the National Council for Voluntary Organizations in 1986. Her recent work includes the publication of *Guidelines for Commissioners and Providers of Cancer Care*, a report on the Dissemination and Evaluation of a CancerLink Project, the review of the King's Fund race and health work, and users' views of community care services in Islington.

Editor's Note

Some of the chapters in this book are extracts from previously published works. Details of original publications can be found in the Acknowledgements.

Acknowledgements

The editor and publishers wish to thank the following for permission to reproduce material:

Dryden Press for ch. 5, reprinted from 'The role of the public sector and public expenditure', from Corry, *Public Expenditure: Effective Management and Control* (1997), pp. 15–40, by permission of the publisher. Copyright © by The Dryden Press, Harcourt Brace & Company, Ltd. All rights reserved;

IPPR for ch. 2, from *The Justice Gap*, Commission on Social Justice Discussion Paper No. 1 (1993); ch. 3, from J. Percy-Smith and I. Sanderson (eds), *Understanding Local Needs* (1992); ch. 4, from A. Coote (ed.), *The Welfare of Citizens* (1992); ch. 6, from *The Family Way* (1990); ch. 7, from *Men and their Children: Proposals for Public Policy* (1996); ch. 8, from *Act Local: Social Justice from the Bottom Up*, Commission on Social Justice Issue Paper No. 13 (1994); ch. 9, from *Building Social Capital: Self Help in a Twenty-first-century Welfare State* (1995); ch. 10, from *Racial Equality: Colour, Culture and Justice*, Commission on Social Justice Issue Paper No. 5 (1994); ch. 11, unpublished paper; ch. 12, from *Citizens' Juries: Theory into Practice* (1997); ch. 13, from Anna Coote and Naomi Pfeffer, *Is Quality Good for You?* (1993); ch. 14, from *Beyond the Citizen's Charter: New Directions for Social Rights* (1996); ch. 15, from *New Agenda for Health* (1996); ch. 16, from *Rationing and Rights in Health Care* (1996);

Rivers Oram Press for ch. 4, 'Citizenship, rights and welfare' by Raymond Plant, ch. 1 of *The Welfare of Citizens*, edited by Anna Coote, London, Rivers Oram/IPPR (1992);

Vintage for ch. 1, from *Social Justice: Strategies for National Renewal*, Report of the Commission on Social Justice (1994).

Introduction: Social Policy in Perspective

This *Reader* brings together for the first time a selection of work on social policy developed by the Institute for Public Policy Research (IPPR). IPPR is a left-of-centre think-tank, based in London, where policy initiatives are generated both to set and to contribute to the political agenda. Its independent yet left-of-centre political status puts IPPR in a unique position to draw on the extensive policy development that takes place in academic, professional and user groups, to pull all these strands together, and to connect this developmental work to the political arena. IPPR stands as a bridge between two spheres.

Though independent of any political party, IPPR has developed a distinct political and conceptual framework which informs its policy development. This could loosely be described as a *democratic liberal* approach, in that it understands the relationship between the individual and society in terms of the primacy of individual rights and responsibilities within the context of a plural and democratic society. This can be distinguished from two perspectives which dominated western political debate in the 1980s: that of the neo-liberal right, which held that free markets were the only sure route to a fair society and an efficient economy, and that of the traditional left, which favoured public ownership and redistributive taxation. It can also be distinguished, more pertinently for the late 1990s, from the communitarian approach, which values the responsibilities of community above individual rights. The Labour government elected in the UK in 1997 can be seen to operate, at least partly, within this new framework.

The Social Policy Programme at IPPR declared its aims as being:

to promote equity so that everyone has an equal chance in life: since individuals have diverse and varying needs, policy should aim to facilitate the just distribution of advantage and risk;

to redistribute power among citizens so that everyone is able to determine and shape their own lives, as far as this is compatible with the freedom of others to do the same;

to encourage shared responsibility for a common future: the well being of every individual is inextricably bound up with that of others – within and between families, neighbourhoods, generations and different ethnic and social groups;

to maximise economic efficiency: social policy should aim to achieve the best value for money and help create conditions for a thriving economy to underpin a healthy society. (IPPR, 1994)

These commitments have also influenced IPPR's method of policy development. It brings together individuals, user groups, professionals, experts and politicians to share ideas and experiences, in order to create a dialogue and to reflect in its policy making the diversity of interests and needs of all stakeholders. For example, in its project on families, children and crime, it included contributions from practitioners working with men who had been violent, academics, family-policy analysts, school teachers, probation officers, journalists, ex-offenders, senior civil servants and the then shadow home secretary, Tony Blair. In this way, IPPR creates a forum for debate in which diverse perspectives have a voice, and the resulting policy initiatives reflect IPPR's broad-based and inclusive political discourse.

IPPR was also the host of the late John Smith's Commission on Social Justice (CSJ). Though the commission was independently constituted, the analysis and policies it developed in its working papers and final report, *Social Justice: Strategies for National Renewal* (1994), echo those of IPPR. The commissioners agreed the following basic principles, outlined in an extract in this volume from its discussion paper, *The Justice Gap* (1993):

The foundation of a free society is the equal worth of all its citizens;

Everyone is entitled, as a right of citizenship, to be able to meet their basic needs;

The right to self-respect and personal autonomy demands the widest possible spread of opportunities;

Not all inequalities are unjust, but unjust inequalities should be reduced and where possible eliminated.

To understand IPPR's approach to policy making, it should be seen within the context of current debates in politics and in social policy. These are largely framed by the shift of emphasis made by recent Conservative governments in the UK in respect of the welfare state. Beveridge's project in 1945 had been to abolish the five giants of want, ignorance, disease, squalor and idleness. This informed the practice which worked towards the alleviation of poverty through the social security system; the development of an education system that laid the foundations of an equal-opportunity society; the establishment of a National Health Service (NHS) which provided free health care at the point of need; and the provision of adequate and affordable housing – all built on an economic system whose logic was based on full male employment. The difficulties and adverse effects of a paternalistic welfare state are well documented. Yet, for all its faults, the post-war welfare state had a considerable impact on people's lives. There remain ample opportunities for adaptation and improvement – to minimize the disadvantages and enhance the benefits that it currently offers.

As Giddens (1994) has argued, the welfare state above all protected the population from risk and uncertainty, promising a secure safety net from cradle to grave. The language itself declared a paternalistic approach. Now times have changed. Since the 1970s, the UK has had to adapt its welfare state to changing economic circumstances. Successive Conservative governments sought to detach the responsibility of the state from individual responsibility, to encourage a low-tax culture, and to impose a strong market ethos on the public sector. The goal of economic efficiency, rather than the needs of individuals, families and communities, was the main imperative.

One important effect was to expose degrees of uncertainty and risk in people's daily lives that were previously hidden. It is this uncertainty, in the context of changing economic and technological conditions, with which social policy makers are now coming to terms. Ulrich Beck (1997) has argued that, although uncertainty is distributed unevenly with a bias towards the less well off, we are all increasingly aware that the securities we once took for granted in the UK are becoming more fragile. The politics and policies generated by this sense of insecurity are experienced in two ways: either as a positive opportunity to build something new, or as triggering an impulse to re-establish past certainties.

The relationship between ideas, politics and policy making is complex. Politicians take up ideas which most closely fit their political goals and their perceptions of social needs and available resources. In the late 1990s, the debate about which set of ideas was most appropriate for the new politics of the centre left became critical to the thinking of New Labour. It took the form of a dialogue between simplified democratic liberal and communitarian positions.

To understand the distinction between the two we can look through two different lenses. The democratic liberal lens takes a wide-angled view of society and social change, which produces a complex picture: a thriving, plural society adapting to change and in need of collective support and political invigoration. The certainties of the post-war world have been undermined; risks and uncertainties are being revealed that were previously obscured by institutions, ways of life and relationships which we took for granted but can no longer rely upon. Policy making within this perspective seeks not to stem the tide of change but rather to accept and work with it, to plan for uncertainty and to enable people to choose their own ways of adapting to new circumstances. It attaches considerable importance to the building of trust between people and policy makers, and between users and providers of services. It acknowledges that trust is forged through mature, adult-to-adult relationships, and is learned, not taught.

Where democratic liberals see a complex society with complex problems that cannot be neatly solved by predetermined formulas, communitarians tend to put forward an idea of how people should live, in order to promote a cohesive society. The communitarian lens zooms in on the family and community as the bedrock of strong societies, and finds fault less with the economic system than with the liberal attitudes of politicians since the 1960s. Popularized by Amitai Etzioni (1995), the communitarian agenda defines the uncertainty experienced today in terms not of the revealed fragility of our institutions, but of the degeneration of moral and social values, brought about by the commitment of liberalism to rights which separate people from each other and lead to the breakdown of families and communities. Communitarian ideas are politically useful to those who wish to re-establish order and certainty in a society lacking a shared sense of right and wrong, and a shared morality to govern the behaviour and responsibilities of individuals and families. This perspective centres on the idea that human beings need the structural stability of generally accepted modes of behaviour and shared moral values to back them up. Liberalism is seen to have dismantled these and to have left society in a state of flux.

In promoting an ideal form of family life, for example, communitarians have made single mothers the scapegoats for the crimes of young men, for latch-key children, and generally for the moral decline in western society. This perspective endorses the argument that the liberal education system has failed the UK's children; it supports the call for stronger discipline in schools and traditional teaching methods. These are seen as strategies that once provided security. Whether they ever did is a moot point; in any event, they obscure the diversity of culture, relationships and daily life that today's children experience.

While the communitarian approach tends to simplify and reduce, the democratic liberal approach starts from the premise that complexities inherent in human experience are better revealed and explored than avoided or restrained. If we try to regenerate the taken-for-granted qualities of traditional institutions, we shall be constantly disappointed and impelled towards increasingly authoritarian policies to enforce the security we desire. If we constrain and coerce people's behaviour, we risk stifling the creativities, capacities and freedoms of individuals and families to adapt and work with change in their own ways.

There is a danger in trying to shift the political focus away from the structural problems of underemployment, poverty, homelessness, under-funded welfare services and a degenerating environment, towards individual behaviour and individual responsibility. For example, saying that poverty is no excuse for crime negates the influence of poverty on the decisions of those who turn to crime for many complex reasons, and hampers the development of effective strategies to combat crime.

IPPR recognizes the strategic importance of economic policy, both for people's lives and for social policy. Funding and resources are key deter-minants, yet they should not be allowed to determine social and political objectives. The economy should be a means, not an end of policy making. A strong framework of rights, and democratic decision making about how money is spent, are required to give people a sense of control over their lives. Individuals do have to make decisions for themselves and their fam-ilies in the context of uncertain futures. Yet it is possible, from a democratic liberal perspective, to create a strong collective framework of adaptable political mechanisms which encourage people to feel a sense of power to engage with the uncertainties of life.

Social policy must be forged in a continuing dialogue between policy makers, providers and users, reflecting and contributing to social change. It stands as a pragmatic bridge between political ideas, political ambitions and the practical needs and necessities of social and economic conditions. IPPR suggests the means by which change and uncertainty can be managed, while the freedom of individuals to make choices and informed decisions about their lives is upheld. It celebrates the fact that individuals are adapt-ing to change and creating new types of relationship. It supports the ways in which individuals and families move with the times, within a framework of individual rights and democratic openness. It rejects the communitarian agenda, which has had some recent influence over policy making on the left. Rather than pursuing an *end goal* of a stable, secure society built on strong families and strong communities, IPPR advocates, within the con-text of democratic and liberal values, a policy-making *process* for the new era of government in the UK. This is open and inclusive, takes account of changing needs and circumstances, and works with the diversity of the choices people make about their lives.

This *Reader* is divided into three parts. In part I, 'New Frameworks for the Twenty-first Century', we set out IPPR's analysis of social, economic and political change, explore the themes of social justice, human need and citizenship which inform our approach to policy development, and ask whether services should be provided by public or private sector. In part II, 'Issues and Debates in Social Policy', this framework is applied to the everyday, practical considerations of policy makers in the spheres of family, community and democracy. In part III, 'Service Design and Delivery', we ask how quality can be assured and whether the Citizen's Charter and a system of rights might provide the mechanism for doing so, particularly in the field of health care.

The extracts in this book were all originally written and published by or for IPPR. For reasons of practical space and intellectual consistency, we have confined ourselves to material produced by IPPR's Social Policy Programme and the Commission on Social Justice. We have not been able to include material from IPPR's Human Rights or Education Programmes, although both have made substantial contributions to the development of ideas and policies in this field.

References

Beck, U. (1997) *The Reinvention of Politics*. Cambridge: Polity Press.

Commission on Social Justice (1993) *The Justice Gap*. Commission on Social Justice Discussion Paper 1. London: IPPR.

Commission on Social Justice (1994) *Social Justice: Strategies for National Renewal*. Report of the Commission on Social Justice. London: Vintage.

Etzioni, A. (1995) *Spirit of Community: Rights, Responsibilities and the Communitarian Agenda*. London: Fontana.

Giddens, A. (1994) *Beyond Left and Right*. Cambridge: Polity Press.

IPPR (1994) Social Policy Programme 1994–6. London: IPPR.

Part I

New Frameworks for the Twenty-first Century

Part I begins with an analysis of social, economic and political change and the context in which an enabling state can work with change and pay attention to the needs of its citizens. In chapter 1, the Commission on Social Justice argues that there is no going back to the stability and security of the 1950s and 1960s, and that a radical and appropriate social policy agenda must work with the three great revolutions that are transforming our world. The *economic revolution* is a global one of finance, competition, skill and technology. Expectation of a 'job for life' has disappeared, and employment insecurity effects us all. The *social revolution* is one of women's life chances and family structures, and has enormous implications for men and women. Social renewal demands that we in the UK rebuild an inclusive society, where rights carry responsibilities, and individuals have the chance to realize their potential. The *political revolution* is a challenge to old assumptions of parliamentary sovereignty and to the growing centralization of government power. Political renewal demands that government be decentralized and democratized – people want to have more say about the things that are important to their lives, from schools to pensions, and government should use its power to devolve responsibility to individuals and communities.

The concept of social justice is a principle which can guide the satisfaction of need and introduce the relationship between rights and responsibilities in the provision of welfare. Chapter 2 outlines the conceptual framework for thinking about ideas of social justice. It explores the theoretical positions of Hayek and Rawls, and debates the nature of social justice through notions of equality of opportunity, needs and life chances.

Rejecting the view that human beings are simply selfish individuals for whom there 'is no such thing as society', it argues that people are essentially social creatures, dependent on one another for the fulfilment of their needs and potential, and willing to recognize their responsibilities to others as well as claiming rights from them. This chapter ends with the four principles of social justice which, the authors argue, articulate widely held feelings about the character of our society.

Ian Gough (chapter 3) looks at how a realistic assessment of need can overstep the ideological tensions between the undermining of collective provision and the role of professionals in decision making. He argues that conventional ideas about meeting needs are being undermined from two directions. On the one hand, individuals who have grown up with a welfare state are casting doubts upon the competence of politicians and 'experts' to decide, behind closed doors, what everyone needs. On the other, those who want to contain costs and achieve better value for money are challenging old certainties about which needs should be met collectively and by what means. All of this lends a special urgency to the question 'How are needs defined and measured for the purpose of planning, delivering and evaluating public services and facilities?' Gough develops a framework and a methodology for testing the potential of a needs-auditing process.

Social and economic rights, Raymond Plant argues (chapter 4), are not categorically different from civil and political rights. He considers ways in which such rights might be enforced in the context of the idea of charters, and argues that they could be regarded as attempts to identify ways in which individuals can have enforceable rights and entitlements to publicly provided goods. However, charters have not been put into a philosophical context which would provide them with a proper rationale. Plant argues that the idea of social and economic rights can provide such a rationale, and that by linking charters of social rights to a Bill of Rights, which protects civil and political rights, it is possible to make them independent but parallel and mutually reinforcing ways of empowering citizens.

Finally, we turn to the question of whether services should be provided by the public or private sector. Dan Corry (chapter 5) takes the view that though governments will always look to the private sector to reduce public expenditure in the provision of services, value for money will never be as important as the need for public-sector activity and democratic control of services. He argues that democracy requires an active public sector, since it is often only through 'political' action that people can influence their own lives. Public action also has an important role to play in creating a sense of community and social cohesion. It does not necessarily follow, however, that all needs should be met by public services. Increasingly, the private sector is involved in the delivery of key public services through contracting out and private-sector financing initiatives. Corry suggests that the ideal arrangement is probably a continuation of a 'mixed economy' of public-service delivery, with a strong commitment to a 'consistent, clear and open approach to policy spending decisions, where accountability and effectiveness are the watchwords'.

1

The UK in a Changing World

THE COMMISSION ON SOCIAL JUSTICE

> The Conservative government elected in May 1979 was more than a change of government; in terms of economic and political philosophy, it was a revolution.
> *Sir Leo Pliatzky, former Second Permanent Secretary, HM Treasury and Permanent Secretary, Department of Trade and Industry,*
> *quoted in Lawson (1993)*

The Conservatives' election victory in 1979 marked a fundamental departure from the governing philosophy of the post-war years. Under Mrs Thatcher, the Conservatives were ambitious and bold: they argued that the United Kingdom was trapped in a cycle of decline, advanced a radical diagnosis of this decline, and sought a mandate to reverse it.

The Thatcherites argued that the post-war drive for a fairer society had produced high taxes, overpowerful trade unions and a bloated public sector. As a result, they said, incentives to entrepreneurship were weak, management could not restructure business or increase efficiency, and the public sector 'crowded out' private-sector expansion. There was relatively slow growth, and slowly increasing equality, and the second caused the first. The argument from the right was that the state had to be rolled back and the market extended, the public sector had to be disciplined and the private sector set free, collectivism reined in and the individual rewarded. Lower direct taxation, less trade union power, and a new emphasis on personal initiative and enterprise would, the Conservatives claimed, build both economic strength and a more responsible society.

This neo-liberal argument was to become conventional wisdom across North America and much of Europe (east as well as west) in the 1980s, but in the UK in 1979 it was a daring and radical credo. For the first time in more than a generation, a political party was trying to challenge, rather than accommodate, the assumptions of the post-war consensus. The Conservatives genuinely believed that they had found the cure for the UK's decline. But they were wrong.

The neo-liberals' medicine has proved worse than the disease. Slow growth continues; taxes have gone up; millions more people depend upon benefits; the state has become more centralized; and crime and the fear of crime have shot up. The dangers of deregulation and untrammelled individualism are increasingly recognized on the right as well as the left of the political spectrum. Right-wing intellectuals diagnose a crisis of conservatism (e.g. Gray, 1993, 1994). The free-market weekly *The Economist* has lamented the government's failure to take responsibility for projects that are crucial to national renewal (Economist, 1992). The Treasury has launched an investigation into the most sacred of free markets – that governing the supply of finance to industry.

But the UK's problems are not simply the product of Conservative mistakes. The causes reach back well before the onset of Conservative administration in 1979, and they will not be tackled by trying to recreate the country that existed before then.

In 1979, the UK was struggling both to compete internationally and to co-operate domestically. After the war, the UK had relied on a combination of national economic management, a mildly redistributive welfare state, and a mixed economy of public and private sectors. The system had seemed to work well enough until 1970, but during the next decade this post-war settlement came under intense strain. The symptoms were clear: the economy suffered 'stagflation' (the previously unknown combination of rising unemployment and rising inflation); the state could no longer resolve conflicts between employers and labour, even when it was itself the employer; and public services and public housing, which had transformed people's lives after the war, had too often come to be seen as dreary and confining.

The reality was that the foundations of the post-war settlement had been destroyed by national and international change. The international economic conditions included the maintenance of free trade, with access to the USA's consumer and capital markets; the creation of a relatively open and stable international financial system agreed at the Bretton Woods conference in 1946; the availability of secure and cheap Middle East oil supplies. Since the early 1970s, however, we have seen the breakdown of the Bretton Woods system; growing instability in world financial markets;

the loss of control over oil supplies by the main western consumers (the UK's North Sea Oil has been a temporary windfall); the rapid industrialization of the Pacific Rim; the increasing recognition that on environmental as well as moral grounds the fate of the Third World is a pressing issue; and the collapse of the Communist 'second' world, with the end of the Cold War.

The *national* conditions were transformed too. The welfare capitalist states that developed in Europe after World War II sought to combine social justice and economic prosperity on the basis of a common set of values. However, the ways in which they expressed these values depended on three specific factors: full employment, the nuclear family, and the interventionist national state. The relations between these three elements took different forms in different countries, the product of particular cultural, institutional and political traditions. In Sweden, for example, an active labour-market policy, highly egalitarian policies towards women, and universal public-sector services combined to produce – until recently – a virtuous circle of low unemployment, high investment and extensive social provision. In Germany, by contrast, the economic miracle of the 1950s and 1960s was based on high-wage and high-skill employment for men, a traditional family structure, and a corporatist partnership between public and private sectors in the organization of the economy (Esping-Andersen, 1990).

In comparison with these countries, the UK was a hybrid. In part, our welfare institutions and practices were at the leading edge of radical social reform (in their creation of a national insurance system to cover people from cradle to grave), in part they lagged behind (in their ambition only to set a minimum floor on the basics of citizenship); in part they were collectivist (council housing, for example), in part individualist (for example, redistributing individual earnings across the life-cycle); in part they were based on social citizenship (the NHS), in part rooted in a contributory system (unemployment benefit); in part the provision was 'universal' (family allowances and, later, child benefit), in part it was means-tested (national assistance and now Income Support).

The tragedy of the 1960s and 1970s in the UK was that the left, which had created the successful post-war settlement, failed to come to terms with these forces of change. The tragedy of the 1980s was that the right, which grasped the need for change, failed to understand what was really needed. Bill Morris, General Secretary of the Transport and General Workers' Union, wrote to the Commission: 'While we cannot afford to indulge in nostalgia for a supposed bygone era of welfarism which never really existed, it is nevertheless true that many of the principles on which the post-war welfare state was based still hold good today.' If the values of the welfare state – opportunity, security, responsibility – are to have real meaning in future, then they will require new institutions and policies to give them practical effect. We have no option but to engage with the three great revolutions – economic, social and political – which are changing our lives, and those of people in every other industrialized country.

The Economic Revolution

The economic revolution is a global revolution of finance, competition, skill and technology in which the United Kingdom is being left behind.

The economic revolution affects every industrialized country. But the United Kingdom, by virtue of its past structures and present policies, is sadly ill equipped to confront the challenge. First, economic globalization is constraining the power of individual nation-states, putting a premium on international co-operation: but the UK government carries little weight within the European Union and uses what influence it has there and internationally to promote deflation and deregulation. Second, the new competitive conditions of the global economy demand that we raise our productivity if we are to maintain, let alone improve, our living standards and quality of life: neither protectionism nor the low-cost, low-value-added strategy offers a way forward. Third, the revolution of technology, skill and organization which is transforming the demand for and nature of work means that economic success increasingly depends upon investment in human, physical and social capital – precisely the factors which have been most seriously neglected in this country.

Economic globalization and national sovereignty

The changing economic power of nation-states starts from the massive increase since the 1970s in the volume of international financial flows. The *daily* turnover on foreign-exchange markets is $1 trillion in the early 1990s. In the early 1970s, 90 per cent of currency flows were based on trade and only 10 per cent on speculation; today, the proportions have been reversed. Deregulation of financial markets, the growth of international telecommunications and the creation of highly sophisticated computer software have not only encouraged aggressive speculation in new financial instruments but effectively created an international market in government policies. Speculators who doubt the ability of a national government to maintain a particular exchange rate can destroy the government's position by betting against the currency, as George Soros did to great effect in 1992. The search for market credibility has already imposed a deflationary strait-jacket on European economies, led by high interest rates across Europe since the late 1970s, and the power of individual economies to buck these trends is severely restricted.

Foreign direct investment is also on the rise. Among the OECD countries, it has grown from $440 billion since the early 1980s to $1,720 billion in 1990. Between 1986 and 1991, the holdings by foreigners of companies registered in the US, Japan and Europe increased from $800 billion to $1,300 billion.

Professor Fritz Scharpf, a leading German political economist, explains the diminishing power of nation-states in blunt terms:

> National governments in highly industrialised countries in the 1970s lost the ability to maintain or regain full employment through demand reflation; in the 1980s they have lost (or abdicated) the power to protect their own industries against intensified competition from other first-world countries; and they are now for the first time confronted with the possibility that world markets may be captured by high-quality industrial goods (and services) produced at very low costs in what used to be third-world or second-world countries. (Scharpf, 1994)

But single countries are not the only economic powers. For European countries today, it is at the pan-European level that effective macroeconomic sovereignty resides. The EU is a significant player in the world economy. Not only does it contain a wealthy market of 320 million citizens (345 million with the entry in 1995 of Austria, Finland, Sweden and Norway), but 93 per cent of European investment and trade takes place between EU countries, and the Union as a whole is broadly in current-account balance with the rest of the world. Since the early 1960s, trade within the EU has doubled as a share of European GDP, while the share of European GDP taken up by global trade has remained constant. The European Union now offers its members the scope to do together what no European nation, except Germany, can do alone: increase economic growth without crashing into unsustainable trade deficits.

Of course, it is not only economic interdependence that is a striking feature of the modern world. Ecological interdependence is no less obvious. The present terms of world trade are desperately disadvantageous to countries that rely on their natural resources, while the pursuit of economic growth without regard to ecological constraints is likely to prove disastrous, possibly to ourselves and certainly to our children and grandchildren. Nationally and internationally, markets need to be shaped by environmental regulation and taxation, providing constant incentives to business to find cleaner ways of producing cleaner goods.

Economic decline can be as disastrous for the environment as economic growth – as is witnessed by the ecological difficulties of the former Soviet Union – and disengagement from world trade will not serve the best interests of the developing world. Rather than try to persuade people in India or China to do without cars, in the interests of holding down CO_2 emissions and protecting the global environment, we would do better to try to develop, for them and for us, cleaner forms of private *and* public transport. Not only is this the ecologically responsible route to follow, there is ample evidence that companies and countries which lead the way in raising environmental standards gain a competitive advantage in increasingly environmentally aware markets. Environmental protection is now big business, amounting to over 2.5 per cent of national income (at least £12 billion a year) (Atkinson and Dubourg, 1994).

Competition: *the new global marketplace*

The World Bank's analysis of growth rates in the twenty-five years after 1960 provides surprising reading. Botswana was the fastest-growing economy in the period, followed by Taiwan, Indonesia, Hong Kong, Singapore, Korea and Japan. Egypt was 10th, Greece 13th, Italy and Spain 22nd and 23rd respectively, with the US and UK 32nd and 33rd (World Bank, 1993).

Of course, these figures do not reveal the size of each economy. None the less, the figures show something important about changes in international wealth and power. Technological change is fuelling growth in developing economies at a scarcely believable pace. Figure 1.1 shows that while it took the UK sixty years to double national output at the end of the eighteenth century (at a growth rate of about 1.2 per cent per year), the Chinese economy doubled its output in the ten years from 1977. If South Korea and Taiwan continue to grow as fast as they did in the 1980s, they could overtake America's income per head by about 2020. The later a country industrializes, the faster it does so.

The result of these fast growth rates among newly industrializing countries is a new international geography of economic strength. In the postwar period, there was one dominant, 'hegemonic' economic power – the United States. As a result, it was the USA that underpinned and policed the international economy. In the late 1960s and early 1970s, however, under the pressure of international entanglements and domestic economic problems, US hegemony declined. Today's international order lacks a dominant power: we are living in a multipolar economic world. Three blocs – North America (perhaps soon to be relabelled 'the Americas' to include Mexico and other countries to the south), Europe and the Far East – are emerging,

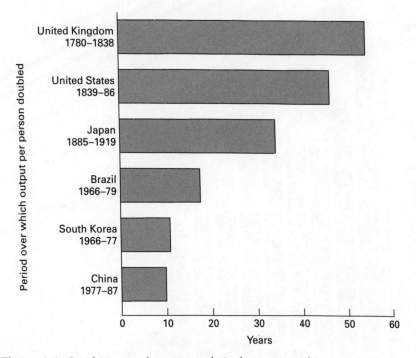

Figure 1.1 Catching up: later growth is faster growth
Source: Wybrew (1994)

and it will be in and through international forums like the G7, not within
the government of any one country, that the world's economic framework
will have to be hammered out.

The success of the high-performing Asian economies – Japan, the 'four
tigers' (Hong Kong, Taiwan, Singapore and Korea), and the new arrivals
(Indonesia, Malaysia, Thailand) – has been an outstanding economic feature since the early 1950s. By 2030 or sooner, it will be the turn of China
and India. The challenge offered by the newly industrializing countries to
the old is partly based on low wage costs, as figure 1.2 shows. It is, however, the quality and productivity of labour, not just its price, which determines the cost of production: the gap in hourly pay between Germany and
Spain is compensated for by the difference in productivity. Internationally,
the competitive challenge to the west is based not only on price, but also
on productivity, quality and innovation. There are now 600 million people in
the world with the literacy and numeracy skills to operate a computer. There
are 60 million Indians with the equivalent of an undergraduate education.
In Bangalore, the 'Silicon Valley' of India, highly skilled computer software

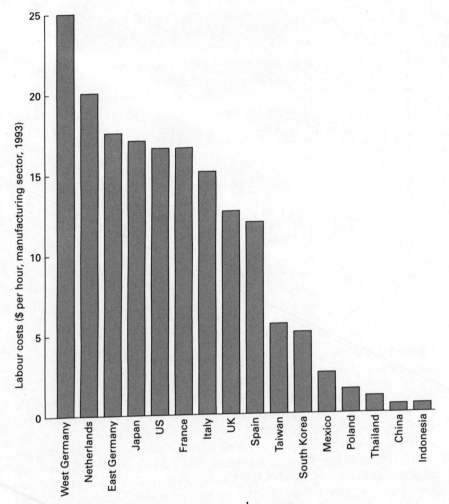

Figure 1.2 The UK cannot compete on low wages
Source: Wybrew (1994)

designers are linked by satellite to western clients: they earn on average $960 a month, one-eighth of the comparable American wage. Eighty per cent of Korean 18-year-olds are heading for higher education. So while we are all familiar with companies shifting low-tech, low-skill production abroad, we now have to contemplate the export of high-tech production and reasonably skilled jobs. Swissair has already relocated its worldwide accounts operation to Bombay.

Faced with this challenge to jobs and living standards, some people in Western Europe and the USA argue that we should put up walls, protect ourselves with import controls against 'unfair' competition. Protectionism can be a popular cry, and if the social and economic exclusion of significant numbers of people continues to grow within the European Union, protectionism may find a dangerous ally in xenophobia. But protectionism is no way forward. Since the vast majority of our trade is with other European Union countries, protectionism for the United Kingdom alone would require us to leave the European Union, turning our backs on our largest export markets and forfeiting the inward investment from overseas which made up nearly one-fifth of total investment in the UK in the five years to 1993, totalling some £40 billion out of £220 billion (Centre for Economic and Business Research, 1993).

Whether at national or European level, there are four main arguments against protectionism. First, putting up barriers to other countries' imports invites them to put up similar barriers to ours. European Union protectionism would risk a trade war with the world's two other large economic blocs – North America and the Pacific Rim. Second, import controls would either increase the price British consumers pay for imported goods, or make such goods scarce: either way, living standards would suffer, just as they did in New Zealand during its protectionist years.

Third, those concerned with social justice in the UK and in Europe should not try to achieve it at the expense of people who are even poorer than the poorest in our country. In what used to be the Third World, international trade is enabling countries like Taiwan and Brazil to raise living standards rapidly. If Poland, Hungary and the Czech Republic are to do the same, they need to be able to sell their agricultural products within the European Union, instead of being penalized by the Common Agricultural Policy. Finally, trade is not a zero-sum game, in which another country's gain must be our loss: as trade increases living standards in Central and Eastern Europe, in the Pacific Rim and elsewhere, it creates new consumers for the goods and services that we can produce.

To argue against protectionism is not, however, to argue for a trade free-for-all, in which social and environmental standards are bid down in a race to the lowest cost. Child labour is becoming an important issue again, 100 years after it was banned in the UK. In China's special enterprise zones, girls under the age of 10 work 14-hour days for less than $10 a month. Anita Roddick, the founder and managing director of the Body Shop, has exposed the 'species-skimming' multinational corporations which claim patent rights over indigenous people's resources. She and other advocates of fair trade argue that, just as national markets are shaped by national standards, liberalized world trade requires new international regulations to prevent the worst excesses of social and environmental dumping.[1]

Global labour standards could do something to stop the poverty of poor nations depressing the living standards of poor people in rich countries. Although those in the poorest countries often argue that today's industrialized countries became rich through precisely the same practices which we now condemn, and that we have no right to pull up the ladder behind us, there is a case for using international trade negotiations to help spread economic growth more fairly within newly industrializing countries – provided of course that wealthy countries are also willing to end practices like child labour at home. Future GATT negotiations and the work of the International Labour Organization and other international bodies should, for instance, consider proposals for an international charter of basic workers' rights, a principle suggested to us in evidence by Professor Peter Townsend of Bristol University. It is furthermore in everyone's interests to create international regimes which will protect the world's environment by promoting sustainable development in both industrialized and industrializing countries. Far more attractive than narrow-minded protectionism is what the US secretary of labor, Robert Reich, has called 'outward-looking nationalism' (which in our case must include 'outward-looking Europeanism') – a conviction that building a country and a region to be proud of depends on engagement with the outside world, not retreat from it.

The new international economic order is not benign; economic and industrial change will continue to impose a painful price on those with the least educational and economic power. The challenge to all those who believe that protectionism is not the answer is to find new ways of enabling all our people to survive and to thrive in radically changed circumstances.

Change in production and work

Debates about economic sovereignty and the implications of Chinese economic development may seem a long way from the everyday concerns of people in the UK. But international competition is rapidly penetrating the domestic economies of the west, while new technologies would continue to transform every workplace even if we could cut ourselves off from international trade. The speed of change leaves many people breathless and scared. In the management jargon:

- Companies are 'delayering' – cutting out the middle-management jobs in personnel, finance and corporate planning that were the heart of middle-class security.[2]

KEIGHLEY COLLEGE
LIBRARY

- Companies are 'downsizing' – breaking up into self-governing units, concentrating on core functions and exporting the rest to independent contractors.
- Companies are 'networking' – joining chains of co-operation and co-ordination to maximize efficiencies of organization.

Throughout the world, many unskilled, routine jobs are being automated out of existence, while the content of jobs is being changed in a continuous process of technological upgrading. German engineering trainees spend six years in apprenticeship; but it is estimated that the 'half-life' of their skills – the time it takes for half their value to drain away – is only four years. Rapidly changing markets and technologies mean that people starting a career today can expect to change jobs between five and eight times in their lives. In a paper circulated to the commission, David Sainsbury, chairman of one of the UK's most successful businesses, stressed that it is 'cumulative learning' that determines the standard of living of a country: 'The world's best companies . . . are using the intelligence and skills of their workers more fully than in the past, and as a result are unleashing major advances in productivity, quality, variety and speed of new product introductions.'

Yet while governments in France as well as Korea and Japan are on course to have 80 per cent of young people reaching university entrance standard by the year 2000, the English, Welsh, Northern Irish, and to a lesser extent Scottish education systems are designed to weed out all but the top third by the age of 18 (Hills/LSE Welfare State Programme, 1993). At Nissan in Sunderland, where the commission talked to management and front-line workers, seven out of ten job applicants fail to score 40 per cent on the company's verbal reasoning test. Skill levels in the UK are 40 per cent below those of our neighbours, and two-thirds of workers have no vocational or professional qualification at all.

It would be foolish to believe that skills alone are enough to build competitive strength. However good the skills, they will be wasted if the tools are poor. But the UK lags behind as much in investment in plant and technology as it does in education. Capital stock per worker is 94 per cent higher in Germany than in Britain, 73 per cent higher in the USA, 49 per cent higher in France and 31 per cent higher in Japan. Business investment in research and development, which was at roughly the same level as in Japan, West Germany and the USA in 1980, is now one-third less. According to the OECD, investment (measured as gross fixed capital formation) rose in the 1980s to reach 20 per cent of our national income but has now fallen back to 18 per cent, compared with 21 per cent in Germany and a massive 32 per cent in Japan and 35 per cent in Singapore. Between 1960 and 1990, total investment in the UK economy was on average 1 per cent less than in other European countries, and 10 per cent a year less than in Japan (Hutton, 1995).

The failure of investment is symptomatic of the short-termism that divides the Anglo-Saxon market economies – particularly the USA and the UK – from those of continental Europe and the Pacific Rim. Since the early 1960s, while companies in Japan have been expected to show an average annual return of 3.1 per cent, in Switzerland 5.3 per cent and in Germany 6.9 per cent, the UK Stock Market has demanded an average return of 9.8 per cent (ibid.).

Even if the UK achieves far higher investment in skills and plant, we will still need organizations capable of using them. The potential of people and technology cannot be fulfilled in a company structured on traditional lines, with vertical hierarchies and strict demarcation of tasks. Driven by technological change and the search for competitive advantage in a crowded market, successful companies are leaving behind the systems of industrial production that powered the first industrial revolution, with their separation of manual from mental labour, where thinkers were not expected to make anything, and doers were not expected to think.

The old model is giving way to new systems of 'mass customization', which combine the innovation and improvisation of craft production with the efficiency of mass production. That requires a fundamental reorganization of production and, above all, a decentralization of decision making, the elimination of unnecessary chains of command, and the promotion of team-working and co-operation. Firms beat off low-wage competition from other countries by moving up market: James Womack and his colleagues, whose book *The Machine that Changed the World* documents the transformation in car production, argue that what they call 'lean production'

Mass production	Mass customization
Efficiency	Value added
Command and control	Empowerment/decentralization
Conglomerates	Enterprise webs
Individuals	Teams
Assets are things	Assets are people
Trade for life	Multiskilling
Training	Learning
Contract	Trust
Us and them	Us and us

Box 1.1 Old economy versus new economy

is more than a match for low-wage mass production; it raises the threshold of acceptable quality, offers a wider variety of products, responds rapidly to changes in consumer tastes, and can fully utilize automation in ways that mass production cannot (Womack et al., 1991).

The director of one of the major Japanese conglomerates, Konsouke Matsushita, argues forcefully that the west cannot compete through the old ways:

> Your firms are built on the Taylor model;[3] even worse, so are your heads. With your bosses doing the thinking while the workers wield the screwdrivers . . . the essence of management is getting the ideas out of the heads of the bosses and into the hands of labour. We are beyond the Taylor model; business, we know, is now so complex and difficult, the survival of firms so hazardous . . . the core of management is precisely the art of mobilising and pulling together the intellectual resources of all employees in the service of the firm.

Rover Cars has learnt this lesson so successfully that it is now a model for visiting Japanese managers. One of Rover's top managers explained to us that as the company struggled to survive it dawned upon the management that 'with every pair of hands, we get a free brain', and that worker involvement was the only route to company success. Unfortunately, most British companies have scarcely begun to use their workers' brains: two-thirds of employees report that they have no significant influence over changes in work organization that could directly affect their jobs (Gallie and White, 1993).

In the best companies, managers do not just eat in the same canteen as other employees (what Professor Jeffrey Pfeffer (1994) of the Stanford Graduate School of Business calls 'symbolic egalitarianism'), they develop ideas with them, and share profits and stock options with them. Conflict between management and workforce is of course not dead: shareholders do not have the same priorities as employees, senior management do not lead the same lives as workers on the office or shop floor. But in the 'inclusive company' – the company which accounts for the varying interests of employees, suppliers, shareholders and the local community – various interests are at least given appropriate weight and consideration, to the benefit of all concerned.

The strategic choice between old and new was vividly illustrated for the commission by our visit to Southampton Docks in May 1993. At Southampton Container Terminals (SCT), TGWU dockers were locked in a bitter dispute with employers who were demanding a pay freeze, longer working hours and job flexibility, while threatening compulsory redundancies. A few hundred yards away, at Southampton Cargo Handling (SCH), TGWU dockers were their own employers, the result of an employee buy-out organized by the union three years earlier. Facing intense competition in an overcrowded industry, one firm was trying to compete by cutting costs and subcontracting, the other by engaging every employee in the drive for higher quality.

SCH's slogan, 'every worker a shareholder', stresses that the worker/owners' commitment to quality and speed guarantees top-class service to customers. Gone are the old demarcations between white-collar and blue-collar workers: today, administrative staff drive vehicles onto waiting ships and nobody stops work until the loading is finished. Gone too are the structures of 'us and them' and the old conflicts between management and workers; the motto today is 'us and us', and the worker/owners elect the managing director. At SCT the dispute seemed set for a bitter lockout, but a few months later union and management had signed a deal which allowed the company to contract out work and make several dockers redundant – but which transferred their work and all the jobs to a new subsidiary of the employee-owned SCH. Both groups of workers earn less than they used to, but, as we were repeatedly told, better to have a job (and still a relatively well-paid one) than just a redundancy cheque, and better still, for the worker/owners who paid themselves their first bonus last year, to have the prospect of sharing future profits as well.

To pay our way in world markets today, and maintain, let alone improve, our standard of living for tomorrow, the United Kingdom needs to compete in the market for quality goods and services by combining Savile Row service, Marks and Spencer quantities and Woolworth prices. In today's global economy, wealth creation depends upon the value which companies and countries add through production. Low skills go with low investment, low productivity, low prices, low profit margins and low wages. The only way to achieve and sustain prosperity is through the high value-added production which requires skilled people using modern equipment in participative enterprises. The aim of public policy must be to help firms respond to the changing demands of global competition, instead of resisting them.

The Social Revolution

The social revolution is a revolution of women's life chances, of family structures and of demography. Although social change has been faster and gone further in the UK than in most other European countries, public policy has failed to keep up.

William Beveridge, like most policy makers of his time, assumed that a woman's place was in the home of a two-parent family – even though he was writing during the war, when millions of married women were being mobilized into industry. 'By definition,' he wrote, 'the family is a group consisting of two parents, male and female respectively, and their offspring.' He envisaged that after the end of the war 'in the next thirty years housewives as mothers have vital work to do in ensuring the adequate continuance of the British race and of British ideals in the world.' Half a century on, the situation is very different. Above all, women must be treated as individuals, citizens seeking autonomy through economic opportunity as well as family security.

Change in families

In 1949, one in three British workers was a woman; today the proportion is nearly one in two, and in many regions women are already the majority of the workforce. A woman whose first child was born in the early 1950s spent an average of ten years out of employment, caring for the family; by the late 1980s, that timespan had dropped to nine months (Hewitt, 1993). In most industrialized countries, growing (although still unequal) economic opportunities for women have been accompanied by a rise in separation, divorce, cohabitation and lone parenthood. A shrinking minority of the population now lives in a traditional nuclear family – male breadwinner, female caregiver. With the exception of Denmark, the United Kingdom now has the highest divorce rate – as well as the highest marriage and remarriage rates – in the European Union. In 1991, 37 per cent of all marriages involved at least one divorced partner (*Social Trends 1994*).

Today, nearly one child in five (18 per cent) is being brought up by a lone parent, usually the mother, compared to 8 per cent in 1972 (*Social Trends 1993*); about half of these lone parents are divorced and a third have never been married. One child in ten lives with one natural parent and a step-parent. The majority – seven out of ten – are living with both their natural parents. A growing proportion of babies – three in ten in 1993 – are born outside marriage, three-quarters of them to couples living together (quoted in the *Guardian*, 26 July 1994).

Family patterns differ significantly within different racial and ethnic groups. In the Afro-Caribbean community, for example, female-headed families are commonplace and not regarded as second best. Afro-Caribbean women with children are more likely than white mothers to be in employment. Within Asian communities, married women are less likely to have paid jobs, although when they are employed they are also more likely to work full-time. Families are often larger and three generations are more likely to live together.

Although statistics provide only a snapshot, it is clear that family life is not static. Children who start life living with their two parents may later become part of a one-parent family and, later still, part of one or more step-families. The rapid rise in the divorce rate suggests that more than one in three new marriages will end in divorce; among couples who cohabit without marrying, the separation rate is even higher (McRae, 1993). Family breakdown is the trapdoor through which women and children most often fall into poverty – itself one of the most important factors in the worse outcomes which, on average, children from lone-parent families experience compared with children of two-parent families (Burghes, 1994).

Although the economic revolution has affected us all, its real victims are the older men who have been made redundant from old industries, and the young men with little education and few skills who have never had the chance to enter industry. The decline in manufacturing employment, which has occurred in almost every industrial country but fastest of all in the United Kingdom, has had a devastating impact on men who could have expected in the past to have acquired a well-paid and secure skilled job. New jobs have been created, but they are in the service sector, often part-time and offering far lower wages than those available to a skilled industrial worker; where they are well-paid, they generally require a high level of education. Men can increasingly expect to share the breadwinner role with women; and some have little prospect of contributing to family income in any way at all. In both cases, economic change is throwing into question traditional definitions of masculinity and what it means to support children.

The demands made by this transformation in domestic relations are wide-ranging:

- For families, a renegotiation of the relationships between mothers, fathers and children.
- For employers, new demands for flexible work patterns, support for child-care and other measures to accommodate caring work within the home.
- For the government, a fundamental review of the social security system, childcare and social services.

Women's growing participation in employment has not been matched by men's participation in the home. Despite the optimistic rhetoric of the 'new man', women are still responsible for most work in the home. As researchers Dr Jane Millar and Dr Caroline Glendinning (1992) have put it, 'women are service-sector workers in and out of the family'. There are, however, some signs of change. Compared with the early 1960s, women are spending less time on routine housework, men a little more. Furthermore, 'time budget' analysis shows that both mothers and fathers are spending more time on childcare – mothers because of the drop in their housework time, fathers because of the fall in working hours throughout the 1970s and (for some workers) the 1980s (Hewitt, 1993).

Although other European countries acknowledge fathers' importance to their families through provision for paid paternity leave, the United Kingdom still fails to do so, and the British government's only significant attempt to come to terms with family change – the introduction of the Child Support Act – has been a near-disaster in practice. Although British women are more likely to be in employment than in most other European countries, British families have less in the way of paid maternity, parental or family leave, and less access to publicly funded nursery education and childcare, than families in any other European country.

In the UK, mothers in part-time employment – despite their lower status and lower pay – consistently report higher levels of satisfaction with the balance they can achieve between employment, family and personal leisure. But full-time employment for men and part-time employment for mothers is an unstable and unsatisfactory pattern: the new challenge is to take advantage of increasingly flexible forms of employment to give men as well as women far greater choice as to how they combine employment, family, education, community activities and leisure in different ways and at different stages in their lives. In other words, we need to make flexibility work for rather than against employees, especially those with family responsibilities.

Fate, class and mobility

Among many changes in traditional structures since the early 1950s, the power of deference has greatly declined. A belief in the equal worth and value of all citizens is now more widely and firmly accepted than ever before. Moreover, as the importance of tradition declines, more and more issues become matters of personal decision (Giddens, 1994). What we wear, how we vote, what we eat, what job we do, where we live – all these are concerns that, two generations ago, were determined for large sections of the population by their birth. This is no longer the case. The UK is more mobile and open, but it is also increasingly unequal.

Perhaps the greatest force for mobility has been greater participation and achievement in the education system. Participation in higher education has long been an assumption of a few; today it is becoming an aspiration for a significant number of the population. There are more than a million undergraduates in higher education, and one thing is almost certain: today's undergraduates will expect their children to go to university.

There are in fact three parallel processes going on – of which two are largely beneficial. The first is the decline of traditional patterns of hierarchy. The second is the development of more flexible and varied patterns of life. The linear progression from education to adult life to retirement is being supplanted by more complex processes: education and training take place throughout the life-cycle; employment is mixed with caring responsibilities through the prime working years; retirement is taken early or late in increasing numbers of cases depending on individual choice.

The third shift is less welcome: social and economic *exclusion* – from work, transport, politics, education, housing, leisure facilities – is an increasingly obvious and depressing feature of life in many parts of the UK. In towns and cities the commission has visited, the accumulated disadvantages of unemployment, bad housing and poor schooling combine to produce areas where there is simply no economy – no banks, no shops, no work.

We do not accept the common assertion that class is dead. Class matters – many of the statistics reviewed elsewhere reinforce our conviction that it is still the most important determinant of a child's life chances. But the class map of the UK is changing. Manual workers formed over half the electorate in the early 1970s; today they make up only one-third. Fewer than four million people now work in manufacturing, once the heart of the industrial working class. Eight million people are now self-employed. The public sector – whose employees do not fit traditional class categories based on labour for the profit of an employer – still employs around six million people. Furthermore, traditional definitions of class structure have always assigned class position to a woman on the basis of her husband's occupation, an assumption which is no longer tenable.

Many of those who profess to see the end of class – or the makings of classlessness – also argue that the United Kingdom is developing an 'underclass' characterized by fecklessness, idleness, dependency and criminality. In the late 1970s Mrs Thatcher talked of 'young single girls who deliberately become pregnant in order to jump a housing queue and get welfare payments' (interview in *The Times*, quoted in Land, 1993). More recently, the Adam Smith Institute, in a pamphlet dedicated to 'ending' the welfare state, argued that the welfare state produces dependency (Bell et al., 1994).

We are unconvinced by such descriptions. Of course there is increasing alienation and disaffection among many people: economic and social exclusion on a grand scale is bound to lessen the stake that people have in society. But the aspirations of the bottom 10 or 20 per cent of the population are remarkably similar to those of the next 60 or 70 per cent – better schools, action against crime, and above all revived economic prospects. The communities we have visited and the people we have met have not been passive victims of fate; they are often active people trying desperately to shore up communities and bring up families in the most deprived conditions.

The UK remains a society corrupted by inequities of class, which intersect with those of gender, race and disability; but the nature of those inequities, and their implications, are changing. In particular, Beveridge could not have anticipated that the UK would become the multicultural, multiracial, multilingual and multifaith society that it is today. Racial discrimination and disadvantage are increasingly complex problems: some Asian communities which are achieving considerable success in education and the economy may none the less find their lives threatened by racist violence. A simple analysis of differences between black and white populations, though they do exist in employment, education and the like, has to be supplemented by a more sophisticated understanding of cultural as well as colour discrimination (Modood, 1994).

Demographic change

In terms of our population, the United Kingdom is a slow-growth country in a slow-growth region of a very rapidly growing world. Today, the twelve countries of the European Union have 6 per cent of the world's population of 5.5 billion. By 2025, the same twelve countries are likely to account for only 4 per cent of a global population of 8.5 billion. The UK's fertility rate, which was 2.7 in 1960, has now dropped to 1.8. In Germany, the fertility rate is down to 1.3 – implying that unless the birth rate recovers, its native population will be extinct in 300 years (*Financial Times*, 8 March 1994)!

A slowly growing or even shrinking population must, of course, mean an ageing population. The eighteen Western European states of the OECD, now home to 50 million people over the age of 65, will by 2030 have 70 million older citizens. In the UK, which had one million people aged over 80 in 1961, there are already more than two million, including 250,000 over the age of 90.

Although many older people remain active and healthy, governments are increasingly concerned about the 'burden' placed upon the working population by older people's entitlement to pensions, health care and other services. The UK, however, has less reason to be worried than other industrialized countries. The 'support ratio', comparing the number of people of working age with those over 65, was low in 1980 by international standards (at around 4:1), but it is expected to fall more slowly than in other countries. By about 2040, it is predicted that the UK will have one of the highest ratios (around 3:1), while Germany, Japan and the Netherlands will have among the lowest ratios (each just more than 2:1). As Dr John Hills of the LSE has shown, the projected cost of ageing by 2020 twenty-five years amounts to a smaller increase than during the 1980s (Hills/LSE Welfare State Programme, 1993).

None the less, the care of the old presents a significant challenge. In the early 1950s, 20 per cent of NHS resources was spent on people over 65; now it is nearly 50 per cent (Field, 1993). Moreover, in 1900 for every person aged over 85, there were twenty-four women in their 50s (the group which carries out most informal care); by 2000 there will be only three (Henwood, 1993). As the woefully inadequate state of community-care services suggests, we have scarcely begun to face up to the financial and social arithmetic of care. Retired people already do a great deal of productive work outside the paid economy (much of it as carers themselves), but as the number of elderly people in our population grows, so the questions of who does the caring, and of how it is paid for, become more acute.

The Political Revolution

The political revolution is a challenge to the UK's old assumptions of parliamentary sovereignty and to its growing centralization of government power; it involves a fundamental reorientation of the relationship between those who govern and those who are governed.

Economic and social reform must be supported in the political sphere. Political factors – power, popular attitudes, institutional structures – make change possible, or serve to block it. The 1990s, however, are a time of particular political openness.

The collapse of Soviet Communism and the limitations of both Keynesian social democracy and Thatcherite neo-liberalism have left a political vacuum. The Communist experiment, far from eliminating inefficiency and waste, fuelled both. Keynesian social democracy promised to smooth the business cycle, and for thirty years after World War II did so, but in an interdependent world economy found its prescription less and less reliable: Keynes had not solved the problem of production after all. And the neo-liberal answer to the limitations of the 1945 settlement, a return to the laissez-faire economics of the minimal state and free markets, has in turn produced a cycle of debt, recession and social polarization in the countries where it has been most vigorously pursued. The polarities of the post-war period – individual versus collective, state versus market, public versus private – are giving way to a new recognition of their interdependence. Since old ideas do not work, it is a good time to develop new ones: 'This is the time to *make the future* – precisely because everything is in flux', says the American economist Peter Drucker (1993).

The welfare state of 1945 was built on the expertise of professionals. Too often, people were treated as passive recipients of services and benefits deemed appropriate by government. Today, people who are active and well-informed consumers of private goods and services want to make more decisions for themselves in the public sphere: about the nature of social services, traffic planning in their neighbourhood, or the future of local schools. Because people have diverse needs, and because they are almost always the best judges of their own needs, they must have a greater say in determining how needs are met. But there is also a need to address the cynicism that afflicts popular attitudes to politics. The 1994 celebration of democratic suffrage in South Africa was a timely reminder of the power of the free ballot, and the extent to which its potential has been corrupted in many countries. A new politics is needed in Europe, and nowhere more so than in the UK.

Reinventing government

There are growing and changing demands on politics and government and growing constraints on what they can achieve. In the 1970s, the right used the idea that advanced and complex democracies were 'ungovernable' to argue that the answer was *less* government. Today, the search is for *better* government.

David Osborne, co-author of the American bestseller *Reinventing Government*, has identified four factors that explain the pressures on public services across the industrialized world: the pace of social and technological change, and the difficulties this poses for traditional, top-down government bureaucracies; the expectations of the public, for quality and choice; the impact of the global marketplace, and the need to attract mobile capital; and finally, the sheer expense of government (Osborne and Gaebler, 1992). To these should be added a fifth, the growing demand from previously excluded groups – women, ethnic minorities, disabled people – for a political system that includes them and better reflects their concerns and demands.

Further demands on government are made by, for example, technical innovation and by medical advance. It has been estimated, for instance, that spending on personal social services needs to grow by 2.5 per cent per annum to meet demand, and that if the NHS were to try to keep pace with the advances of medical technology, it would need to grow by 2 per cent per annum in real terms (Glennerster, 1992). There are constraints on the supply side of government spending because the electorate is sceptical about increased taxation, and there is international pressure for a convergence of tax levels.

In addition, public services suffer from a 'relative price effect'. Although doctors, nurses and other staff in the NHS have recently achieved substantial increases in productivity, it is always more difficult to achieve and to measure rising productivity in services than it is in traditional manufacturing. Service-sector activities like teaching children or helping elderly people look after themselves necessarily involve a high input of labour. Because wages rise fairly consistently across the economy, the faster productivity is increased in the trading sector in the face of world competition, the faster the relative costs of services grow.

Political leadership

Just when imaginative political and civic leadership is most needed, people feel great distrust of the designs – grand or otherwise – of politicians. One councillor in Newcastle summed up the situation very succinctly for the commission: 'The issue on the doorstep is not "Why should I vote Labour?", but "Why should I vote at all?"'

This is in part a legacy of the 1980s, when the dominant ideology was that economic and social decline were the products of government intervention, and that markets, not politics, held the solution to our problems. But the decline of people's faith in politics goes deeper: the claims and actions of politicians seem increasingly distant from the people who vote for them. One source of this is to be found in the structure of politics at Westminster.

The functions, structures and powers of the UK Parliament are peculiar. The sovereignty of the crown in Parliament, the UK's unwritten constitution, an electoral system which tends to give very great power to the winning party, and the power of party whips and prime ministerial patronage combine to make the British system uniquely centralized, unusually confrontational in its debates, and notably weak in its ability to implement policy in a flexible and effective way. The problems that have in the early 1990s arisen with alarming regularity – the confusion of democracy with majority rule, the equating of public interest with ministerial interest, the neglect of local diversity and difference, the failure to consult on legislation – come from the top of the system. This is why there is such widespread demand for constitutional reform. 'High-performance government', government which is a catalyst for renewal and change, is alien in a system that revolves around administration and legislation, not persuasion and negotiation.

The policies of the post-war period were largely conceived in terms of the national state, but the national arena is increasingly too small for the large problems, and too large for the small problems. The Conservative government has passed dozens of Acts of Parliament dealing with local government, which have promised to shift power away from local government to the users of services; yet power has in fact been transferred from local government to central government and to unelected quangos . . . The irony of this centralization of power is that there is unremitting outside pressure for the transfer of responsibility away from the national level. In some matters, such as transport policy, there are calls for decentralization to local government at regional and city level; by contrast, in the case of environmental or macroeconomic policy, a European level of debate is essential. This is the 'double shift' faced by all advanced industrial societies.

It is not only the peculiarities of the Westminster system that make the UK increasingly hard to govern from the top down. The welfare state developed after 1945 has been undermined politically, as well as economically and socially, because it failed, with the exception of the NHS, to make citizens feel that it was theirs. The traditional Fabian conception of society was one in which people were profoundly dependent on government. Problems were to be solved by experts, and there were few mechanisms for ordinary people to participate in decisions affecting their own lives. Perhaps most revealing is the treatment of disabled people: the concept of 'need' is central, but its definition has been controlled by professionals, too often to the exclusion of disabled people themselves. There was in various public-service activities a powerful ethos of 'government knows best'.

The government's response to this situation has been to try to impose market disciplines on public services – through contracting out, market testing, Next Steps and a number of other initiatives. Whatever the details of the various policies that have been established, at their heart has been a view of the individual as *consumer* in the marketplace – a consumer of health care, refuse collection or social services, in much the same way as he or she consumes ice cream, cars or clothes. The problem with this view is that it takes into account only a part of the relationship between the users of public services and the people who provide them. Individuals are sometimes joint producers of public services: in the case of education, for example, parental input is one essential complement to good teaching in the development of successful schooling. It is vitally important that individuals are seen not just as consumers but as citizens. While we are not particularly affected by our neighbour's choice of holiday, we are profoundly affected if neighbouring children are poorly educated. Good public services for all who use them are in all our interests.

In its attempt to change the structure of public service, the government has been right to emphasize the needs and views of individuals. But it has neglected the potential of public-service workers to contribute constructively to change. And choice, real or imaginary, is not the whole answer: people do not have equal power to choose from equally satisfactory alternatives, and high-quality public services depend on supply-side action as well as demand-side strength. The important point is to provide responsive and efficient services, and their design must be grounded not in paternalism but in participation and democracy. Citizens should be able to shape the service, not merely buy it and complain about it.

There is a final paradox in the current debate about the renewal of social policy. Everyone agrees that expenditure of £80 billion per year on social security is not halting the increase in poverty and social division; few people believe that anyone actually likes paying taxes; yet the polls suggest that a substantial and (more significantly) increasing majority of the population says that it is in favour of spending more on social welfare and public action. *British Social Attitudes* surveys report that the number of people supporting an increase in taxation to provide better public services doubled between 1983 and 1991 (Social and Community Planning Research, 1992). A *Breadline Britain* survey for London Weekend Television showed that in 1983 25 per cent of people were willing to pay an extra 5p in the pound in tax to help everyone afford items agreed to be necessities, while 59 per cent rejected the idea; by 1991, 44 per cent supported the idea, although 44 per cent were still against it (London Weekend Television, 1991).

The UK today does not, in J.K. Galbraith's phrase, display a 'culture of contentment' (Galbraith, 1992). We are a nation hungry for the satisfaction of aspirations rather than bloated by contentment; we are increasingly insecure rather than benignly content. Greater personal independence, paradoxically, means increasing social interdependence. Whether the issue is environmental protection, team-work in the workplace, or the promotion of safety in local communities, we are more and more dependent on others for what we are able to do. The challenge is to develop new mechanisms of collective action which will at the same time meet common goals and liberate individual talent. Far from living through the death of politics, we depend on its resurrection for national renewal.

Notes

1 The North American Free Trade Agreement (NAFTA) represents the first major trade agreement that secures rights, albeit minimal ones, for workers.
2 British Telecom have cut 6,000 middle-management jobs during their restructuring.

3 Frederick Winslow Taylor developed the principle of 'scientific management', relentlessly subdividing work tasks into their smallest constituent units.

References

Atkinson, Giles and Dubourg, Richard (1994) Green approaches. *New Economy*, 1 (2), Summer.

Bell, Michael, Butler, Eamonn, Marsland, David and Pirie, Madsen (1994) *The End of the Welfare State*. London: Adam Smith Institute.

Burghes, Louie (1994) *Lone Parenthood and Family Disruption*. London: Family Policy Studies Centre.

Centre for Economic and Business Research (1993) *US and Japanese Investment in the UK*. London: CBI.

Drucker, Peter (1993) *Post-capitalist Society*. Oxford: Butterworth Heinemann.

Economist (1992) The case for central planning. *The Economist*, 12 September.

Esping-Andersen, Gøsta (1990) *The Three Worlds of Welfare Capitalism*. Cambridge: Polity Press and Princeton NJ: Princeton University Press.

Field, Frank (1993) Don't sell granny short: the role of care pensions. First Annual Pegasus Lecture, Royal College of Medicine, 27 October.

Galbraith, J.K. (1992) *The Culture of Contentment*. London: Sinclair-Stevenson.

Gallie, Duncan and White, Michael (1993) *Employee Commitment and the Skills Revolution*. London: PSI.

Giddens, Anthony (1994) *Beyond Left and Right*. Cambridge: Polity Press.

Glennerster, Howard (1992) *Paying for Welfare*. London: Harvester Wheatsheaf.

Gray, John (1993) *Beyond the New Right*. London: Routledge.

Gray, John (1994) *The Undoing of Conservatism*. London: Social Market Foundation.

Henwood, Melanie (1993) Presentation to the Commission on Social Justice.

Hewitt, Patricia (1993) *About Time*. London: Rivers Oram/IPPR.

Hills, John/LSE Welfare State Programme (1993) *The Future of Welfare: A Guide to the Debate*. York: Joseph Rowntree Foundation.

Hutton, Will (1995) *The State We're In*. London: Jonathan Cape.

Land, Hilary (1993) Money isn't everything. Submission to the Commission on Social Justice.

Lawson, Nigel (1993) *The View from Number 11*. London: Corgi.

London Weekend Television (1991) *Breadline Britain 1990*.

McRae, Susan (1993) *Cohabiting Mothers*. London: PSI.

Millar, Jane and Glendinning, Caroline (1992). Introduction. In Jane Millar and Caroline Glendinning (eds), *Women and Poverty in Britain*, London: Harvester Wheatsheaf.

Modood, Tariq (1994) *Racial Equality: Colour, Culture and Justice*. Commission on Social Justice Issue Paper 5. London: IPPR.

Osborne, David and Gaebler, Ted (1992) *Reinventing Government*. New York: Addison-Wesley.

Pfeffer, Jeffrey (1994) *Competitive Advantage through People*. Cambridge MA: Harvard Business School Press.

Scharpf, Fritz (1994) Unpublished paper presented to a seminar organized by the Socialist International, March.

Social and Community Planning Research (1992) *British Social Attitudes Cumulative Sourcebook: The First Six Surveys*. Aldershot: Gower.

Social Trends 1993 (1993) London: HMSO.
Social Trends 1994 (1994) London: HMSO.
Womack, James, Jones, Daniel and Roos, Daniel (1991) *The Machine that Changed the World: The Story of Lean Production.* New York: Harper Perennial.
World Bank (1993) *The East Asian Miracle.* Oxford: Oxford University Press.
Wybrew, John (1994) *Global Forces for Change: The Challenge to UK Business and Society.* London: Shell UK.

2
What is Social Justice?

THE COMMISSION ON SOCIAL JUSTICE

In deciding to develop a conceptual framework for thinking about social justice, the commission made a big assumption, namely that there is such a thing as 'social justice'. Some people (particularly of the libertarian right) deny that there is a worthwhile idea of *social* justice at all. They say that justice is an idea confined to the law, with regard to crime, punishment, and the settling of disputes before the courts. They claim that it is non-sense to talk about resources in society being fairly or unfairly distributed. The free-market theorist, F.A. Hayek, for example, argued that the process of allocating wealth and property 'can be neither just nor unjust, because the results are not intended or foreseen, and depend on a multitude of circumstances not known in their totality to anybody' (Hayek, 1976).

What libertarians really mean, however, is not that there is no such thing as social justice, but rather that there is only one criterion of a just outcome in society, namely that it should be the product of a free market. But this is not as simple as it may sound, because ideas of fairness (and not merely of efficiency) are themselves used in defining what counts as a free market. While it is often said that a given market competition is not fair because it is not being played 'on a level field', it is not clear what counts as levelling the field, as opposed to altering the result of the match. For example, anti-trust laws can be seen as an interference in a free mar-ket, or a device for making the field level.

In fact, people in modern societies *do* have strong ideas about social justice. We all know this from daily conversation, and opinion polls regu-larly confirm it. We are confident that at least in our belief that there is such a thing as 'social justice', we reflect the common-sense of the vast majority of people. However, polls are not easy to interpret, and they make it clear that people's ideas about social justice are complex.

There is more than one notion associated with the term 'social justice'. In some connections, for example, justice is thought to have something to do with *equality*. Sometimes it seems to relate to *need*: for example, it can seem notably unfair if bad fortune prevents someone from having something they really need, such as medical care, less unfair if it is something they just happen to want. Yet again, justice relates to such notions as *entitlement, merit* and *desert*. These are not the same as each other. For example, if someone wins the prize in the lottery, they are entitled to the money, and it would be unjust to take it away from them, but it has nothing to do with their merits, and they have done nothing to deserve it. Similarly, if talented people win prizes in an activity that requires no great practice or effort, they are entitled to the prize and get it on the strength of their merits (as opposed, for instance, to someone's getting it because he is the son of the promoter), but they may well have not done anything much to deserve it. People who are especially keen on the notion of desert may want there to be prizes only for effort; or, at least, think that prizes which command admiration (as the lottery prize does not) should be awarded only for effort. Humanity has shown so far a steady reluctance to go all the way with this view.

As well as being *complex* in this way, people's views about justice are also *indeterminate*. This means that it is often unclear what the just outcome should be – particularly when various considerations of social justice seem to pull in different directions, as they often do. Most people, for instance, think that inheritance is at least not intrinsically evil, and that parents are entitled to leave property to their children. But no one thinks that one can leave anything one likes to one's children – one's job, for instance – and almost everyone thinks that it can be just for the state to tax inheritances in order to deal with social injustice, or simply to help the common good.

The mere fact that people's ideas about justice are both complex and indeterminate has an important consequence for democratic politics. There is more than one step from general ideas to practical recommendations. There have to be *general* policies directed to social justice, and these are going to be at best an interpretation of people's ideas on such matters. General policies will hope to offer considerations which people can recognize as making sense in the light of their own experience and ideas (this need not exclude challenging some of those ideas). *Specific* policies, however, involve a further step, since they have to express general policies in a particular administrative form. A given scheme of taxation or social security is, in that sense, at two removes from the complex and indeterminate ideas that are its moral roots.

This is not to deny that some administrative practices may acquire a symbolic value of their own. In the 1940s, the death grant was a symbol of society's commitment to end paupers' funerals and ensure for every family the means to offer deceased relatives a proper burial. It is a matter of acute political judgement to decide whether one is dealing with an important example of such a value, as opposed to a fetish (in the more or less literal sense of an inert object that has been invested with value that does not belong to it in its own right). Not every arrangement that has been taken to be an essential embodiment of social justice is, in changing circumstances, really so.

Theories of Social Justice

There are important theories of social justice. The most ambitious give a general account of what social justice is, explain and harmonize the relations between the different considerations associated with it, do the same for the relations between justice and other goods, notably liberty, help to resolve apparent conflicts between different values, and in the light of all that, even give pointers to practical policies. The most famous such theory in modern discussion is that of John Rawls (1971), which gives a very rich elaboration to a very simple idea: that the fair division of a cake would be one that could be agreed on by people who did not know which piece they were going to get.

Rawls invokes an 'Original Position', in which representatives of various parties to society are behind 'a veil of ignorance' and do not know what role each party will occupy in the society. They are asked to choose a general scheme for the ordering of society. The scheme that they would reasonably choose in these imagined circumstances constitutes, in Rawls's view, the scheme of a just society.

Rawls's theory, and others with similar aims, contain important insights, and anyone who is trying to think about these problems should pay attention to them. But there is an important question – one acknowledged by Rawls himself (1992) – of what relation such a theory can have to politics. Rawls thinks that his theory articulates a widely spread sense of fairness, but it is certain that the British public would not recognize in such a theory, or in any other with such ambitions, all its conflicting ideas and feelings about social justice. Even if the commission, improbably, all agreed on Rawls's or some other such theory, we would not be justified in presenting our conclusions in terms of that theory. The commission has a more practical purpose.

Our task is to find compelling ways of making our society more just. We shall be able to do so only if we think in ways that people can recognize and respect about such questions as how best to understand merit and need; how to see the effects of luck in different spheres of life; what is implied in saying, or denying, that health care is a morally special kind of good which makes a special kind of demand.

The commission has to guard against all-or-nothing assumptions. It is not true that either we have a complete top-down theory, or we are left only with mere prejudice and subservience to polls. This particularly applies to conflict. Confronted . . . with an apparent conflict within justice, or between justice and some other value, we may tend to assume that there are only two possibilities: the conflict is merely apparent, and we should understand liberty and equality (for instance) in such a way that they cannot conflict; or it is a real conflict, and then it can only be left to politics, majorities, subjective taste, or whatever. This will not do. Reflection may not eliminate all conflicts, but it can help us to understand them, and then arrive at policy choices.

The Equal Worth of Every Citizen

Social justice is often thought to have something specially to do with equality, but this idea, in itself, determines very little. A basic question is: equality of what? Furthermore, not all inequalities are unjust. For example, what people can do with money varies. Thus disabled people may well need more resources to reach a given quality of life than other people do, and if you are trying to be fair to people with regard to the quality of their life, unequal amounts of money is what fairness itself will demand. What this shows, as the philosopher and economist Amartya Sen has insisted (1992), is that equality in one dimension goes with inequality in another. Since people have different capacities to turn resources into worthwhile activity (for instance, because they are disabled), people will need different resources to be equally capable of worthwhile activity.

In fact, virtually everyone in the modern world believes in equality of *something*. All modern states are based on belief in some sort of equality and claim to treat their citizens equally. But what is involved in 'treating people equally'? Minimally, it implies political and civil liberties, equal rights before the law, equal protection against arbitrary arrest, and so forth. These things provide the basis of a 'civil society', a society of equal citizens.

However, these rights and freedoms cannot stand by themselves. More than this formal level of equality is needed if the minimal demands themselves are to be properly met. It is a familiar point that equality before the law does not come to much if one cannot afford a good lawyer. The 'equal freedom' of which modern democratic states boast should amount to more . . . than the freedom to sleep on park benches and under bridges. Everyone needs the means to make use of their equal freedom, which otherwise would be hollow. Formal equalities have substantive consequences. Perhaps the most basic question about the nature of social justice in a modern society is what those substantive consequences are.

Meeting Basic Needs

People are likely to be restricted in what they can do with their freedom and their rights if they are poor, or ill, or lack the education which, to a greater extent today than ever before, is the basis of employment opportunities, personal fulfilment, and people's capacities to influence what happens to them. These concerns define areas of *need*, and it is a natural application of the idea that everyone is of equal worth that they should have access to what they need, or at least to what they basically need.

Some basic needs are met by providing resources, or by helping people to save or acquire resources. This is the case with paid work; with financial security in old age; and with provisions for dealing with lack of resources, such as benefit in case of unemployment. In the case of health care and education, however, the most appropriate way of meeting needs seems to be not through money, but in kind; we think that someone who is ill has a right to access to treatment for their illness, but not that they have a right to funds which they can choose to spend on treatment or not. One way of expressing this commitment is that the state should itself provide the service. Another is that the state should provide means which command health care or education, but which cannot be converted into money. In the case of health, this may take the form of public insurance, though this can raise basic questions of fairness (with regard to individual risk) as well as of efficiency.

The case of health now raises a fundamental question which was not present in the early 1940s. Health care has always seemed a very special good, in relation to social justice as in other respects. It involves our most basic interests, gives great power to certain professionals, and carries heavy symbolic value (brought out, for instance, in Richard Titmuss's (1970) famous discussion of blood donation, *The Gift Relationship*). Treating health as one commodity, to be bought and sold like any other, is found offensive in most parts of the world (and Americans, though used to that attitude, seem to be turning against it). Our sentiments about health care merge with our sense of some very basic obligations: most people feel that resources should be used to save an identified person (as opposed to a merely statistical casualty) from death.

But today it is a fact that medicine's resources to extend life are expanding at an accelerating rate, and so is their cost. This raises hard questions not only about the distribution of resources devoted to health care (who gets the kidney machine?), but also about the amount of resources that should be devoted to health care at all. These hard questions are questions of justice, among other things. Confronted with the opportunity to save someone in the street from death, we will think that we should stop to save them even if the cost is not taking the children to school, but is it fair to save every saveable person from death at the cost of sending many children to quite inadequate schools?

To answer these questions, there is a need to consider what *sort* of goods we take health and health care to be. This was a less pressing question in the past, but it is now harder to avoid the issue of what we are distributing when we distribute medical care, and of what we most want it to do.

Education is also a good to which everyone has a right, because it is so closely tied to basic needs, to personal development, and to one's role in society. But it is also connected to equality in another way. Disadvantage is, notoriously, inherited, and an unfair situation in one generation tends to mean an unfair start for the next. Educational opportunity is still what it always has been, a crucial means for doing something about this unfairness.

This brings out a further point, that the ideal of 'equality of opportunity', which has often been thought by reformers to be a rather weak aspiration, is in fact very radical, if it is taken seriously. The changes required in order to give the most disadvantaged in our society the same life chances as the more fortunate would be very wide-ranging indeed.

Opportunities and Life Chances

Self-respect and equal citizenship demand more than the meeting of basic needs for income, shelter and so on. They demand the opportunities and life chances central to personal freedom and autonomy. In a commercial society (outside monasteries, kibbutzim, etc.), self-respect standardly requires a certain amount of personal property. As Adam Smith remarked, a working man in eighteenth-century Scotland needed to own a decent linen shirt as a condition of self-respect, even though that might not be true of every man everywhere.

This does not mean that Adam Smith's man should be issued with a shirt. In a commercial society, his need is rather for the resources to buy a shirt of his choice. This is connected with his needing it as a matter of self-respect, which suggests something else, namely that where resources are supplied directly, for instance to those who are retired or who are caring for members of their families, it must be in ways which affirm their self-respect. But most people, for most of their lives, want the opportunities to earn the resources for themselves. The obvious question is whether everyone therefore has a right to a job, or the right to the means to gain a job.

The trouble, clearly, is that it may not be in the power of government directly to bring this about. Having a job, at least as the world is now, is closely connected with self-respect and hence with the equality of citizens, and for this as well as other reasons it must be a high priority for any government to create the circumstances in which there are jobs for those who want them. To insist, however, on a right to work – a right, presumably, which each person holds against the government – may not be the best way of expressing this aim. It is important therefore to consider not only ways in which employment may be increased, but also what provision social justice demands for those who are unable to do paid work, or who are engaged in valuable unpaid work, or when significant levels of unemployment persist, even for a temporary period. Tackling unemployment is, of course, central to the realization of social justice.

There are questions here of how resources and opportunities can be extended to the unemployed. But there is a wider question as well, that extends to the provision for other needs: how opportunities may be created for the expression of people's autonomy and the extension of their freedom to determine their own lives. There is no doubt that advocates of social justice have often been insensitive to this dimension. The designers of the welfare state wanted to put rights in the place of charity: the idea of *entitlement* to benefit was meant to undercut any notion that the better off were doing the worse off a good turn. But the entitlement was often still understood as an entitlement to be given or issued with certain goods and services, the nature of which it was, in many cases, the business of experts to determine. There is a much greater awareness today that what people need is the chance to provide for themselves: . . . 'there is a limit to what government can do for people, but there is no limit to what they can be enabled to achieve for themselves' (Commission on Social Justice, 1993).

Relatedly, there is a stronger sense today that the aims of social justice are served not only by redistribution, by bringing resources after the event to people who have done badly. Social justice requires as well that structures should be adapted and influenced in ways that can give more people a better chance in the first place. That is why opportunities, and breaking down barriers to them, are so important.

There are, without doubt, conflicts between these various considerations. You cannot both encourage people's freedom to live their own lives as they choose, and guarantee that they will not suffer if they do not live them well. You cannot both allow people to spend money, if they wish, on their children's education – a right that exists in every democratic country – and also bring it about that everyone gets exactly the same education whether they pay privately for it or not. Here there are questions, too, of how far publicly supported provision to meet need should aim only at a minimal level, available to those without other provision, and how far it should seek to provide a high level of service for everyone. The view of most people is probably that the first answer applies to some needs and the goods and services that meet them, while in the case of health care and education, at least, no one should be excluded by disadvantage from a very high level of provision. Exactly how those different aims should now be conceived, and the extent to which they can realistically be carried out, are central questions . . .

Unjustified Inequalities

Proponents of equality sometimes seem to imply that *all* inequalities are unjust (although they usually hasten to add that they are not in fact arguing for 'arithmetical equality'). We do not accept this. It seems fair, for instance, that a medical student should receive a lower income than the fully qualified doctor; or that experience or outstanding talent should be rewarded, and so on. Different people may have different views about what the basis of differential rewards should be; but most people accept, as we do, that some inequalities are just. There is, however, a question about the justifiable *extent* of an inequality, even if we accept that the inequality per se is not unjust.

Similarly, most people believe that it is fair for people to bequeath their property as they see fit, even though this means that some will inherit more then others. None the less, it is also accepted that society may claim a share of an inheritance through the taxation of wealth or gifts, particularly when the estate is large. It is, after all, offensive to most ideas of social justice that a growing number of people own two homes while others have nowhere to live at all. This does not imply that one person's property should be confiscated to house another; but it does suggest the need for a fundamental reform of housing policy . . .

But if some inequalities are just, it is obviously the case that not all are so. It would, for instance, be unjust to allow people to inherit jobs from their parents: employment should be open to all, on the basis of merit. Inheritance of a family title offends many people's views about a classless society, but could not be said to deny somebody else something which they deserved. But inheritance of a peerage, in the UK, carries with it automatic entitlement to a seat and vote in the Second Chamber of Parliament: and that is an inequality of power which seems manifestly unjust.

Entitlement and desert

Parents can, however, pass on intelligence, talent, charm and other qualities, as well as property or titles. Rawls (1971) in his theory rests much on the fact that a person's talents, and his or her capacity to make productive use of those talents, are very much matters of luck and are also, in some part, the product of society. Nobody, he has rightly insisted, *deserves* his or her (natural) talents. From this he has inferred that nobody, at a level of basic principle, deserves the rewards of his or her talents. He argues that no one has a right to something simply because it is the product of his or her talents, and society has a right to redistribute that product in accordance with the demands of social justice.

This is a very strong and surprising claim. Some people might agree that no one deserves a reward that they get on the basis of some raw advantage, without any investment of effort. (Of course, given the existing rules, that does not mean that they are not entitled to it, or that it can merely be taken away from them. It means that it would not necessarily be an injustice to change the rules.) But those who agree to this are very likely to think that people who *do* invest effort deserve its rewards, at least up to a certain point. But Rawls's argument applies just as much to effort as to raw talent. First, it is practically impossible to separate the relative contributions of effort and talent to a particular product. Moreover, the capacity to make a given degree of effort is itself not equally distributed, and may plausibly be thought to be affected by upbringing, culture and other social factors. Virtually everything about a person that yields a product is itself undeserved. So no rewards, on Rawls's view, are, at the most basic level, a matter of desert.

Few people believe this. If someone has taken a lot of trouble in designing and tending a garden, for instance, they will be proud of it, and appropriately think of its success as theirs. The same applies to many aspects of life. This does suggest that there is something wrong with the idea that basically people never earn anything by their talents or labours – that in the last analysis all that anyone's work represents is a site at which society has achieved something. Yet, certainly, one does not 'deserve' the talents of birth. It must be true, then, that one can deserve the rewards of one's talents without deserving one's talents. As the American philosopher Robert Nozick (1974) forcefully put it, why does desert 'have to go all the way down'?

What the various arguments about entitlement and desert suggest seems to be something close to what many people believe: that there is basic justice in people having some differential reward for their productive activities, but that they have no right to any *given* differential of their reward over others. It is not simply self-interest, or again scepticism about government spending programmes (though that is certainly a factor), that makes people resist the idea that everyone's income is in principle a resource for redistribution; that idea also goes against their sense of what is right. They rightly think that redistribution of income is not an aim in itself.

At the same time, they acknowledge that the needs of the less fortunate make a claim. Luck is everywhere, and one is entitled to some rewards of luck, but there are limits to this entitlement when one lives and works with other people. Even if one is entitled to some rewards from the product of one's efforts and talents, there is the further point that in a complex enterprise such as a company or family, there is rarely a product which is solely and definitely the product of a given person's efforts and talents.

This is no doubt one reason why people are sceptical about vast rewards to captains of industry. It is also a question of the relation of one person's activity to that of others. Few people mind that Pavarotti or Lenny Henry are paid large sums – there is only one of them, and they are undoubtedly the star of the show. But in some cases, one person's reward can be another person's loss. The Nobel Prize-winning economist Professor James Meade argued in a submission to the Commission that:

> Keynesian full-employment policy . . . collapsed simply and solely because a high level of money expenditures came to lead not to a high level of output and employment but to a high rate of money wages, costs and prices . . . It is very possible that to absorb two million extra workers into employment would require a considerable reduction in real wage costs.

This raises a crucial point, concerning the power to determine one's own rewards, and the relationship of that power to questions of justice and desert. In contrast to a simple focus on the distribution of rewards, this raises the question of the *generation* of rewards, the processes whereby inequalities are generated.

Unequal incomes are inherent in a market economy. Even if everyone started off with the same allocation of money, differences would soon emerge. Not all labour commands the same price; not all investments produce the same return; some people work longer hours, others prefer more leisure, and so on. The resulting inequalities are not necessarily unjust – although the extent of them may be. In the real world, of course, people start off with very different personal and financial resources. The problem is that too many of these inequalities are exacerbated in the UK's system of market exchange.

But market economies are not all of a piece; different kinds of market produce different outcomes. For instance, Germany, Japan and Sweden all have more equal earnings distributions than the UK, where the gap between the highest and lowest paid is wider today in the early 1990s than at any time since 1886. Social justice therefore has a part to play in deciding how a market is constructed, and not simply with the end result.

Fair reward

Most people have some idea of a 'fair reward'. For example, it is clear to the vast majority of people that disadvantage and discrimination on grounds of sex or race or disability are unjust. However, once one gets beyond the general idea, there is less agreement on what fair rewards should be. Even if there were more agreement about this, it is very difficult, both practically and morally, to impose such notions on a modern economy. The very idea of a society that can be effectively managed from the top on the basis of detailed centralized decisions is now discredited. Moreover, our society does not stand by itself and happily does not have walls around it, and people can go elsewhere.

Ideas of social justice in this area are not, however, necessarily tied to the model of a command economy. It is often clear, at least, that given rewards in a market economy are not fair, because they are not being determined by such things as talent, effort, and the person's contribution to the enterprise, but rather by established power relations. Real life does not conform to economic models: people are not paid for the 'marginal product' of their labour. They are paid, among other things, according to social norms. In one sense, such distortions are the product of the market: they are what we get if market processes, uncorrected, are allowed to reflect established structures and habits of power. Examples of this are the huge salaries and bonuses distributed to the directors of some large companies ... [T]hese salaries and bonuses are often quite unrelated to the performance of the company concerned, and are sometimes actually inversely correlated with company performance.

In another sense, unjust inequalities are themselves distortions of the market: it is not a fair market in talent and effort if it is not talent and effort that determine the outcome. This is most obviously demonstrated in the case of inequalities of pay between men and women. Although the 1970 Equal Pay Act eliminated overt pay inequities, it had a limited effect on the gap between men's and women's pay, which resulted in the main from job segregation and gender-biased views of what different jobs and different qualities were worth. Hence the concept of 'equal pay for work of equal value', which permits comparisons between two very different jobs performed for the same employer. Although designed to eradicate gender as a consideration in earnings, equal-value claims may in practice require a complete transformation in an organization's pay setting. Equal pay for work of equal value, after all, implies unequal pay for work of unequal value: thus, the basis for differentials has to be made explicit and justified.

Different organizations and people will have different views of what constitutes a fair basis for differentials: it should not be an aim of government to substitute its own view of fair wage settlements. It is, however, a legitimate aim of policy concerned with social justice to develop social institutions (of which equal-value laws are one example) which will enable people to express their own ideas of a fair reward.

The Meaning of Social Justice: A Summary

In arriving at our principles of social justice, we reject the view, so fashionable in the 1980s, that human beings are simply selfish individuals, for whom there is 'no such thing as society'. People are essentially social creatures, dependent on one another for the fulfilment of their needs and potential, and willing to recognize their responsibilities to others as well as claiming their rights from them. We believe our four principles of social justice, based on a basic belief in the intrinsic worth of every human being, echo the deeply held views of many people in this country. They provide a compelling justification and basis for our work:

1 The foundation of a free society is the equal worth of all citizens.
2 Everyone is entitled, as a right of citizenship, to be able to meet their basic needs.
3 The right to self-respect and personal autonomy demands the widest possible spread of opportunities.
4 Not all inequalities are unjust, but unjust inequalities should be reduced and where possible eliminated.

This summary completes the description of our conceptual framework for thinking about ideas of social justice. We have attempted to articulate some widely held feelings about the character of our society and to describe them in a way that makes sense.

References

Commission on Social Justice (1993) *Social Justice in a Changing World*. Commission on Social Justice Discussion Paper 2. London: IPPR.

Hayek, F.A. (1976) *Law, Legislation and Liberty. Vol. 2: The Mirage of Social Justice*. London: Routledge and Kegan Paul.

Nozick, R. (1974) *Anarchy, State and Utopia*. Oxford: Blackwell.

Rawls, J. (1971) *A Theory of Justice*. Oxford: Oxford University Press.

Rawls, J. (1992) *Political Liberalism*. Oxford: Oxford University Press.

Sen, A.K. (1992) *Inequality Re-examined*. Cambridge MA: Harvard University Press.

Titmuss, R. (1970) *The Gift Relationship: From Human Blood to Social Policy*. Oxford: George Allen and Unwin.

3

What are Human Needs?

IAN GOUGH

What are human needs? We all use the term 'need': 'We need to fix this roof' . . . 'That family really needs some financial assistance' . . . 'My mother needs a home help.' Yet the idea of common human needs has been criticized and denounced in recent years. From the New Right, needs are viewed as the impositions of professionals and other do-gooders. To gear social policy to common human needs, it is argued, is to risk paternalism at best and dictatorship at worst; far better to listen to and meet people's wants or demands via the market. This hostility finds an echo on the left and among social movements and community groups. Needs are defined by those with power, whether experts, men, whites, the able-bodied, and are imposed on the powerless – women, blacks, people with disabilities, the poor. A needs-based strategy, far from being a path to liberation, is all too often a source of oppression.

The result of all this has been either scepticism that human needs exist, or a belief that all needs are relative. Most researchers in Britain and other developed countries accept that deprivation is relative to place and time, that the meanings of food and shelter, for example, are defined by the roles and expectations which membership of a social group entails. Representatives of social movements argue that particular groups have needs, but that they can only be truly known by members of those groups, whether elderly, blacks, people with disabilities, single mothers and so on. Clearly, if this is so, any common yardstick of welfare is unattainable, and a comprehensive audit of needs cannot succeed.

Yet despite all this, the idea of common or universal human needs won't go away. And for good reason: the notion that all people have basic human

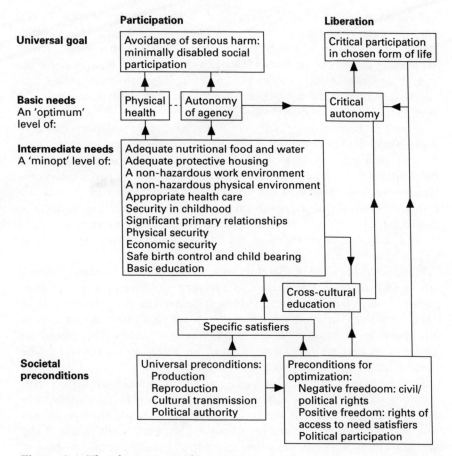

Figure 3.1 The theory in outline

needs and that we can chart how far they are met or not met is central to any coherent idea of social policy and social progress. This chapter uses a theory developed by Len Doyal and myself which attempts to overcome these limitations (Doyal and Gough, 1991). It is summarized in figure 3.1.

The Meanings of 'Need'

To begin with, some conceptual clarification is necessary, since 'need' is such an ubiquitous word in the English language. Let us distinguish three common usages of the noun and verb 'need'. First, it can refer to a 'drive' or motivational force, such as the need to sleep or eat. Maslow (1943) interprets the term thus in his famous hierarchy of needs. This meaning draws our attention to the biological aspects of human behaviour over which we have no choice. For example, ultimately we all have to sleep. But over a far broader spectrum of behaviour biology constrains rather than determines human choice, hence we are only indirectly concerned with needs interpreted in these terms.

Secondly, 'need' is universally used to refer to any necessary means to a given end. For example, to say 'I need a new hi fi' implies that I have the goal of a better quality of reproduced music. It is this protean use of the word (and its equivalents in other languages) that in part explains the widespread view that needs are essentially relative. The truth behind this is that all needs statements conform to the relational structure 'A needs X in order to Y.' We will refer at times to the means necessary to attain specific ends, but when doing so we will qualify the word need in some way, or use the term 'need satisfier'.

Thirdly, the question is, therefore, whether or not there is some Y which can be said to be in the interest of everyone to achieve, whatever their culture. Generally speaking the answer is clearly yes. All persons have an objective interest in avoiding serious *harm* which in turn prevents them from pursuing their vision of the good, whatever that is. This pursuit of the good entails, as others have argued, an ability to *participate* in the form of life in which they find themselves.

If there are preconditions for social participation which apply to everyone in the same way then universal needs can be said to exist. Needs can thus be distinguished from wants. To repeat a hackneyed example, a diabetic may want sugar, but she needs insulin. She even needs insulin if she does not know of its existence. She needs it ultimately because without it her social participation will become more and more impaired. This is an objective situation and is not necessarily reflected in subjective feelings such as unhappiness. Nor is it an 'individualist' concept. We all live our lives in groups and build our conceptions of ourselves through participating with others in social life. Nor, lastly, is it a static concept: we may wish to participate in a social form of life other than that which we grew up in.

If human needs are the universal preconditions for participation in social life, we contend that all people have a strong right to need satisfaction. This follows because membership of all social groups entails corresponding duties, yet without adequate levels of need satisfaction a person will be unable to act in accordance with those duties. It is contradictory to ask of someone that they fulfil their social duties, yet to deny them the prerequisite need satisfaction which will enable them to do so. This is why social rights of citizenship follow from an unambiguous concept of human need.

Basic Needs

Basic human needs, then, are the universal prerequisites for successful and, if necessary, critical participation in a social form of life. We identify these universal prerequisites as *physical health* and *autonomy* (see figure 3.1).

The bottom line, so to speak, of physical health is survival: to act and to participate we need to be at least alive, so survival chances are an important indicator here. However, much more than this is required if social participation is not to be seriously impaired. We must also enjoy a modicum of good physical health. Health can be conceptualized in negative terms as the absence of specific diseases, where disease is defined according to the biomedical model. This is best operationalized via measures of disease patterns and disability. 'Disability', according to the WHO, is any restriction on a person's ability to perform an activity in the manner or within the range considered normal for a human being. It is distinguished from 'handicap', which is an explicitly social notion referring to limits on a person's ability to fulfil a social role.

Yet physical health alone is insufficient to tap impairments to successful social participation, as the broader WHO definition of positive health acknowledges. Autonomy of agency – *the capacity to make informed choices about what should be done and how to go about doing it* – is the definitive attribute of human beings. We contend that autonomy is impaired when there is a deficit of three attributes: mental health, cognitive skills and opportunities to engage in social participation.

The concept, even the very existence, of mental health has, of course, aroused fierce debate and relativist criticism. Yet mental illness, defined as an 'extreme and prolonged inability to deal in a rational way with one's environment', undermines a person's confidence and competence to participate in social life in all cultures. The second component of autonomy of agency comprises the cognitive skills necessary for social participation. These include a person's understanding of the rules of her culture and her ability to reason about them and interpret them. These require both culturally specific skills and universal skills, such as language use and literacy. The opportunity to participate in significant social roles constitutes the third component of autonomy of agency. We identify four social roles common to all human societies which we label production, reproduction, cultural transmission and political authority. To be deprived of the opportunity to participate in any of these, let alone all of them, is a serious restriction of personal autonomy. This restriction can of course stem from many different factors, including cultural rules (e.g. the exclusion of women from certain roles), economic circumstances (e.g. unemployment or poverty) or role stress stemming from conflicting demands (e.g. the 'dual burden' of many women).

We have specified the general preconditions for successful participation in any social form of life. But some forms of life are extremely oppressive to their members, and all harm some of their members. Successful participation in a cruel or exploitative system is hardly a recipe for welfare. Beyond the goal of successful participation lies the goal of critical participation in a social life form which is, as far as possible, of one's own choosing (figure 3.1). Beyond autonomy of agency lies critical autonomy – the ability to situate, criticize and, if necessary, challenge the rules and practices of the culture one is born into, or presently lives in. Critical autonomy entails the same levels of physical and mental health as autonomy of agency but wider cognitive skills and social opportunities.

Intermediate Needs

So a needs audit should try to assess the levels of physical health and critical autonomy of different individuals and groups. But this does not get us very far. These basic needs can be met in numerous different ways. Common needs do not imply uniform satisfiers – far from it. There is an almost infinite variety of goods, services, activities and relationships which, to a greater or lesser extent, meet basic needs. It is this open-endedness which has led many researchers who accept the theoretical possibility of universal needs to argue that their objective assessment is beyond our reach. How is relativism of this second sort to be rebutted? There are two levels at which this problem can be handled.

The first level involves the identification of those characteristics of need satisfiers which everywhere contribute to improved physical heath and autonomy. Let us call these intermediate needs. For example, provision of energy and/or protein is (or should be) a common property of foodstuffs, protection from the elements is (or should be) a common property of dwellings, and so on. These intermediate needs are grouped into eleven categories in figure 3.1. Nine of these apply to all people, one refers to the specific needs of children, and another to the specific needs of women for safe birth control and child bearing. All eleven are essential to protect the health and autonomy of people, and thus to enable them to participate to the maximum extent in their social form of life, whatever that is. So a needs audit should try to measure the levels at which all these intermediate needs are satisfied.

But even this is insufficiently detailed if we want to get at the level of welfare of small-scale communities, and if we want an audit to inform social policies in the community. We need, secondly, to identify those specific satisfiers which best meet local needs, and to monitor people's access to these. Here the focus is on more specific goods, services and policies which do, or could, improve human welfare in particular social situations such as in a particular area of a city.

It is this task which the Leeds audit set itself (Percy-Smith and Sanderson, 1992). The ambit of the study is very broad – and necessarily so. Human needs are a complex set of prerequisites for effective human action and social interaction. If any one of them is absent, people suffer and their health and autonomy are impaired. So auditing human needs cannot simply mimic market research, which can quite reasonably enquire into people's views about a particular brand of cigarette or soap powder. Assessing needs means gaining some overview about all aspects of life vital to people's capacity to participate in society.

How should Needs be Audited?

If this much is agreed, we still face the question of how to assess need satisfaction in practice. Further awkward problems are then posed. What indicators of basic and intermediate needs should be used? What standards of need satisfaction should be set in order to calculate shortfalls in welfare? Above all, who should decide the answer to these and other thorny questions? Two extreme approaches have traditionally been adopted in answer to these questions, each suffering from different deficiencies and entailing different dangers.

On the one hand, there is the 'expert knows best' approach. If objective needs are not necessarily the same as subjective wants, then you cannot simply ask people what they need. You must instead rely on the knowledge of experts, professionals, researchers and so on. For example, a doctor has specialized knowledge which enables her, given the appropriate information, to judge people's state of health in a more informed way than can people themselves. Similarly, nutritionists can specify objective criteria with which to evaluate diets, whatever our own views about what is good for us. Yet this 'top-down' approach to determining and auditing needs has drawbacks and dangers which are only too well known. Experts and professionals can put their own interests before the well-being of their clients or research subjects. Often too they will be so ignorant of the reality of life for ordinary people that their proposals can be counter-productive or just plain stupid.

A general revulsion against professional and bureaucratic dictat has fuelled support for the opposite approach. This stresses the right and ability of different communities and groups to decide on their own needs and to do their own need audits. The detailed knowledge we have of our own communities can be tapped and the participation and empowerment of ordinary people encouraged. Many of the progressive community initiatives of recent years have advocated and practised this 'bottom-up' approach to needs auditing. Yet this too has its drawbacks and dangers. For one thing it can advantage the already privileged in a group, or those groups with more resources. For another, it can simply endorse prejudice and ignorance, whatever the evidence against them. Lastly, it offers no way of reconciling different notions of need and cannot establish common criteria of welfare other than the lowest common denominator of whatever the separate groups will endorse.

A needs audit, we would argue, must accept and seek to overcome this profound antinomy between top-down and bottom-up approaches. Related to this, it must also situate the 'codified knowledge' of researchers in all the fields of basic and intermediate needs listed above alongside the 'experientially grounded' knowledge of ordinary people in their everyday lives. More than this, it must enable them to confront each other and try to reconcile any differences which emerge . . .

This methodology is open-ended but cumulative. Though basic and intermediate needs are universal, the forms in which they can be met, and the levels at which they can be satisfied, are continually open to improvement. Yet this does not endorse a relativist position of 'anything goes'. The test of what to include, of what measures to use, of what policies to back, is always the idea of universal human need outlined above, and an acceptance that we can learn about, and judge between, better and worse methods of meeting needs.

References

Doyal, L. and Gough, I. (1991) *A Theory of Human Need*. Basingstoke: Macmillan.

Maslow, A. (1943) A theory of human motivation. *Psychological Review*, 50, 370–96.

Percy-Smith, J. and Sanderson, I. (1992) *Understanding Human Needs*. London: IPPR.

4

Citizenship, Rights, Welfare

RAYMOND PLANT

Since the 1950s those on the left have become used to the idea of talking about welfare in terms of rights. The influence of T.H. Marshall was
crucial: he argued in his great essay *Citizenship and Social Class* that the
social and economic rights of citizenship provided the twentieth century's
contribution to the idea of rights. Civil and political rights had been gradually won since the seventeenth century. However, it was in the modern
period that rights came to be seen in terms of rights to resources (to welfare, health, education, income and social security) rather than being treated
as immunities and being seen in terms of procedures such as due process of
law or fair elections. This dimension of rights is also a central part of the
United Nations Declaration of Human Rights: here, no sharp distinction
is drawn between civil rights such as freedom from coercion and assault,
political rights such as a right to vote and to political participation, and
rights to health, education and welfare.

This is a fundamental shift in emphasis. Earlier it was assumed that civil
and political rights alone were central to the status of citizenship. The level
of economic well-being people might be thought to enjoy, the education
they could get and the degree to which they could enjoy health and health
care were essentially private matters. They were private in the sense that
they were to be attained through the market, by the individual's own
efforts. Being a citizen did not imply a social and economic status so much
as a political and civil one. Civil and political citizenship could be attained
and enjoyed, so it was thought, despite the inequalities in social and economic status that would inevitably follow from this status being secured
through the market. Of course, it was recognized that some would be

unable to attain even a minimal status through the market. For the disabled and the feeble-minded the remedy was either private charity, or public provision under the Elizabethan Poor Law or, later, under the system introduced by the Poor Law Amendment Act 1834. But whether private or public, relief from poverty or from illness was not to be construed in terms of rights and citizenship. There could be no right to private charity since charity was essentially discretionary, a gift to which the recipient had no moral or legal right. In the case of public provision after 1834, there was certainly no right to resources. The indigent person's claim to relief was to be met only in a kind of contractual way: public provision was tied to a set of incentives to work and, for those within workhouses, to a punitive regime.

The idea that there is a right to welfare and to resources is a fundamental challenge to the idea that citizenship is only a civil and political status, and to the capitalist idea that a person's status in economic and social terms is to be determined by the market. The idea of rights to welfare has also become linked with the idea of social justice. According to this view, market outcomes should not be just accepted with all the resulting inequalities; rather, citizenship confers a right to a central set of resources which can provide economic security, health and education – and this right exists irrespective of a person's standing in the market.

The idea of welfare rights, contrary to some of the basic ideological assumptions of laissez-faire capitalism, confers an economic and social status outside the market; it involves the idea of a just distribution of resources and, therefore, a correction of market outcomes. It also entails the idea that citizens' obligations do not stop at mutual non-interference, for citizens have positive obligations to provide resources for welfare which can be collected coercively through the tax system. Additionally, it implies some limit to commodification and commercialization, in the sense that the basic welfare goods to which individuals have rights are not ultimately to be subject to the market mechanism, since the market cannot guarantee the provision of these goods, as of right, on a fair basis to all citizens. These social rights of citizenship are also to be ascribed independently of any character assessment of the individual bearer of social rights. They are unconditional, based upon the status of citizenship alone and not on whether the individual lives the kind of life that others in society would wish. In this respect, too, social rights are on a par with civil and political rights. Civil and political rights are not dependent on living a virtuous life; nor does one have to be a member of the deserving poor to qualify for social rights.

It is not surprising, therefore, that from the late 1970s to the early 1990s (years which saw the ideological ascendancy of capitalism and the intellectual retreat of socialism and social democracy) the idea of welfare rights should have been high on the agenda for attack and criticism by the intellectual defenders of free markets. Part of this chapter will be concerned with looking at the nature of this attack and defending the intellectual and moral coherence of the view that welfare can be considered as a right.

However, I want first to explore another issue relating to social and economic rights. It might be thought that those who have followed Marshall, as well as Marshall himself, have made a kind of intellectual error in thinking of these sorts of social and economic claims as rights in the first place. It might be argued that there is some kind of logical link between something being claimed as a right and the possibility of its enforceability. That is to say, what distinguishes a right from other things, such as desires or interests and claims, is that rights can be enforced. Critics then go on to argue that many social and economic rights are not enforceable, or they are non-justiciable because in many cases, such as health and education, there is not and cannot be any mechanism for rendering such rights amenable to enforcement. I shall consider later why this might be thought to be so, but for the moment it looks like a powerful argument: rights must be connected to some mechanism of enforcement; there is no such mechanism for rights to health and education and hence they are not genuine rights. This is a particularly salient issue at the moment when there is a strong movement on the left towards constitutional reform and the entrenchment of a Bill of Rights. Many on the left have argued that such a Bill would be defective if it dealt only with civil and political rights. Others meanwhile argue that large parts of welfare cannot be considered in terms of rights in the necessarily strict sense of enforceability.

In this chapter then I shall try to do two things: first to demonstrate that social and economic rights are not in fact categorically different from civil and political rights as capitalist critics maintain; and second to consider ways in which such rights might in fact be enforced. This latter issue will connect with a salient political issue, namely the ideas about citizens' charters[1] offered for consideration by all the main political parties. These can plausibly be regarded as attempts to identify ways in which individuals can come to have enforceable rights and entitlements to publicly provided goods. However, as they are presented, these various charters are not really put into a philosophical context which would provide them with a proper rationale. The argument of this chapter is that the idea of social and economic rights can provide such a rationale. Furthermore, it can link charters of social rights to a Bill of Rights to protect civil and political rights, so as to make them independent but parallel and mutually reinforcing ways of empowering citizens.

The Critique of the Social Rights of Citizenship

Before we can get to the practical political implications of this view, how-ever, we need to grapple with some basic theoretical issues. While these may appear abstract, they do concern the underlying rationale of the idea that there can be genuine rights to social and economic resources and that citizenship has an intrinsic social and economic dimension as much as a civil and political one.

The New Right in its economic liberal form, as found for example in the writings of Hayek, Buchanan, Friedman, John Gray,[2] Norman Barry, Lord Joseph and others who contribute to the Institute of Economic Affairs and the Adam Smith Institute, has mounted a substantial onslaught on the idea of social and economic rights. That was to be expected: to accept such rights would pose a major threat to the coherence of free-market capitalism.

The New Right argues, first of all, that such rights differ fundamentally from civil and political rights in terms of the corresponding duties which acceptance of these rights place upon citizens. It claims that the civil and political rights of citizenship imply corresponding duties of non-interference and abstaining from action. These rights are essentially about protecting a set of *negative* liberties or immunities, that is to say freedoms from inter-ference of various sorts. The right to life is the right to be free from being killed, the right to freedom of speech is the right to speak and not to be silenced, the rights to physical integrity and security are rights to be free from assault, rape and coercion of various sorts. Because these are rights to be free from interference of specific types, the corresponding duties on the part of fellow citizens, government and social agencies are to abstain from killing, interfering, raping, coercing and so forth. So for example, the right to life is not the positive right to the means to life. This is a distinction of the first importance for understanding the critique of *positive* rights to resources put forward by the New Right.

First of all, it is assumed that because civil and political rights are rights not to be interfered with in specific ways, they are always capable of being respected since the corresponding duties are essentially duties to abstain from action; duties of abstinence are in fact costless and can therefore always be discharged. Social and economic rights, however, are categorically different in the sense that they always imply the commitment of resources and in that sense are always going to involve costs. If the resources are not in fact available then the rights cannot be met. Social rights always run up against resource constraints and therefore there is always a possibility of their not being respected – unlike negative rights, which imply costless duties and therefore can always be respected.

Second, because social and economic rights run up against resource constraints these resources may have to be rationed, which undermines the idea that they can in fact be rights. If something is a right then it ought to be able to be claimed in an unconditional way. This cannot be true of social rights. From this it follows that social rights are inherently non-justiciable in that there cannot be a legally enforceable right to a scarce resource.

It is also argued that the defender of social rights operates with a defective view of liberty. Civil and political rights essentially codify a set of negative liberties; social rights, however, seem to trade on an idea of positive freedom – to be able to do certain things for which health, education and income are necessary. Social rights therefore seem to link the idea of freedom and ability, implying that being free to do something is the same as being able to do it and therefore having the appropriate resources to do it. If we have a right to liberty then we have a right to those resources which bear directly upon our capacity for agency and our ability to act freely.

In the view of the neo-liberal critics of social rights this is a fundamentally mistaken notion of freedom. Freedom has to be distinguished sharply from ability. No one is able to do all that they are free to do. To assimilate the two, so that freedom implies ability and thus a right to those resources which would enable one to do what one is free to do, is just conceptual confusion. Freedom has to be restricted to negative liberty in terms of *freedom from*, and the rights that protect those liberties are essentially negative rights.

It is also argued that underlying the idea of positive rights is a concept of needs: that people have a need for certain sorts of resources in order to live adequately. However, it is then argued that the idea of needs is essentially open-ended and therefore that the needs which underpin positive rights are also open-ended – and thus social rights themselves are without any clear limit. They can and will expand inexorably under interest-group pressure, since there is no clear limit to health, welfare and education. It is claimed that the position is fundamentally different with civil and political rights. Here, there are clear limits to the rights and, since the duties connected with them are ones of abstinence, these duties are clear, categorical, always capable of being discharged; they will not grow inexorably. We know when we have discharged our negative duty not to interfere with someone under the negative right to security. We do not have such a clear idea of what our duty is with regard to a positive right to security – in terms of the resources necessary to provide it – since the content of that right can expand.

The link between the ideas of social rights and social justice is also rejected by critics. What fuels the argument for social rights is the concern with the alleged unjust outcome of pure market allocations. Because markets cause injustice for the worst off there is then a claim that there should be a collective responsibility to correct market outcomes in terms of justice, by conferring on all citizens a right to those resources which may not be secured to each person in a fair and predictable manner by the market. This claim is disputed by the New Right for several reasons.

It is argued first of all that the idea of social justice is incurably vague and contested. In a morally pluralist society it is not possible to arrive at a consensus about social justice. We can distribute resources according to a wide range of criteria: merit, need, desert, entitlement, equality, and so forth. There is no uniquely compelling criterion or principle on which citizens in a pluralistic society can actually agree and thus the idea that social justice can ground a set of welfare rights is a delusion.

In addition it is claimed that markets do not produce injustice in terms of their outcomes. If people experience poverty or disadvantage in markets, then so long as these outcomes are the consequence of individual acts of free exchange, no injustice is caused. The argument here trades on the idea that injustice has to be caused by intentional action. However, the distribution of income and wealth produced by markets is not intended by anyone and therefore injustice cannot arise. Market distributions arise as the result of millions of individual acts of free exchange. This cannot produce injustice because market outcomes are unintended. Hence there is no moral case for a set of citizen rights to resources, conferred outside the market by political means, being based on an idea of social justice, because that idea is illusory.

It is further claimed that if social justice were supposed to govern the distribution of resources, public authorities charged with distributing those resources would have to act in arbitrary and discretionary ways. The argument is that we lack a clear idea about the appropriate principles of just distribution, whether based on need, desert, equality or any other criterion; we cannot therefore write rules of law which could govern just distribution. This is part of Hayek's critique in the second volume of *Law, Legislation and Liberty*: a regime of social justice would strengthen the hands of professionals and bureaucrats in the public sector who are charged with the task of operating justly in a context in which there cannot be any clear rules of justice since we lack the social consensus that would underpin these rules. This would entrench at the heart of the public sector a wholly undesirable, but equally unavoidable degree of professional and bureaucratic power, since such resources under their control would have to be distributed and rationed in an ethical vacuum in which there cannot be any rules of justice to guide the rationing of scarce resources.

A Defence of Social Rights

The arguments outlined above add up to a pretty fundamental assault on the idea of social rights and there are clear practical implications for the public sector. Essentially it puts the whole weight of citizenship on the civil and political realms. The public sector is not to be construed as essential to citizenship. Few of the New Right now argue for wholesale privatization of the public sector, but this has more to do with political possibility than with any belief in the principle that citizenship entails a right to public provision of resources and services. It has to be remembered that in 1983 a paper sponsored by Sir Geoffrey Howe and prepared by the Central Policy Review Staff did in fact argue for a thorough privatization of state-provided services. What defeated the proposal was the ensuing outcry and the need to win the 1983 election, not the thought that it might be inappropriate to privatize services which were to be seen as a right of citizenship. Obviously, if one does see provision of social resources in terms of rights then there is an objection of principle to their wholesale privatization, because no market can possibly guarantee delivering these basic resources as rights of citizenship.

Implicit in this argument are two profoundly different philosophies of the public sector and public provision. There are also two contrasting views of the nature of citizenship. One sees it in civil and political terms. The other sees it not only in those terms but also in social and economic terms, and contends that the freedoms and immunities which are guaranteed in a Bill of civil and political rights remain wholly abstract if people do not have the social and economic resources to be independent citizens.

So can the critique of social rights in fact be met? In my view most of the arguments outlined above are extremely weak. They are weak either in an absolute sense, in that they are not very good arguments, or because, if they were to be accepted, then they would apply equally to civil and political rights. Those who criticize social rights are not usually impugning civil and political rights as well, yet if they take their own strictures on social rights seriously this might well be the consequence of their own arguments.

The first argument against social rights trades on the idea of scarcity. Social rights intrinsically involve the commitment of scarce resources and there cannot be a right to scarce resources. However, it is difficult to see why this argument does not apply equally to civil and political rights. While these rights are essentially rights to be left alone in various ways, with corresponding duties of abstinence, nevertheless in the real world those rights have to be enforced and methods of enforcement involve the costs of police, courts, prisons, etc. It might be argued that this is a more incidental feature of civil and political rights, whereas costs are intrinsic to social rights. However, this is doubtful. What is it that marks something out as a right? If it is that rights, unlike other claims, have to be *enforceable* then there has to be an enforcement mechanism, and therefore the costs of enforceability are intrinsic to all sorts of rights, not just social ones. To put the point more simply, if one believes that there is a right to the protection and enforceability of rights (and how would they be rights otherwise?) then one cannot draw a sharp distinction between one set of rights and another by arguing that one set intrinsically involves costs and thus the commitment of scarce resources, while the other does not. If we have a right to enforceable civil and political rights then this is a positive right to resources.

It is argued by critics that there cannot be a right to, for example, the services of a doctor or teacher, since these are inherently in short supply, compared with the potential need. Again, though, it is difficult to see that this marks out social rights as uniquely problematic. There must be a right to the protection of civil and political rights, but there cannot be a right to the services of a policeman, as these are subject to the same problems of scarcity as doctors and teachers. It is currently illegal for a chief constable, as a matter of policy, not to enforce a particular set of laws. Nevertheless a chief constable has to decide how to deploy his forces and individual members of the public have no legally enforceable right to particular policing services in relation to any specific incident, any more than they have rights to the services of a doctor or teacher. It is difficult therefore to believe that the difference between civil and political rights on the one hand and social rights on the other can be defined in terms of costs – once it is accepted that there is, in effect, a *positive right to the protection of negative rights*.

The same argument applies to the duties that go with rights. The critic of social rights argues that the duties that correspond to negative rights are clear and categorical and involve abstaining from action and interference; whereas the duties corresponding to social rights always involve resources and are therefore inherently vague and open-ended. You never know, according to this critique, when enough has been done to satisfy the claims embodied in social rights. Such rights and the corresponding duties are always going to be subject to political possibility and political negotiation, but this is not true of civil and political rights. However, if the argument outlined above goes through, then again the distinction cannot be upheld. Let us take two examples: the right to privacy and the right to physical security. In the case of the latter, as we have seen, the enforceability of that right depends on the police force and the degree of enforceability depends on the resources available to the police. The amount of resources which we as a society decide to allocate to the police to defend these sorts of rights is as much a matter of political negotiation as are the resources allocated to health care or education. In the case of the right to privacy it can be argued that the resources needed to enforce this right also change with time. The invention of information technology has created new poss- ibilities for infringing this right and new mechanisms are needed to protect and enforce it. Again, the resources we commit to this are going to vary and will depend upon political negotiation and political judgement. It is not the case, therefore, that civil and political rights are in some way pure and unsullied and detached from the sordid world of political decision mak- ing. Both sorts of rights, as enforceable claims, necessarily involve resources – and the quality and quantity of resources will depend on politics.

This brings us to needs. The critics' argument here is that an idea of needs underpins the claim to social resources embodied in the doctrine of social rights. However, say the critics, the idea of needs is vague and open- ended and therefore social rights can expand without clear limit, turning more and more of civil society away from private provision for which the individual is responsible towards politically conferred rights. Again, the assumption is that civil and political rights are clear and obvious and do not have this tendency to expand. It is also argued that in relation to health and, to some degree, education too, there is an interaction between needs and technological change, because needs develop with advances in technology. The discovery of ways of treating heart disease with bypass surgery has created a whole class of new needs; the invention of the computer has created a whole class of educational needs. This again leads to the expansion of social rights and with it public expenditure and the growth of the public sector.

Yet here, too, it is difficult to draw sharp distinctions between civil and political rights and social rights. Presumably such rights as freedom from assault or interference, or rights to privacy and physical integrity, are rooted in some idea of what the basic needs and interests of citizens are. These needs too may be without clearly defined limits. Physical security depends on all sorts of things from police forces to street lighting and there is always more that could be done. Also these needs change with techno- logy. As we have already seen the need for privacy changes in relation to information technology; the need for physical security, for example, in air travel has changed since the invention of plastic explosives and depends upon newly invented security devices. Again the enforceability of rights in relation to such needs changes with technology and it is not possible to draw a categorical distinction between two sorts of rights on these terms.

It is also difficult to see that questions of social justice can be avoided in relation to the enforceability of civil and political rights. Once it is accepted that the enforceability of these rights involves costs and resources and thus political negotiation and political decision, then there are going to be questions about the fair distribution of resources *between* different types of public expenditure to meet different sorts of rights; about the fair distribution *within* particular sorts of rights (such as physical security or privacy to take the two examples discussed earlier); and about the fair distribution of resources *between* particular sections of the population in regard to such rights. If, as New Right critics argue, we do not have a sense of social justice as a society, then it is difficult to see that this claim does not impinge directly on the distribution of resources to protect civil and political rights, just as it does with social rights.

The critics argue that we do not have such a conception in a pluralistic society. However, the issues with which we are concerned here have to do with needs of various sorts, whether these needs be to do with a sense of autonomy and therefore being free from interference, a sense of physical integrity and a sense of private space, or with security of income, or with education or health. It would be a very ardent relativist who could deny that there is a consensus that income, health, education and welfare are needs bearing on the capacity for agency,[3] which all citizens have in common in a society like ours.

Of course, there might be an argument that even if we accept that these are common needs, there is in fact no consensus about how to satisfy them in relation to social rights. This argument has to be treated with some care. Up to a point it might be true – in the sense that there may be no consensus on where the limits of public provision should be set. However, two comments are apposite at this point. The first is that yet again there is no reason to think that this is uniquely a problem for social rights. Take again the right to physical security and the right to privacy: the limits of provision to meet these rights might well be controversial and a matter of political dispute.

Second, we are able through political negotiation to get some degree of consensus, despite these differences, on what it is fair to allocate to help to enforce these rights, and there is no reason of principle why this should not equally be so in regard to the resources allocated to meet social rights. Obviously this consensus can only be built politically if there is an agreement that there has to be some limit at any particular time on the resources to meet these sorts of needs. But there does not seem to be any reason of principle why it should not be possible to develop a consensus about what it is reasonable to do and then to define rights in relation to this consensus. The main point for the moment though is that if all rights involve the commitment of resources then the issue of social justice in their distribution will arise for all of them – since the very fact that they are rights means that the resources involved in their protection cannot be left wholly to markets. Once there is public provision to protect rights then questions about the fair allocation of resources are bound to arise. If the New Right's critique of social justice is allowed to stand in the sense that we accept that we cannot develop through political negotiation a conception of a fair allocation of resources, then the problems here will arise in relation not only to social rights, but to other rights as well.

The critics' view of the moral redundancy of social justice does not, in any case, hold water. They argue that free markets cannot produce injustice in distribution since the outcomes of markets are not intentional and the question of injustice can only arise when it has been caused by intentional action. This argument is defective because our moral responsibility for the consequences of our actions arises not just in relation to the *intended* consequences but also to the *foreseeable* consequences. If it is a foreseeable consequence of extending markets, let us say in the field of health care or education, that the worst off may actually not experience as much welfare as they would under public provision, then while this may not be anyone's intention, if it is a foreseeable consequence there is a case for saying that we bear moral responsibility for those consequences, even though they are not intended. If the general principle here is accepted, namely that we are responsible for the foreseeable albeit unintended consequences of our actions, then the issue becomes an empirical one: the extent to which consequences are foreseeable and what in fact they are in relation to the worst-off groups in society. If this is accepted, then there is scope for a moral critique of markets in terms of social justice and for conferring on citizens rights to resources as a matter of social justice, given that they would not be able to command those resources in the market and this failure is socially unjust. Hence, there is moral purchase in the idea of social justice and an idea of social justice can in fact underpin a set of welfare rights.

The critics will still argue that social rights are defective because they trade upon a false conception of liberty. Liberty has to be defined in terms of the absence of intentional coercion and these liberties are secured by civil and political rights which define the limits of legitimate and illegitimate coercion. Social rights, according to this view, operate with a false view of liberty, namely that liberty is linked with ability and the associated resources that people need to exercise liberty. This argument is central to the Hayek-inspired critique of social rights and the roots of the argument are to be found in *The Constitution of Liberty*. However, while the issue is extremely complex there are at least three arguments that reduce the force of this centrally important critique. The first is that if liberty is categorically different from ability, then we seem to be involved in a paradox.

If there is no possibility of performing an action, that is, we are clearly unable to do it (like jumping from Southampton to New York), then the question of whether we are free to do it does not arise. If this is accepted then it cannot be true that liberty and ability are categorically different. Rather the possibility of doing X is a necessary condition of whether we are free or unfree to do X.

Second, if liberty is defined in terms of the absence of intentional coercion, then the issue of whether society A is more free than society B is to be settled by identifying and counting the range of intentionally coercive actions permitted in each society. This might make a very primitive society with few regulations and forms of interference more free than modern western society. Few would be prepared to accept this and the reason for not accepting it would be that in our sort of society we are in fact able to do far more things. If this is the reason for regarding our society as more free than a primitive society then again freedom and ability cannot be regarded as categorically different. The judgement turns on an evaluation of what people are able to do in these societies, and the normative judgement that some of the things they are *able* to do in one are more important than those they are able to do in another.

Third, there is the question of the worth of negative liberty. Why do we want to be free from coercion? Presumably we find liberty in the sense of being free from coercion valuable because of the range of things that we are able to do within the space secured by mutual non-coercion. If this is so then freedom and ability are not categorically different since what makes freedom valuable to us is what we are able to do with it. If this is rejected by New Right critics, then they have to explain why human beings value freedom and, if they are to be consistent in separating freedom from ability, this answer has to make no reference to ability and what people are enabled to do. There is no compelling reason for rejecting the idea of social rights on the ground that it trades on a false view of freedom: it does not.

Finally, the critic argues, as we have seen, that because social rights are rights to scarce resources there has to be rationing, which means that public officials will have to act in arbitrary and discretionary ways in the distribution of resources, and this in turn will entrench professional power which cannot be made accountable. This is certainly a problem, and will be the focus of the rest of the chapter. However, again the problem is exactly the same in relation to civil and political rights. In the same way as the hospital consultant has the professional discretion to ration scarce resources, so the chief constable has to choose how to allocate resources to protect civil and political rights.

It is therefore false to think that there is an account of civil and political rights that is pristine and pure and does not involve all the problems that critics ascribe to social rights. Both sets of rights involve much the same sorts of difficulty and it would be better to think through these common difficulties, rather than falsely assuming that all the problems can be laid at the door of social rights.

Rights, Scarcity and Discretion

The central practical issue is how to define a set of rights, against a background of scarcity, in terms of those things which are necessary to enforce them and make them a reality – whether these be hospital services, educational institutions or the police. Is there really any way to secure the enforceability of social rights at the individual level? This has not been properly confronted in the literature since Marshall put social rights of citizenship on to the political agenda in *Citizenship and Social Class*. The assumption has been that the general provision of public services is what social rights require, but equally it is clear that these have not led, by and large, to individually enforceable rights. If the idea of rights is linked to the idea of enforceability, then Marshallian social rights are actually a bit of a sham, and in fact possibly a rather cruel deception. People might think that they do have individually enforceable rights when they do not. The secretary of state for health has a general duty to maintain a National Health Service, but this does not yield an enforceable right to health care of a specific sort to individuals. The central issue then becomes whether this can be remedied at all, and, if not, whether it is sensible to carry on speaking the language of rights.

The point also links to professional power and discretion. If individuals do not have enforceable rights and the distribution of services is to a large degree at the discretion of professional providers, then the providers of services have every incentive to provide them on terms that suit them – rather than seeing themselves as responding to the rights of individuals to a set of services or resources. The idea of rights therefore can be seen as a way of empowering the citizen in the public sector in relation to those services which are provided, in response to the idea that there is a social dimension to citizenship. This idea of linking rights and entitlements to empowerment is one which marks a departure from the traditional approaches of both right and left.

On the right it has been assumed too frequently that the only way to empower the individual is as a consumer in the marketplace and therefore that the only real way of empowering people in the public sector is by transferring publicly provided resources to the market. However, leaving aside the question of whether market empowerment is as powerful as people believe, there are crucial problems in privatizing public services such as health and education, and I have tried, earlier in this chapter, to give reasons why we should not go down that road in any case. These services should be seen as an integral part of citizenship, supporting its political and civil aspects. Those from the right who press the case for a citizen's charter seem to see it as a second best to privatization and a way of strengthening market mechanisms within the public sector, which in their view is the only effective way of empowering people.

On the left the issue of professional power in the public sector has often been seen in terms of greater regulation or democratization. The only way to limit professional power is either to make it accountable to a higher bureaucratic level, such as an inspectorate or a regulatory body, or to make professional power more accountable to democratic bodies. There are considerable problems with both of these approaches. In the case of bureaucratic regulation, it is difficult to believe that this empowers the citizen in any direct or meaningful way and there is also the problem that the inspectors or the regulators, in order to know what they are doing, have to come from the same professional groups as those whom they are regulating, and are therefore in danger of 'going native' and being persuaded more by the needs of the professionals than by the rights of the citizen.

The case with democratic accountability is rather different, but it is quite difficult to have confidence in the view that elected representatives can in fact effectively monitor and hold to account the behaviour of professionals. First, there is an asymmetry of information in the sense that the professional has much more knowledge and experience of what he or she is doing than an amateur representative. This may well inhibit effective control and accountability in the delivery of services. Second, there is an asymmetry of motivation in that the professional provider of services has a greater incentive to limit the degree to which his or her activity is monitored than the elected representative has to get to the bottom of what is going on. We do not have to look very far to see ways in which professional service providers have frequently been able to get away with quite outrageous practices while elected representatives were wholly ignorant not just of particular practices in individual cases but rather of a whole policy. The recent 'pin-down' case is the most blatant example of an elected social services committee not having any idea of a practice over a number of years in the residential homes run by professionals who were nominally accountable to elected representatives.

The idea of rights in the public sector provides a new way forward between the market and democracy as two models of empowerment. This is not to decry either markets or democracy, only to say that there is a case for looking at a new way and seeing how far we can get with it. If these rights could work and be made clear and enforceable, whether they are rights to have certain procedures followed, or actual rights to resources, then this would clearly be a more direct way of empowering the citizen than either the market, or bureaucratic regulation, or greater democratic accountability. Rights will not be a panacea and there will be areas of the public sector where we shall have to rely on both inspection and greater democratic accountability, but rights should be looked at very carefully on a case-by-case basis to see how far they can be taken.

It is essential, if they are to be more than rhetorical, that these rights be linked to enforcement procedures, and to compensation or the provision of alternatives if the rights fail. There will be different mechanisms in different areas. For example, there can be changes to the contracts of public service professionals, as doctors' and teachers' contracts have already been changed, specifying more clearly what their duties are. There can be administrative definitions of rights, particularly in relation to procedures. There can be a requirement to meet performance indicators with the possibility, if these are not met, of individuals being able to go elsewhere for a service, or receive compensation – and so forth . . .

Where mechanisms for securing individually enforceable rights can be made to work, these changes will strengthen the social dimensions of citizenship, as well as helping to strengthen civil and political rights and increasing the accountability of service providers to the citizens whose needs and interests they are supposed to serve.

Hence, it is important to put the idea of citizen's charters in the context of a new philosophy of the public sector. Public provision should not be seen as second best to the market as it is by the New Right. Nor should it be dominated by service providers, as a consequence of the idealistic but rather limited assumption on the left that democratization can increase the power of the ordinary citizen in relation to professionally organized bureaucracies. Instead, we have an opportunity to embrace a new philosophy of the public sector, based upon the social rights of citizenship – one which is not only consistent with civil and political rights, but would also enhance the quality of citizenship in those spheres.

Notes

1 The discussion of citizen's charters has tended to focus on how the issue came to be put on the agenda of the Conservative government under Mr Major and as such has concentrated on the recent work of the Adam Smith Institute and

the Institute of Economic Affairs. However, I could perhaps take this opportunity of pointing out that I argued for this kind of approach from a left-wing perspective at a conference held by the IEA early in 1989 and in a series of articles in *The Times* in 1988 and 1989. The paper from the conference was published by the IEA in Plant and Barry (1990).

2 John Gray has now changed his mind; see Gray (forthcoming).
3 John Gray once held this highly relativist view; see Gray (1983), p. 182. However, he has now retracted this view as is seen in Gray (forthcoming).

References

Gray, J. (1983) Classical liberalism, positional goods and the politicisation of poverty. In A. Ellis and K. Kumar (eds), *Dilemmas of Liberal Democracies*, London: Tavistock.
Gray, J. (1992) *The Moral Foundations of Market Institutions*.
Plant, R. and Barry, N. (1990) *Citizenship and Rights in Thatcher's Britain: Two Views*. London: IEA.

5

The Role of the Public Sector and Public Expenditure

DAN CORRY

In the old days, people thought they knew what services the public sector should provide. The police, the post office, water and even swimming pools all seemed an integral part of the UK public sector, while clearly only the state could provide all that was needed for social welfare policies. However, recent experience in the UK has put a question mark over all this. Services that were once regarded as part and parcel of the public realm have been privatized and the world has not ended.

One result is that many on the centre left have become confused as to the proper role of the public sector. But if there is no clear conception of what government should do, a centre-left approach to public policy appears much less attractive. This hesitancy is unnecessary. There are certain goods and services that all sensible people regard as essential in a civilized society and which the private sector on its own will not deliver. There is still, therefore, a vital role for the public sector in many areas of life. What have changed are conceptions of exactly how that action should take place.

The first part of this chapter sets out some philosophical arguments for and against public action. At its root, the case for public sector activity is closely bound up with the concept of democracy. The libertarian arguments against public action, though important, are seen to be warnings about the way the power of the state is used, not against its existence per se.

We go on to describe the public sector's current functions and how its role has developed over time and why. This leads on to a discussion of one of the main technical reasons for public provision of services: market failure.

Public provision, however, appears to bring with it a number of practical problems, and some of these are discussed. Increasingly, the private sector is involved in the delivery of key public services, even where these continue to be financed (in the final analysis) by public funds. We look, in particular, at two such methods – contracting out and private-sector financing initiatives. While there are potential gains from using the private sector in this way, there are also a number of disadvantages, including loss of democratic control of the service. An alternative, regulation of activity carried out and financed entirely by the private sector, suffers particularly from the hidden costs of regulation. The conclusion draws together the strands of what is a complicated, theoretical debate and suggests how a more consistent and open approach to public spending might be achieved. Such an approach would revitalize and relegitimate the role of public action and expenditure.

Case For and Against Public Action

The democratic case

Democracy requires an active public sector. Without the capability for public-sector activity, democracy has given way and people collectively and individually have lost the ability to make decisions about how their society should run. That is why the concept of public action is so important.

The concept of a welfare state, for instance, evolved as people came to the view that it was their democratic right to be protected from the worst ravages of laissez-faire capitalism. Their views were expressed through the democratic process and there was a clear demand that the power of the state should be used to do what the market clearly could and would not.

More generally, it is only through 'political' action that people can often influence their own lives. If something is going wrong, be it with a noisy neighbour, or in the local community or at a broader spatial level, action from government is frequently crucial to the solution.

Some argue that the market is the most practical application of genuine democracy. The only tolerable role for government, then, is to ensure that the market applies to all things. This, however, is a thin agenda. Sometimes people have political views about not wanting to use market mechanisms. This may be because there is a (correct) sense that the market-based approach would not work, but it is certainly not based on detailed analysis. There are also some areas in which, even if there is a view that the private sector could do things a bit better, we do not want them. This may be inefficient in the narrow economic sense – and one may want to try and influence opinions – but it is the democratic prerogative.

At a technical level, however, the call for public action can be – and often is – seen as a response to failures of the market. Here, there is an underlying assumption that, in an ideal world, the public sector would provide no services other than those judged desirable and which the market cannot deliver. The aim, therefore, would be to minimize the role of the public sector. Each public intervention would need to be justified strictly against the inability of the market to deliver.

Much of the opposition, in principle, to market-type solutions has now disappeared. However, even where a service is provided by the private sector, people still often want the potential for democratic control. This is particularly the case when there is danger of a monopolistic situation, as with many examples of privatization.

Delivery of a service by the private sector under contract to the public sector leads to a loss of day-to-day democratic control and of accountability to individual citizens. Direct accountability is considerably weakened if the public sector provides very little, and if everything is guided by legalistic controls or regulation. In this sense contracts do little for the democratic process. The role of the citizen as stakeholder has been reduced to the extent that the citizen only now has a say as a consumer.

On the other hand, the contract approach does have the advantage of keeping control over strategic decisions and focuses democratic control on these key policy issues. When direct public provision of public services was near universal, the producer interest – be it trade unions or the professionals – was often able to block the sensible exercise of democratic control let alone steps to increase efficiency. Producer capture was not only bad for consumers but also bad for citizens.

Putting aside efficiency arguments (which are considered later), there may be something intrinsically useful about public-sector involvement in the provision of public services. A public sector as only purchaser – or regulator – . . . operates differently from one that also acts as a provider. A body that merely writes, signs and monitors contracts and regulates private-sector behaviour loses the ability to be flexible and to respond quickly to new situations. It no longer has direct responsibility for the pay and conditions of a large segment of the workforce. And, inevitably, the responsibility it takes for any mistakes and inefficiencies is diluted.

The public sector also has an important role to play in binding individuals together, in creating a sense of community and social cohesion. While often romanticized, the position of a local school in creating some sense of community is clear. A world in which one group of people within a local community used one type of school and another group a different type would clearly lack this; a world with quasi-markets for schools or no state schools at all might tend to this situation (although this is not to deny the existence of geographical segregation by income). As Self (1989, p. 24) has put it: 'there is a certain intrinsic value in the public provision of some services for cementing common citizenship and a sharing of common values . . . ideals of solidarity and community are given some expression which otherwise would be lacking.'

Finding out what individuals want

Given that public activity should be governed and steered by the democratic will, we need to find out what society wants. Democracy is never perfect. Representative democracy is indirect, it often works with methods (first past the post) that fail to give power to the majority, and it is ill equipped to discover what individuals think about particular issues (especially when individuals themselves are ill informed). This is why, where there are no market-failure or policy reasons to the contrary, using the market has so many attractions.

Nevertheless, however imperfect, discovering the democratic will must be our starting point. In general terms, elections tell us the broad strategy. For many years it seemed that this was all that was needed. Issues such as the type, quality and responsiveness of public services, let alone their value for money, were not keenly debated. This is no longer acceptable.

However, some commentators are pessimistic as to whether it is ever possible to ascertain individuals' true preferences, for example regarding either the quantity or the quality of services they would like provided. In the early 1960s Walter Heller, chairman of the US President's Council of Economic Advisors, asked: 'how are preferences of voters for governmental services to be revealed, measured and appropriately financed' and concluded that while economists have done good work on the subject and 'have made some intriguing suggestions as to its solution . . . [they] . . . have concluded that it is next to insoluble'. Moreover, not only do the democratic processes have to be sophisticated to work any of this out, people may actually have incentives to give 'false signals' (Barnett, 1993).

Given these difficulties, there are those who conclude that it would be best, in almost all cases, to apply market-type mechanisms to the provision of public services. However, the market itself is not good at revealing true demands in many of the areas covered by public services. Indeed, this is one reason why the public sector became involved in the first place. Price signals do not necessarily reflect true costs and information problems may mean that perceived demands are not the 'true' ones. We are also talking about areas where we believe that the individual as citizen should have a say even if they are not actual users of the service. For instance, just because someone has no children does not mean that their views on the development of education locally should be discounted.

Currently, more sophisticated techniques are being developed that might enable policy makers to get a better handle on the quality and kind of public services that are wanted. Such methods include greater use of referenda and opinion polls, as well as citizens' juries and methodologies that use the willingness-to-pay approach (see Cave and Hulme in Corry, 1997).

Case against public action

The philosophical case against public action is traditionally voiced by the libertarian right. This has much resonance nowadays, particularly for a new left that has rediscovered individualism and shies away from paternalism. At its most basic, the belief is that publicly provided services – whether provided directly by the state or contracted out – offend against liberty because they give the citizen no choice. According to one commentator, when we provide, for example, free or subsidized housing we are 'in effect requiring the minority to accept services they might or might not have bought had they been handed an equivalent amount of cash. Perhaps they would have preferred to spend it on wine, women and song' (Heller, 1965, p. 156). A related argument is that free services will, in time, sap the will of individuals to run their lives, thus encouraging welfare dependency.

Both arguments are, however, confused and contradictory. Much of the case against state action is, in fact, against the provision of welfare defined in its widest sense. However, if the need for some kind of welfare provision is accepted, the key question is whether this is best done directly, or by cash hand-outs. There is no doubt that the former restricts choice, while benefit payments do not. As Phelps (1965) has pointed out: 'transfers raise many of the same issues raised by public expenditures . . . but they do not directly reallocate resources in the economy [between the private and public sectors]. Thus they do not interfere with consumer sovereignty, nor with free enterprise in any fundamental way' (p. xiii). On the other hand, cash payments are inevitably means-tested and this gives rise to major disincentive problems since they are withdrawn as income rises.

There are, however, possible solutions. For instance, provision in kind can be made more responsive to individual preference by providing choice within prescribed limits. Vouchers are one method of achieving this, although these are not without disadvantages of their own (Self, 1989, p. 25; OECD, 1995, p. 43).

Taken to its logical conclusion, the voucher approach leads to a world where the public sector does almost nothing in terms of services. Instead it redistributes income, either through issuing vouchers (that can be as progressive as it chooses) or directly through, for example, minimum wages and social security. Consumers are then left to make their own choices in the private market. However, these two aspects, no public-sector activity and radical redistribution, are probably incompatible. In a world dominated totally by the private, market economy, the political conditions would not exist for anything but the most minor redistribution of income (Self, 1989, p. 21).

Finally, it is worth saying that while the maintenance of liberty is fundamental, one should not be over-obsessed about the need to protect the individual from encroachment from the state, but should be looking to a more 'positive' concept of freedom. If certain basic social goods such as health care, employment and education are necessary in order to give individuals the capacity to enjoy life, a case can be made for the state to provide these services universally (Dasgupta, 1989).

To recap: there is an enduring need for public action in many areas of life. While this does not need to involve direct provision by the public sector, there are drawbacks in the sector withdrawing entirely from such activity.

What the Public Sector Provides

Over a third of all public-sector spending is, in fact, on transfers (social security benefits); in other words, the distribution of resources from one set of individuals to another (Public Finance Trends, 1995, table 1.4). Of the remainder, much is consumed by health, education and defence (see Gray and Cooper in Corry, 1997).

The combination of public services in which government plays a role, as purchaser and/or provider, may be categorized into four main types of activity:

- the core functions of law, order, income support and redistribution;
- defence and other public goods;
- merit goods: services that society believes individuals should have access to at uniform price and without the usual market constraints such as having the service cut off if payment is not made on time. The definition of these varies over time and across nations;
- services such as education and health.

It is difficult to envisage the core functions being performed by anyone other than government. However, it is not immediately obvious why government should have a major role to play in the provision of education and health services.

In practice it seems that public intervention goes far beyond providing the classic 'public goods'. These are goods that are non-rival (one person's use does not reduce their value to someone else) and non-excludable (where it is impossible to get anyone to pay). Education is an example of a good that is rival and could be excludable. However, government, reflecting public views, chooses to make it a 'publicly provided private good' (Barnett, 1993). One rationale for this is that such services are provided by professionals that society does not want to be guided by profit-maximizing considerations. The BBC also comes into this category.

There have been changes over time in the type of services provided by the public sector, in how much is spent and how. These have been the result of a number of factors, including:

- changes in *ambitions or targets*. For instance, the growth in individualism has changed the nature of the products that people want and the degree to which they will accept uniform services. Beliefs about the appropriate degree of egalitarianism also change.
- changes in *needs or circumstances*. Such exogenous changes include the collapse of the USSR, which has reduced the need for defence spending. Demographic factors tend to affect expenditure on, for example, health, while changes in unemployment and inequality affect spending on social security and law enforcement.
- *the discovering of new ways of delivering an existing service*. This may result in the internal reorganization of the public sector, changes in planning and control procedures, or new forms of service delivery.

Criteria for Public Action

For the past decade and a half, UK governments have been mainly concerned with a strict and narrow definition of market failure (as defined in the neo-classical economic paradigm). Only where the market palpably fails is there a role for public action and, potentially, public expenditure. Given the requirement to identify a specific market failure, it is not surprising that there has been a concerted attempt to marketize and privatize as much as possible of what were generally regarded as 'publicly provided services'.

As we have argued, ultimate decision making about what should and should not be done must rest with the democratic process. Analysis of market failure is useful in that it encourages vigorous examination of possible options (and probably cost-effective interventions). However, goals of fairness and equity also play an important role in determining public policy for most governments. It is undoubtedly the case that market provision of goods and services usually results in different outcomes for people with different incomes. Free marketeers either do not see this as central, or argue that any equity issues should be dealt with by the tax and social security systems (Dilnot, 1995), a solution with problems of its own (Corry, 1995b; Waterson, 1994).

Moral criteria

Using a broader approach to the concept of market failure than that of recent governments, what general criteria may be used to justify public action? First, there is the argument that some services, such as prisons, the army, the police and the judiciary, should not be provided by the market. Direct provision is therefore required. Furthermore, there appears still to be consensus within the UK that education and particularly health broadly come under this category of service where the profit motive would not be appropriate (even though the private sector is involved in the UK and, in some countries, such services are provided totally by the private sector).

In the UK, for example, most people object to the idea of paying for blood donations, or would find it unacceptable to allow a poor person to sell a spare kidney. The idea of someone being involved in providing health or primary-school education primarily to make money is also met with disapproval. Many also believe that as people are in prison because of the coercive power of the state, it would be morally wrong to let the private sector play a role in any but the most peripheral aspects of prisons. As opinion polls carried out prior to privatizations show, similar views were held on issues such as water and (to a lesser extent) electricity.

Moral values are crucial and, as expressed in a democracy, cannot and should not be ridden over roughshod. Nevertheless, they should not be a barrier to innovative thinking.

Market failure criteria

There are some limited areas where the private sector would simply provide nothing if left unprompted. For instance, it is highly unlikely that the private sector would choose to produce driving licences. Here, there is

How valid is the claim that social security/welfare expenditure has to be provided by the state? Some of this activity is redistributive across time, essentially for the same individual (ABI, 1995; Falkingham and Hills, 1995) and there is a case that government need not be involved: people could make their own provision and, it appears, increasingly are (Hills, 1995, pp. 30–2). But aspects of the nature of insurance markets, like asymmetric information, moral hazard, myopia and so on, make a purely private solution problematic.

Alternatively, compulsory saving for things like pensions (with top-ups for the poor) could replace taxation and public expenditure. Although it is unclear that in the long run such a switch will lead to a lower PSBR, since 'traditional' taxes would have to go down as well, private provision carried out under compulsory regulation by the state (quasi-taxes) does seem to be increasing in areas like Child Support Act payments and firms paying maternity or sick pay for employees (Hills, 1995).

However, a certain degree of the social security system is undoubtedly redistributive between individuals. While the administration of such activity could in principle be done by the private sector, there seems to be no way of transferring this redistributive activity to the private sector. If the state does not help the poorest in society, no one else is likely to do so.

Since there are arguments that there are wider benefits from supporting the poor than those that go to the direct beneficiaries, and that some of these benefits are very intangible, it is right in principle too that government should assess their value and run the system.

Box 5.1 Social security/welfare

clearly a need for government action to stimulate a market by bringing in a legal requirement that all drivers hold a licence. However, government need not necessarily deliver the service, rather its role is to put the appropriate legislation in place. This is also true of some policies that involve an element of redistribution (see box 5.1 for a discussion of the role of the state in the provision of these services).

The main reason for government action, however, is where the market would not provide an appropriate service. Clearly, the market is capable of delivering some service when it comes to water, telephones, research establishments, hospitals, trains and so on. This does not mean, however, that the provision would always be of the desired quality (including price) or quantity. At the very least, public regulation is needed, especially where monopoly power may be an issue.

Markets only respond to the desires of individuals fed through their market demands. But the prices charged cannot capture the wider social benefits of, for example, an educated or healthy society. The market therefore provides too little of things with positive 'externalities' at the same time as it provides too much pollution – where the externalities are negative. Here, again, there is a role for government.

Public action is also required because of asymmetric information (where the user of a service has less information than the provider and so can be exploited). Moral hazard is also associated with markets, particularly insurance provision. Here, individuals have an incentive to adjust their behaviour once they are insured. Knowing this, the private sector may only provide cover at a very high price, if at all. Adverse selection is also a problem. Only those who are likely to become ill actually take up insurance, so that the insurer would not be able to spread risk in an efficient way. Finally, there is the much-debated issue of short-termism that tends to bedevil the private sector in the UK. (See Helm, 1989, for a good summary of the market-failure rationale for public action.)

A related advantage of public-sector action is that it is different from the private sector and therefore avoids some of its constraints. In particular, because of its size, the public sector is able to spread risk. It also has the unique possibility of raising money through taxation. As a consequence the public sector can borrow money more cheaply than any private-sector organization. There are therefore intrinsic advantages in having it finance services and capital projects, whether or not it provides them itself. In addition and because of its ability to escape the constraint of short-term profit maximization, it can take on tasks that the private sector never would.

A final reason for the market's failure to provide the desired service is the issue of equity. If equal access to particular services and equal treatment by that service matter, then private provision may not deliver. If cherry picking and cream skimming occur, one may well find that the rich end up paying less than the poor for the same service (if the poor can get it at all) and that one region may get a poorer service than another. Fairness and social cohesion disappear. The voucher idea is one way of sidestepping this problem – so we all enter the market with the same 'income'. But this, of course, does not escape the need for public action and public expenditure.

Arguments For and Against Public Provision

In addition to the reasons for public involvement in the delivery of services outlined in the previous two sections (democratic accountability and market failure), there are a number of advantages associated with public-sector provision. They broadly fall into two categories: first, that certain problems associated with private-sector provision are avoided; second, that accountability and flexibility are easier to maintain. These may be briefly summarized as follows.

Avoiding the private-sector problems

1 The public sector, at least in theory, is not vulnerable to short-term pressures from the financial markets or from the structure of private-sector corporate governance.
2 Incentives to reduce quality or exploit workers in order to raise profits are absent.
3 The public sector is less likely to 'waste' money on advertising and PR.
4 Direct provision can deal more easily with imperfect and asymmetric information. There are for instance fewer market incentives for the experts (doctors) to give the users (the patients) expensive treatment that they do not really need.
5 The public sector can be more efficient than the private sector, at least for some services. This is because the monopsony power that, for example, a national health service or education system gives to employers allows wages to be held down.
6 The absence of a need to make a profit means that the break-even point is lower for the public sector. If efficiency were the same in both sectors, the public-sector provider would always have the edge.

Flexibility/accountability

1 Direct provision is more flexible, being able to respond to new policy objectives faster than any arm's-length, purely contractual relationship can.
2 The absence of rigid budget constraints may have beneficial effects on behaviour. When, for instance, hospital cleaners were directly employed they would have picked up a book dropped by a patient. Now, for fear of losing time, the contracted-out cleaner might not.
3 Publicly provided services ensure that national standards are met directly, especially those that encompass equality.
4 The public sector as provider is likely to be more responsible than one that just purchases since it has to answer for the consequences of its actions not just for its policy aims or contract-writing abilities.
5 Direct public-sector provision of service delivery makes democratic accountability clear and obvious.

Disadvantages of public provision

Not everyone is convinced by the above arguments. Some commentators take the view that everything that government touches will turn to disaster. 'There are now considerable doubts about the capacity of governments necessarily to improve outcomes even when there is acknowledged to be some degree of market failure, lack of competition, or a particular concern about equity' (Keating, 1991, p. 235). These thoughts have dominated the academic literature for some time now.

In addition, the problems of using the private sector that are held to arise from the particular objectives and ethos of the private sector can to some extent be avoided by use of voluntary organizations and other not-for-profit organizations, if their motives are held to be more sound (Finley, 1989). The question then is whether the accusation of government failure is clinching or not.

There is no doubt that there are severe disadvantages associated with the public sector's involvement, particularly as the provider of public services. Decision makers, in the absence of both strict budget constraints and reasonable freedom to manage their own budgets, often act inefficiently. Ministers often want to involve themselves in operational decisions which they are poorly qualified to make. The political cycle causes short-term factors to dominate decision making. Vested interests often dominate at the expense of individual consumers. Large, bureaucratic structures can be slow to adapt, lack the thirst for innovation of the private sector and often seem obsessed with paperwork.

Recent efficiency gains and improvements in the quality of services following privatization and contracting out have drawn attention in some areas to previously low levels of efficiency, producer capture and a focus on everything but the user of the service. However, it is important not to exaggerate these supposed inefficiencies. The only major detailed work on this aspect of the public sector in the UK, carried out before many of the recent market-based reforms, strongly suggests that government departments carry out their business as efficiently as most private-sector organizations. Levitt and Joyce (1987, p. 66) concluded: 'There is no overwhelming evidence that the government departments considered are markedly inferior in their performance to private institutions, despite significant differences in the financial incentives to the staff concerned.'

In any case, if we go down the private-sector 'partnership' or contracting-state routes to delivering public services we must believe that the public sector is good at writing contracts, setting regulations and so on. It is not obvious why this should be. If the public sector is inherently bad at things then it is likely to fail here too. Ending direct provision would not solve all the problems.

Clearly, we want to reduce incentives for inefficient decisions within the public sector. To some extent, recent reforms, particularly the introduction of agencies, means that there is now less short-term interference by politicians and reduced power for vested interests. Other positive changes include the proposed move to resource accounting; the relaxation of end-year spending restrictions; the delegating of running-cost control to lower levels; the introduction of small teams working as business units with clear accountability to achieve certain performance measures; and the giving of tough personal contracts to senior managers, who become accountable, publicly as well as financially, for hitting targets set for them. One sees therefore that the scope to overcome many of the government failure problems does exist. However, two key questions need to be asked:

- Is the public sector capable of further reform?
- Should it abandon its role in the delivery of services?

These issues are considered in the next section, which describes the alternative methods of providing public services introduced in the UK over the past decade or so and examines the advantages and disadvantages associated with each.

Alternative Ways of Providing Public Services

If one wants to avoid public provision of services, various options are available (see box 5.2) each with different implications for total public expenditure and spending priorities. One option continues to involve full state funding. It offers the possibility of the public sector defining the service wanted and contracting out its provision to the private sector. A second option, that has some strong links with the first approach, is the currently fashionable private finance initiative (PFI), in which the private sector puts up the initial finance and also contracts to build and operate the infrastructure (for example, a hospital, a road, an IT system).

In principle, it should be possible to provide excellent public services through either option. If one believes that the private sector will be more efficient and innovative, partly because of the problems and dangers of public provision, then even if the public sector funds the project, the delivery should be private (Blankart, 1985, p. 196). However, such methods are not without costs and the key question that needs to be asked is whether the potential benefits are worthwhile.

(a) public provision, public payment (e.g. water pre-privatization; the army)
(b) private provision, public payment (contracted-out swimming pool)
(c) private provision (including the finance), public contract (PFI deal for a new bridge or a franchise to run a motorway service area)
(d) private provision (including the finance), public regulation (e.g. water post-privatization)
(e) private provision (e.g. bread)

Box 5.2 Options for the funding and provision of services to the public

Contracting out

In a contract relationship, the decision maker, or principal, has an object-ive but the work to achieve it is carried out by someone else, the agent. In the case of contracting out in the public sector, there is a strong like-lihood that the principal (in this case, the public sector) and the agent (the private sector) will have divergent objectives and incentives. Essentially then, the principal has to try to write down what it wants, monitor that it is getting it and enforce its desires. This process is not straightforward.

In practice, it may be impossible to draft contracts that deliver what is required from public services. One might, for example, want those provid-ing a particular service to be polite or caring or even 'helpful' – such as dinner ladies helping out at playtime when a school is short of staff. In the case of a complex service such as education (where one objective might be to teach children the joy of learning as well as exam techniques) it would be difficult, if not impossible, to specify a sensible contract, let alone to monitor and enforce one.[1]

In addition, consumers seem to respond quite differently to a privatized provider, suspecting the motives of the company and not giving them the benefit of the doubt when things go wrong. One consequence may be that tight monitoring conditions are placed on the contracting company. The likelihood then is that it will act only to meet them and skip other things (Le Grand, 1996).

The conclusion, then, is that the absence of complex contractual arrange-ments and shareholder pressures that characterizes public-sector provision may, ironically, make it easier to achieve complex goals. Where transac-tion costs are likely to be high, delivering the service in-house may there-fore make a lot of sense. According to Marchese (1985, p. 213) 'In a world

CCT is the name given to the legislative position where the UK government has insisted that local authorities put out to tender many of their services. Authorities are generally obliged to accept the lowest bid (although they have some room for manoeuvre on this). Thus in theory, the in-house provider can win the contract.

CCT began in services such as refuse collection and cleaning. It has since been applied more extensively to white-collar activities such as accountancy, information technology and architecture.

Box 5.3 CCT

where information is costly and people also pursue their interests by misrepresentation, transaction costs . ... may be higher than the organizations' costs of producing directly.' Furthermore, it goes without saying that, if the public sector's stringent conditions for greater efficiency are to be met, there needs to be a healthy, competitive and honest private sector. There are reasons to doubt that this is always the case in the UK (see, for example, Public Services Privatisation Research Unit, 1996).

Many of these issues have arisen clearly in the UK context from the application of compulsory competitive tendering (CCT) in local government (see box 5.3).

Although driven too much by ideology and dislike of public-sector unions, CCT has had some positive results. In particular, the need to specify a contract has made local authorities focus more on what they are trying to achieve and has encouraged thinking on efficiency and innovation (Szymanski, 1994). It is, however, difficult to say how much the improvements made in this area have been the result of CCT and how much the result of the tight financial controls under which local authorities have been operating. However, a number of disadvantages along the lines discussed above have also become apparent.

First, local authorities have lost a degree of flexibility. Typically, councils draw up a contract and put it out to tender. The contract the council signs usually runs for five years. This makes it difficult for service specifications to be changed in the interim, or for the nature of the relationship between the purchaser and provider to be refined. The result can be both costly and inconvenient. Although more flexible contracts could be agreed, the private sector would charge a much higher price.

This lack of flexibility can endanger efficiency objectives. Efficiency is not just a static concept. It must relate to the achievement of objectives which, due to changes in technology, prices, tastes and the democratic process, change over time.

Second, where a service is contracted out to a monopoly provider, there is no certainty that the service will be provided more efficiently. The reality is that competition for the contract is often partial at best (because there are few contractors in a position to bid). Where the private sector wins a contract, it is likely that any future capability to operate the service in-house disappears, removing another source of competition. Furthermore:

> Even if there is competition among suppliers before the contract is made, the supplier and the demander are locked in a bilateral monopoly position after the contract has been signed. Ex ante competition and ex post monopoly encourage opportunistic behaviour of the contractors, which is detrimental to efficiency. In order to avoid such difficulties it may be more advantageous to buy. (Blankart, 1985, p. 197)

Some of these disadvantages might be overcome by a more rigorous competition policy that encouraged a competitive private sector, by more flexibility in the contracting process itself and minimum standards of pay – since some of the much-vaunted efficiency gains may simply reflect pay cuts for workers and therefore not do much for overall welfare in society (Kerr and Radford, 1995). However, it has to be remembered that many of these services were taken on by the public sector in the first place because it was generally felt that the private sector was oligopolistic, was inefficient and exploited its workforce. (See IPPR, 1996, for more discussion of these issues.)

All the available evidence suggests that CCT works best in a number of limited circumstances: where a market existed previously (e.g. catering and cleaning); where there is scope for the private sector to be truly innovative and add extra services (e.g. breakfasts in schools); where the contracts are big so that the costs of bidding and so on are a small percentage of the contract price; and where there is potential to casualize the workforce.

This is not to say that contracting out is never worth it. Far from it. But the conditions for it to be a real success and to really save major amounts of money are limited. Indeed, one notices that despite massive amounts of contracting out and claims of savings, government spending has not obviously declined.

Private finance

There is a great deal of interest currently in the concept of using the private sector not only to construct and operate major infrastructure projects but to finance them as well. This also involves a contracting relationship between state and private company, but this time the contract includes the financing factor.

1 *Financially free-standing*, when a bridge is financed by tolls paid to the private-sector provider.

2 *Services sold to the public sector*, where the public sector agrees to 'rent' a new hospital (and its services) to be built and financed by the private sector, for a period of time.

3 *Leasing*, when a private company supplies an asset to a public body (for instance, trains to the Northern Line), in return for a stream of payments over time. In other words, the private sector buys the train in the first place and is so taking on some of the risk.

4 *Joint ventures* between public and private sector, so that returns (as well as finance) are shared, are another way of using private finance. Examples of these include housing associations and urban development corporations. There are also increasing numbers of 'GoCos' (government owned, contractor-operated companies) where the private sector takes over a public asset and runs it (and makes incremental investments) on commercial lines. Finally, 'corporatization' is where public managers have more freedom to borrow on private markets (OXERA, 1996; Watson, 1995; London Economics, 1996).

Box 5.4 Types of private finance arrangement

The immediate attraction of the private finance approach is that it appears to offer the prospect of someone other than the public sector paying for public projects and services (see box 5.4).[2] In this way, the public expenditure constraint on delivering public services is avoided. As we discuss below, this view is mistaken. Nevertheless, there may be some advantages to such an approach. In particular, it is argued that the full benefits of private-sector expertise cannot be secured without them putting their money in (although the All Party Treasury Select Committee's report of 1996 argued that 'many of the assumed benefits of PFI would appear to be available to . . . conventional procurement'. See also Flemming in Corry, 1997).

There are, however, four main disadvantages associated with using private finance in this way (Corry 1995a, 1996; Watson and Heald in Corry, 1997).

First, using private-sector finance for public-sector projects delivers no free lunch. Unless the private sector is able to raise capital that the state could not, then private finance does not ease any macroeconomic constraints on the resources available for public services (unless it increases the efficiency of resource use) (Heald, 1996; Treasury Committee, 1996). For example, where the public sector pays for the service, the private sector finances, builds and often operates the facility in return for a contract with the public sector that specifies payments for the use of that facility for a number of years (up to sixty in some recent PFI negotiations). The state (taxpayer) still pays, all that has happened is that the time profile of payments has changed.

Second, the costs of borrowing are higher for the private than for the public sector. This means that there would need to be strong efficiency reasons for involving private-sector finance in the first place. One estimate of the cost of a PFI approach to a road project assessed it at more than 80 per cent higher than the conventional approach (Metropolitan Transport Research Unit, 1996).

Third, it is not clear what advantages there are where the end-user is made to pay. For example, if the private sector is to be allowed to charge for the service it provides (for example, road or bridge tolls), why could not the public sector itself have applied tolls in the first place? This would have had the effect of reducing the PSBR without the need for recourse to the PFI. Furthermore, charging in this way does qualitatively affect the service provided. What is being provided is no longer a 'free' road, but a 'toll' road.[3] And if one is searching for self-financing projects, there may well be a downgrading of the importance of non-financial benefits, or externality gains. This is true even when additional spending in one area – for example, roads – reduces spending in another area such as health. In a 'privatized' system, the incentives do not allow for these spill-overs.

Fourth, it is difficult to negotiate a fair PFI contract because of the problem of allocating risk. The private sector will be looking to minimize the risk it takes on – often by looking for guarantees (to provide a higher expected return). For instance, a private-sector firm may not want to build a tube line, even if it could have all the receipts, because it would not know for certain that demand would continue or that fares would not be altered by the state. It will be looking for clauses to protect it from such events.

It is arguable, however, that the government cannot avoid taking on, at the very least, the risk associated with the project collapsing completely. Will government actually stand by if and when a project fails or when a purchaser like a major NHS trust or a grant-maintained school goes bankrupt? In reality, in any major project the state guarantees and takes on all the project risk. This means that a whole host of contingent liabilities are being built up. Furthermore, private lenders are, in effect, being underwritten by the taxpayer, and there is no incentive for the private sector to monitor the project. There is also an asymmetry in the distribution of risks, for if the project goes well the private sector gets all the rewards (unless complex clawback deals are arranged and enforced). Joint ventures can avoid some of this (as well as other problems) and are probably a more fruitful line of progress.

If risk is not transferred to the private sector, there are no efficiency gains and it is unclear what gains there are for the public sector.[4] The Conservative government's attempts to encourage private-sector finance for large-scale projects have been riddled with difficulties of allocating risk and designing contracts that are fair to the public sector and do not discourage private investors. In practice, the private sector has been demanding a high price for taking on any of the risk involved (knowing that the government is committed to bringing in private finance). The Treasury has been criticized for the slow pace of the PFI. While some of the criticism may be valid, the danger is that a 'more relaxed' Treasury may just be a euphemism for less insistence on value for money.

The danger then with PFI is that it is being pushed primarily because of the political attraction that it appears to provide investment in public services without public spending and increased PSBR. Out goes a great lump of spending which makes the financial markets scream. In comes some kind of commitment to a stream of payments over thirty or so years. The danger, however, is that reducing the PSBR in the short term is merely piling up massive liabilities in the future. If the PFI is in fact mainly being used as a way to evade tough public-spending decisions, then at some point the financial markets will cotton on to the fact. It will then collapse in a heap with severe consequences for the private sector, for the public sector and for the citizens of this country.

One way of avoiding this would be the introduction of more transparent, balance-sheet accounting (Smith, 1996). In particular, more information must be provided on the efficiency gains that are expected to be and are being achieved and the additional financing costs that are involved. In this way the public can check that value for money is being achieved.

To sum up: there is nothing wrong with the PFI per se and it may produce extra efficiency gains that we cannot secure in other ways. But we need proof of this because PFI is not 'costless' to the public. A PFI-driven deal will be different from a conventionally financed project. The way that the service is delivered, the way management behaves, even the projects that are started will change and so the PFI will start to determine the shape of our public services. Over the long run, this may have important implications both for the Exchequer and for the public.

User charges

Charges for users are another way of introducing the disciplines of the market to public services and of reducing the need to raise money for public spending. These are only feasible when the service is not totally a 'public' good (for example, entry to a museum), and it is not widely used at present. The OECD estimated that charges represented only around 5 per cent of total government revenue in member countries (Oxley et al., 1990, p. 20).

Proponents of charging argue that people resist these less than they do taxes because payment is linked to specific services. It is also argued that charges reduce 'fiscal illusion' and so reduce the demand for services that individuals are not willing to pay for. A further argument in favour of charges is that services become more tailored to what consumers want. This is especially true if the public agency that provides the service is allowed to keep the revenues raised through charging. Finally, charges provide an incentive to new suppliers to enter the market (Marchese, 1985, p. 224).

As with the other forms of public-service delivery discussed above, charging raises a number of issues. One might ask why if one is prepared to charge more than a token amount, one pulls back from privatizing fully. In fact, the costs of a particular service are usually only partially met by user charges. This raises concerns about equity without eliminating the funding issue.

Consequences of Market-type Mechanisms

Do they ease the public-sector size problem?

Market-type mechanisms (MTMs) now apply to large areas of the public sector. When used appropriately, they have the potential to improve cost effectiveness and to make services more responsive to user requirements. Such mechanisms also have the potential to ease the role of the public sector as provider and, possibly, as payer. If all goes well, then, they may reduce the pressure on public spending. However, there are also a number of disadvantages, including loss of control and the costs of regulation (Corry, Le Grand and Radcliffe, 1997).

First, however, what of the view that the public sector in the UK is too big? Are MTMs a way out of this problem?

In the first place, we have seen that contracting out probably only offers marginal changes to public spending overall. Second, we have found that the PFI does not really alter the scale of the public spending over the long term. MTMs therefore should not really be addressed at the size issue but at the efficiency one.

In any case the major critique of the bloated public sector is essentially that public-sector activities are using too many of the resources of the economy, not that public spending (however this is defined) is too high. The old criticism of 'too few producers' (Bacon and Eltis, 1976) does not go away if private money is being diverted into what are essentially public-sector projects. In this sense, just looking at spending/GDP ratios is misleading (see also the discussion of regulation below).

Furthermore, attempts to twist the rules and structure of organizations, either to reduce the need for public money or to make it seem legitimate to exclude their spending and borrowing from the PSBR (Heald in Corry, 1997) may result in important and unintended changes to the services being produced.

In the case of housing, for example, the government has insisted that housing associations raise more and more of their money from the private sector. This has led associations to squeeze unit costs and to build on large, greenfield sites. These are likely to be the problem estates of the next decades. Rents being charged are also higher, to pay for the private finance, with major implications for housing-benefit bills, poverty traps and future public expenditure.

It is now being suggested that arm's-length local housing companies take over existing council housing stock (Institute of Housing, 1993). These would have only a small percentage of council representatives on the board and the hope is that their spending would not count as public expenditure. But this too would undoubtedly lead to a different type of housing service being provided.

There are also suggestions that the Post Office be restructured within the public sector, such that its borrowing would no longer count as public spending. The idea is that the restructured body would have no guarantee from government to secure its lending and would be run by a board of directors made up of business people, with no interference from politicians (London Economics, 1994). If adopted, these proposals would result in a very different Post Office. Indeed, it is difficult to see what the advantages of such a system would be over a fully privatized and regulated Post Office.

Public policy must focus on the desired outcome. Playing about with the structure of the organization for financial reasons may well lead one to take one's eyes off this. This suggests that MTMs and other changes to the organization of public services are no short cut to reducing the spending/GDP ratio.

Loss of control

There are other more general problems associated with the use of MTMs. In the case of leasing and the PFI, both involve long, binding contracts that have implications for the scale and flexible use of public spending in the future. Future governments may find their hands tied on policy issues, particularly if contracts give compensation to the private sector in the event of major policy changes. This raises interesting constitutional issues with risk implications. A government today effectively signs up future parliaments to contracts. Is this democratic? Will they hold if a government twenty years later prefers to spend on something else?

There is also a problem arising from the fact that the PFI seemed to be intended by the Conservative government as a replacement and not a supplement to existing resources. This means that there is a danger that the investment decision itself has become 'privatized', with private-sector interests coming to dominate public-welfare ones.

PFI deals offer another possibility of 'losing control'. Some are attracted by the idea of PFI only for the basics, like the construction of hospitals. But it is difficult to see the benefits of the PFI when used for construction-only contracts over a straightforward contracting-out approach. The real gains in involving the private sector (innovation and so on) will only result if the sector runs and operates a large proportion of the service. Then, for instance, they look at how to design the hospital so as to reduce the costs of delivering the other services they run.

This is also true of other services. A recent study on social housing, for example, pointed out that 'a firm that is interested in development only may not be as concerned about the long-term implications of building standards for the maintenance and management of the property as one which sees the provision of social housing as a long-term enterprise' (Day and Klein, 1996).

If, however, the private sector is allowed to take over the running of, for example, clinical services, there is a danger that it will manipulate demand for these services (as many commentators believe happened with Medicare in the US).

Overall, then, MTMs must not be introduced simply to reduce public expenditure. It is their potential to improve cost effectiveness that matters, and this too should be considered with an open mind. As the market-orientated OECD has concluded: 'the notion that market arrangements are inherently more efficient than non-market arrangements has been shown to be rather naive' (OECD, 1995, p. 112;[5] see also Martin, 1993, for a critique of the move to privatization and market-type mechanisms in general).

Regulation

Public provision and contracting out involve public expenditure. So too, in most cases, does the PFI. In addition we have seen that there are problems with all of them.

There are several other approaches to delivering 'public' services through public action that have only minor public-expenditure implications. We can use revenue-neutral changes in subsidies and/or taxes to shift the private sector in the way we want.[6] We can use industry levies to try and alter behaviour. Or we can try and change the objective of a private-sector firm, perhaps by altering corporate governance arrangements. The most important idea, however, is of using regulation, instead of ownership or funding of any kind, to help deliver required services.

It is difficult to put in place a regulatory system to deal with the private sector that delivers public-sector objectives (including accountability) and also provides the private sector with the right incentives to deliver services efficiently. For these reasons, the privatization/regulation approach needs to be motivated by the belief that it can help to achieve public-policy objectives more easily than other measures.

Outside the utilities, regulation is often a response to information asymmetries (hence restrictions on the behaviour of insurance companies, health and safety legislation and so on) or because of externalities (for example, control of polluting emissions from industry). In the case of the utilities, issues of natural monopoly and social-policy objectives are often as important.

In theory, the regulation of a private-sector monopoly would appear to be fairly straightforward. Left alone, the monopoly would restrict output and raise prices. The regulator therefore places restrictions upon its behaviour. In the UK, restrictions imposed by the regulators on the utilities have taken the form of ceilings on the prices that can be charged to consumers.

In practice, the regulator does not have perfect information on crucial aspects of a utility's business – for example, its cost structure. This makes it difficult for the regulator to put appropriate restrictions in place. As recent events in the electricity industry show, the regulator often only has the information that the monopoly wants it to have. This has resulted in outcomes (particularly in terms of very high profit levels) that many consumers have found intolerable.

There is also the difficulty that regulation will often have multiple public-policy objectives. In the utilities, for example, there are concerns over equity, quality, shareholder interests, potential new entrants, management, workers, prices, possible strategic interests specific to that industry (such as diversity of energy sources) and environmental objectives. This means that regulation has to try to balance the conflicting interests in a way that is both open and accountable. Where this turns out to be difficult, the question that has to be asked is whether public provision would have been better.[7] (See Corry, 1995b, for more discussion.)

A more general point is that a 'desire to comply' or 'trust' may be essential if regulation is to work. Day and Klein (1996), for instance, note that the Housing Corporation can focus on efficiency while regulating essentially non-profit-making housing associations, assuming that the ethos of the housing associations will take care of quality. However, the opposite will hold if and when for-profit organizations are brought into the social housing field (Day and Klein, 1996, p. 12).

A very important argument against regulation is that it involves costs that do not appear in the accounts. Some estimates of the total cost of regulation, especially made by those on the right of the political spectrum, are enormous (Stein, 1995). The aggregate cost of all regulation in the US has been put as high as 10 per cent of GDP (OECD, 1995, p. 69). Although these figures are open to debate, there is no doubt that regulation of the private sector often hides the true costs of delivering either a service or a particular standard. Regulation may, in fact, be a mechanism for government spending through indirect taxation. This means that policy makers and the electorate cannot judge whether the cost of providing a service is worthwhile. As the OECD rightly says, 'if governments are finding it difficult to control fiscal costs, which are highly visible, how much more difficult will it be to control the invisible costs of regulation?' (ibid., p. 70).

Some use this as a reason not to regulate at all: however bad the private sector, at least it is clear and transparent. However, if one is trying to achieve a policy objective, then if the cost of regulating in some cases seems too high we should reject the privatize-and-regulate approach in favour either of a contracting approach or, if that is deemed to be a problem, of direct provision.

Conclusions

Policy makers starting with a clean sheet of paper at the end of the twentieth century might well devise a public sector that did things differently from our present arrangements. But while there is always a case for thinking from first principles, of performing fundamental expenditure reviews and zero-based budgeting, we have to take where we are as a starting point and focus on several key issues in guiding our decision making.

There will always be a need for public action in order to make the world a better place in which to live. It is right that we constantly debate how wide this remit should go and how best to do this. In the long run, value for money will never be as important as the fundamental reasons for public action discussed at the beginning of this chapter. This does not mean that the current expenditure constraints, which are likely to persist for the next few decades, can be ignored. All future governments, in an attempt to reduce public expenditure, are likely to look to the private sector. The result will be more market-type mechanisms, either of the contracting-out or PFI type, 'corporatization', or privatization with regulation.

What must not happen is that an unjustified bias in favour of public provision is replaced with an unrigorous bias towards market-based solutions. The semi-privatized world creates a strong lobby for increases in government activity since the private sector values highly these safe and reliable contracts (Bosanquet, 1995). Add to this the attraction of keeping spending off the books and, from the new left, a desire to look fashionably pro-market and the dangers are clear.

The ideal is probably a continuation of a 'mixed economy' of public-service delivery. This will enable learning from trying different approaches, testing the public sector to be as efficient as the private, keeping in-house provision as a way of providing competition to the private sector (de Fraja, 1995) as well as coping with situations where transaction costs are high and keeping flexibility is essential.

Above all, we must be rigorous in demanding a consistent, clear and open approach to public spending decisions, where accountability and effectiveness are the watchwords. Openness is important because the knowledge that the decision-making process and analysis of public-policy decisions – both in a technical and in a political sense – are subject to public scrutiny would help ensure that decisions were carefully thought through and evaluated properly. It would also help to ensure that resources were devoted to services that individuals valued most. Rational decision making might be forced on politicians and the electorate might come to trust its politicians more. When they picked a particular delivery mechanism it would be because it was the best option available.

For any public project, the following sort of details should be discussed in the public domain:

- the degree to which public good and equity issues are raised;
- the value for money of the project, and different ways of delivering the service, to include specific estimates of the alternative costs (including financing costs) and (assumed) benefit and efficiency gains of each option;
- the degree to which any arrangement incurs future and contingent liabilities (massively aided if one had real resource accounting and budgeting – see Pallot and Ball in Corry, 1997);
- an assessment of the long- and short-run risk in using the private sector;

- an analysis of the likely disadvantages involved in using or continuing to use the public sector as a provider;
- evaluation to see if the assumptions were correct.

Finally, it is worth noting that no 'expert' really knows what the long-run consequences of letting the private sector genii out of the bottle will be. Public scepticism with regard to many of these issues may reflect a sensible risk aversion rather than just a blind defence of the status quo.

Christopher Hood (1989) has suggested that the limits to the contract and subsidiarity state will lie 'in terms of transactional convenience and constitutional answerability'. To these might be added value for money, given ever-changing needs and desires of the electorate, as well as the capability of the private sector. In exploring these issues an open mind must be the starting point.

Notes

1 Barrow et al. (1996) talk of the importance of 'atmosphere', the idea that 'social networks and non-price competition may be more important than conventional incentives' and the belief that institutional form may lead to more altruistic behaviour (p. 4).
2 In fact all finance is ultimately private, be it funded through general borrowing by the public sector or via taxation raised from private firms and individuals.
3 Much the same applies in 'partnership' deals that involve transfer of assets, development rights, planning gain, exemption from tough regulation and so on (see Brown et al., 1994). None of these [is] a case of something for nothing: the public sector is in essence paying the private sector in kind. Some of these issues would become clearer if the public sector had proper accounts.
4 Of course exactly what risk is transferred has to be clearly assessed. There may be little point in transferring risk to the private sector that they can do little about. On the other hand, there are dangers that the public sector isolates the private sector to too great an extent. Under pressure from the private sector the Conservative government has gone some way to underwriting private-sector involvement in PFI in hospital trusts (see e.g. *Health Service Journal*, 7 March 1996), and has also had to amend ideas for regulating private finance in housing associations (Roof, 1996).
5 The OECD (1995) points out that in theory at least it is better to add in lots of elements that mimic a competitive market rather than just one or two. 'Market outcomes are predictable, generally speaking, but not when isolated elements of private practices are incorporated into large public organizations' (p. 113). In other words, go the whole hog or not at all.
6 However, tax reliefs have costs which are essentially the same as public expenditure so we do not really relax the spending constraint by switching from grants, for example, to tax breaks. They also have efficiency and distributional consequences that are too rarely examined (Kvist and Sinfield, 1996).

7 This of course is not to say that one avoids the need for regulation within the public sector. Many of the answers to traditional government failure may well lie in this sort of approach.

References

ABI (1995) *Risk, Insurance and Welfare: The Changing Balance between Public and Private Protection.* London: Association of British Insurers.

Bacon, R. and Eltis, W. (1976) *Britain's Economic Problem: Too Few Producers.* London: Macmillan.

Barnett, R. (1993) Preference revelation and public goods. In P. Jackson (ed.), *Current Issues in Public Sector Economics*, Basingstoke: Macmillan.

Barrow, M., Johnson, P., Smith, P. and Taylor, J. (1996) *Targeting and Control in the Finance of Local Governance.* Paper presented at ESRC Local Governance Seminar held at the Department of Environment, 12 March.

Blankart, C. (1985) Market and non-market alternatives in the supply of public goods: general issues. In F. Forte and A. Peacock (eds), *Public Expenditure and Government Growth*, Oxford: Blackwell.

Bosanquet, N. (1995) Public spending into the millennium. London: Social Market Foundation.

Brown, G., Cook, R. and Prescott, J. (1994). *Financing Infrastructure Investment.* London: Labour Party.

Corry, D. (1995a) Public and private partnerships. *Renewal*, 3 (2).

Corry, D. (1995b) Why should we regulate and why is it so complicated? In D. Corry (ed.), *Regulating in the Public Interest: Looking to the Future*, London: IPPR.

Corry, D. (1996) Making the PFI honest. *Private Finance Initiative Journal*, 1 (4).

Corry, D. (ed.) (1997) *Public Expenditure: Effective Management and Control.* London: Dryden Press.

Corry, D., Le Grand, J. and Radcliffe, R. (1997) *Public private partnerships: a marriage of convenience or a permanent commitment?* London: IPPR.

Dasgupta, P. (1989) Positive freedom, markets and the welfare state. In D. Helm (ed.), *The Economic Borders of the State*, Oxford: Oxford University Press.

Day, P. and Klein, R. (1996) *The Regulation of Social Housing.* London: National Federation of Housing Associations.

de Fraja, G. (1995) In praise of public firms. *New Economy*, 2 (3).

Dilnot, A. (1995) *What Role for the State in the Economy?* ESRC State of Britain Seminars. Swindon: ESRC.

Falkingham, J. and Hills, J. (eds) (1995) *The Dynamic of Welfare: The Welfare State and the Life Cycle.* Herrel Hempstead: Prentice-Hall/Harvester Wheatsheaf.

Finley, L. (1989) Alternative service delivery, privatisation and competition. In L. Finley (ed.), *Public Sector Privatisation: Alternative Approaches to Service Delivery*, New York: Quorm Books.

Forte, F. and Peacock, A. (eds) (1985) *Public Expenditure and Government Growth.* Oxford: Blackwell.

Heald, D. (1996) *Privately Financed Capital in Public Services.* Paper for the Local Governance Programme of the Economic and Social Research Council, March.

Heller, W. (1965) Reflections on public expenditure theory. In E. Phelps (ed.), *Private Wants and Public Needs*, New York: Norton.

Helm, D. (1989) The economic borders of the state. In D. Helm (ed.), *The Economic Borders of the State*, Oxford: Oxford University Press.

Hills, J. (1995) Funding the welfare state. *Oxford Review of Economic Policy*, 11 (3).

Hood, C. (1989) Rolling back the state or moving to a contract and subsidiarity state? In P. Coldrake and J.R. Nethercote (eds), *What Should Government Do?*, Sydney: Hale and Ironmonger.

Institute of Housing (1993) *Local Housing Companies: New Opportunities for Council Housing*. York: Joseph Rowntree Trust.

IPPR (1996) Submission to the House of Lords enquiry into relations between central and local government, February.

Keating, M. (1991) Management of the public sector. In J. Llewellyn and S. Potter (eds), *Economic Policies for the 1990s*, Oxford: Blackwell.

Kerr, A. and Radford, M. (1995). CCT challenged. *New Economy*, 1 (2).

Kvist, J. and Sinfield, A. (1996) *Comparing Tax Routes in Denmark and the United Kingdom*. Copenhagen: Danish National Institute of Social Research.

Le Grand, J. (1996). The thinkable. *Prospect*, July.

Levitt, M. and Joyce, M. (1987). *The Growth and Efficiency of Public Spending*. Cambridge: NIESR/Cambridge University Press.

London Economics (1994) The future of postal services: a critique of the government's Green Paper. *London Economics Newsletter*, 1.

London Economics (1996) What price commercial freedom? Economics in action. *London Economics Newsletter*, 3.

Marchese, C. (1985) Market and nonmarket alternatives in the public supply of public services: some empirical evidence. In F. Forte and A. Peacock (eds), *Public Expenditure and Government Growth*, Oxford: Blackwell.

Martin, B. (1993) *In the Public Interest? Privatisation and Public Sector Reform*. London: Zed Books in association with PSI.

Metropolitan Transport Research Unit (1996) For whom the shadow tolls: the effects of design, build, finance and operate on the A36 Salisbury Bypass. *Transport 2000*, May.

OECD (1994) *New Ways of Managing Infrastructure Provision*. Public Management (PUMA) Occasional Papers No. 6. Paris: OECD.

OECD (1995) *Governance in Transition: Public Management Reforms in OECD Countries*. Paris: OECD.

OXERA (1996) *Infrastructure in the UK: Public Projects and Private Money*. Oxford: OXERA Press.

Oxley, H., Maher, M., Martin, J.P. and Nicoletti, G. (1990) *The Public Sector: Issues for the 1990s*. Department of Economics and Statistics Working Paper No. 90. Paris: OECD.

Phelps, E. (1965) Introduction. In E. Phelps (ed.), *Private Wants and Public Needs*, New York: Norton.

Public Finance Trends (1995) London: HMSO.

Public Services Privatisation Research Unit (1996). *The Privatisation Network*. Report by the Public Services Privatisation Research Unit. London: PSPRU.

Radcliffe, R., Hawksworth, J. and Glanville, G. (1996) *Consensus for Change: Public Borrowing, Housing Investment and the City*. Coventry: Coopers and Lybrand/Chartered Institute of Housing.

Roof (1996) Private finance warnings. *Roof Briefing*, April.

Self, P. (1989) Redefining the role of government. In P. Coldrake and J.R. Nethercote (eds), *What Should Government Do?*, Sydney: Hale and Ironmonger.

Smith, A. (1996) The state of the public finances: Labour's approach. Speech to the Opening Plenary Session of CIPFA Conference, 11 June, Labour Party.

Stein, P. (1995) Measuring the costs of regulation. In P. Stein, T. Hopkins and R. Vaubel (eds), *The Hidden Cost of Regulation in Europe*, London: European Policy Forum.

Szymanski, S. (1994) CCT: a clean solution? *New Economy*, 1 (2).

Treasury Committee (1996) *The Private Finance Initiative*. HC 146. London: HMSO.

Waterson, M. (1994) The future of utility regulation: economic aspects. In D. Corry (ed.), *Regulating our Utilities*, London: IPPR.

Watson, S. (1995) Innovative approaches to the financing of infrastructure and public service projects. *Local Work*, 68.

Part II
Issues and Debates in Social Policy

In Part II, IPPR's conceptual framework informs a discussion of issues and debates in social policy, organized around three main themes: families, communities and democracy. IPPR's distinctive approach to family policy is outlined by Anna Coote, Harriet Harman and Patricia Hewitt in chapter 6. They begin with the idea that policy should work with rather than against the grain of change in families and society, aiming to support all kinds of family and not just a particular 'ideal' type. They take children's needs as the focus for policy development with the premise that every child should have the right to be dependent and to grow up in conditions which enable her or him to become a dependable adult. Policies should enable women, who are the mainstay of most families, to be strong and self-reliant, providing the opportunity to combine paid employment and parenthood. They should encourage a sense of responsibility in men, as fathers, to form strong, lasting and loving bonds with their children and as partners, to consider their role in the household and to learn to respect and treat women as individuals of equal worth.

In chapter 7, Adrienne Burgess and Sandy Ruxton develop this position, as they explore the experience of men within families. Men are just as passionate about their children as women are and if fathers are seen to be more than breadwinners they can be active, caring parents, no less able than women to perform the intimate day-to-day tasks of parenting. However, increased participation by men in the care and upbringing of children will mean rethinking motherhood as well as fatherhood, and rethinking patterns of working time so that women can be good earners as well as good mothers and men can be good fathers as well as good workers. Burgess and Ruxton look at the benefits to employers of designing father-friendly workplaces which offer a flexible approach to men's needs as fathers and employees.

Communities have become the focus for political rhetoric and policy making. David Donnison (chapter 8) stresses the need for social policy to work with communities to reinforce the positive things that are happening, rather than develop policies which suggest how people should live. The capacity and potential of people are too often ignored in debates about tax, social security, employment and housing. Social injustice is experienced at street level in local communities and Donnison asks what can be done to build social renewal from the bottom up. He traces the economic, social and political factors which together can divide and brutalize our society, calling for comprehensive action to build on and support existing initiatives.

Self-help and mutual-aid activities have grown dramatically over the last two decades across Europe and North America, a development that has important political implications. As Mai Wann argues (chapter 9), this runs counter to the conventions of post-war welfarism as well as to the older traditions of charity and voluntarism. Self-help and mutual aid stress personal responsibility and interdependence, as well as direct, local action. They present an ethos which is empowering and enabling rather than protective, prescriptive or philanthropic, challenging the power and expertise of professionals, especially in the field of health.

Tariq Modood (chapter 10) argues that racial discrimination is a major barrier to social justice in Britain, denying opportunities for people in minority communities to develop their talents to the full. But racial discrimination is a complex phenomenon, linked to class inequalities and experienced differently by different racial groups. How can it be understood and what can be done about it? Modood attempts to answer these questions and provides a vigorous, original and challenging contribution to the debate about how to combat racism in Britain and Europe more generally.

Public participation in decision making is a key aspect of social-policy development at IPPR. Anna Coote (chapter 11) looks at the development of public discontent with the welfare state in relation to questions of power and participation and considers the case for 'empowerment', as seen from the right and left of the political spectrum. She assesses the main strategy for empowerment adopted by the Conservatives in the 1980s and 1990s, describes a range of options for increasing public participation in decisions about public services, and examines some problems and possibilities associated with them. In the following chapter, Anna Coote and Jo Lenaghan develop a critique of the relationship between electors and elected, which, they argue, is immature and induces passive citizenship. They consider the value of citizens' juries, a process of decision making which combines features of other forms of public involvement such as referendums and citizens' panels in one mechanism to enhance and strengthen representative democracy.

6

Family Policy: Guidelines and Goals

ANNA COOTE, HARRIET HARMAN AND PATRICIA HEWITT

Family policy is high on the agenda as politicians try to understand the implications of rapid changes in family circumstances.

This is, however, a difficult subject for policy makers. There is a widespread, and proper, reluctance to encourage the state to interfere in people's domestic lives. At the same time, there is a growing concern, equally justified, about the impact of these changes on children.

Policy makers of very different political views have generally failed to adopt any coherent family policy or even to reach agreement on what they mean by the 'family'. The word has a strong symbolic value, but its meaning is vague. 'Family' is something everyone is *for*, rather as everyone is against sin. In real life, 'family' means different things to different people – each according to his or her personal experience.

None the less, governments in every country have a 'family policy'. It may be implicit in policies about divorce, education, abortion, women's employment and so on, rather than explicit. It may be overtly designed to increase the birth rate . . . or to reduce it . . . It may be contradictory; for instance, where government seeks both to increase women's participation in the labour force and to increase their level of responsibility for children and elderly dependents in the home.

The community's interest in family relationships – specifically in how children are brought up and how elderly relatives are cared for – is so great that no government can be 'neutral' on the family. The question is not whether government has a family policy, but whether it is explicit or implicit, whether it is coherent or inconsistent, what purpose it is meant to fulfil and whom it benefits.

With this in mind, we set out below the guidelines and goals, first published in 1990, which continue to inform IPPR's approach to family-policy making . . .

Guidelines

Families are social, not natural, phenomena

Contrary to the assertions of some, families are not natural phenomena, like the fall of snow in winter or the blossoming of trees in spring. They are social phenomena; they change over time; they are susceptible to – and shaped by – economic and political developments.

What counts is the process, not the label

It is important to be clear about the focus of policy making in this area. What does the 'family' in 'family policy' mean? Drawing on what we know about the ways in which families are changing, as well as the causes and consequences of change, it seems sensible to focus on *what happens* in families, rather than on the label or status attached to different living arrangements. In other words, it is useful for the purposes of policy making to think in terms of process and relationships.

Of course, all sorts of things happen in families. Where does public policy come in? Which parts of the process do we wish to focus upon?

Children come first

This approach to family policy is based on the premise that we all bear responsibility for all our children. They are society's most precious resource and everyone has an obligation to them, whether parents themselves or not. They are tomorrow's producers, who may help pay the pensions of today's workers. They are tomorrow's carers, who will raise the next generation of children and look after today's fit young adults, when they cease to be so. They are tomorrow's politicians, who will govern (or try to govern) society in the twenty-first century. While they are young, they cannot defend themselves against neglect, abuse or exploitation, which may come from within their own families; there is therefore a social obligation to ensure that they are properly protected.

Family policy should be primarily concerned with the process of bringing up and caring for children. That is not to say it should be unconcerned about the problems of adults whose marriages become intolerable for them, about single people, child-free couples or families looking after adult dependents: we are simply identifying the starting point for a family policy . . .

Policy must work with, not against, the grain of change

Long-term, cross-national trends in the patterns of family life cannot be halted, let alone reversed, by the efforts of any government (unless it is totalitarian and extraordinarily powerful). It is vital to acknowledge that change can be painful – as it so often is for children who have to live with changes in their family circumstances. The aim of public-policy makers should be to understand the nature of change and make the best of it – not to engage in a futile mission to restore 'the good old days'. Nostalgia fills the air with resentment, breeds taboo and stifles political creativity. One sure way to stunt the healthy development of children growing up in one-parent or reconstituted families is to give them the impression that they are abnormal, or that their families are incomplete or deviant. Rather than accuse increasingly large numbers of people of living in the 'wrong' kind of family, the aim should be to make sure that policies are adapted to suit changing practice and – as far as possible – to mitigate the painful effects of change.

Encouragement, not coercion

Public policy can encourage some kinds of behaviour and discourage others. It should not attempt coercion – which is undemocratic and likely to be counter-productive.

A long-term perspective

It is important to recognize that significant changes in the nature of family life develop slowly over a long period of time. There is a lag between cause and effect. Policy makers must therefore take a long-term perspective and anticipate the effects of change over two or three generations.

A European perspective

A family policy designed for the UK must take account of what is happening in Europe. The UK can learn from the example of other countries. In matters of parental leave and child care, in particular, Britain has lagged behind most of Western Europe. Moreover, closer integration of the EU means that individual countries can no longer develop social policy in isolation from each other.

Policy Goals

Having suggested some ground rules for a new approach to family policy, we turn to the question of what it should try to achieve . . .

1 Children

Every child should have the right to be dependent and to grow up in conditions which enable it to become a dependable adult.

This is the cornerstone on which all else rests. We are not suggesting that children should be forced into dependency; of course, it is important that they also learn to be independent. The point is that every child, for part of its life, needs to depend on others. The quality of the child's relationships with those on whom it depends, and the conditions in which it experiences dependency, are crucial to its development.

One important test of a successful childhood is whether the child grows up to be a dependable adult. We use the word 'dependable' in a broad sense to convey the psychological maturity and personal autonomy which enable individuals to take responsibility for themselves, and provide for others who need them the conditions in which they can be dependent.

2 Women

Families need strong, self-reliant women.

In most families, women are the mainstay, on whom children depend; almost invariably, they do most of the caring work involved in bringing up children and, often, women bear sole responsibility. They are also usually the ones who care for dependent adults in the family.

If children are to have a right to be dependent and grow up in conditions which enable them to become dependable adults, it is essential that women themselves have the opportunity to be dependable and to provide those conditions for their children.

Yet for many women with dependent children, being dependable is a struggle against considerable odds. Their own lives are shaped by enforced dependency. They are neither prepared, nor expected, nor given the opportunity to be autonomous adults. They are trapped in a cycle of dependency which works (approximately) like this. Women, according to convention, are the ones who look after children. They are not expected to be the main family breadwinners. They are less likely than men to be educated and trained for the kinds of job that will enable them to be the main family breadwinners. They earn less than men. When they have children, it 'makes sense' for the man to stay in work and the woman to look after the children, because his earning power is greater. She takes time out of the labour market, or opts for part-time work, and further reduces her prospects of earning as much as a man. Employers feel justified in giving preferential treatment to men, because they are the main family breadwinners. Women continue to depend on men – or on the state if they cannot – for part or all of their livelihood . . .

Women derive varying degrees of joy and satisfaction from bringing up children; men, in many families, provide financial support. There are still many households where the traditional model of family life suits all parties, although their number appears to be declining. As Heather Joshi has observed, the 'traditional domestic bargain does not work to the advantage of all women': 'it involves loss of earnings, future earnings potential and pensions rights; it can involve social obligation, loss of autonomy and self- and social-esteem; and perhaps most important, loss of security' (Joshi, 1990).

If they are financially dependent on men, women have little or no control over how much money they get, or for how long. There is evidence that within marriage, money is not shared equally between husbands and wives; men spend more on themselves and women have relatively little personal spending money, even if they contribute to the family's earned income (Pahl, 1989, p. 169). There is also the danger that the male 'breadwinner' may become unemployed and be less able to support his family; or he may decide to leave and take his breadwinning capacity elsewhere . . .

The cycle of female dependency is not simply about money. It is about power. Men who have superior financial power in the household tend to dominate decision making (ibid., p. 174). Women who are economically dependent cannot easily decide to make changes in their lives. For instance, if the family money isn't 'theirs' they don't feel free to spend it on child care or a training course, so that they can repair their prospects of earning a living. If they depend on a man for support, they cannot – without risking considerable hardship – choose to leave him, even if he is violent or prone to other 'unreasonable behaviour'. Their dependency may encourage them to swap one unsatisfactory partner for another, as the only way of escaping poverty.

Inequality is not a recipe for wedded bliss. It is, on the contrary, one of the main causes of marital breakdown. Moreover, an unequal power relationship can feed upon itself, compounding the inequality with abuses of power. In many families, men exert power over women with acts of violence. According to the United Nations' Group of Experts on Violence in the Family, 'the root cause of abuse of women stems from the position of women in society and the unequal power structure therein.' 'Socialisation which assumes gender stereotyping was therefore seen as one of the causes of violence towards women in the context of the family . . . Economic independence for women was regarded as crucial' (Expert Group Meeting on Violence in the Family, 1986).

Nowhere are the ill effects of the cycle of female dependency more keenly felt than in lone-parent families. We described earlier the degrees of poverty suffered by women living alone with children. They seldom have access to childcare arrangements which enable them to earn enough to lift themselves and their children above the poverty line. They have little opportunity to improve their earning power. Many depend upon the state for their income and that, for the most part, traps them in poverty. Most of them feel – and are – powerless to influence the course of their lives, except by swapping one form of dependency (on the state) for another (a man). In her study of lone parents in EU countries, Jo Roll concludes:

> it is clear, given that most lone parents are divorced or separated, that were financial dependence within marriage to disappear, the financial problems of the majority of lone mothers would be greatly reduced. It is even possible that fewer lone parent families would be formed as a result of greater equality within marriage. (Roll, 1989)

This cycle of female dependency, which brings with it poverty and powerlessness, is bad for women. It is also, ultimately, bad for men. More important still, it is bad for children. It undermines the personal resources of those who are the primary carers of dependent children. That is why enabling women to be strong and self-reliant rather than dependent is one of the main goals of a new family policy.

3 Men

Changing times require a new sense of responsibility in men.

The idea that men must be 'responsible' for their families is an old one – older than the Victorian era on which our traditional family model is based. It has been central to the Conservative government's approach to the family and has inspired their . . . intiative to enforce the payment of maintenance by errant fathers.

According to traditional thinking, male responsibility is primarily about *financial support*. It is this notion of responsibility which lies at the heart of the current crisis in family life – for three main reasons.

Firstly, the policies of the state (for example, in relation to childcare and social security) are organized around the assumption that men are the main family breadwinners and that women stay at home to do the unpaid caring work. Yet increasing numbers of children are being raised in families where there is little or no financial support from men. It is largely as a result of the mismatch between policy and reality that these children experience the material deprivation common to most lone-parent families.

Secondly, the assumption that men are financially responsible for their families is at the root of women's disadvantage in the labour market – and it is this disadvantage which makes it so hard for women alone to provide adequately for themselves and their children.

Thirdly, the traditional emphasis on men as breadwinners has deterred many of them from forming close and lasting bonds with their children. Men who are out at work for nine hours or more, five days a week, are effectively exiled from their children. If men feel they have no role except as financial providers, it is scarcely any wonder that so many abandon their children, not only ceasing to pay, but cutting off contact altogether. As we noted earlier, there is evidence that within two years of divorce, more than a third of the children involved have no contact with the non-custodial parent (usually the father). After ten years, more than half had lost contact altogether (Bradshaw and Millar, 1990). We have seen how children can suffer from this loss.

Quite apart from questions of money, a new family policy should encourage new kinds of responsibility in men:

• Responsibility as fathers. It is important for men to form strong, loving bonds with their children. That implies giving men the opportunity to spend more time with their children, especially when they are young. The closer a man's involvement with the day-to-day lives of his children, the more likely it is that he will develop a sense of commitment to them at an emotional – rather than simply a material – level. This will be of great value to the child in any circumstances – but as we have seen, it may be especially important where a marriage breaks down and the father leaves the home. A father who is deeply committed to his children is more likely to maintain a loving and affirming relationship with them after the breakdown of his relationship with their mother.

- Responsibility as partners. Public policy should aim to create the conditions for men to be responsible in ways which do not perpetuate female dependency, but help to break the cycle. For women to be more autonomous, it is essential for men to change their role in the household, and do more of the unpaid work. We have seen how unequally tasks are divided at present and we have noted the inconsistency between what people say ought to happen and what really does. We have also seen how people's expectations of marriage (especially women's) do not match reality – this being a significant factor when marriages break down. Men's responsibility as partners should go beyond simply 'doing more housework'. They must learn to respect – and treat – women as individuals of equal worth. That, more than anything, would seem to be the key to a stable partnership and one which works in the best interests of the children.

We now come to the question of men's financial responsibility. The long-term aim should be to create the conditions for men and women to be equally capable of supporting themselves and contributing at least half to the support of their children. While inequality persists, it seems sensible to encourage men to pay a level of maintenance which reflects their earning capacity and makes an appropriate contribution towards the cost of bringing up their children. However, any initiative in this area should give priority to the first two goals of this family policy. In other words, a strategy to recover maintenance from errant fathers should be tailored to serve the interests of children first and foremost.

4 Interdependence

Public policy should recognize that the essence of successful family life is neither enforced dependency, nor isolated individualism, but interdependence.

In this context, we are interested in two main expressions of interdependence:

1 *Within families.* Interdependence implies a relationship between equals. For women and men to be interdependent within families, they need to have equivalent skills, status and power and to look to each other for

mutual support. This suggests the end of the 'separate spheres' model of family life, which produces unequal power relations, locking men into exile from their children and women into dependency on men.

2 *Within communities.* Public policy should also recognize the interdependence of family and community. Families cannot exist in a vacuum, isolated from each other. They are, as we have seen, profoundly affected by their social and material environment. At the same time, that environment is profoundly affected by what happens in families. Social institutions should support families (by furthering the goals outlined here) without trapping them in dependency. Schools and health services play an important part in the process of bringing up children – not just by providing education and medical care, but by supporting parents in their own work of caring for children. Teachers, doctors, health visitors and other staff are often best placed to anticipate and identify problems and to provide extra support, especially when things go wrong within the family.

It should be recognized that supporting families is not an act of philanthropy or charity, but is central to the interests of society as a whole.

5 Flexibility

Policies should be adaptable, to support all kinds of family.

In these changing times, fewer families conform to the traditional model of family life – and we know that this trend is likely to increase. Public policy should therefore seek to support the process of family life, whatever the shape or size of the family unit. In a multi-ethnic society, public policy must be sensitive to the different experience and needs of families with different racial and cultural identities.

References

Bradshaw, J. and Millar, J. (1990) Lone parent families in the UK. Final report to the Department of Social Security, May. (Unpublished).

Expert Group Meeting on Violence in the Family (1986) Report of the Expert Group Meeting on Violence in the Family with Special Emphasis on its Effects on Women. Vienna, 8–12 December.

Joshi, H. (1990) The cash opportunity costs of childbearing: an approach to estimation using British data. *Population Studies*, 44, 52–3.

Pahl, J. (1989) *Money and Marriage*. Basingstoke: Macmillan.

Roll, J. (1989) *Lone Parent Families in the European Community*. Family Policy Studies Centre.

7

Men and their Children

ADRIENNE BURGESS AND SANDY RUXTON

Worldwide, fathers' roles and responsibilities are being reassessed. Many factors are forcing this: changes in family structure and the equal opportunity debate; restructuring of the labour market and diminishing opportunities for men within it; changes in women's lives, education levels and labour-force participation; concerns about morality, criminality and education; and advances in genetics.

Within families, fathers have become increasingly marginalized: long-hours working limits many; family breakdown alienates others. Today mothers are the 'preferred parent' among children of all ages, and teen-agers discuss education and employment as well as personal issues more frequently with mothers than with fathers ...

There are clear distinctions between the approach that we adopt and that of thinkers on the right. Where those on the right regard the father as the ultimate authority figure, and identify financial responsibility and discipline as his proper functions, we maintain that these functions, like all other day-to-day parenting functions, are best shared by both parents. Where the politics of the right seems to favour returning women to the home and restoring men's former dominance in the labour force, we want women and men to have equal opportunities to be both breadwinners and carers. A goal of IPPR's 1990 report *The Family Way* was to encourage the formation of strong, loving and lasting bonds between fathers and their children. That goal we now extend into a policy for fathers, recognizing the need to:

- widen cultural images of fatherhood;
- improve education and support for fathers;

- adopt a children's-rights perspective;
- develop a positive legal framework which encourages men to be involved with their children;
- reduce conflict between parents post-separation;
- maintain contact between children and their fathers . . .

What are Fathers For?

It is now established that men can be competent caretakers of children including newborns, that most are deeply attached to their infants, and that some are already centrally involved in child rearing.[1] The parenting styles of mothers and fathers within couples have been revealed as remarkably similar; and where fathering differs from mothering, this is more strongly associated with situation than with gender (Lewis, 1996). As soon as men take on similar levels (to mothers) of responsibility for young children, parenting approaches generally become indistinguishable. (Gbrich, 1987).

Fathers are of potential value to their children in many ways: through individual father–child relationships – both real and symbolic; through the resources (time and money) they contribute to the household; through the networks (family and other contacts) attaching to them; through the support they can provide to mothers; and through their potential to be 'irrationally emotionally involved' with their children – that is, to 'love them madly and remain loyal to them for life' (Ochiltree, 1994). Children and biological parents measure themselves against each other in unique ways, and while father substitutes can, and often do, fulfil many of the functions listed here, they can never fulfil them all.

Fathers are a resource within families – in many ways a greatly underused resource – and their absence is a source of stress which, when combined with other stresses, such as poverty, racism, maternal failure, can seriously inhibit their children's life chances. Despite the many variables in child development, children are shown to experience a similar range of benefits from interaction with fathers and with mothers; and strong association has been shown between support and involvement by both parents and positive outcomes for children as they grow up, including academic achievement, psychological adjustment, self-concept and social competence (Biller, 1993).

Paternal participation also increases marital satisfaction, and other benefits to men are now becoming clear: the concept of 'generativity' has been invoked, to explain how fathers develop socially and psychologically through participant fathering (Snarey, 1993).

Involving Fathers

To date, men's interest in undertaking family work has been greatly inhibited – first and foremost by the fact that caring for children has been seen as the ultimate in 'women's work', and women's work has been of such low status. This has led to some men developing little or no interest in caring for children, and seeing it as a task which they feel offers them little reward, status or power – an attitude which has, in itself, reinforced the low status of such work.

This view has been confirmed by recent debates on family work, which have been mainly conducted in a 'feminist voice'. Child rearing has been depicted as a burden, and its pleasures and satisfactions downplayed – understandably, since women's love and concern for their children have been so unremittingly exploited. Attempts to increase men's participation have relied on inducing guilt – a strategy that has met with only limited success and has, counter-productively, fostered the belief that the only people who are losers in the 'work/family dilemma' are women.

'Men should play a bigger role at home, to free their wives to go out to work' declared the then employment secretary, Norman Fowler (somewhat surprisingly) in 1989 (Purves, 1989). What he could not say – would have been laughed out of the House for saying – is that 'women should play a bigger role in the workforce to free their husbands to spend more time with their families.'

So convincing has been talk about the disadvantages of spending time with children, that even males who have a strong personal wish to be involved fathers usually present their participation as a justice issue ('she's had them all week, it's only fair I should take them out at weekends').

Also masked has been an important truth: that, in terms of the 'work/family dilemma' men are losers too – most obviously, in their relationships with their children. At all ages in most families mothers are the 'preferred parent' (Lamb and Oppenheim, 1989), and analysis of visiting patterns reveals that while elderly couples or mothers living alone are regularly visited by their adult children, fathers living alone – either due to the death of, or separation from, their partners – receive visits only rarely (Jalmert, 1990).

The function of the family has changed. It is no longer a site of training and production, but a place of privacy and intimacy. The relationship between parent and child is seen as having more force and durability than the relationship between sexual partners, and fathers no longer rate 'breadwinning' as their key function. They assess their own value to their children in terms of 'being there' and 'emotional availability' (Snarey, 1993).

A majority of men see their own fathers as 'negative role models', and say they wish to be very different kinds of fathers themselves: they will usually declare that they want to be 'closer' to their children – both emotionally and physically. And a Europe-wide survey in 1993 revealed that neither men nor women think child rearing should be left mainly to women: 86.3 per cent of men and 87.4 per cent of women think it is better for a father to be 'very involved in bringing the child up from an early age' (Eurobarometer, 1993) . . .

In raising issues for consideration by policy makers and individuals, with a view to enabling men to take a more active part in the care and upbringing of children, we take as our starting point the observations that, over many centuries, British fathers have been discouraged from playing a full and rewarding role in the intimate lives of their families; and that latterly, men's supposed 'rationality' has been used to exclude them from the world of home, as surely as women's supposed 'emotionality' has been used to exclude them from the world of work . . .

Fathers, Mothers and Employment

Although within families, a number of factors, including the attitudes of fathers (and, particularly, of mothers) to paternal involvement have a bearing on fathers' levels of participation, work patterns are the single greatest determinant of fathers' relationships with their children. In the main, involved fathers work shorter hours than other men; and their partners work longer hours outside the home than other women (Cowan, 1988).

Most British fathers with children under 10 in two-parent families are in employment – 82 per cent full-time, and 2 per cent part-time. Of the rest, since some are retired, disabled or in prison, fewer than one in ten is actually unemployed. Although some of the employed fathers will have experienced periods of unemployment during the preceding years, fathers' employment rates are down only 1 per cent since 1985.

Since young men and men over 50 are the most likely to be un- or underemployed, men's working lives are increasingly crammed into the years between 25 and 50 – the very time when they are raising children. Fathers in two-parent families with children under 10 work an average of 47 hours a week – not including time spent travelling to and from work.

This is in sharp contrast to the children's mothers, only 53 per cent of whom are employed – 18 per cent averaging 25 hours a week and the remaining 35 per cent, 17 hours.[2] Even among mothers working more than 30 hours per week, one in six is home by 3.30 p.m.; and only one in sixteen puts in more than 47 hours a week. Since mothers are more likely to work locally, their commuting times are often considerably shorter than fathers' (Hewitt, 1993). Mothers, of course, work as long hours as fathers – and mothers of young babies somewhat longer – but their additional hours are worked inside their homes, and in the presence of their children.

Long-hours working is an increasing problem for many fathers. One-third work more than 50 hours a week,[3] and while their children are young, they clock up four times as much paid overtime as childless men (Study Commission on the Family, 1983). Increased working is often presented as the 'natural' male response to becoming a parent. In fact, it is more likely to be a response to crises in family finances, occasioned by mothers' withdrawal from the labour market: in Sweden, where 76 per cent of mothers of under-3s are in paid employment, fathers with very young children work the shortest hours of all fathers (Nasman, 1991).

British fathers are, overwhelmingly, still functioning as their families' primary or sole breadwinners, for while women's wages lift the family above the poverty line in one-third of families, part-time working mothers bring in – on average – one-fifth of the 'family wage' and full-timers two-fifths (Hewitt, 1993).

Interestingly, married or cohabiting men with children are less likely to be in work than their child-free counterparts. The least likely of all to be employed are fathers of under-5s (Sly, 1994). As children become older, fathers, like mothers, are more likely to be employed, which seems to indicate that a small group of fathers may be 'opting' for unemployment in order to care for their children.

However, because three-quarters of families with unemployed fathers also contain unemployed mothers, the traditional 'parental balance' remains unchanged in many families, although unemployment certainly increases the time men spend on housework and childcare (Mintel International, 1994). Only seventeen fathers out of every thousand have role-reversed to become 'househusbands' while their partners work full-time (Sly, 1994).

Fathers Negotiating Work and Family

As might be expected – given the patterns of paid work outlined above – women still retain major responsibility for family work. However, men's contribution in this arena is growing steadily – both in real and in relative terms. Between 1961 and 1985, while UK women reduced the time they spent on routine housework by six and a half hours a week, men doubled their contribution – by six hours. The time men spent on childcare also increased during these years – four-fold (Hewitt, 1993).

More recently, in Australia, some interesting trends are emerging, which may prove to be replicated in the UK. Between 1987 and 1992, childcare (as a primary activity) increased for both sexes, but the increase, both relative and absolute, was greatest for fathers – up a full two hours per week. Furthermore, the fathers' involvement was with much younger children: Australian men are no longer waiting for their offspring to leave infancy before becoming active fathers (Bittman, 1995).

The average employed British father and mother work around the same number of hours per day – when family work, paid work and commuting times are added in (Niemi, 1995). The division of labour within individual families varies considerably, but the rule of thumb is that where partners are equal breadwinners in terms of the amounts earned, 'core' domestic tasks are most likely to be equally shared (Clift and Fielding, 1991).

US research has revealed that, in New York City, the proportion of men reporting significant conflict between work and family ('role strain') increased from 12 per cent to 71 per cent between 1977 and 1989, and 28 per cent of male workers in the US report that 'family matters' regularly interfere with their concentration at work (Rodgers, 1992). In Britain, the Institute of Management found 71 per cent of managers saying they believe their relationships with their children are badly affected by their working lives. Since half these men were in late middle age, it is likely that among managers with young children 'role strain' is nearer 100 per cent (Institute of Management, 1993).

Work/family conflict tends to be different for men and women. Whereas women worry about the practicalities of childcare, men are guilty and concerned about lack of time spent with their children. This, in a 'loop effect', has implications for cost effectiveness in industry: an American study of 300 dual-career couples found the only consistent predictor of men's bad physical health to be whether they had worries or concerns about their relationships with their children (Levine, 1994).

As women increasingly choose work which uses their qualifications rather than jobs with hours that 'suit the family', fathers' working hours are beginning to form part of working-time negotiations within families. A recent Australian study revealed that one-third of the parents who had taken time off in the previous twelve months to be with sick children were men; and in Britain 50 per cent of fathers in dual-earner households share the care of sick children equally with their wives – a proportion that has risen sharply in recent years (Jowell et al., 1992).

Working fathers attempt to accommodate family responsibilities to a far greater degree than is generally realized. A quarter of 'first-choice' applicants refuse relocation for family reasons (Catalyst, 1983) and a recent Nordic study has shown 'work-oriented men' to be just as concerned with adapting work to family as 'family-oriented' men – obtaining flexible working for family reasons, cutting down on overtime and refusing promotions which would further disturb family life (Bjornberg, 1994).

Increasing numbers of fathers today have ongoing direct responsibility for childcare. Fathers miss work and are late for work more frequently than non-fathers (Levine, 1994). Fathers are the most usual 'baby-sitters' when mothers work, and when mothers work part-time, fathers do more childcare than when mothers work full-time: in Britain, half of female part-timers work evenings, weekends or nights (Hewitt, 1993).

Almost all British fathers desire paternity leave and take at least two days off work, with at least a third taking eight days or more. Much of this is unofficial, and taken as sick leave or 'on the nod' (Lewis, 1986). Take-up of official paternity leave remains low if it is not paid or is not known about or is not seen as acceptable.

While many men struggle with the 'work/family dilemma' privately, few dare raise it publicly. In a recent British survey of long-hours working, more than half the men thought this put their family relationships at risk – but, given their time over again, only a quarter would take a stand against it (Austin Knight UK, 1994). Studies of flexitime programmes and of 'compressed' working (when people work, for instance, three or four twelve-hour shifts, and have the rest of the week off) show clearly that this kind of non-standard working increases fathers' involvement with their children, but the men themselves do not advertise this fact.

Those who must work standard hours devise a range of coping strategies: parking in the back lot (so others won't see them leaving early) or saying they're going to 'another meeting' – without admitting that it's a meeting with their children.

Father-blind Employment Policies

'Work/family is not an issue here' wrote an American manager in the late 1980s 'because there are no women in this firm' (Andrews and Bailyn, 1993). In Britain, too, this perspective informs the debate – or lack of it – on men, work and family. Throughout both public and private employment sectors, so called 'family-friendly provision' really means 'mother-friendly'.

In corporate publications in the UK, such policies are often listed under 'women' or are clearly directed only at women. Paternity leave, if offered (National Power provide adoption leave for both women and men – but no paternity leave! (Income Data Services, 1995)), is almost invariably found under 'maternity leave' and even there can be heavily sidelined. The

Royal Bank of Scotland mention it only in a footnote; and Sussex County Council have renamed it 'Maternity Support Leave', listing fathers (in a subclause) as potential 'support' people, alongside 'the partner of the expectant mother' or her 'nominated carer' (cited in IRS Employment Trends, 1995).

Initiatives from voluntary organizations have generally betrayed a similar mind-set. 'Opportunity 2000' is (of course) specifically for women; publications by Parents at Work have been preoccupied with women; and when Exploring Parenthood devised a New Parents Service for IKEA, the promotional literature, while claiming to be for both 'fathers and mothers', announced: 'You have access to the service during pregnancy, after you have left work and when and if you return.'

During the International Year of the Family, when evidence on 'work and family' was given to the All Party Parliamentary Group on Parenting, not one man was brought in as a 'witness' to praise day-care initiatives – although it is plain that men, no less than women, can only take part in the work of paid employment if someone else is looking after their children.

Things, however, may be changing. The All Party Group, in its report (1994), addressed fathers as an important issue; New Ways to Work have recently produced a document focusing on men – *Balanced Lives* (1995); Exploring Parenthood have been studying black fathers; and Parents at Work say that men will be the subject of their next report.

An Equal Opportunities Review survey of paternity-leave entitlements in Britain noted that over two-thirds of respondents now provide paid paternity leave, and that most of this was introduced post-1990 (Equal Opportunities Review, 1994). However, the review also noted that the most usual reason given for instituting paternity leave was 'equal opportunities legislation'. This applies to US provision, too, where a recent survey has revealed that paternity leave is not always meant as a 'real' benefit, but is there simply to prevent challenge under equality legislation: few of the US companies surveyed informed the labour force of the entitlement, and a full 41 per cent did not expect them to take paternity leave. Nor, as in the UK, was take-up monitored – a clear indication of lack of commitment (Pleck, 1993).

Although it is rare for a business to do a thorough 'cost-benefit' analysis when introducing family-friendly benefits ('copycat' behaviour is common – if a leading player in a sector introduces an entitlement, others will follow), the business case for mother-friendly employment has been well argued in the UK, taking as its starting point employee retention. Career breaks, flexible working, job sharing, permanent part-time working, workplace nurseries, childcare vouchers and other childcare support – all these have been offered to workers (women) on the understanding that without them, they will not be 'able' to work, or will not be able to work full-time.

The case for father-friendly employment, however, has never been put. It has not even been compiled. In so far as fathers have been considered at all in Britain, their work/family needs have been assumed to be the same as mothers'.

Reframing Family-friendly Employment for Fathers

In presenting the case for father-friendly employment, several things need to be borne in mind. Firstly, that it is necessary to set out the context for the argument, along with the argument itself: listeners will tend to assume, unless it is proven to them otherwise, that (a) fathers do not have responsibility for childcare, (b) fathers do not suffer from 'role strain', and (c) father–child intimacy is not necessary, or even of particular value.

Secondly, the 'employee retention' argument does not hold for fathers: all but a few men will work anyway, whether or not childcare support is available. Thirdly, career breaks, job shares and permanent part-time working are currently of interest only to a tiny minority of fathers: most, as their families' main breadwinners, cannot afford to work less (because of reduced income or perceived reduced career opportunities) or would feel compromised 'as men' if they did so.

Fourthly, the direct benefits to men of 'family-friendly' policies need to be detailed: when men use childcare support or avail themselves of non-standard working opportunities, they may not perceive these as being for their benefit. They may, rather, see them as a benefit to their partners – enabling 'her' to work.

In the light of this, it is necessary to reframe some family-friendly benefits, to demonstrate their value to males. Involved child rearing can be shown as personally satisfying for men, and a route to personal development. In Norway, fathers now perceive developing good relationships with their children to be part of career success, and regard the skills they learn at home as useful to them at work (Bjornberg, 1994).

Paternity leave should be seen as an opportunity for fathers to spend time with their newborns, and develop confidence as parents, rather than primarily as a 'support' provision for mothers. We disagree strongly with any suggestion that paternity leave be defined as maternity support leave.

Childcare support as an indirect benefit for fathers can be emphasized. Without it, few mothers can take more than low-paid, part-time employment, and this in turn defines fathers as their families' sole or main breadwinners. This – the primary cause of men's current marginalization within their families – then continues as the predominating constraint on father–child intimacy. Families do not then have a second line of defence against unemployment, and fathers who might like to reduce their working hours cannot even consider this as a possibility. If a divorce occurs, fathers who have played little part at home are unlikely to be viewed sympathetically by the courts, even if their home involvement was limited by dutiful observance of the breadwinner role.

Benefits to Employers

Although offering standard family-friendly benefits does not yet attract men into the workplace (a fair sign that men do not perceive them as being 'for me'), once experienced they inspire in male employees both company loyalty and workplace satisfaction (Families and Work Institute, 1993).

Workplace-based parent education in men-only groups (including 'mentoring' programmes for new fathers) is popular with US fathers, who identify this as a specific need. Such initiatives have proved extremely cost effective (US Personnel Journal, 1992).

Flexibility to balance work and family life through individual scheduling or compressed-week working is highly valued by men. Fifty per cent of UK male white-collar workers want truly flexible working arrangements, and 41 per cent also feel their companies would benefit if they worked flexibly (Austin Knight UK, 1994). The benefits to employers – in terms of reduction in absenteeism, tardiness and employee turnover, together with increased productivity – are similar to those found when such working arrangements are provided for employed mothers (Gonyea and Googins, 1992).

Of particular interest in respect of fathers is that flexible working is especially prized by the 15 per cent of employees ranked as 'high performers' by their companies. These individuals – men as well as women – rate it second only to 'remuneration' as a reason not to leave a company (ibid.).

Father-friendly employment policies deliver diversity in the kinds of men employed. Employers who admit only one kind of male to their teams – the man 'married to the job' – limit their options as surely as if they exclude other groups, such as women. It is now accepted that diversity in work teams delivers competitive advantage; and that 'workaholic' employees are not necessarily the best employees. Men who are successful at work have been found often to retain a surprisingly good work/family balance (Snarey, 1993).

There is empirical support for the desirability of work and family organizations emphasizing both instrumental and affective values. Not only is this, in itself, associated with men's better physical and mental health, but enabling fathers to have more satisfying relationships with their children also helps reduce their stress levels, and can improve both their health and effectiveness at work (Lobel, 1992). And since involved fathers tend to have more satisfying relationships with their partners, it would seem probable that work disturbance due to divorce and other family disruptions will be reduced.

Employers may therefore find it a 'business benefit' to introduce parenting-skills training for male employees. Since many fathers are poorly equipped to relate well to their children and satisfaction in father–child relationships is determined not only by time spent together but by the quality of the interaction, such training may enable fathers to optimize the time they spend with their children, thereby reducing work/family stress, and providing spin-offs in the shape of 'transferable' people skills for use in the workplace (Delong and Delong, 1992).

Employers should also be aware that if they do not provide family-friendly benefits equally to men and women, they may be vulnerable to legal challenge. While the European Council of Ministers' Recommendation on Childcare, adopted by the UK Government in 1992, is not legally binding, it may be taken into account by industrial tribunals – for instance, in the case of a man claiming sex discrimination due to refusal of access to an adoption-leave policy (EOC, 1992).

Reconciling the needs of workers for individual scheduling with the needs of companies for non-standard working can make good business sense. The Australian insurance company, MLC Life, where customer-service teams have been redesigned to accommodate younger workers part-time at university, older people scaling down to retirement, and parents of young children, claims this has also improved customer service and has increased customer satisfaction (Clarke, 1994).

When father-friendly policies are approached in the right way, they can sometimes be adopted company wide with surprising ease. In another Australian firm whose (male) employees expressed a desire for three days of their sick leave to be designated family leave (emergency time off for family reasons), the board were implacably opposed to the idea until they reviewed the results of a pilot study: finding the cost to the company to be marginal, they promptly offered three family leave days on top of sick leave.[4]

Parental Leave

Parental leave is now a major issue for family-friendly employment worldwide. Parental leave (sustained childcare leave) differs from paternity leave (time off at or near the time of the birth) and from family leave (emergency days/hours off for family reasons).

The Parental Leave Directive from the European Union's Council of Ministers allows for a minimum entitlement of three months' non-transferable and continuous parental leave per worker per child. Whether or not parental leave is to be paid is left up to individual member states, but payment, if made, is to come from public funds. This directive was adopted by all member states, with the exception of Britain, in June 1996 under the Agreement on Social Policy (the Social Chapter). With the recent change of government in the UK, the process for applying the EU Parental Leave Directive in this country is expected to be completed before the end of 1997. The government will have to implement it within two years.

Although the last government set its face against statutory provision, parental leave has been entering Britain by a side-door. Due to the Framework Agreement on Parental Leave drawn up between European employers and trade unions, which provides for company workers in multinationals to have similar entitlements wherever in Europe they are employed, some European employers with British operations will have been extending parental leave to their UK workers (European Commission, 1995).

However, parental leave is not per se a father-friendly benefit. In its full-time form and as a benefit to care for infants (which is how it was originally designed), fewer than 3 per cent of fathers take it. Although few 'lay' people understand this, parental leave is often a method of extending or redefining maternity leave (in Sweden, only the six weeks directly before and after birth can be taken as maternity leave; any other leave taken around this time is termed parental leave), and unless parental leave is non-transferable or maternity provision extensive, mothers use it all, usually without discussion and frequently for breast-feeding (Carlsen, 1994).

The reasons for low take-up by fathers are simple: many are unaware of their entitlement; unless the leave is paid at full salary, the loss to the family is substantial; employers are less likely to hire replacement labour for the relatively short time the men are away, so a backlog develops; full-time stay-at-home parenting is more difficult for men than women, because at present local parent support networks are invariably mother based; and men fear that taking leave will negatively impact on their careers (European Commission Network on Childcare, 1994).

The reasons for high take-up of parental leave by mothers are equally straightforward: breast-feeding mothers need sustained time off when their babies are young; the idea of the 'innate' superiority of mother-care over any other kind of care is still being proclaimed; more mothers than fathers find paid work unattractive (they are more likely to be employed below capability and for low wages); fathers are often committed to long and/or erratic working hours, for which mothers are seen as having to cover; and quality, affordable childcare is not universally available.

However, once parental leave is designed with fathers in mind, take-up increases. Two different approaches are currently being tried in Denmark and Sweden, the outcomes of which are being watched with interest throughout Europe.

Denmark has opted for retaining (paid) parental leave as a full-time one-block benefit, observing that fathers who stay 'home alone' with their children for a minimum of three months develop independent relationships with them and remain highly involved after they return to work. Denmark also stands by the 'equality perspective': that full-time leave taken extensively by fathers would help equalize disadvantage in the workplace; or, to put it another way, could help 'change the workplace culture'.

Denmark has now also introduced a 'use it or lose it' 'daddy-month' quota (alongside a 'mummy month' – to avoid equal opportunities' challenge) recognizing that without this many families will not even discuss fathers' participation, and that a non-transferable quota gives men a stronger case when they approach employers: taking parental leave is then seen less as an indulgence, and more as a necessity (Carlsen, 1994).

In Sweden parental leave looks very different. Here it can be taken part-time or in small 'blocks' and beyond the months normally required by mothers for breast-feeding. Take-up by fathers is now running at 40 per cent – a figure which should rise even higher now that a 'daddy-month' quota has been introduced here, too. For some Swedes, parental leave is rapidly becoming a subsidy for reduced-hours working. This is because it can be combined with another family-friendly benefit – the right of parents of pre-school children to work 75 per cent of normal working hours, but with no payment for lost earnings (European Commission Network on Childcare, 1994).

Designing Father-friendly Workplace Policies for Britain

Although the Nordic countries have latterly turned their attention to fathers, the history of family-friendly policy making in these countries reveals what happens when focus is only or mainly on mothers: differences between male and female workers are exacerbated; and the workplace becomes more and more sharply divided by gender. Thus true reconciliation between work and family remains an illusion, and gender roles go unchallenged (ibid.).

It would seem wise, therefore, for Britain to learn from these mistakes and for those whose interest is in family-friendly policy making to seek to nurture and design father-friendly and mother-friendly employment policies side by side, with clear understanding of how and where needs differ and converge.

British trade unions and professional associations, as well as employers, should be encouraged to consider the issue of men and their children, and to work towards a synergistic model in respect of work and family. Negotiators should be made aware of the different kinds of policies which may be attractive to fathers and mothers, and be provided with separate data to support claims for these. Policy development should be accompanied by information campaigns to improve the status of fathers and inform men of their entitlements. In Sweden, a decisive factor in increasing take-up of parental leave by fathers was the 'best dad in the world' campaign run by the Swedish TUC (ibid.).

The need for training requirements – particularly of line managers – if father-friendly policies are to be followed must not be underestimated. Monitoring of take-up is also crucial. Take-up will be more rapid in workplaces where work is organized on a group basis, and where career structures are least individualistic and competitive (Carlsen, 1994). It is important, therefore, that particular attention be paid to promoting and monitoring take-up in hierarchical and competitive career environments.

As far as parental leave policies are concerned, the British government, along with the Confederation of British Industry, has so far taken a non-interventionist and isolationist stance. This position is no longer tenable. If leave is not statutory, then individuals desiring leave will work for those bound to offer it (e.g. the large European employers), who will then find provision prohibitively expensive (Rapoport and Moss, 1990).

Furthermore, declaring – as the government has done in its response to Article 6 of the European Recommendation on Childcare (which refers to the sharing of responsibilities between men and women) that 'each family must decide what is best for them and their children' – ignores the fact that families can only make positive choices within the context of supportive legislation and policy. It should also be pointed out that the British government has agreed all the European Union Recommendation Articles – including Article 6 (Balls, 1996).

For paternity leave – time off at the birth of a child – the first goal should be five days at full pay. Statutory, paid paternity leave is important as a signal to men that their relationship with their children is of value. If holiday leave is used, this limits the already limited time fathers have available to spend with their babies. The cost to employers would be negligible (Equal Opportunities Review, 1994). Within five years, the entitlement should be ten working days fully paid per child.

For family leave – time off to accommodate family emergencies – the first demand should be for three days paid leave per year per child per worker, together with an entitlement to use three days of the parent's own sick leave. Fathers-to-be should be permitted to use this leave for antenatal visits and/or parent education. The goal, again within five years, should be for ten days per child per worker. Where the father is not available, the mother should be entitled to appoint a co-carer, but non-resident fathers' participation should be strongly encouraged.

For parental leave – sustained time off to care for children – the initial demand should be three months per worker per child, unpaid at the outset, but within ten years fully paid. Attention must be paid to the relationship between parental leave and maternity leave. It is our opinion that the Swedish system of specifying maternity leave as a leave to cope only with the demands of late pregnancy and recovery from birth is appropriate. The Swedish system allows for six weeks' maternity leave before and after the birth, outside of which parental leave is taken, and this seems to permit maximum flexibility to include fathers without penalizing mothers.

Introducing such a programme in Britain would require skilled nego-tiation and detailed evaluation at each stage. As an interim measure, and before full parental leave entitlements are in place, maternity leave should be transferable to the father in the event of maternal illness or death.

In our view, maximum flexibility is necessary if parental leave is to be a viable option for fathers and acceptable to employers, who may absorb in their work teams the 'shortfall' left by a parent working shorter hours more easily than if she or he removes from the workplace entirely.

We therefore support parental leave available in shorter or longer 'blocks', full-time or part-time – 90 per cent, 80 per cent, 70 per cent and so on, for negotiation between employers and employees. The period over which parental leave can be taken should be no less than five years. Special provi-sion must be made in the case of chronic illness or disability, and in respect of lone parents, although again wherever practicable the participation of non-resident parents should be sought.

What is striking about Sweden, where parental leave is both extensive and long established, is that it does not seem to present any major prob-lems to employers. As Rapoport and Moss (1990) have written: 'experi-ence has shown that parental leave is workable . . . initial worries went as it became apparent there are no really big problems . . . Parental leave is predictable and employers get advance notice of an employee taking it. It only affects a small part of the workforce at any one time.'

A recent and comprehensive study published by the US National Bur-eau of Economic Research found that short to moderate periods of leave (whether paid or unpaid, and three months was well within the range) impose no burdens on the economy at all. In fact, the effect is positive, because parental leave enables parents to stay in employment and improve their skill levels (Balls, 1996). Requirements for day-care provision are also reduced. Flow-back to the Exchequer from reduced unemployment also provides savings. And when parental leave is taken part-time or in short blocks, its impact is often absorbed by other workers within a section with relatively little difficulty and no extra expense to the company.

The same applies to emergency family leave. Furthermore, when this is made an entitlement, it does not necessarily result in workers spending more time away from the workplace; when granted family leave, they take fewer 'sick' or unauthorized leave periods. And when they return to work, their supervisors often report increased productivity (Families and Work Institute, 1993).

Although in Britain a great deal of noise is made about 'core' workers being overstretched and being unable to take time off, much long-hours working is seen to be a result of poor work organization (and to result in lowered productivity). Only 17 per cent of workers ascribe their last advancement to the hours they put in, and 'presentism' (workers being required to be seen at work, even when there is nothing substantial to be done) is widespread (Institute of Management, 1993; Austin Knight UK, 1994). There is undoubtedly scope for reorganization to accommodate the needs of parents – fathers as well as mothers – without imposing significant burdens on industry.

Future Possibilities

While we are well aware that individuals have caring responsibilities throughout their lives, we would place priority on the relationship between parent and child during the early years. Children are especially vulnerable to carer turnover during the first two and a half years of life, and parents should be assisted to be major (though not necessarily exclusive) carers during this time. It may be that, since parenting skills are best learned by parents together at the outset, a month's paternity leave will ultimately be considered appropriate – to include parent education and training.

It is our hope that, ultimately, both parents should be enabled to work less than full-time hours while their children are young, and/or structure their working lives in order to develop and maintain satisfying family relationships while simultaneously retaining substantial contact with the labour market. Most families today exist on one and a half salaries, built out of one full-time salary and one half-time salary. There is no reason why, in many cases, the same family wage should not be constructed from two three-quarter salaries (Hewitt, 1993).

It seems likely that as job losses due to the information revolution continue, and as women become more entrenched in the workplace, family services will be increasingly professionalized, and employers will be encouraged – possibly via financial incentives – to share work more thinly among more people. This could provide a unique opportunity for parents' and children's needs to be taken into account, for family-friendly policies to have meaning for both sexes, for people's lives to be allowed to develop in richer and more diverse ways, and for unemployment to be reduced.

Here, government will need to play a strategic role, ensuring the development of an infrastructure of affordable, quality childcare; monitoring trends; stimulating public debate; defining and prioritizing policy objectives; setting a timetable for these – and implementing them. Pilot programmes to explore the impact of family-friendly working should be established, with data on men and women listed separately. Possible topics for research include the impact of family-supportive leave policies; projects to challenge long-hours working; reconciliation of the needs of employers and employees involved in 'non-standard' working; and 'time-bank' initiatives.

At an early stage, a feasibility study should be undertaken to establish the real cost of paid parental leave, taking into account the potential for savings in unemployment benefit, when workers on leave are replaced by unemployed workers. In Belgium a career-break system has been introduced specifically to reduce unemployment, with an estimated possible net reduction in public expenditure of BF 7.85 billion in 1992 (European Commission Network on Childcare, 1994).

Britain will not be taking such initiatives alone. Throughout the world, programmes to facilitate the reconciling of work and family are under way. And while, in any country, radical redesign of the relationship between paid and unpaid work requires a positive partnership between government, employers and trade unions, we feel that there is much that can be done immediately – by individuals.

Men have a long tradition of 'covering' for each other at work – making time available for commitments to trade unions and professional organizations, sports and the Territorial Army, and facilitating 'moonlighting' or second jobs. A relatively slight culture change could enable that flexibility to be extended to men in their role as fathers.

Until recently the gold standard against which fathering has been measured – and by which it must inevitably fail – has been mothers' full-time involvement with their children at home. But as working mothers become more and more visible, a new blueprint is emerging and it is becoming plain that it is not necessary to be a full-time parent to develop profound and satisfying relationships with your children.

Even mothers who work exceedingly long hours rarely spend less than an hour on a (working) day interacting intensively with their children. They struggle to get home in time and resist 'switching off' when they walk in through the front door – not because they love or value their children more than fathers, but because they value themselves at home, because they believe their contribution there to be of the highest importance. When fathers hold that belief too, much will be achieved.

Notes

1 For critical review see Lamb and Oppenheim (1989).
2 Figures [here and in the two preceding paragraphs] supplied by the European Commission Network on Childcare.
3 [Figures supplied by the] European Commission Network on Childcare.
4 Graeme Russell, Macquarie University, Melbourne, personal communication, 1994.

References

All Party Parliamentary Group on Parenting (1994) Report of the All Party Parliamentary Group on Parenting. London: HMSO.

Andrews, S.A. and Bailyn, L. (1993) Segmentation and synergy. In J.C. Hood (ed.), *Men Work and Family*, Beverly Hills: Sage.

Austin Knight UK (1994) *The Family Friendly Workplace: An Investigation into Long Hours Culture and Family Friendly Employment Practices*. London: Austin Knight UK.

Balls, E. (1996) New man faces up to parental leave dilemma. *Guardian*, 16 February.

Biller, B. (1993) *Fathers and Families: Paternal Factors in Child Development*. New York: Auburn House.

Bittman, M. (1995) Changes at the heart of family households. *Family Matters*, 10, Autumn.

Bjornberg, U. (1994) Family orientation among men. In J. Brannen and M. O'Brien (eds), *Childhood and Parenthood: Proceedings of an International Conference*, London: Institute of Education.

Carlsen, S. (1994) Men's utilisation of paternity and parental leave schemes. In S. Carlsen and J.E. Larsen, *The Equality Dilemma*, Copenhagen: Munksgaard International.

Catalyst (1983) Human factors in relocation. New York: Catalyst.

Clarke, D. (1994) Family-friendly employment: the business perspective. Paper delivered at the Balancing the Partnership conference, Work and Family Unit, Commonwealth Department of Industrial Relations, Canberra.

Clift, C. and Fielding, D. (1991) *The Balance of Power*. London: Lowe Howard Spink.

Coote, A., Harman, H. and Hewitt, P. (1990) *The Family Way*. London: IPPR.

Cowan, C.P. (1988) Working with men becoming fathers: the impact of a couples group intervention. In P. Bronstein and C.P. Cowan, *Fatherhood Today: Men's Changing Role in the Family*, Chichester: Wiley.

Delong, T.J. and Delong, C.C. (1992) Managers as fathers: hope on the home front. *Human Resource Management*, 31 (3).

EOC (1992) *Guidance Note on the European Council Recommendation on Childcare*. Manchester: EOC.

Equal Opportunities Review (1994) Paternity leave. *Equal Opportunities Review*, 55 (24), May/June.

Eurobarometer (1993) *Europeans and the Family*. Brussels: European Commission (DGV).

European Commission (1995) Framework agreement on parental leave. 14 December. Brussels: European Commission.

European Commission Network on Childcare (1994) Leave arrangements for workers with children. Brussels: European Commission Directorate-General V.

Families and Work Institute (1993) *An Evaluation of Johnson and Johnson's Work/Family Initiative*. New York: Families and Work Institute.

Gbrich, C. (1987) Primary caregiver fathers: a role study, some preliminary findings. *Australian Journal of Sex, Marriage and Family*, 8 (2).

Gonyea, J.G. and Googins, B.K. (1992) Linking the worlds of work and family. *Human Resource Management*, 31 (3).

Hewitt, P. (1993) *About Time*. London: Rivers Oram/IPPR.

Income Data Services (1995) *Maternity and Parental Leave*. Income Data Services Study 578. Income Data Services.

Institute of Management (1993) *Managers Under Stress: A Survey of Management Morale in the 90s*. London: Institute of Management.

IRS Employment Trends (1995) Happy families. *IRS Employment Trends*, 593.

Jalmert, L. (1990) *Increasing Men's Involvement as Fathers in the Care of Children: Some Gains and Some Obstacles*. Stockholm: Department of Education, Stockholm University.

Jowell, R., Brook, L., Prior, G. and Taylor, B. (1992) *British Social Attitudes*. 9th Report. Aldershot: Dartmouth.

Lamb, M.E. and Oppenheim, D. (1989) Fatherhood and father–child relationships: five years of research. In S.H. Cath, A. Gurwitta and L. Gunsberg (eds), *Fathers and their Families*, Hillsdale NJ: Analytic Press.

Levine, J.A. (1994) Daddy-stress. *Child*, June/July.

Lewis, C. (1986) *Becoming a Father*. Milton Keynes: Open University Press.

Lewis, C. (1996) Fathers and preschoolers. In M.E. Lamb (ed.), *The Role of the Father in Child Development*, 3rd edn, Chichester: Wiley.

Lobel, S.A. (1992) A value-laden approach to integrating work and family life. *Human Resource Management*, 31 (3).

Mintel International (1994) Men 2000. London: Mintel International Group.

Nasman, E. (1991) Parental leave in Sweden: a workplace issue. Stockholm Research Reports in Demography No. 73, Stockholm University.

New Ways to Work (1995) *Balanced Lives: Changing Work Patterns for Men*. London: New Ways to Work.

Niemi, I. (1995) A general view of time use by gender. In I. Niemi (ed.), *Time Use of Women in Europe and North America*, New York: United Nations.

Ochiltree, G. (1994) *Effects of Child Care on Young Children: Forty Years of Research*. Melbourne: Australian Institute of Family Studies.

Pleck, J.H. (1993) Are 'family supportive' employer policies relevant to men? In J.C. Hood (ed.), *Men Work and Family*, Beverly Hills: Sage.

Purves, L. (1989) Fathers of the future? *The Times*, 27 October.

Rapoport, R. and Moss, P. (1990) *Men and Women as Equals at Work.* London: Thomas Coram Institute.

Rodgers, C.S. (1992) The flexible workplace: what have we learned? *Human Resource Management*, 31 (3).

Sly, F. (1994) Mothers in the labour market. *Employment Gazette*, November.

Snarey, J.R. (1993) *How Fathers Father the Next Generation.* Cambridge MA: Harvard University Press.

Study Commission on the Family (1983) Families in the future: a policy agenda for the 1980s. London: Study Commission on the Family.

US Personnel Journal (1992) Work/family ideas. *US Personnel Journal*, October.

8

Act Local: Social Justice from the Bottom Up

DAVID DONNISON

The Machinery of Social Injustice

The processes which together lead towards greater inequality and hardship are well known but rarely put together in a way which shows how they interlock. Stated very briefly, these are the seven main elements in the story – the working parts of the injustice machine. They are not separate influences; they are different dimensions or patterns of injustice, each of which has many causes. By distinguishing them we make it easier to explore these causes and to start thinking about solutions. By linking them together we are reminded that they interact with each other, and that none of them can be reversed if it is tackled in isolation from the others.

(a) Economic trends

Once a country has passed through the first phases of industrialization and urbanization, its distributions of incomes and of wealth – very unequal at that stage – usually begin to grow slowly more equal. That basic trend is reinforced by the growth of trade unions and democracy, which in time help to protect workers from exploitation and to create social benefits and taxes which together redistribute incomes over people's lives, providing help in childhood, early parenthood and old age, and during periods of sickness and unemployment.

All that has changed. Since 1972, in most of the richer capitalist countries the basic distribution of incomes, before taking account of taxes and benefits, has been growing more unequal. The upper half of the labour force has continued to make fairly good progress, but the wages of the lower third have fallen further and further behind the nations' averages. Unemployment has risen through successive cycles which proceed with a ratchet effect, so that each downswing in the economy sees the numbers out of work rising from a higher base level than that achieved in the previous boom. Over these years, growing proportions of the unemployed have been out of work for a very long time. Since employers scarcely ever hire workers who have been out of work for more than a year, these people have, in effect, been excluded from the labour force. Non-workers are, for many purposes, 'non-persons'. Men feel this particularly keenly. In a society where so much of the citizens' self-confidence, status, credit-worthiness, pension rights and other social benefits depend on their position in the labour force, many feel that this exclusion is a sentence of social death. Suicide rates for males rise steeply as unemployment extends.

The spread of new technologies, the gradual integration of the world economy and the reorganizations of industry which those changes have brought about are the main (but not the only) causes of these trends. They are replacing predominantly male, full-time, manufacturing work with predominantly female, white-collar work in service industries, much of it temporary and/or part-time. As the European and world economies become increasingly integrated, these basic economic trends will go a lot further. They have been well summarized by Edward Balls and Paul Gregg (1993).

That is only the beginning of the story. These trends are mediated and exacerbated by other influences which interact with each other. We distinguish three of them.

(b) Household and family patterns

People are not just workers. They live in households (even if those consist only of one person) and they rely on support from their families. For various reasons, the better jobs, housing, health and other good things which many people have secured tend to be concentrated in the same families and households. Meanwhile unemployment, homelessness, deteriorating health and other bad things tend to concentrate in other families and households. We have more households than hitherto with several earners, and more with none; more living in excellent housing and more who are homeless; more young people going to universities, and more who drop out of schools as failures – and we know that educational attainment depends heavily on the support which students gain from their families. Meanwhile the differences in the life expectancies of the upper and lower social classes continue to widen, and these differences are real – not a statistical accident arising from the changing numbers in different social classes, or the tendency of healthy and unhealthy people to rise and fall in the social scale.

Those who have borne the brunt of this growing inequality have been families with children: three overlapping groups of them – low-paid workers, the unemployed, and lone parents. Although there are single, childless and elderly people who are having a hard time too, most of them have continued to make reasonably good progress in relation to the living standards of the average citizen.

These are trends which threaten everyone. The growing stresses borne by children and young people ultimately damage all of us. It is on their future health, skills, productivity and tax-paying capacity that everyone else's pensions and tax burdens will depend, just as their civility and willingness to abide by the law will affect everyone else's safety and peace of mind.

(c) Divided neighbourhoods

Households do not live by themselves; they are based in a neighbourhood of some sort, and the poorer and more vulnerable of them rarely venture far from home: the 'city' actually inhabited by these people is often no more than a tiny patch of the place named on the maps. For various reasons, the growing good and bad fortune experienced by different families has become increasingly concentrated in different areas. Markets work that way; and the administered marketplace of social rented housing too often works that way too. Neighbourhoods in which deprivation has been increasingly severe and widespread have become a problem in their own right – their citizens so excluded that even if we 'get the economy right' and return to high levels of employment, special steps will be needed to help them find a way back into the mainstream.

Being poor in a poor neighbourhood is worse than poverty which is more thinly scattered among richer people: there are fewer opportunities for work, the streets are more dangerous, the air more polluted, the junk shops and jumble sales less well stocked, it is harder to get your property insured, to get credit or to get shortlisted for a job. Even the tomatoes in the shops cost more.

(d) Political power

The poverty of those who suffer these hardships arises from inequality, which is exacerbated in many ways by the powerlessness which is its most fundamental feature. Whether deliberately or by unthinking neglect, public policy and commercial practice further penalize the poor. Those political effects operate in complex ways at all scales and call for a fuller explanation.

These influences can be seen at the global level. We know who is likely to benefit most from the free-trade agreements being negotiated through NAFTA and GATT; we have seen the social priorities which the IMF imposes on Third World countries.

Similar patterns can be seen at the national level. In Britain, massive changes have been made in taxes and in social benefits in the 1980s and early 1990s, and both have generally penalized the poor and rewarded the rich. Some have calculated that most of the sharp increase in inequality which has occurred since 1985 is due to changes in taxes and benefits – due, that is to say, to political decisions. Even changes originating in the labour market have their political origins. We have been told by a previous chancellor of the exchequer that unemployment is 'a price well worth paying' to beat inflation. That was a political, not a technical, statement: governments pay a lower political price if they can solve the nation's problems at the expense of the unemployed. But the 'problems' in question are caused by the excessive wage increases, the inadequate productivity, the excessive expenditure on imported goods and the inadequate savings of those who are still in work.

Similar political influences operate at local and neighbourhood levels. When schools close it is those used by the poorest families which usually go first; bus services to town centres are often more frequent and fares lower from the leafiest suburbs than from bleak housing estates with poor local services and few cars.

The political powerlessness of the poor is not inevitable. Poor blacks in the USA and South Africa, poor Arabs in Palestine, Polish workers in the shipyards of Gdansk have all shown that this need not be the unalterable order of things. But the changes which they have brought about were not achieved overnight: they called for long years of thought, organization and education, and much suffering; also – we should be warned – a good deal of violence.

It has always been the case that those who do best in commercial marketplaces tend also to do best in the administered marketplaces of the state, getting their children into the better schools and the more expensive courses, getting more subsidies for the recreations (opera, for example) which they enjoy, keeping the motorways out of their neighbourhoods, and so forth. But in recent years more profound political forces have been at work.

For the best part of a century, the ruling classes in capitalist societies knew they lived under threat. Before World War I these threats came from political turbulence which might have turned to revolution – and did, across much of Central and Eastern Europe, a few years later. Then there followed the war itself, which could only be won if working-class people could be persuaded to suffer and die in their millions to defend the regime. After that there was renewed turbulence, leading in many places to fascism; then a new war, and yet another generation of militant ex-servicemen, the threat of economic and social chaos, and always – across the German frontiers – the millions of men under arms in the Soviet bloc.

Suddenly, at the end of the 1980s, all that changed. It was not that capitalism had solved the world's problems. Despite its many achievements, growing unemployment, pollution and disorder make it clear that it is failing, and now threatens to destroy the whole planet. But for the first time since the beginning of the century capitalism was no longer under threat . . . Working conditions, security of employment and fringe benefits for those in the lower reaches of the labour market have been eroded. This happened first and most aggressively in Britain, but similar trends are now to be seen in many other countries – even in Sweden, long the exemplar of democratic socialism. That means that action to rebuild social protection and more civilized human relationships will have to be taken on an international scale: otherwise, any country taking an initiative will fear that it will be undercut by competitors elsewhere.

Meanwhile, at the top, greed has been unbridled: senior managers, who have already been given huge reductions in tax, award themselves vast increases in pay, almost without regard to the success of their (frequently failing) enterprises.

Recently, even the head of the CBI and the chancellor of the exchequer have been moved to protest at their rapacity: but not to do anything about it. In more anxious times, public opinion among the nation's elites would have held such greed in check. No longer.

(e) Hardship

These patterns do not account for all the influences at work, but they bring us to the central stage of the processes, the growing hardship experienced by poorer people – particularly among families with dependent children. It could also be called inequality, social injustice or stress; but hardship seems the best description. In Britain, the outcomes of these growing hardships are now appalling . . .

A good deal can be done to sharpen or soften these hardships. The growing numbers of local authorities now developing anti-poverty strategies show that many believe something has to be done at the local scale.

They often begin by offering concessions for people with low incomes on public transport and at swimming baths, support for credit unions in deprived areas, more help for the homeless and so on. But to make much impact these priorities have to be built into mainstream services and to tackle other phases of the processes which create social injustice ...

The impact of these hardships and how people respond to them depend on two other groups of factors.

(f) Character of the community

First we have to ask, who are the people involved? If there are lots of old people in a poverty-stricken area they will not be tearing around in stolen cars 'ram raiding' the shops; but there will probably be more loneliness and isolation, and more diseases related to cold and damp than will be found elsewhere. If there are many lone parents in the area, there will probably be more depression, more diseases related to smoking, more children showing difficult behaviour in school, and more minor social security frauds and shoplifting than elsewhere. If there are lots of young males there will probably be more homelessness, more people using drugs and dealing in them, and more crime of many kinds. But all these patterns change. The youngsters become parents and eventually grow old; people move in and out of the area, which may become 'gentrified' or may decline into deprivation, decay and disorder.

We also have to ask, how long do people stay in the area, and why do they leave? And what does the rest of the community think of the area? If people no longer know who their neighbours are because they change so often and many flats are left empty or taken over by squatters, then civility, order and a sense of social responsibility inevitably decay. If the rest of the city regards the area as notorious for these things, that encourages its more successful citizens to escape from it.

(g) Responses to hardship

Even when all six of the influences so far identified have been taken into account, we still do not have an equation which produces a unique, predictable outcome. Some communities have a tradition which fosters capacities for collective action and protest. Others have no such experience; or they have for too long relied on a paternalistic regime; or they are too deeply divided by race or religion to work together. Each place is different.

Individually and collectively, people learn, and relearn, to respond in different ways to hardship. They may, at worst, be completely apathetic. They may clamber out of apathy into a state of depression – feeling and resenting pain, but unable to do much about it. The route out of depression usually leads through anger: for a while they become quite difficult to deal with, but the prospects are more hopeful. From there they may move either into delinquency – which at least shows a capacity to assert themselves and take their fate into their own hands for a while – or into collective action and protest. It may be difficult to distinguish between these responses. (When tenants of Manchester City Council threw bags of cockroaches from their infested flats across the counters of the housing office, whether that was called delinquency or protest depended on which side of the counter one stood.) If protests are taken seriously and prove effective and if the protesters learn to negotiate successfully with power holders, they may then become very creative. This is when housing co-operatives and credit unions are formed, drama groups and youth clubs flourish and new enterprises are founded. People are gaining confidence, and learning to make friends, to work together and support each other.

That is the optimistic scenario. But if the protests of those who suffer injustice are brushed off and they are humiliated and neglected, if the turnover of tenancies rises so that all sense of community is destroyed, then the same people may be driven back through helpless anger to cynicism and apathy. Like all human relationships, these are in a continuing state of evolution: if they are not getting better, they are probably getting worse. 'He not busy being born is busy dying' sang Bob Dylan.

Which of these routes is followed depends heavily upon the ways in which public authorities deal with the communities concerned. In the short run, these authorities will often feel that depression and apathy are easier to handle than protest and creativity. More people may escape from their plight into addiction to alcohol or drugs, into mental breakdown or imprisonment, but politicians and officials will spend less time coping with anger in turbulent meetings and in lengthy negotiation about decisions which they have been accustomed to take without consulting anyone.

What Can Be Done at a Local Scale

'Civic leaders' is a deliberately vague term. Here it means a group of people who have a lasting commitment to their 'place' – be it village, town or county. They have a vision of its future, and a capacity to work with each other, with the private sector, with community groups and with higher levels of government to bring that future about. Conflict there is bound to be. Their task is not to suppress it but to manage it in reasonably constructive ways for the sake of their place and its citizens.

Some places have such a group; others do not. Various people may play a part in it. In the United States an elected mayor and leading business people often play central roles. In many of the continental countries of the European Union the leaders of the political parties which have gained a majority of council seats and their senior officials play central roles. In Ireland the bishop and some of his clergy will usually be key figures. It is the role, rather than the specific members of the cast, which is important.

So what can be done at a local scale to arrest and reverse the deepening division of Britain, which is excluding growing numbers of people from opportunities available to those in the mainstream of this society? Books could be written to answer that question. Here we must confine ourselves to the main points which should appear in that answer...

(a) Strategies for economic regeneration

People working in cities stricken by worldwide economic trends cannot isolate themselves from the infection and reverse those trends. But, in collaboration with colleagues speaking for other cities with similar problems, civic leaders can press national and international authorities to give higher priority to that task. Meanwhile, with help from the private sector and higher levels of government, they can over a period of years do a great deal to reorganize a city's economy, to prepare it to take advantage of new opportunities, developing new industries as old ones die and training people who will need new skills to work in them.

In Britain the main instruments for achieving that lie outside local government in the TECs [Training and Enterprise Councils], the development agencies appointed by central government, the local universities and the private sector. Civic leaders, who may be found in all these agencies, have to work together on behalf of their city, county or region. Leading councillors elected to represent the area can speak with greater authority than anyone else on these matters.

Economic regeneration does not depend only on construction work. People have become rightly suspicious of property-led strategies for renewal which collapse when property prices fall; but where more houses are needed or old ones need renewal, that investment can make a significant contribution to wider economic development, particularly where it helps to attract or to retain a resident population. When the construction phase is over, a resident population of 1,000 people generates demands for about

400 jobs in public and commercial services – more in richer neighbour-hoods, less in poorer – ranging from doctors and teachers to bus crews and hairdressers. But those demands need to be foreseen and workers need to be trained to meet them.

We have frequently been told that employers, even when funded by public money, cannot be pressed to train or hire those whose employment is likely to benefit the whole community. Yet policies of this kind have in many places been successfully adopted. There is clearly a need for civic leaders to consult their counterparts in other cities and to learn from each other's experience.

Culture and the arts have become industries in themselves, capable of employing large numbers of workers, and engaging people from all classes and ethnic communities. But probably more important than this direct impact is the indirect influence which these resources have on the city's worldwide image and its capacity to attract people who, previously, might not have contemplated living and working there. Enterprises which are growing (including corporate bodies like hospitals, universities and broad-casting companies) have to recruit skilled staff, patients, students and other people who have a good deal of choice about where they go. The reputa-tion of the city for security, civility, education and culture plays a signi-ficant part in their decisions. These lifestyle factors help to shape a city's future.

Most major local authorities now have strategies of some sort for eco-nomic and cultural development, but whether the more excluded people gain much from them will depend on civic leaders' determination to develop opportunities for them to do so, and to provide the kinds of education, training, childcare and other services which they will need for that purpose. There are now enough constructive examples of that kind to give civic leaders everywhere some encouragement.

Strategies for extending opportunities for work and training will not develop successfully unless they become the responsibility of special units, located close to the centres of civic power and with strong links to the private sector. The TECs, the urban development corporations, the city challenge projects and other initiatives launched by the central government have important parts to play, but none of them is concerned with a whole city – still less with its more disadvantaged people. Every major local authority needs an economic development unit of some kind, but it has to deal with a labour market which extends beyond the authority's bound-aries. It must therefore operate within a regional framework and in close collaboration with neighbouring authorities.

In future, major local authorities should be required to formulate an employment policy. This would be prepared in consultation with groups representing women, ethnic minorities, people with disabilities and people out of work, and would produce plans to meet identified needs, together with the training and employment required for these purposes. Temporary employment for people coming out of training schemes has been so often abused by employers who use it to save them the costs of offering long-term jobs: it should therefore be abolished or replaced by longer contracts.

The contracting out to commercial and voluntary agencies of a growing amount of work previously done, in-house, by public services is creating in some areas what one of the trade union participants in a Warwick University seminar described as a 'casualized industrial peasantry' of under-paid, exploited staff. Trade unions and public services should, between them, insist that contractors, and any major employer seeking public support, adhere to minimum standards of performance which protect staff as well as service users. These are complimentary, not contradictory, obligations. To reduce staff complements, rates of pay and security of employment in homes caring for frail and elderly people – a development we have witnessed – is bound in time to lead to a deterioration in standards of care.

If citizens are to secure good opportunities in an attractive place, without massive costs, then 'green' priorities and 'justice' priorities will have to be carefully meshed. That is more likely to be achieved if older houses can be rehabilitated rather than replaced, if improved insulation and heating systems ensure that they provide affordable warmth, if older towns can be made nice enough to attract and retain people rather than dispersing them to distant suburbs, and if investment in public transport takes priority over investment in roads. That will call for strategic planning which reconciles both priorities. Neither unregulated private enterprise nor independent housing, energy and transport agencies will achieve that.

Places experiencing economic decline contain large numbers of people for whom job opportunities are – for the moment at least – of little inter-est: the retired, the sick, lone parents and others who wish to devote their full time to caring for others. These people will benefit far more from an efficient and aggressive welfare rights service which helps them to get the benefits they are entitled to. With a little training, these same people can make very effective welfare rights workers. Since people with low incomes are likely to spend a high proportion of what little they have on goods and services produced not far away, getting benefits for them will help every-one else living in the same place. A good welfare rights service is rooted in good case work, but it does far more. By monitoring poverty, the take-up of benefits, and the impact of tax and benefit changes on local people, it enables civic leaders to speak with greater authority on behalf of their city to the media and higher levels of government.

(b) Helping families and young people

There are several reasons why deprivations of various kinds tend to concentrate in the same families and households. In our present culture, the psychodynamics of family relations make it difficult for many couples to tolerate a reversal of roles which makes the man a 'house-husband' and his wife the breadwinner. In countries like Britain, which support their unemployed mainly with social assistance payments based on a household means test, no one in the household has much incentive to work unless they can earn enough to lift the whole household above the social assistance level. At lower rates of pay their earnings are deducted from social assistance payments and they find themselves, in effect, working for the state. This is why the growing numbers of low-paid, insecure jobs offered to women tend to be taken by those who already have a full-time earner in the household. Lone parents are in a particularly difficult position, and more likely than any other kind of household to be in poverty.

Policies for the family should reflect the experience of women contending with these difficulties, and of ethnic minorities, who often include many households with young children. If women and ethnic minorities are not already well represented on the council, they should be; but there are various other ways in which they can gain a voice in public debate. Experience shows that they are likely to give high priority to education and training for themselves and their families, and to childcare arrangements which enable them to use these opportunities. They will also want decent, accessible housing with economical heating systems, safe play spaces for children, and security of tenure. A social security system which does not imprison people in poverty traps is likely to be another high priority, but that has to be created by the central government.

Exactly the same points need to be made on behalf of young people, who, if taken seriously and given opportunities to develop their own projects, have so much to offer. If ill-trained, unemployed and neglected, they become outlaws provoking fear and hostility.

Without adequate services of the basic kinds for everyone, special provision for people with special needs will provoke opposition from the rest of the electorate. The poorest people always tend to be the losers in conflicts of that kind. Already in the early 1990s, the Conservative government is reducing the rights of homeless families because, with growing shortages of affordable housing, their needs are said to conflict increasingly with those of ordinary families on the waiting lists.

New forms of evaluation and social accounting should be developed to help in planning and evaluating these policies. It is now widely known, for example, that policies which open up opportunities for people suffering from discrimination, coupled with investment in good pre-school education and support for the most vulnerable families, eventually repay society many times over in higher employment levels and tax payments among the families affected, lower demands on social security, health and police services, and less incarceration in prisons and hospitals. But these pay-offs take a long time to reveal themselves and then benefit other services, not those which made the original investment.

(c) Renewing impoverished neighbourhoods

The processes which create great concentrations of poverty in particular neighbourhoods arise partly from the failings of past urban policies: the building of poorly serviced public housing estates with few jobs within easy reach, the concentration in these places of many people who are having a hard time – the homeless, lone parents, people coming out of prisons and long-stay hospital care – and from failures to maintain buildings and their surrounding environment. Together, these can lead to high turnover, squatting, vandalism and the erosion of constraints on behaviour maintained by more stable communities.

Now that by deliberate policies the UK has created a public sector of the housing market which, in many cities, consists largely of people living on state benefits, any big housing estate is likely to be a poverty-stricken neighbourhood. Thus special steps must be taken to improve local opportunities, to diversify housing and tenures and to integrate these communities more closely into the rest of the city.

Meanwhile there remain inner-city areas of run-down housing, public and private, owner-occupied and rented, which have been badly neglected. They may offer a first foothold in the housing market for recently arrived migrants, together with cheap business premises for people starting their own enterprises. If they are to be renewed and diversified without damaging vulnerable people, local residents have to be actively involved in planning for these areas.

This kind of social polarization and segregation would not be allowed to happen if it did not, at least in some respects, suit powerful people quite well. Housing managers may find it useful to have a 'Siberia' in which space can always be found for people with urgent needs, and which also serves as a kind of punishment camp for poor rent payers and troublesome tenants. Police chiefs, who know they cannot eliminate drug traffickers, may find it convenient to concentrate the trade in a low-status area where they can keep an eye on it and middle-class citizens will not be disturbed. As the populations of economically failing cities decline, those responsible for health and education services have to find hospitals and schools which can be closed without politically damaging protests. Planners need reserve supplies of land and buildings which can be brought forward for redevelopment or neglected till they are required. Meanwhile powerless people and their children have to live out their lives in these landscapes of despair.

It follows that purely technical or commercial solutions will not work. Initiatives which are to put these things right must be launched by political leaders who have the authority to change public priorities and focus resources in new and sustained ways on such areas. They will need support from central government and the national tax payer – a point we return to below. If the area to be renewed is a large one, it will need a local committee or agency capable of pulling together the efforts of the private sector and the many different public services operating there, and gaining support from local community groups and the central government. Women, people with disabilities and the varied ethnic groups often found in such areas must gain a voice in the project. There are encouraging examples of such initiatives led by local authorities and the central government. No single formula can be guaranteed to work: success depends on the people involved.

Local residents must be given an independent voice in the formulation of priorities through some association or an umbrella group speaking for existing associations, with resources which enable them to hire their own staff and to own some of the initiatives and enterprises that will be set up. Again, we have seen encouraging examples of this kind.

The private sector has an interest in the social and economic regeneration of deprived areas – an interest best carried forward by focusing on particular places in collaboration with local authorities and community groups, as Scottish Business in the Community has tried to do, not riding roughshod over local people in pursuit of killings in a fickle property market.

Local needs, resources and traditions differ, even in areas which appear uniformly deprived. In some, people will give first priority to housing (as in Manchester's Hulme estate); in others it will be jobs and training (as in Moss Side, next door), or culture and celebration (as in the early days on Edinburgh's Craigmillar estate, and, on a larger scale, in (London) Derry), or economic opportunities coupled with the reduction of violence and crime (as in Glasgow's Barrowfield estate). Given time and some support, people will usually take up all these issues – together with welfare rights, childcare, mental health and other issues.

The flexible way in which the government has sought bids for public funds from the new Single Regeneration Budget shows that this lesson is being learned. The broad objectives are clear, but the initiators of such projects and their first priorities are expected to vary from place to place.

Political action will be needed to ensure that the public services which have to respond to these demands work effectively together for neighbourhoods with special needs. Left to themselves, each agency will usually retain a different pattern of area management, making it impossible for their staff even to talk about – let alone act for – the same area. If regeneration projects focused on areas with special needs are not just to sweep social problems around the urban map, their priorities have to be built into the operations of mainstream services in ways which will prevent the emergence of new problem areas as soon as old ones are improved. Areas entitled to priority treatment need to be agreed by all services, and their requirements built into the priorities of education, health, training, housing, planning, transport and other services. That is bound to be difficult at a time when more and more of these services are being contracted out to independent agencies or placed in the hands of semi-independent quangos. Local politicians, securely based in the communities which elected them, have greater authority than anyone else to call upon these agencies to adopt priorities of this kind, and to call upon a future Parliament to give civic leaders greater powers to make such priorities effective.

We have stressed the importance of focusing attention on areas with special needs; but, within a framework of that kind, public services must be capable of operating at many different scales. A housing co-operative usually works best when it is small, serving perhaps 200 or 300 households; an urban secondary school needs a much larger catchment area with at least 5,000 people living in it; a modern health centre may serve an area three times as large; and a training and placement programme that is designed to give people the best opportunities for work will serve a region extending beyond even the larger cities. The complex requirements of a strategy which has to operate at these different scales make this a task for civic leaders responsible for a whole city or county.

(d) Opening up the power structure

We are, under this heading, concerned mainly not with party politics, but with broader aspects of the exercise of power, already broached under the previous heading. Yet party politics has a part to play too. Every council needs a lively opposition. Otherwise it may decay into stagnation or be taken over by spokesmen of the public-service unions or the private sector. It will then no longer speak for the community as a whole – and least of all for its most excluded members. Monopolies of any kind are bad news for the poor.

The main conflicts in British society used to divide manual from non-manual workers. These were related to differences in working conditions and pension arrangements, the distribution of income over people's lifetimes, their education, housing conditions and tenure, car ownership and much else. All that has changed. The main social distinctions and conflicts of our society now divide those securely placed in the core of the economy – manual workers, many of them, but with mortgages, cars, occupational pension rights and high educational aspirations – from those on the margins of society who lack many of these things. These are the people sometimes called 'the underclass'. That is a misleading phrase which suggests that they are a distinctive group, and even that their plight is their own fault. In fact their diversity is a major reason for their difficulties. They include some (but never all) members of a wide variety of groups: recent immigrants, pensioners with intermittent work records, older workers with obsolete skills, youngsters who never had a proper job, lone parents, and people with disabilities of various kinds. People move in and out of this 'exclusion zone' and have few lasting, shared interests which link them together.

Those whom Seebohm Rowntree identified as being poor in three classic studies spanning the first half of this century were not excluded from the rest of their society. They were having a hard time at predictable phases of their lives – during childhood, early parenthood and old age; but most of them were firmly rooted in the working class, which created movements that spoke for them and ultimately helped to build a protective welfare state. Labour politics were based on an alliance between these people and the workers recruited to provide the public services they depended on. Today that alliance is falling apart. The excluded are not spoken for by trade unions to which they do not belong, by public-service workers who control the resources on which they depend for survival, or by the movements created for people still securely based in the core of society. For those in the core, unemployment – and many other causes of hardship for the excluded – may be 'the price worth paying' to keep society on the rails.

Government spokesmen have claimed that they are addressing this problem by using market mechanisms, coupled with charters of citizen's rights, to make public services more accountable even to their most vulnerable customers. No one can confidently claim that the old, bureaucratic styles of municipal administration could be relied on to do better. But we have to note the dangers of the new pattern now taking shape. Citizen's rights and charters are unlikely to deal effectively with the plight of the excluded. For a start, the evidence of nationwide surveys shows that they are less likely than most to engage in political action, to protest, to demand their rights or to join organizations which can speak up on their behalf. There are sound reasons for their apathy. Customer's rights are a flimsy weapon for people who have only one landlord to turn to, only one school to which they are entitled to send their children, only one doctor who serves their neighbourhood, and – at best – only one employer who might give them a job.

If the needs of poorer people are the same as those of richer people, others may speak up for them, but we are developing a more divisive system of public services which makes that much less likely than it used to be. Less and less do people stand shoulder to shoulder to demand better services; more and more do they feel compelled to fight their own corner as best they can. That is why the rights of the homeless and the educational opportunities of pupils excluded from school are being eroded; that is why most forms of social security payment have fallen further behind average wages, and why the patients of non-fund-holding general practitioners have to wait longer for a hospital bed than the patients who go to fund-holders.

There is also a more fundamental criticism to be made of the whole charter approach. It offers customer's rights for individuals dissatisfied with the service they receive – because their train was late or their leaking roof took weeks to repair, for example. Useful though those are, they are not the citizen's rights which enable people to question the way in which their society is evolving – to ask for a different kind of transport system, for more public housing or for housing allocated to different kinds of people, for example.

Some people have tried to tackle exclusion head-on by mobilizing and organizing the unemployed or the poor. Others – particularly in some of the New England cities of the United States – have tried to mobilize 'rainbow coalitions' of many excluded groups, together with peace groups, women's groups and the more radical church groups, to formulate common programmes and press mayors and candidates for public offices for action. None of these strategies should be dismissed, but in Britain it has generally proved more effective to mobilize around broader interests which include unemployed and poor people but are not confined to them: tenants' and residents' associations speaking for everyone in their street, disability forums speaking for people with many kinds of disabilities, arts groups offering opportunities for anyone wanting to paint, sculpt, write or act, church groups speaking for a whole parish, ethnic associations speaking for their communities – all these can provide a basis for breaking down exclusion.

New patterns of governance and voluntary action are developing to give hitherto neglected people a voice in local and public affairs, to make public-service staff more directly accountable to them, and to extend genuine rights of citizenship. These initiatives include:

- the creation of voluntary bodies with local branches designed to act as advisors, advocates and pressure groups. Some speak for people with particular needs – like women's refuges, Age Concern and many more. Some, like the tenants' and residents' associations, speak for their neighbourhood or housing estate. Some speak for larger groupings of poor people in general – like the Child Poverty Action Group. Local authorities have found various ways of supporting and responding to these groups.
- the deconcentration or outstationing of public services in smaller, more accessible offices from which a team of staff from different services operate with greater commitment to a local community in which they are better known and more exposed.
- The creation of new, community-owned or at least community-based agencies providing particular services such as the credit unions, and the management and ownership co-operatives which have developed in the housing field. More ambitious development trusts of various kinds have an open brief to develop a wider range of services and enterprises.
- the development of community enterprises, producing and trading like other businesses, but on terms which make them accountable to their local communities while feeding back any profit made into the development of the enterprise or to benefit the community. These can in principle serve any kind of place, but they have made a particularly important contribution in deprived neighbourhoods where they have helped people who have been out of work for a long time to find a way back into the labour market.
- attempts to link up some of these initiatives in ways which begin to create new forms of governance linking providers and users of services in new ways. Some of the more venturesome examples are to be found in Islington's neighbourhood offices, to which active neighbourhood forums of local people are attached, and in Tower Hamlets' neighbourhood councils, which work through neighbourhood offices and smaller 'one-stop shops' in consultation with local tenants' associations. Other authorities are experimenting with similar strategies, sometimes in selected areas of deprivation (as in Glasgow, for example) and sometimes wall-to-wall across their territory (as in Manchester, for example).

As power begins to be handed over at the local scale to community groups it becomes very important to foresee problems of incompetence, dishonesty, discrimination and other abuses of power which may arise, to discuss these frankly with community representatives, to work out agreed methods for monitoring and auditing their operations, and to train them to deal with such matters. There is no magic about 'community': civic leaders have to ensure that the basic tasks of government are still performed.

Critics of community-based projects often complain that they are 'not really representative'. In fact, they are often more representative than municipal councillors are – in the sense of resembling the communities they serve in age, gender, race and so on. But that is not their main purpose. The main questions should be: 'Are they efficient and effective?' and 'Are they accountable?' – to their staff and customers, to their funders and backers, to the law and the community at large. Those questions must be answered at three different levels:

- at the local, day-to-day level: where, for example, do the aggrieved customers and staff of a housing co-operative go if they feel badly treated?
- over a somewhat longer term and larger scale: to whom, for example, can the neighbours appeal if they believe the co-operative is polluting their street or competing unfairly with local enterprises?
- at the larger, city-wide scale: who ensures that the co-operative does not act in racist or financially dishonest ways?

Exactly the same questions must be asked of the growing numbers of quangos appointed by central government to wield great powers at the local level: development agencies, hospital trusts, the Housing Corporation, and so on. Only if accountability can be assured at all these levels will people gain rights, not only as customers concerned with the quality of the services they get, but also as citizens, concerned with the way in which their society is developing. Local councillors empowered to speak for the whole community will have to play a central part in those processes if the poorest people are not to be further excluded.

(e) Easing hardship

This leads us to the central phase of the processes we have traced: the stresses imposed on people who are being excluded from the mainstream of their society – and particularly the hardships of families and young people.

A society can still respond at this stage in ways which ease or exacerbate such hardships. If (as has happened in Britain) lone parents living on income support are placed in flats which no one else will live in because they are impossible to keep warm at a price which people living on low incomes could afford, if the discretionary grants which used to help such people pay for fuel are eliminated and VAT is added to their fuel bills, if the local school is closed and school meals deteriorate, then the hardships of these families grow worse. But none of the policy changes which have exacerbated these hardships were inevitable. Things could instead have been made easier for them.

A similar story can be told about the ways in which social security and housing benefits have been withdrawn from young people between the ages of 16 and 25, while at the same time economic changes were making it harder – in many places impossible – for them to find jobs which confer any sense of the dignity of labour. The rise in homelessness, addiction and crime which has occurred since the mid-1980s was widely predicted. But again, none of these policy changes was inevitable.

Many of the policies suggested by these examples would have to be initiated by central governments, but there is scope too for action to be taken at a local scale. Many municipal and health authorities in Britain are now trying to formulate more systematic anti-poverty policies and the local authorities have set up a National Local Government Forum Against Poverty to help in carrying forward this work.

(f) Rebuilding communities

Much of the action required under this heading has already been outlined. The ways in which deprived communities respond to hardship depend partly on their social composition, and that can be shaped, wittingly or unwittingly, by urban policy. If housing is provided in a place where public and commercial services are poor, the environment is neglected and good jobs are hard to find, then the more successful families will move out to rent or buy a home elsewhere and more hard-pressed people will take their places. If turnover then rises and the sense of community decays, crime and fear are bound to become more widespread. Only a comprehensive, long-term programme of regeneration will arrest this kind of social decay. To provide training and jobs alone will hasten the outflow, enabling some people to pay off their debts and buy their way into better neighbourhoods while others are left in a community even more deprived than before.

(g) Working with the people

People may respond more or less creatively to exclusion and injustice. How they respond will depend heavily on the way in which they are treated by the politicians and officials whom they encounter. For every creative, community-based project there is usually at least one support worker, chosen by the community but paid from public funds, and, somewhere in the background, at least one supportive official, empowered to devote a lot of time to helping the activists, with the backing of local politicians.

Too often, official initiatives to renew and regenerate stricken parts of a city's economy are launched, and then local people are asked to participate in them – quickly. The procedures decreed for estate action and city challenge projects permit no other approach. It rarely works well. Individuals and communities lying fairly close to the bottom of the scale we outlined which runs from apathy to creativity will be suspicious of invitations to 'consult' and 'participate'. They've heard it all before; and, in their experience, nothing much gets done. Moreover, people lacking long experience in the rituals of government are seldom at their best in large meetings with formal agendas. Initiatives which are designed to respond to their needs and feelings, and to help them to play effective parts in the action, will usually provide the best starting points and training grounds for what may later become more ambitious community-based action. Initiatives which tap the vigour and imagination of women often do best of all – possibly because their commitment to their children makes them more determined than men to fight for a better future; possibly because they have depended less on wage labour to give their lives meaning and so they are less demoralized by unemployment. There are many encouraging examples of this kind ranging from community colleges to food co-ops.

Many renewal and regeneration projects cannot – or are not allowed to – proceed in this informal way. For them it may be better frankly to explain that there will be one stream of decisions leading to action which has to proceed according to a tight timetable. Every effort will be made to consult people about those things, and to respond to their views or explain why that is impossible; but they will not 'own' that stream of events or be able to delay them for long. Meanwhile there will be other developments which can proceed according to a more relaxed timetable, and the community will be helped to take over full ownership of those parts of the work.

The arguments in this chapter are developed at greater length by David Donnison in *Policies for a Just Society* (1997) London: Macmillan.

Reference

Balls, E. and Gregg, P. (1993) Work and welfare: tackling the jobs deficit. Commission on Social Justice Issue Paper No. 3. London: IPPR.

9

Building Social Capital

MAI WANN

Across Europe and North America,[1] the last two decades have witnessed
a vast expansion in the activities of groups devoted to self-help and mutual
aid. This development has important political implications. It runs counter to the conventions of post-war welfarism as well as to the older traditions of charity and voluntarism. Self-help and mutual aid stress personal
responsibility and interdependence, as well as direct, local action. They
present an ethos which is empowering and enabling rather than protective,
prescriptive or philanthropic. They challenge the power and expertise of
professional groups, especially in the field of health. All this comes at a
time when the search is on for new strategies to tackle social problems and
meet individual needs.

There is broad agreement that self-help and mutual-aid activities can be
beneficial. The consensus has developed among participants as well as among
community workers and professionals in health and social care – from
observation and experience, since there has been no systematic research.
Such activities are thought to bring benefits not only to the individuals
who take part in groups, but also to communities and sectors of society
who experience change as a result of the groups' endeavours.

The development has occurred without any significant intervention from
political parties or governments. Groups spring to life and expire spontan-
eously and randomly; together, they have an anarchic quality which defies
external regulation. For a range of reasons, they are viewed with both
favour and suspicion on the left and right of the political spectrum. They
have few powerful champions, perhaps because they lack any clear political identity (except that they are antithetical to centralized and *dirigiste*

regimes: the collapse of Communism led to a sudden surge of self-help and mutual-aid activity in Eastern Europe). Should governments continue to turn a blind eye, or is there a case for a new public policy for self-help and mutual aid? Should these activities continue to be regarded as marginal, or should they be brought into the mainstream as policy makers attempt to reinvent the welfare state for the twenty-first century? . . .

Self-help without mutual aid, as a purely private activity, is not relevant to this discussion. Mutual aid implies helping oneself as well as – and through – helping others. However, 'self-help' is used throughout this discussion to denote a combination of both activities, simply because it is the more familiar term.

What Is Self-help?

To understand what is meant by self-help, we consider its ideological roots, the characteristics shared by most self-help groups and their core activities.

Sources of inspiration

The concepts of self-help and mutual aid have been inspired, on the one hand, by Samuel Smiles and his Victorian faith in individual effort and, on the other hand, by Peter Kropotkin, the anarchist and atheist who lived in Russia at the turn of the century.[2]

In his work *Self Help: With Illustrations of Character, Conduct and Perseverance*, Samuel Smiles (1958) famously declared:

> Heaven helps those who help themselves . . . The spirit of self help is the root of all genuine growth in the individual; and exhibited in the lives of many, it constitutes the true source of national vigour and strength. Help from without is often enfeebling in its effects, but help from within invariably invigorates.

For Smiles, self-help was essentially about individual and self-improvement, and antithetical to the activities of governments and charities. Kropotkin stressed the importance of collective action. In his book *Mutual Aid: A Factor of Evolution* (1972), he described mutual aid as a natural force which bound people together. Like Smiles, although for different reasons, Kropotkin rejected central and local state aid that imposed formal discipline and hierarchy. He also rejected the church and religion for preaching charity and thereby conferring superiority on the giver. But for him the essence of mutual aid was co-operative endeavour – an idea manifested in friendly societies, trade unions and the co-operative movement.

Since the 1970s, self-help has been influenced by other forms of voluntary action, notably community development and the women's movement. Both have been committed to enabling individuals and groups to become more powerful and determine their own destinies, to gain in confidence and learn new skills, to stand up for their rights and to negotiate with professionals and others in authority. Their ideas and experience have helped to nourish the development of self-help activities.

More recently, self-help has become a symbol of renewal for civil society, a means of asserting autonomy and self-determination for individuals and communities, against the centralizing power of the state. The idea has been particularly salient in post-Communist Eastern Europe, but also resonates in western welfare states. The Czech president Vaclav Havel, writing in 1991, expressed this vision for the twenty-first century:

> The whole country will be criss-crossed by a network of local, regional and state-wide clubs, organisations, and associations with a wide variety of aims and purposes. This network will be so complex that it will be difficult to map thoroughly. Through it, the rich, nuanced and colourful life of a civilised European society will emerge and develop.

Common characteristics

Self-help groups are formed by people who, directly or through family or friends, have the same problem or life experience. They get together for mutual support and to share information and understanding. In a safe environment members of a group learn new ways of coping from each other. Individuals develop by being in the group through difficult times. People learn to give and take support, to value others and to feel valued themselves.

Essential characteristics of self-help groups include informality, equality among members, a common concern and a decision to do something about this concern. Self-help groups are often formed as a spontaneous response to an absence of services or to a hierarchical and formal organization of services which people find unsatisfactory. Unlike statutory services or those provided by charitable organizations, self-help groups are run by and for their members.

An elaborate definition is offered by the German Association of Self Help Supporters. Not all groups comply with the formula, but it covers the most common components of self help:

Self help groups are voluntary, mostly loose associations of people whose activities are directed towards common coping with illnesses, psychological or social problems, by which they – either themselves personally or as relatives – are affected. They don't want to make a (commercial) profit. Their goal is a change in their personal life situation and often influence on their social and political environment. In regular, often weekly, groupwork they stress authenticity, equality, a common language and mutual aid. In doing so the group is a means to counteract outer (social) as well as inner (psychological) isolation. The goals of self help groups focus on their members, and not on outsiders; in that respect they differ from other forms of citizen's initiative. Self help groups are not led by professional helpers; some consult experts now and again on particular questions however. (Matzat, 1993)

Core activities

Whether or not they fit this description precisely, all self-help groups share certain core activities, which can be summarized as follows.

Emotional support   People join a self-help group to give and receive support of a kind that can only be provided by others with similar experiences and problems.

Information   There is great need for clear, simple and appropriate information about the condition or problem around which the group is formed. Most self-help groups build up a small resource of literature and audio-visual material. Many produce their own leaflet or booklet to explain in accessible language the particular condition and suggest where to go for practical help. Another common strategy is to organize open meetings at which talks are given by professionals with specialist knowledge.

Advice and practical help   People who contact a self-help group have queries and practical difficulties. Members of the group offer advice based on their own experience and their wider knowledge of the condition they share. Members often accompany each other on visits to hospitals and clinics, and increasingly self-help groups run telephone helplines.

Recruiting   Most self-help organizations, whether large or small, are concerned to recruit new members. Building membership is a way of adding to the group's store of knowledge about the conditions around which it is formed; it is also a way of spreading the knowledge it has to a wider range of people. Attracting members from different social and ethnic backgrounds can be a problem. Recruiting people from black and ethnic minority communities is a particular concern of many groups.

Publicity and education   Most groups publicize their meetings at some stage of their development in order to attract new members, to make themselves known to potential funders and to gain recognition among professionals. Leaflets, annual reports and newsletters are used to keep in touch with members and promote their activities. Groups use local radio, newsletters and journals to educate the wider public about their issue of concern. Giving talks to trainee and qualified professionals is a common activity.

Fundraising   Depending on how much money the group is hoping to raise, this activity varies from running jumble sales to applying for funds from charitable trusts.

Campaigning   Some groups undertake campaigning and lobby local councillors and MPs. There is a continuing debate among self-help groups about how far they should get involved in campaigning and other pressure-group activities. Some contend that trying to bring about change is a natural step to take when a group has identified bad practice or a lack of suitable services; in this sense, campaigning is seen as an extension of self-help. Others maintain that self-help is essentially about group members doing things for themselves and each other, and that campaigning for changes in the world beyond the group would contradict their purpose.

What Can Self-help Achieve?

What can self-help groups achieve for their members and for society at large? Here we use case studies to illustrate the main benefits which self-help can bring to individuals and the ways in which groups can have a wider impact at local and national levels. We also consider their limitations.

Benefits for individual members

There are clearly a great many ways in which self-help groups have an impact on their members. The following examples focus on two of the most common: ending isolation and lending practical support.

East London Cancer Group: ending isolation   The first step in joining a group is to break the isolation that individuals feel when they experience a problem on their own. This is perhaps the most important benefit for anyone joining a self-help group.

Vi Mitchell started a self-help group in East London in 1979 when she came out of hospital after major surgery for cancer. She knew through her personal experience that there was no support locally other than individual families and friends. Anyone who came out of hospital after surgery was likely to feel isolated and to have little or no access to information or advice.

There were five of us who had met at hospital having had surgery. Other people heard about the group. We did not advertise it anywhere. Word of mouth went around. There was so much need in the area. We were approached by new people all the time. We had to keep the numbers down. The maximum number my flat could take was 18. The others were turned away.

The group gradually became a cancer group. We gave each other a lot of support. And we learned from others. People facing death or people learning to live with devastating effects of surgery. There was honesty and openness in the group. At times we all cried together. But we had evenings where each of us had to tell a funny story about something that happened in hospital.

We had good fun discovering the various alternative cures practised in the USA. We dreamed of going to luxury hotels in Mexico and having new therapies. We argued about sugar versus honey. We discovered that Babycham sweetens the pills we had to take. The group had both men and women. We talked about sex. Some surgery destroys many people's ability to have sex. Nerves are sometimes severed in men and women often have their vagina affected. This wasn't the kind of conversation you could have anywhere else.

Credit Unions: practical help for individuals Some self-help groups are concerned less with ending personal isolation than with providing practical support. Credit unions are a case in point. A credit union is a way of saving and borrowing money without using a bank. Members of the union save as much or as little as they want. This process keeps the money in the community. Loans are governed by each credit union's regulations. Most of the people who borrow money from a credit union could not go to a high-street bank and ask for a loan. According to a study by the University of Sheffield (Dibben, 1993) the number of credit unions trebled in three years to a total of over 200 in 1992. The researchers found that credit unions helped not only to alleviate debt problems but also, just as importantly, to bring communities together and to provide social and educational support.

One of the twenty-two founding members of the Rotten Park Winson Green credit union gives this account:

I knew a little about credit unions in the West Indies. In some parts of Jamaica, where I come from, there are 14 or 15 miles before you can see a bank. Every district has a credit union office called Loan Bank, where farmers get loans before planting yellow banana or cane. The idea came from the Rotten Park Winson Green Employment Project. The suggestion struck a chord with everyone. Some people had heard about credit unions from Ireland where they are quite common. The Council was very keen and supportive.

There was a lot to be done; recruiting members, learning how to run a credit union, registering as a Friendly Society. Within twelve months we had 100 members. The membership fee is £1. Then people can save whatever they can. Their ability to borrow depends on the consistency of their saving. Money is collected every week in a personal account. People are given a book which records their savings and shares. Annual dividends are calculated on the basis of profit margins. A member's request for a loan has to be approved by the Credit Committee, which decides according to the member's track record as well as their need.

Members borrow to go on a holiday back home or to pay a high bill. For many of them the alternative would be a loan shark. Members get an annual dividend on savings even though they may still have an outstanding loan. Say you have shares of £200 and a loan of £150: you can pay the loan and increase savings or ask for a top-up loan to pay a high bill or deal with a crisis.

When people get into bad debts we write to them. Ultimately the credit union could take them to the small claims court, but it does not happen very often. In the last three or four years it only happened five times. The rate of bad debts is 0.35 per cent. Bank managers would be happy with a rate of 4–5 per cent. Unlike bank debts, credit union debts die with the borrower. All the policies are there to benefit the members.

Effecting wider changes

The activities of self-help groups can do more than just benefit their own members. For example, if a group is successful in improving services there are gains for all users, whether or not they are members of the group. Some groups help to shift the balance of power from providers to users of public services; to influence public policy by bringing lay people's views to the attention of policy makers, to challenge established values and traditional roles, and to promote research. The following examples have been chosen to illustrate these functions, although it will be clear that there is considerable overlap between them.

Positively Women: shifting power from providers to users Positively Women was set up in 1987. Initially it was for women who, like its founder, had become HIV positive through drug use. The founder felt doubly isolated: women's AIDS groups excluded drug users and other groups consisted mainly of gay men. At first, women drug users responded to a poster advertising the group. Gradually they were joined by women infected through sexual activity, who eventually made up the majority of members. About thirty women participated in the first group with an average of ten to fifteen attending each fortnightly meeting. One of the members had experience in fund raising and together with the founder provided the drive, expertise and skills to set up an organization which grew in six years from a small support group to a large, London-wide organization.

Positively Women runs a network of support groups; organizes training days for women and service providers; distributes information; provides representatives for health and social services working parties; and raises awareness through the mass media about HIV and AIDS. It is funded by most London Boroughs and Health Authorities as well as by charitable foundations.

According to Positively Women, women find that from the moment of diagnosis, they are at the mercy of experts who are sometimes intolerant and judgemental. They feel powerless and out of control of their lives. They are sometimes pressed by social workers to tell their children about their illness, irrespective of their own ability to cope with the consequences. They are not always clear whether they are being given a new treatment for their own benefit or as part of a research exercise. Often their children are subjected to tests because, doctors argue, it can benefit research about the disease. African members of Positively Women are sometimes told by service providers that they are lucky to receive treatment and that they would not get it in their own country.

There is a general feeling among women that they are told what to do by professionals instead of being given information and choices. The way they are treated by service providers increases, rather than relieves, their sense of vulnerability. They therefore find it helpful to meet in a setting where there is support, trust and respect for confidentiality.

The support groups run by Positively Women are exclusively for HIV-positive women. Feeling safe to be open about HIV is very important for the women who come to the groups. Each group has a paid worker who is also HIV positive, trained to facilitate the group, organize the activities and provide counselling. The groups meet between from 11 a.m. and 3 p.m. so that women can take their children to and from school.

In addition to sharing experiences and giving and receiving support, women can have training in safer sex, assertiveness, counselling skills and coping with loss and bereavement. Newly diagnosed women have the opportunity to meet others who are living with HIV. The groups build up information about symptoms, ways of coping, different therapies and their side effects.

Positively Women has built up a wealth of knowledge which they use to influence professionals in health and social care. Members give talks to professionals, organize presentations at conferences and seminars, act as consultants to professional bodies, work with the media to promote awareness, and produce health education for specific groups of vulnerable women such as women in prisons and hostels. The organization is represented on the Medical Research Council's Collaborative Study of HIV in Women.

The Grandparents' Federation: influencing public policy The Grandparents' Federation was founded in 1987, two years after a group of grandparents got together to share their concern about the plight of grandparents who had no contact with their grandchildren. Most of their difficulties occurred when children were taken into care and grandparents were forbidden to help in a family crisis.

The Federation was set up with funds from Children in Need and Age Concern, in order to respond to telephone calls and letters from grandparents seeking advice and support. Further grants have since been secured to finance specific projects. Membership is open to anyone, regardless of creed or colour, who shares its aims and objectives. Members receive a quarterly newsletter and information about meetings. People join because they feel powerless to influence social services, resentful about their lack of legal rights and unjustly deprived of their grandchildren through no fault of their own. They also experience the stigma attached to families with children in care, who are so often assumed to have been abused by their parents.

The Grandparents' Federation campaigned to raise public awareness about the range of reasons why families break up, including mental illness and long hospital stays. They highlighted, through personal stories, the contribution grandparents make when they are allowed to help look after their grandchildren. They involved retired social workers in their support groups, who acted as advocates for families and provided a bridge between them and the professionals.

Members of the Grandparents' Federation lobbied MPs who were debating the Bill which became the 1989 Children Act. The Act simplifies and rationalizes the grandparents' position in seeking contact, particularly with children in care. It is also helpful to grandparents in internal family disputes. It became clear that grandparents would need help in order to benefit from the legislation. The federation continues to offer support, advice and information. It is involved in a pilot project in Newcastle to enable people to act as surrogate grandparents for children in care. Having started life as a single self-help group, it is now a national organization striving to develop a network of local self-help groups.

Southall Black Sisters and the Everyman Centre: challenging established values Domestic violence has been described as part of a wider social, institutional and political framework that 'subordinates women, trivialises their abuse and addicts men to the maintenance of power and control over them'. Southall Black Sisters in West London and the Everyman Centre in Brixton, South London, are two organizations which help individuals involved in domestic violence to change their behaviour. In doing so they challenge the values that prevail in the communities to which the individuals belong, as well as in society at large.

Southall Black Sisters was set up in 1979 to address the needs of black, Asian, African and Caribbean women. They carry out casework, advocacy and counselling with women facing violence and abuse at home. The majority of their clients are Asian women. They have found that women and girls who experience violence in their families have been traumatized and often suffer from depression and suicidal tendencies as a result. Many are also under pressure to conform to cultural and religious norms and values.

The support they give to Asian women and girls is met with disapproval by many Asian men and local institutions. For challenging the status of women within the family and the community at large, Southall Black Sisters are criticized for letting the community down and for losing their ethnic and cultural identity. In response, they cite evidence that domestic violence damages women's mental health and argue that the services available to them are not providing appropriate support. They are seeking to develop innovative models of intervention.

The Everyman Centre is a project run by men offering a range of support services for men who want to stop behaving violently. It is based in Brixton in South London and accepts men from London and the neighbouring counties. More than 250 men were seen at the Centre in the first two years (1991–3).

The Everyman Centre recognizes that many factors may contribute to a man's violent behaviour but that he always has a choice. Violence is neither inevitable nor inherent. The centre's counselling programme consists of a combination of short-term individual counselling followed by a further three months of group work. The aim is to challenge and change the attitudes and behavioural patterns of men, to redress male stereotyping, and to foster understanding of power dynamics and inequalities. Men must choose to attend the centre; they are not referred by outside agencies. Men from different backgrounds are encouraged to help each other in a safe, careful environment.

The British Diabetic Association: promoting research   The British Diabetic Association (BDA), set up in 1934, is a lay association which provides a number of services including support for self-help groups. It represents the interests of people with diabetes and maintains contact with them through local branches and groups. It has three main objectives:

- to provide education and information for people with diabetes and their professional advisors;
- to represent the interests and welfare of people with diabetes;
- to promote research into the causes, prevention and cure of diabetes.

The association provides an umbrella for self-help groups formed around diabetes. It helps them get in touch with each other and provides training for members and group leaders. It has more than 400 local groups in the UK. These groups provide a local point of contact for people with diabetes and their families. They also raise funds for BDA and to provide equipment for a local diabetic clinic or day unit.

BDA recognizes that the diagnosis of diabetes comes as a major shock to the individuals concerned, causing loss of self-esteem and undermining their view of themselves as competent and healthy. By sharing and venting feelings in a group with other diabetics, they can regain confidence, become competent in dealing with diabetes and form a new image of themselves which feels comfortable.

According to a study undertaken for BDA in 1990 (Kelleher, 1990), group members found it helpful to share personal difficulties including feelings of anger and anxiety about the disease. There was a mutual understanding about not always doing the right thing: a degree of non-compliance to the demands of diabetes was seen as necessary for a full life.

There have been some attempts to set up groups outside BDA for those who felt it was not catering for their needs. For example, some women with diabetes felt that BDA only mentioned women in relation to pregnancy. There was also a view among young people that their needs were overshadowed by those of older people and parents of diabetic children. Members of ethnic minorities found that diets suggested by BDA took no account of their culinary traditions. In response the organization has been trying to broaden its scope and devote space in the newsletter to issues such as these. However, at the time of writing in the early 1990s, financial difficulties had caused BDA to cut back some of its services and give priority to research.

Limitations

For all the benefits they offer, self-help groups are not suitable for everybody. For many people it is bad enough thinking about their own problems let alone listening to other people's. Some think that participating in a self-help group would simply increase their preoccupation with their own difficulties. Others worry that self-help groups, particularly for people with learning difficulties, may make them more stigmatized by isolating them further from the rest of society.

Like other forms of social gathering, self-help groups harbour as much opportunity for conflict as for positive development. As members draw closer to each other and become more committed to the group, the chance for disagreement and conflict increases. Some groups have 'difficult members' who can be disruptive. When individuals become disappointed with a self-help group, this can exacerbate the problems which brought them to the group in the first place. A common difficulty is finding members who are willing to take on organizing tasks. The same few people do all the work while others seem to get only the benefits. For example, a group's treasurer often occupies this position year after year because nobody else wants it.

Signs of fragility and informality in self-help groups may worry professionals who wish to protect their patients or clients from negative experiences. Doctors may worry about misinformation and confusion or even crankiness in a group, or about groups being too dogmatic about how members should help themselves. These fears reflect the gulf between expert and experiential knowledge and are rarely founded in fact. Professionals do not always take kindly to lay people criticizing or supplementing the services they provide. They may feel threatened by self-help groups if they see them as pressure groups prepared to campaign for change . . .

There are, of course, some practical limits to the effectiveness of self help groups. When members are unwell, tired or live far away from each other their contribution to the group is severely cut back. People with few resources and little access to information may not be able to bring into the group what it needs in order to develop. These limitations are more marked in self-help groups in rural areas and among disadvantaged communities.

Notes

1 There is also a very lively and well-organized self-help movement in Australia. For a brief description see Wilson (1987).
2 Both Smiles (1958) and Kropotkin (1972) are quoted in Vincent (1985).

References

Dibben, M. (1993) Credit where it's due. *Search*, 17 September.
Havel, V. (1992) *Summer Meditations*. London: Faber and Faber.
Kelleher, D. (1990) *Patients Learning from Each Other: Self Help Groups for People with Diabetes*. Presented at Forum on Medical Communication, 1 June.

Kropotkin, P. (1972) *Mutual Aid: A Factor of Evolution*. Harmondsworth: Allen Lane.

Matzat, J. (1993) Away with the experts? Self help groupwork in Germany. *Groupwork*, 6 (1), 30–42.

Smiles, S. (1958) *Self Help: With Illustrations of Character, Conduct and Perseverance*. Centenary edn. London: John Murray.

Vincent, J. (1985) *Constraints on the Stability and Longevity of Self Help Groups in the Field of Health Care*. Centre for Research in Social Policy.

Wilson, J. (1987) Self help speaks out. *New Society*, 13 February.

10

Racial Equality: Colour, Culture and Justice

TARIQ MODOOD

Racial discrimination is an important contributor to economic, social and political injustice in the UK today. It works in a number of direct and indirect ways, wastes talent and potential, and, by creating bitter feelings of resentment and alienation, undermines respect for and desire to participate in the political system. Discrimination is a brake on the material and social progress of the country as a whole, and while not an absolute bar to the progress of minorities, it prevents success on equal terms or in proportionate numbers to that of the white majority.

The groups that suffer from the cumulative disadvantages of historical and current racism in Britain today are in the main those whose origins are from outside Europe. Such minority groups are diverse, originating as they do from different parts of the former British colonial world and shaped by different aspects of its history. While their presence in Britain pre-dates the large post-war immigration, it is only in the last few decades that they have become a feature of life in the UK, above all England. While primary immigration was effectively stopped by the mid-1960s, family reunification and natural growth have created communities that now form over 6 per cent of the population of England (and about 1.5 per cent in Scotland and Wales), with much higher proportions in urban areas (over 20 per cent in London and Birmingham). The growth rate of some minority groups is declining to a level comparable with the rest of the population, but other groups, being younger and having larger families, are still growing.

Ethnic minorities entered British society at the bottom. The need in Britain was for cheap, unskilled labour to perform those jobs in an expanding economy which white people no longer wished to do, and the bulk of the immigration occurred in response to this need. Research from the 1960s onwards established quite clearly that non-white people had a much worse socio-economic profile than white people and that racial discrimination was one of the principal causes. Anti-discrimination legislation was introduced in 1965 and strengthened in 1968 and 1976. While this eliminated the open discrimination that was common up to that time, there is much evidence that racial discrimination is a persisting feature of our society today (see, for example, Brown and Gay, 1985).

The evidence of inequality

Despite the persistence of racial discrimination, the ethnic minorities in Britain are reversing the initial downward mobility produced by migration and racial discrimination.[1] All ethnic minority groups, however, continue to be employed and to earn below the level appropriate to their educational qualifications and continue to be grossly underrepresented as managers in large firms and institutions. Moreover, while the Chinese and African Asians have achieved broad parity with whites, the Indians and Caribbeans are relatively disadvantaged, and the Pakistanis and Bangladeshis continue to be severely disadvantaged.

The qualifications, job levels and earnings spread in 1994 are roughly what one would have predicted from the spread of qualifications in 1974, if racial exclusion were relaxed but not absent. Those groups that had an above-average middle-class professional and business profile before migration seem to have been able to recreate that profile despite the occupational downgrading that all minority groups initially experienced.

The progress of ethnic minorities has also depended on their studying harder and longer than their white peers, and their working harder and longer in their jobs. The high representation of most of the Asian groups in self-employment may represent the same phenomenon. Certainly, self-employment has been critical to the economic survival and advancement of some groups, and to narrowing the earnings gap with whites.

There is severe and widespread poverty amongst Pakistani and Bangladeshi households, with more than four out of five having an income below half the national average – four times as many as white non-pensioners. This is related to their poor qualification levels, collapse of the northen manufacturing industries in which they were employed, large families, poor facility in English amongst women, and the very low levels of economic activity amongst women.

While many Caribbean people seem to have escaped from disadvantage, others are probably worse off in some ways than their equivalents twenty years ago. Young black men are disproportionately without qualifications, without work, without a stable family life, in trouble with the police and in prison. Many young black women are in work, with earnings higher than white women's; but others are disproportionately likely to be lone parents, unemployed and in social housing – with all that implies for poverty. While for most groups disadvantage may be diminishing across the generations, this is less clearly the case for the Caribbeans.

A *new concept of equality*

The concept of equality has been under intense theoretical and political discussion, especially in the English-speaking world; what is often claimed today in the name of racial equality is more than would have been recognized as such in the 1960s. Iris Young expresses well the new political climate when she describes the emergence of an ideal of equality based not just on allowing excluded groups to assimilate and live by the norms of dominant groups, but on the view that 'a positive self-definition of group difference is in fact more liberatory' (Young, 1990, p. 157). She cites the examples of the black power movement, the gay pride assertion that sexual identity is a matter of culture and politics, and the feminism which emphasizes that women's experiences should be celebrated and valued in their own right. These movements have not had the same impact in Britain as in parts of North America, but are certainly present. In particular there is an ethnic assertiveness in Britain which has parallels with North America. It has been less evident amongst recent migrants and their descendants in other European Union countries, where cultural assimilation is still regarded as essential to citizenship and political equality (Baldwin and Schwain, 1994). This assertiveness counterposes positive images against traditional or dominant stereotypes, and projects identities in order to challenge existing power relations or to negotiate the sharing of physical, institutional and discursive space. Anti-racists have challenged the presumed stigma associated with not being white or conventionally British (Modood, 1994).

The shift is from an understanding of equality in terms of individualism and cultural assimilation to a politics of recognition, to equality as encompassing public ethnicity. Equality is not having to hide or apologize for one's origins, family or community, but expecting others to respect them and adapt public attitudes and arrangements so that the heritage they represent is encouraged rather than contemptuously expected to wither away. There seems, then, to be two distinct conceptions of equal citizenship, each based on a different view of what is 'public' and 'private'. These two conceptions of equality may be stated as follows:

1 the right to assimilate to the majority/dominant culture in the public sphere, and toleration of 'difference' in the private sphere;
2 the right to have one's 'difference' recognized and supported in both the public and the private spheres.

These are not, however, alternative conceptions in the sense that to hold one, the other has to be rejected. Multiculturalism requires support for both conceptions. For the assumption behind the first is that participation in the public or national culture is necessary for the effective exercise of citizenship, the only obstacles to which are the exclusionary processes preventing gradual assimilation. The second conception, too, assumes that groups excluded from the national culture have their citizenship diminished as a result; offers to remedy this by accepting the right to assimilate yet adds the right to widen and adapt the national culture and the public symbols of national membership to include the relevant minority ethnicities.

Racial Discrimination and Racial Disadvantage

Discrimination can be based on colour-racism in the direct form of discriminatory behaviour, or in the indirect form of policies and practices which have a disproportionate, even if unintended, unfavourable impact upon some or all non-white groups. The cumulative effects of this discrimination, especially when intergenerational, is what is meant by 'racial disadvantage', namely a socio-economic gap between white and (some) non-white groups which would persist even if discrimination were to disappear tomorrow.
    Racial discrimination, however, is:

● not a discrete form of disadvantage: in other words, it is connected to other disadvantages;
● not a unitary form of disadvantage: it takes various forms;
● not necessarily linked to racial disadvantage: despite discrimination, some groups can achieve significant socio-economic mobility.

Race and class

Racial discrimination is not a discrete form of disadvantage because many forms of indirect discrimination ('institutional discrimination') and racial disadvantage are closely related to structural inequalities better understood in terms of class. For example, if a merchant bank favours Oxbridge graduates in the recruitment of trainee managers, it is operating a discriminatory policy; for, because of the make-up of the student population at

Oxford and Cambridge, its actions will proportionately disadvantage more non-whites than whites. Yet the policy is colour-blind; it is a form of class discrimination. For it clearly has a discriminatory impact upon large sections of the white population, and indeed it is *through* its class bias that it negatively impacts upon racially disadvantaged groups. Its racially exclusionary effect is brought about through the conditions of disadvantage rather than racism. It perpetuates racial disadvantage but the discrimination is effected through what the disadvantaged have in common across racial boundaries, rather than what separates them.

In this case, to attack the class bias of the policy is in effect to attack the racial bias and vice versa; a policy aimed at removing the conditions of racial disadvantage would make little headway if it did not challenge the existing structure of opportunities created by class divisions. Hence, an attack on certain kinds of racial inequalities is only possible within a much more extensive commitment to equality and social justice. In so far as race-specific policies can provide opportunities for education, training, employment and social mobility, restrictions upon which can all be forms of indirect racial discrimination, they can only be wholly effective as refinements of broad social programmes to improve the relevant opportunity structures for all racial groups. The relevance of the race dimension of such programmes would be to ensure that those most disadvantaged were not overlooked by the programme and got the particular kind of assistance they needed in a culturally appropriate way; it could not be a substitute for a social equality programme – even in respect of disadvantaged racial groups (Wilson, 1987).

Cultural racism

Racial discrimination is not a unitary form of disadvantage because not all non-white groups are discriminated against in the same way or to the same extent. Colour-racism may be a constant but there are other kinds of racism at work in Britain. Colour-racism is the foundation of racism rather than the whole edifice.

Direct discrimination depends upon stereotypes and there are no stereotypes about 'blackness' as such: the stereotypes are always about specific groups or quasi-groups ('Jamaicans are lazy', 'Asians don't mix', 'Muslims are fanatical', etc.). Hence, different groups will be affected differently, and some groups can become or cease to be more 'acceptable' than others (white people have in surveys always stated more prejudice against Asians than Afro-Caribbeans and this is now rising, especially amongst the young; see Young, 1992). Moreover, stereotypes, like all social generalizations, allow for counter-examples, so that individuals of any group who are able to demonstrate, for example in an interview, that they are a counter-example to the stereotype, will receive less unfavourable treatment.

Indirect discrimination depends on policies and practices which (unintentionally) disproportionately disadvantage one group compared to others. Groups whose language, religion, customs, family structures, and so on are most different from the white majority norm will experience the most disadvantage and exclusion. So, just as colour-blind class discrimination can be a form of indirect racial discrimination, membership of a minority community can render one less employable on the grounds of one's dress, dietary habits, or desire to take leave from work on one's holy days rather than those prescribed by the custom and practice of the majority community.

This direct and indirect discrimination, taken together, constitutes 'cultural racism' (in contrast to colour-racism) and is targeted at groups perceived to be assertively 'different' and not trying to 'fit in'. It is racism which uses cultural difference to vilify or marginalize or demand cultural assimilation from groups who also suffer colour-racism. Racial groups which have distinctive cultural identities or community life will suffer this additional dimension of discrimination and prejudice. This form of racism is least acknowledged, debated or repudiated (sentences beginning: 'I am no racist but . . .' are most likely to be expressions of cultural racism), and is not properly outlawed (the courts have deemed discrimination against Muslims to be lawful) and yet is the racism that is on the increase, has the greater impact upon Asians and is an important cause of the rising levels of racial violence in Britain and Europe.

It is quite clear from BNP [British National Party] leaflets and graffiti in the East End of London which refer to 'Pakis', and of Front National statements in France about Arabs, where in both cases Islam is explicitly a dimension of the racial abuse and incitement to hatred, that the contemporary attacks upon Muslims are not a case of straightforward religious bigotry or of colour-racism but of the phenomenon I am calling 'cultural racism'. It is because of its complex character that it cannot be properly defeated by the politics of religious harmony or by anti-colour-racism, but only by a movement that understands the pluralistic phenomenon of cultural racism. This approach can also explain some of the contradictions in contemporary racism, such as the observation that white working-class youth culture is incorporating, indeed emulating, young black men and women while hardening against groups like South Asians and Vietnamese (Cohen, 1993, p. 83; Back, 1993).

One way to understand the emergence and growth in cultural racism is to see it as a backlash against the emergence of 'public ethnicity'. Minority ethnicity, albeit white ethnicity like that of the Jewish community, has traditionally been regarded in Britain as acceptable if confined to the privacy of family and community, and if it did not make any political demands. However, in association with other socio-political movements (feminism, gay rights, etc.) which challenge the public–private distinction or demand a share of the public space, claims are increasingly made today that ethnic difference is not just something that needs 'mere' toleration but needs to be publicly acknowledged, resourced and represented.

Thus there is a vague multiculturalism as a policy ideology and it has perhaps contributed to a new ethnic assertiveness, so that many of the race-relations conflicts today (for example, the Honeyford affair, the Rushdie affair) arise out of a demand for public space, for public respect and public resources for minority cultures and for the transmission of such cultures to the young. Yet, because our racial equality legal and policy framework is premised on colour-racism, rather than cultural racism, there is no clear view from any part of the political spectrum (except perhaps from the nationalist right) about to what extent these political demands are justifiable, especially in relation to religious communalism, and how cultural racism should be tackled.

In many ways prejudice and antipathy against ethno-religious groups pose a challenge the seriousness of which has yet to be appreciated. For there is a challenge not only to recognize and oppose cultural racism, but, additionally, to the taken-for-granted secularism of the multiculturalists and indeed of British public life. While a secular framework need not necessarily be insensitively hegemonic, I think that contemporary secular multiculturalists are unaware of the contradictory signals that they are sending out. Multiculturalism which states that public recognition of minority cultures is essential to equal citizenship, combined with a denial of an equivalent public recognition of religion, can only convey the message that religious identity has and ought to have less status than other forms of group identity (Modood, 1994, 1997a). Why should it be the case that groups proclaiming themselves to be 'black' are to be empowered and given distinctive forms of political representation, but equally disadvantaged groups that mobilize around a religious rather than a colour identity are to be discouraged? While such questions are not answered, non-white religious groups may rightly complain of double standards.

Disadvantage and equality

Racial discrimination is not necessarily linked to racial disadvantage because some groups migrate with skills and capital, and because some discriminated groups put in extra time and energy, work and study harder, develop self-help and/or other networks to compensate and, therefore, avoid the socio-economic disadvantages that would otherwise result from discrimination. There is now growing evidence that some Asian groups experience discrimination in selection processes *and* are over-represented in higher-education admissions and in entry to prestigious professions such as medicine, accountancy and law (Modood, 1992, ch. 6; Modood, 1993). This is quite a confusing development for race egalitarians, even though it is not unique to Britain, and the signs of it happening have been there for some years. Egalitarians have in general given it little thought and do not know how to respond to it (except to deny that it exists). In considering the implications of such developments for rethinking racial equality, the following in particular need to be borne in mind.

First, it is not necessarily the case that the upwardly mobile groups experience less discrimination than the less mobile groups; on the contrary, Asians suffer as much prejudice as any group and it is not obvious that the successful Asian groups experience less discrimination or hostility than the others. Moreover, it is not the case that as a group is perceived to be successful and separated out from other minorities, it will attract less prejudice and discrimination: as the Jews know, those considered to be 'too successful' can suffer more prejudice than those thought to be inferior.

Secondly, if measures to eliminate discrimination are successful, it will mean that groups like Indians or Chinese will increase their over-representation in fields such as higher education and management, for some of those presently kept out will get in. At whose expense should this be? Is it clear that it should be at the expense of whites rather than, say, Pakistanis? The Jews were able to consolidate and are able to maintain their over-representation because they are not easily visible, and, above all, because they are not counted. This is not the case with groups such as Indians, and as ethnic monitoring becomes more extensive, this argument about over-representation will force itself into debates.

It has already done so at prestigious US universities, at a number of which Chinese and Asians have complained that making entry easier for some minorities has the effect of imposing a ceiling upon them. The universities do not deny the charge but say it has to be offset against the wider goal of 'proportional representation'.

An alternative egalitarian defence might be that equal opportunities is about process not outcome, about fairness in selection, not numbers in outcomes. If so, this would mean a major shift or retreat as most equality statements (sex as well as race) currently say the opposite. It is therefore important to see why egalitarians currently think of equality in terms of outcomes. Ethnic-origin data collection was first introduced on the basis of the reasonable assumption that differential statistics would be *prima facie* evidence of discrimination, of practices that needed to be investigated and justified. Where justification was not possible, the practices were to be eliminated. Yet even where this was done, further monitoring revealed that there was still an inequality in outcomes.

Moreover, arguments about the fairness of procedures (for example, whether a recruiter should discount knowledge about a candidate's abilities acquired in a way not repeatable with other candidates, as would be the case with an internal candidate whose strengths and weaknesses are known to an extent not possible with external candidates) were proving to be time-consuming and intractable and were perceived as too academic or formalistic by both egalitarians and recruiters alike. The simple goal of 'mirroring' the population, or achieving proportionality in outcomes as the definition of absence of discrimination, cut through this knot, and made possible the setting of numerical targets or quotas.

While this has now become the understanding of equal opportunities at policy level (for gender even more so than for race), Bhikhu Parekh has argued that to commit policy to proportionality is: 'to ignore [the disadvantaged groups'] diversity of talents and aptitudes, to control and curtail their right of self-determination, and to mould them in the image of the dominant world' (Parekh, 1992, p. 270). If one accepts that different groups legitimately have different norms, priorities and cultural commitments, it is difficult to see why the measure of equality should assume that all groups equally pursue the same experiences, education, occupational and other personal goals and make the same compromises between work, family and recreation. Without such an assumption, equality has to be much more complexly interpreted as outcomes that are the product of free choices. Yet this surely, especially on a macrosocietal level, is even more difficult to measure than fairness in procedures at an institutional level.

Hence it is difficult to see how we can altogether give up on equal opportunities as proportionality in outcomes. It must at least figure at the start of equality debates, even if it does not tell the full story. In talking of racial *disadvantage* we must necessarily be talking about comparative outcomes, about socio-economic profiles. What we cannot assume is that racial discrimination is the effective cause of racial disadvantage or that the elimination of discrimination will of itself eliminate the conditions of disadvantage, let alone produce freely chosen outcomes. Conversely, the commitment to the elimination of discrimination cannot be put aside just because the discriminated group has managed to avoid relative disadvantages. The right to not be discriminated against by public institutions and in civil society is fundamental.

It is worth spelling out one important corollary of this. Given the 'over-representation' of some ethnic minorities in higher education and amongst entrants to some professions, to pursue a more vigorous, US-style, affirmative-action approach to achieve equality of outcomes (inevitably based on soft or hard quotas) will create *prima facie* cases of injustice to individuals (for example, individuals denied entry onto a university course because of a policy which prefers others with lesser qualifications) not just against whites but also against some minorities. Such a policy is not likely to be considered just or necessary unless it can be demonstrated that it is the only way to overcome racial disadvantage, but this would be difficult to sustain at a time when some minorities were being visibly successful. A broad, class-based attack on socio-economic disadvantage is more likely to win public support and avoid racial and ethnic conflict.

Policy Dilemmas

Racial equality thinking, where it reduces racial discrimination to colour-discrimination, and/or fails to think through the implications of public ethnicity, and/or assumes too close a linkage between discrimination and disadvantage, fails to keep up with the socio-cultural developments that are taking place. At the very least, these changes challenge the assumptions of political 'blackness': the view that colour-racism is the most important determinant in the outcomes of non-white people who, therefore, form a quasi-class with a common socio-economic position and interests. They should also challenge the view that the only remedy for their disadvantage is through political power. For the reality is that those groups who evidence social mobility (Indians and Chinese) have no special access to state power and have assiduously kept a low political profile (in so far as they seek political power, it is to consolidate rather than to initiate social mobility). This should encourage sober reflection on the nature and extent of state intervention in this area. Yet the first conclusions one may come to are hardly unproblematic.

Ethnicity – norms, group solidarities and patterns of behaviour which are not merely the products of majority exclusion, and which may be valued by the community in question, which may inculcate them in its young – can clearly be a resource. It can provide the strength to cope with racism and majority contempt, to instil group pride, to organize forms of welfare and cultural needs satisfaction, to create business opportunities and enclaves, to maintain across the generations the discipline of deferred gratification needed to climb educational, business and career ladders, and so on. It may, therefore, be thought that sound policy should endorse ethnicity and encourage communities to use their own traditions to develop themselves.

Not only would this be in keeping with multiculturalism but it would mean less direct state intervention and state management of services, and would, therefore, also be in keeping with the 'enabling state' idea.

Two problems, however, immediately suggest themselves. First, some communities may be too fragmented or too resourceless to benefit from this approach. It does not follow, however, that this approach is not appropriate for any groups. Secondly, the legitimizing of 'difference' that this approach involves might increase group consciousness and therefore encourage the potential for group competitiveness rather than intergroup social solidarity. Moreover, it would tend to harden boundaries that may otherwise become fluid, and strengthen intragroup authority in ways not wholly consonant with a political culture of individual rights. Perhaps we need an open recognition that multiculturalism is a legitimate limit on individualism.

This, however, is not as simple an idea as it might sound, or easy to use as the basis for political consensus. Consider equal opportunities recruitment policies. The principle often enunciated is of overcoming stereotypical bias by treating everyone the same: but how can one do that if people have different norms, sensibilities and needs? It is not possible to treat someone as an individual if one is ignorant about their cultural background and the things that matter to them, for the greater the ignorance about a group of people by an outsider or observer, the greater the reliance on a stereotype. To decrease the use of unfavourable stereotypes one has to increase the level of knowledge about the groups and to make sure that the knowledge used is not only of the outsider's generalizing type but includes some understanding of how the group understands itself, of what it believes to be some of its distinctive qualities or virtues.

An abstract, culture-blind individualism will necessarily impose majority norms and expectations upon all candidates and, therefore, discomfort and disadvantage some minority candidates. On the other hand, to treat the latter differently from white candidates can be difficult to justify in any particular case, let alone to institutionalize through policies and procedures and to build the necessary consensus for amongst managers, staff, etc. Where active multiculturalism contradicts such a basic (if partial) intuition of fairness as uniformity of treatment, it will be very difficult to get public support for differential policies that are not merely about tolerating difference but involve large-scale resource commitments. A debate about the implications of cultural difference for equality is therefore unavoidable if multiculturalism is to mean more than tokenistic recognition of minority cultures.

Not only is there a clash between some of our intuitions about fairness and equality, but well-meaning policies may well collide. Some have expressed concern that policies of multiculturalism which allow Asian girls to be withdrawn from certain activities at school (activities such as sex education, sport, dance), or not to be entered for certain subjects, collude with traditional views on gender difference and sex roles. Similarly, though less noticed as an example of how tackling some forms of discrimination actually reinforces other forms of discrimination, is how many racial equality policies currently act as a barrier to recognizing the needs of Muslims, for instance. The numerous examples of the latter include: same-race adoption and fostering policies which place black Muslims with black Christians, and Asian Muslims with Hindus and Sikhs; social work based on Asian needs, which can lead to a Muslim being given a Hindu home-help who does not know about Muslim sensitivities or whose own inhibitions (about meat for example) prevent her from fulfilling her duties; the recent decision by the Housing Corporation to reverse its policy of registering housing associations catering for religious communities in favour of race; and recruitment monitoring and targeting in terms of 'black' or 'Asian' statistics which obscure the level of Muslim disadvantage and under-representation.

The Muslim example is not simply illustrative but urgent. By the usual socio-economic measures of disadvantage Muslims are among the very worst-off group, and yet, unlike religious groups such as Sikhs and Jews, they are not deemed to be an ethnic group and so are outside the terms of existing anti-discrimination legislation (UKACIA, 1993). Their level of representation in mainstream institutions and forums is chronic: in the early 1990s no Muslim has ever sat in either House of Parliament or even been chosen by a political party to fight a winnable seat. Given that they form nearly half the non-white population (Anwar, 1993), it is difficult to see how there could be a British race-relations settlement without the Muslim communities. Combining as they do the facets of being a socio-economic underclass, targets of colour-racism and victims of cultural racism, they combine in their person the three 'cs' of race: colour, class and culture. Muslims are an important test of whether racial equality policies can be extended to meet the new challenges of the 1990s.

Conclusions

Despite these various tensions and dilemmas, some of which cannot be resolved without considerably more thought and debate than they have received so far, I offer the following six conclusions as the basis for re-thinking racial disadvantage in the context of the new pluralism.

1 The first principle of racial equality should be anti-discrimination, that is to say, the right of the individual to full participation in all the major aspects of the common social life without being penalized for their racial, ethnic or religious identity, regardless of the socio-economic standing of the group to which the individual may belong. In failing to protect groups such as Muslims, existing anti-discrimination law is in need of urgent extension. It should be unlawful to refuse to employ someone because of their religious background, as is currently the case for Sikhs and Jews. We also need more effective measures against racial and religious attacks and harassment. It is long overdue for the police and the law courts to treat these crimes much more seriously. To assist in this process a new criminal offence of 'racial violence' should be created, taking full account of how religious bigotry can be intertwined with violent racism. Moreover, the Northern Irish 'incitement to religious hatred' law should be extended to cover the whole of the UK to complement the existing law on incitement to racial hatred.

2 Colour is a factor in the total analysis of social disadvantage and inability to achieve full citizenship, but it is a weak indicator of need over and beyond the elimination of discrimination, for while some non-white groups may have more members in need of assistance, others may have less, and the needs in question will not always be based on race but will sometimes be identical to those of white people.

3 Some aspects of racial disadvantage can only be tackled within wide-ranging needs-based or class-based programmes, though the knowledge that non-white groups have been overlooked or discriminated against in the past (for example, in allocation of public housing), and as a result may be sceptical about provisions of new opportunities and benefits, may mean that explicit monitoring and outreach are required to ensure take-up by all individuals with the relevant needs.

4 Because racism is wider than colour-racism, we need to be far more informed [of] and sensitive to cultural and religious differences both in *identifying* racial discrimination and in strategies for its *elimination*. This will include training for relevant professionals in the complex character of racial inequality and difference, and in the appropriate cultural backgrounds; and also the recruitment, training, and promotion of individuals who can positively relate to one or more of the marginalized minority groups and can infuse their understanding into the policy-making and implementation processes.

5 We need to allow communities to use their traditions and values to meet their problems and disadvantages. Communities should be involved as partners at the level of strategic planning (for example, of an urban development programme) as well as in the provision of services (for

instance, housing associations, community centres, social and health services). This has to some extent been happening in the development of black and Asian housing associations; it is time that non-European traditions of medicine and therapy were taken more seriously and that social work was able to incorporate the kinds of family-orientated counselling services that are developing in the Asian voluntary and private sector.

6 Where supporting ethnic community structures is not a viable approach, effective ethnic monitoring should ensure that action is *targeted* to those who are actually disadvantaged (for example, in the labour market) and not simply to those who are not white. To this end it is essential that racial equality monitoring goes beyond the use of a black–white analysis or even a black–Asian–white analysis. The inclusion of an ethnic question in the 1991 Census allows us to do this, for not only was the question sensitive to diversity (though there is scope for improvement, for example giving proper recognition to the growing numbers of mixed-race individuals) but it provided both at a local and national level benchmark data critical to education, health and welfare services, employers, training agencies and so on. It would be a step backwards to reduce the plural findings of the census into a frame of just two or three categories. Above all, it would be to let down those who are 'the truly disadvantaged' and to whom policy must be targeted.

Among European countries, Britain has been considered to be at the forefront of recognizing and dealing with racial inequality (Modood, 1997b). But racism remains a major barrier to social justice in the UK, and our concern must go beyond narrow colour-racism. We now need to re-emphasize the connections between issues of race and the other concerns of social justice, in particular that racial disadvantage compounds class inequality and social deprivation and exclusion. To make these connections is at the same time to recognize that racism has different dimensions and affects different groups in different ways and to different extents. The most neglected form of racism is that which exploits physical *and* cultural difference. That knowledge must be a key component of any struggle for social justice. To emphasize any 'difference' may seem to make social justice and social cohesion more difficult, yet these multiple factors of inequality are integral to the challenge of achieving social justice. Multiculturalism is not just about the appearance of society; it is about refashioning concepts of equality to take account of the ethnic mix that exists in most British cities today. Ethnic and religious diversity has the potential to make society more interesting, more dynamic and more enriching for all its members, but will only do so when its complexities are understood and made integral to social justice.

Note

1 The evidence for the factual claims in this and the next four paragraphs is in Modood et al. (1997).

References

Anwar, M. (1993) *Muslims in Britain: 1991 Census and Other Statistical Sources*. Centre for the Study of Islam and Christian–Muslim Relations Papers, Birmingham.
Back, L. (1993) Race, identity and nation within an adolescent community in south London. *New Community*, 19 (2), 217–33.
Baldwin-Edwards, M. and Schwain, M.A. (eds) (1994) The Politics of Immigration in Western Europe. *Journal in West European Politics*, 37 (2), Special Issue.
Brown, C. and Gay, P. (1985) *Racial Discrimination: 17 Years after the Act*. London: Policy Studies Institute.
Cohen, P. (1993) The perversions of inheritance: studies in the making of multi-racist Britain. In P. Cohen and H.S. Bains (eds), *Multi-Racist Britain*, Basingstoke: Macmillan.
DFE (Department for Education) (1993) A new deal for 'out of schools' pupils. Press release. 23 April.
Home Office (1993) *Statistical Bulletin*, 7, 30 March.
Jones, T. (1993) *Britain's Ethnic Minorities*. London: Policy Studies Institute.
Modood, T. (1992) *Not Easy being British: Colour, Culture and Citizenship*. London: Runnymede Trust/Trentham Books.
Modood, T. (1993) The number of ethnic minority students in British higher education: some grounds for optimism. *Oxford Review of Education*, 19 (2), 167–82.
Modood, T. (1994) Establishment, multiculturalism and British citizenship. *Political Quarterly*, 65 (1), 53–73.
Modood, T., Beishon, S. and Virdee, S. (1994) *Changing Ethnic Identities*, London: Policy Studies Institute.
Modood, T. (ed.) (1997a) *Church, State and Religious Minorities*. London: PSI.
Modood, T. (ed.) (1997b) *The Politics of Multiculturalism in the New Europe: Racism, Identity and Community*. London: Zed Books.
Modood, T., Berthond, R., Lakey, J., Nazroo, J., Smith, P., Virdee, S. and Beishon, S. (1997) *Ethnic Minorities in Britain: Diversity and Disadvantage*. London: PSI.
Owen, D. (1993) *Ethnic Minorities in Great Britain: Economic Characteristics*. 1991 Census Statistical Paper No. 3, University of Warwick.
Parekh, B. (1992) A case for positive discrimination. In B. Hepple and E. Szyszczak (eds), *Discrimination: The Limits of Law*, London: Mansel.
UKACIA (UK Action Committee on Islamic Affairs) (1993) Muslims and the law in multi-faith Britain: need for reform. Memorandum to the home secretary, London.
Wilson, W.J. (1987) *The Truly Disadvantaged: The Inner City, The Underclass and Public Policy*. Chicago: University of Chicago Press.
Young, I.M. (1990) *Justice and The Politics of Difference*. Princeton: Princeton University Press.
Young, K. (1992) Class, race and opportunity. In R. Jowell, L. Brook, G. Prior and B. Taylor (eds), *British Social Attitudes*, 9th Report, Aldershot: SPCR.

11

Bridging the Gap between Them and Us

ANNA COOTE

How far can – or should – ordinary citizens participate in decisions about public services? What is desirable and what can be achieved? What are the effects of citizens having little or no involvement in the processes of planning or delivery? What are the likely consequences of any increase in citizen participation?

These questions have preoccupied theorists, practitioners and politicians for decades, and they are no less pressing today. In this chapter I look first at the development of public discontent with the welfare state in relation to questions of power and participation. I then consider the case for 'empowerment', as seen from the right and left of the political spectrum. Next, I assess the main strategy for empowerment adopted by the Conservatives in the 1980s and 1990s, and look at the trouble with choice. Finally, I briefly describe a range of options for increasing public participation in decisions about public services, and examine some problems and possibilities associated with them.

Growing Discontent

No one would say that the Keynes/Beveridge model for a welfare state was intended to disempower the people it sought to help. On the contrary, the explicit aim was to create secure conditions in which individual enterprise and creativity could flourish. But nor could it be said that the model was designed to empower individuals and communities to seek their own solutions to the economic and social problems they faced. It expressed the confidence of a relatively well-heeled and powerful minority in their own ability to create a better life for a disadvantaged and powerless majority. It was a top-down approach to meeting the urgent and basic needs of the masses, and it suited the times. A useful, if simplistic, analogy has been drawn between the post-war welfare state and the 'Fordist' model of production. When Henry Ford told his customers 'you can have any car you want so long as it's black', he could get away with it as long as most people were thankful to have any car at all.

As the volume and scope of public services grew in the 1950s and 1960s, so did expressions of discontent about the size and power of the state and the negative consequences for individuals and communities. The machinery of government was perceived by some as overlarge and overbearing, distant, out-of-touch and unresponsive; controlling rather than liberating; creating a sense of alienation and apathy; stifling initiative and encouraging dependency. Its personnel – the new elite battalions of bureaucrats and 'caring' professionals – spoke in tongues incomprehensible to the average citizen; its procedures spewed forth tangled webs of red tape and visited countless indignities upon its patients and 'clients'. It acted upon them, rather than making it possble for them to act for themselves. They did not own it; it owned them.

These criticisms are one-sided and glibly put; they do not cover the full range of problems associated with 'the crisis of the welfare state'. Nor do they represent anything like a fair picture of public opinion, either then or now (much of which was and remains favourable). But such views were felt and expressed in the 1960s, and have gradually gathered support and exerted greater influence until, by the 1908s, they were firmly embedded in current debates about social policy.

The welfare state depended for its legitimacy and public support upon a model of representative democracy which could not – or did not – adapt to the new conditions. While the role of government augmented in scale and sophistication, the opportunity for citizens to direct and check its activities scarcely evolved at all. Over the years there were some attempts to create new channels of communication between the state and the people: an example that springs to mind is the community development projects of the 1970s. But none made any substantial impact on the political ecology of the welfare state. They had insufficient time to evolve in a suitably favourable climate. Even where the left was in government – national or local – there remained an uncertainty about how much power could safely be allowed to seep out into the community (unless it were through the trusty conduits of the trade unions, who were themselves suspicious of grassroots politics they did not control). After 1979, conditions became increasingly inauspicious.

It is not surprising that the welfare state in general and local government in particular was so vulnerable to attack from the Thatcher government. When neo-liberal Conservatives announced their intention to 'roll back the state' in the 1980s, they were echoing sentiments which had been expressed by the libertarian left since the 1960s, and which struck an immediate chord with citizens whose day-to-day experiences led them to believe that the state was for 'Them' and not for 'Us'.

But if the tune was an old one, it was sounding very different by the 1980s. Increasingly, as the post-war baby-boomers gave birth to a new generation, the welfare state fell victim to its own success. People had been brought up, housed, educated and kept, on the whole, in good health and material comfort courtesy of the Keynes/Beveridge plan. They no longer had urgent and basic unfulfilled needs, but they still had many needs and finely tuned desires. They had not lived through war or slump; instead, an unprecedented number had been to college and taken up relatively well-paid, white-collar jobs. They felt themselves to be individuals with a right to distinguish themselves from the crowd and their desires from those of others. This lot would not be fobbed off with 'any car so long as it's black'. They wanted to shop around. Their critique was quite different from that of the anti-statist, community-activist left of the 1960s.

The needy masses of the post-war period became the demanding and individualistic 'contented majority' of the 1980s. A significant minority remained for whom needs were as urgent and basic as ever. But the welfare state appeared to be failing the minority *and* the majority. The 'haves' were fed up with paying taxes and being pushed around. The 'have-nots' found they could not look to the welfare state as a route out of poverty and deprivation; they were trapped in dependency and assailed by all of Beveridge's 'five giants' as they beat a retreat from the middle classes. Both groups wanted more respect, and more control over the kind of services they received. But they were not *united* in this – because respect and control had significantly different meanings for each. And different consequences might accrue from involving – or failing to involve – either group in decisions about planning and delivering public services. This raised the question of whether their respective claims could be met by strategies which tended to polarize or consolidate their interests.

The Case for 'Empowerment'

The word 'empowerment' has certainly become fashionable. Politicians of the right and the left have recently laid claim to it as they have been developing strategies for the public sector. What does it mean? Is it worth pursuing? These are big questions. All I can do here is briefly suggest how the idea of empowerment may be thought to serve different political purposes.

For the right, 'empowerment' speaks to the neo-liberal ideal of the free individual operating in an open market which, if left to its own devices, is believed to produce just outcomes. The citizen is to be empowered against the 'nanny state', which threatens this freedom, both by regulating market activities and by sending in cohorts of public-sector busy-bodies who interfere with people's lives. This is a selective judgement, as the right has no trouble supporting some kinds of intervention, such as by police, child-support procedures, school testing, etc. 'Empowerment' means people taking responsibility for themselves and their families, and thereby reducing their demands on the public purse. It does not address satisfactorily the problem of those who may need to be empowered from, rather than by, families or communities, such as women dependent on unreliable or abusive men; carers saddled with overwhelming responsibilities for elderly or disabled relatives; black families stranded in racist neighbourhoods, etc. It is an individualistic concept which does good service in preparing public opinion for rolling back and marketizing the state, but fails to address the complex interdependence of citizens, both within and between families and communities.

For the left, 'empowerment' can be seen as an integral goal of a more active and interventionist welfare state. The aim is not merely to provide a minimal safety net, but to enable all citizens to have an equal chance in life: to participate in society, to enjoy its fruits and to fulfil their own potential. Yet there is no 'level playing field'. Many individuals suffer unfair disadvantages, some of which are avoidable, some not. Some are there at birth, others accumulate during a lifetime, or occur at random, at any age. An important goal of the welfare state is to create the conditions for eliminating avoidable disadvantages and compensating for the unavoidable ones; or, put another way, to promote the distribution of advantage and risk in such a way that everyone can have an equal chance of determining the shape of her or his own life.

This view acknowledges that all individuals are essentially of equal value. But they have diverse and varying requirements, for which they are dependent upon each other. Broadly, these fall into two categories, which might be described as security and empowerment – and these they need in different measures at different times, according to their circumstances. The two are interrelated. Genuine security cannot be a gift from the powerful to the powerless; it has to be something the citizens themselves control, or else they remain dependent on the interests and whims of others, which is hardly a secure state of affairs. Conversely, the conditions of security (such as good health, education, income, protection from crime, etc.) make the individual's self-determination and exercise of power possible and sustainable.

There are more pragmatic reasons for pursuing the goal of empowerment which might be shared by policy makers of right and left. One is that it may make for more effective policies. The failure of the top-down approach of the post-war welfare state to shift a large minority out of poverty and dependence suggests that the people at the 'top' do not understand what the people at the 'bottom' really need. Would it not be better if more decisions were taken at the level at which they are implemented? (In EC-speak, this is subsidiarity.) A bottom-up approach might aid the development of more creative and productive ideas. Secondly, empowerment may help to sustain public support for social policies. If people feel some sense of ownership in, and control over, the services which affect them, they are more likely to take a positive attitude towards them – whether as tax payers or as beneficiaries, or as both.

It does not follow from any of this that empowerment is an unproblematic objective. Much depends on how the goal is pursued.

The Conservative Approach

In so far as they responded to the claims of the minority, the Conservatives stressed the importance of targeting benefits more closely upon those who are most 'in need'. It is beyond the scope of this chapter to assess the pros and cons of targeting, but two points can be made in relation to this discussion. First, targeting is about increasing *provision* for certain groups; it does not pretend to give those groups any more *voice* in decisions taken about themselves, or any more *control* over what happens to them; it suggests a way of moderating poverty, but not a route out of dependency. Secondly, it is a strategy which tends to polarize rather than consolidate the divergent interests of the majority and the minority.

The Conservative government responded to the discontent of the contented majority by rolling back as much of the state as far as it could without undermining their basic contentedness, and by introducing to what remained of the public sector a new consumerism. This has been associated with the 'post-Fordist' model of production and supply exemplified by such companies as Benetton and Marks and Spencer. It is customer-driven, not producer-driven; flexibility and diversity of output and a plurality of suppliers are seen as the keys to success, rather than monopoly and uniformity.

The patient or client of the welfare state was recast as customer in a quasi-marketplace. Individuals were to be 'empowered' with the help of the Citizen's Charter, which aims to enhance choice through increased competition, to specify what is on offer and to set up procedures for complaint and redress in case specifications are not met. Individuals, or the new institutional purchasers acting as their agents, are supposed to exercise power in the delivery process by choosing between alternative suppliers, and indirectly to influence the planning process by the accumulated weight of choices. This, at least, is the theory. Whether it can work in practice is another matter.

The Trouble with Choice

Few would argue with the Conservative government's drive to ensure that services are specified, standards made explicit, customers treated with courtesy and proper procedures set out for complaint and redress. But the customer-orientated approach will not make the citizen more powerful, if we take 'the citizen' to mean not just some, but all of us.

Public services operate according to economic and social rules which are quite different from those of the commercial world. There is a shared responsibility for serving the long-term interests of the community as a whole, as well as the immediate interests of individuals. Resources are finite. At Benetton or Marks and Spencer, what matters is keeping the customers satisfied, so that they choose to buy more. As long as demand keeps rising and profits are buoyant, managers are doing their job. They need not worry about people who cannot buy. Those in charge of the Health Service or the Benefits Agency have a responsibility for all who may need the services, and for making sure needs are met. There is no happy correlation between 'customer satisfaction', rising demand and increased profits. If more people want their services, it may or may not be in response to improved quality; either way, it spells trouble, because all the extra customers must be served with the same limited resources. Under these perverse incentives, choice cannot be the key to operational success. It is frequently irrelevant and sometimes counter-productive.

Individual choice

Choice is useful only where individuals can choose freely without pushing up public costs and without harming the interests of others. One example might be maternity services, if they are organized so that women can choose how their babies are delivered. But what about other forms or treatment? If all those whose health would benefit from high-tech heart surgery or an expensive new drug regime could have the treatment when they chose, the public purse could not take the strain without diverting resources from elsewhere. My choice of a heart operation may undermine your choice to have regular cervical smears, or a new hip joint. As far as possible, these conflicting interests must be reconciled – a complex process involving medical, economic and political judgement. The consumerist approach does nothing to enable ordinary citizens to participate in that process, although such a move could be genuinely empowering.

In some cases choice is feasible only within narrow limitations, except where individuals have the economic power to add to what the public sector provides. For instance, offering a range of menus in an old people's home can make a big difference to the residents. They want to choose what they eat – but so long as funds are curtailed, so too are their options. Deciding to eat pie and chips instead of pizza and salad is better than eating pie and chips willy-nilly, but it falls far short of dining à la carte – a luxury few can afford.

If you break an arm, you want to get your bones set quickly, not choose between a variety of hospitals offering different services. Here, choice is irrelevant: what matters is providing a first-class service to all comers. Likewise, if you are a severely disabled person dissatisfied with your residential home, you may not want to pack up and move, because that could be even more upsetting – and how can you be sure that the next place will be better? You may prefer to stay put and see the causes of your dissatisfaction removed.

Suppose all parents in one neighbourhood want to send their children to the same school: if the school is not big enough to take them all, it must select. If the parents themselves do not choose the selection criteria (and how could they all?), their freedom to choose that school becomes meaningless. Even where parents do select, their choices can affect other parents' freedom to choose. If all the pushy, middle-class families decide to send their children to a 'desirable' school at one end of town, other families can no longer have their children educated with classmates from a broad mix of social and economic backgrounds. The choices of one group can adversely affect the quality of schools available to another.

In the public sector, some citizens have more power to choose than others – because of where they live, how much they earn, how much they know, or how deftly they can manipulate the system to their advantage. The choices of the powerful can override and further disempower the powerless.

Institutional choice

Where public-sector purchasers acquire more power, this is not necessarily passed on as a benefit to the individual. When my GP chooses where to buy hospital services, she will presumably make some accommodation between her clinical judgement and the business interests of her practice. If as a result I get the hospital care I would choose if I knew what else was available, that is a matter of luck. There is no guarantee that her choices will be in what I (rather than she) perceive to be my best interests. If they are not, my power is limited to chosing another GP, who may make another set of choices that do not suit me.

Institutional customers often have limited power to choose. Unless there is a steady demand for services outside the public sector (for instance, in building, catering or cleaning) competitive conditions cannot be sustained. In a small town or rural area, there may be just one hospital, residential home, or day-care centre, with sufficient capacity to serve local needs. It would make no economic sense to set up another, unless the aim were to take over and close down the competition. Here, the power to choose is short-lived, and the power of choice to drive up quality ends when one monopoly succeeds another.

Yet even sustained choice and competition may fail to meet the needs of the citizen/user. Where resources are scarce, there is always a tension between cost containment and quality assurance. How that problem is addressed depends on whose interests are given priority, how 'quality' is defined and how resources are allocated – and that depends on the political values which guide decisions and on who takes part in decision making. The new post-Fordist consumerism does not give citizens any real power to affect the criteria by which institutional purchasers make choices on their behalf.

Strategies for Public Participation

In this section, I consider different strategies (other than choice) for enabling members of the public to take part in decisions about public services. I set out with certain assumptions. First, in a democracy, informed and active participation in a decision-making process should, as far as possible, be spread evenly among members of the community affected by the decisions. Secondly, where public and 'expert' opinions diverge, the public is not necessarily right (but then neither are the 'experts'). And last but not least, it is neither possible nor desirable for everyone to participate in all political decisions: so the ideal of maximal participation is tempered by the practical requirements of modern government.

Members of the public have a dual relationship with this area of decision making: as 'customers' and as 'citizens'. We are defined as 'customers' by our use of public services. As customers, we are concerned with how we ourselves and our immediate family are affected by various forms of provision at the point of use. We are defined as citizens not by our use of services but by our membership of the community. As citizens, we have much wider concerns – not just about ourselves, but about our neighbours and other members of the community, both now and in the future.

Decisions about public services take place at different levels. There are microlevel decisions about provision to individual customer/patients, and macrolevel decisions about planning and purchasing. Generally, members of the public relate to microlevel decisions as customers and to macrolevel decisions as citizens (although the distinction is often blurred). What follows is a brief and inevitably oversimplified range of options for involving members of the public in decision making, bearing in mind the citizen–customer distinction, as well as that between macro- and microlevel decisions. They are offered not as a definitive list, but simply as a means of further examining questions of public participation and empowerment.

Democratic representation

As I noted earlier, the main way in which members of the public have been able to exercise power in decisions about public services has been through the 'normal channels' of representative democracy. Individuals elect a representative who makes decisions on their behalf. Beyond that, they can try to exert further influence over the representative's decisions by lobbying them on an *ad hoc* basis, by joining a political party and participating in its policy-making processes, or by voting (or threatening to vote) for someone else next time.

Representative democracy is a form of collective decision making which, in theory at least, addresses the diverse and shared interests of the population as a whole. It is geared to macrolevel decision making. Electing a representative is an expression of the individual's status as citizen rather than as customer. Compared with other options it is relatively inexpensive and straightforward; it is also relatively inclusive, in that it is accessible to most people.

However, in a large and complex society, the distances between the decision and the representative, and between the representative and the elector, are so great that the amount of power actually exercised by the individual citizen is negligible. At a national level democratic representation is a vast and unwieldy system, poorly tuned to respond to shifting needs and circumstances. Voters may not know how their choice of candidate will impinge on different decisions about public services – either because political parties have no policies on particular issues or because they fail to define them explicity.

The power of the citizen may be enhanced, and responsiveness increased, by cutting the distances between elector and decision (for example, by devolving decisions, by increasing local representation) and by improving the means by which elected representatives account to the electorate for the substance and consequences of their actions. Crucial in determining the power of citizens are the nature of communication between citizens and their representatives, both during and between election campaigns, and how much citizens (and their representatives) know about the decision-making process and about the issues at stake.

Issue voting

This is where members of the public are asked to vote on a specific question or series of questions, in a local or national referendum. It is simply a form of consultation if the vote is not binding. However, if it is binding, and appropriate action is taken as a result, it becomes a form of participative democracy in which citizens decide for themselves. In a democracy, power to decide whether there will be a referendum and to determine the questions that are asked usually remains with the elected government. But there are examples (in the US) of 'people's referenda' where an issue is raised in the community and, if sufficient support is demonstrated, must then be put to the vote. In Italy, there are similar opportunities, although a referendum can only repeal existing laws, not make new ones, and they cannot decide on tax questions as the Californians did with Proposition 13.

Referenda are generally used for macro- rather than microlevel decision making. A referendum may be an opportunity for an extensive and well-informed public debate (some might cite the French vote on Maastricht as an example). Alternatively, it may be an occasion for railroading public opinion with a lot of rhetoric and little data. Or it may involve over simplified decisions about complex questions, to the detriment of many. A great deal depends on how much the public knows and understands about the issue in question, on how the question is worded, and on how power is distributed between those who campaign for and against. But in any case a referendum is a blunt instrument.

Consultation

There are various ways in which consultation can take place. It may involve asking a single question, or a set of questions; these may be put to individuals chosen at random or selectively. It may involve quantitative and/or qualitative surveys; these may be aimed either at specific sections of the community, at a representative sample of the whole community or at everyone in the community. Documents may be circulated to which responses are invited – from groups which represent special or general interests (community health councils are an example). Such groups may be invited to meetings to discuss the matters in question. Or consultative meetings may be held which are open to any members of the public who are able and willing to attend.

Consultation can be used in macro- and microlevel decisions. How effective it is at either level, from the 'public's' point of view, depends on what questions are asked, by whom, of whom, by what means and on the basis of what information; on whether any *dialogue* takes place and, if so, with whom; on how the answers are processed and conclusions drawn; and on what action is taken as a result. All these decisions remain in the hands of those who consult – as does the decision whether or not to consult in the first place. At worst, it can be a highly manipulative process, benefiting no one but the consulting body. At best, it can be a route towards more open and appropriate decisions, more enlightened decision makers and a better-informed public. If the process is thorough it does not come cheap. It cannot directly empower the public.

Negotiation

A thorough-going consultation involving dialogue with the public may come close to a negotiated agreement. The critical difference between consultation and negotiation is that the latter culminates in some form of shared decision making. One model is provided by the local-service agreement pioneered by a handful of local authorities including the London Borough of Islington and York City Council. It probably works best if there is a decentralized approach to local administration. It entails the setting up of neighbourhood forums, each one catering for a relatively small area. Well-publicized open meetings are called at which members of the public are invited to discuss in detail the planning of a local service. Islington selected refuse collection as its first candidate for an agreement. The neighbourhood forums were asked to make suggestions as to how the service might be improved. Officers were able to respond and to discuss any practical difficulties they might have in carrying out local suggestions. A dialogue took place, leading to a negotiated agreement which embodied changes to the service. The agreement was then published and distributed in each neighbourhood as a form of guarantee, with a procedure for complaining if the terms were breached.

Different kinds of service require different procedures: refuse collection is a universal service and cannot be dealt with in the same way as an elective service such as swimming pools or a needs-based service such as community care. So, for example, the process would include not just neighbourhood forums, but discussions, in the first case, with swimmers at the pools and, in the second case, with carers and care users. Each case has its own problems and pitfalls, which this rudimentary summary cannot begin to explore. The common component is that the procedure involves a dialogue aimed at reaching an agreement which users and providers both feel they share.

Negotiated agreements represent an approach to decision making which addresses members of the public both as citizens and as customers. It is concerned with planning and delivery. Assuming that this approach operates smoothly and achieves its full potential (a big assumption), the following observations can be made. Unlike representation, negotiation attempts to build as short a bridge as possible between the individual citizen/customer and the decision. Unlike issue voting, it insists upon dialogue as an integral part of the decision-making process. Unlike consultation, it enables the public not just to offer an opinion which might inform the decision, but to participate directly in the decision itself. Unlike all of these, it calls for clear and thorough communication of relevant information. It sets high standards of participative democracy and can be expected to raise the expectations of the public about the quality of service.

On the minus side, negotiation may exclude the views of people who are unable or unwilling to participate in discussion (individuals can be encouraged but not forced to participate). It may thus be dominated by unrepresentative individuals or groups. At best, negotiated agreements can work only if they are highly localized, in conditions which maximize the opportunity for wide and representative public involvement. So this approach cannot be applied to regional or national planning decisions. While members of the public have no formal right to negotiate agreements, it is up to the authority in question to decide whether or not to share power in this fashion.

The success of this approach depends upon a supportive political culture, not just on the part of the authority, but within the local community. Without such a culture, the process will deteriorate into a ritual dominated by unrepresentative minorities, raising hopes only to dash them. A supportive culture can be nurtured but, where it does exist, it is unlikely that it can be sustained unless the formula is applied *sparingly*. Negotiation takes time and energy on the part of residents as well as authority representatives. Time and energy are scarce and precious resources – especially among women. If every service were subjected to local negotiation, the likely result would be increasing apathy and disbelief, leading to anger and resentment.

Social rights

How might the introduction of social rights affect the power of the public in decisions about public services? It is useful at the outset to distinguish between *substantive* and *procedural* social rights. Substantive rights are rights to actual services and facilities – for example, a hospital bed, an appointment with a consultant, or an operation. Procedural rights are rights to ensure that individuals are dealt with fairly when they come into contact (or try to come into contact) with the providers of a service. It could be said that substantive rights are for citizens and procedural rights are for customers – although this distinction is not clear cut.

Unlike 'voice' or choice as empowerment strategies, rights are definitive. Once set up, they are supposed to be fairly inflexible. This can be a strength or a weakness. It depends how they are introduced and what they relate to. Social rights may be established by statute which may or may not be entrenched against a simple majority vote in Parliament. Alternatively they may be introduced by voluntary codes of practice or protocols, or by means of negotiated local agreements. They may be expressed as duties imposed on institutions, or as entitlements held by individuals. They may be enforceable ultimately through the courts, or they may be statements of intent or aspiration, which may guide the interpretation and formulation of legislation, or simply help to create a certain climate of opinion. Substantive rights may serve a limited but useful purpose if they are expressed only in aspirational terms; procedural rights are of little use if they cannot be enforced.

Is it possible to envisage all citizens of the UK having certain substantive social rights, enforceable ultimately through the courts? In times of scarcity, how would this affect the setting of priorities and the allocation of resources? For example, suppose I have an enforceable right to 'health care on the basis of clinical need': doctors agree that I should have a kidney transplant. But someone else needs a hip replacement and she has the same rights as I do. The health authority cannot afford to provide both operations. Whose 'right' takes precedence? Will a judge decide? By what criteria and in whose interests will judgement be made? It is hard to see how substantive rights which depend upon publicly funded intervention (unless severely limited) can be enforced effectively while public resources are limited.

What about procedural rights? There are six basic principles of fair treatment, already well established in UK law. They include the right (1) to a fair hearing, (2) to equal and consistent treatment, and (3) to unbiased decisions. (4) Where a decision involves an element of discretion (for example, an expert's assessment of an individual's predicament) it should follow explicit guidelines. (5) When a decision is reached, reasons should be given. (6) The person concerned should have a right to appeal against the decision, or to complain about any action that is taken. These principles safeguard our civil liberties if we are brought before the courts in criminal or civil actions. One possibility, explored in detail in *The Welfare of Citizens* (Coote, 1992), would be to extend them to the administration of public services. There is no simple formula for this. It would mean taking a long, hard look at each area of health and social services, to find appropriate ways of putting the six principles into practice. Open decision making and rights to information and advice are a vital part of the picture.

Procedural rights can help to distribute the power of choice. For example, if Citizen A and Citizen B both have a right to information and advice about the options from which they can choose, it matters less that Citizen A already knows, through personal contacts, about the options and Citizen B does not. Suppose Citizen A and Citizen B have vouchers to buy education for their children: both choose to send their children to the same school; the school has only one place, but Citizen A knows the head teacher and Citizen B does not and consequently the A child gets the place. The right of appeal could help Citizen B to fight through the web of privilege which divides her from Citizen A. If choices are made within a framework of judicial fairness, they are less likely to compound existing inequalities.

Procedural rights would not normally have a direct effect on macrolevel decisions such as setting priorities and allocating resources for health and social care. They would, however, have an impact on microlevel decisions, such as those made by doctors and social workers about treatment for individuals. For better or worse it is at this level that a lot of 'rationing' takes place – for instance, when a social worker assesses a client's needs or when a doctor decides on a course of treatment, the decision is affected by (among other considerations) the professional's estimate of how much money he or she can spend on the intervention. Here, procedural rights could help to prevent the irrational, arbitrary or unfair allocation of resources.

By setting up clear procedures, they would facilitate the fair and equal treatment of individuals. By establishing individual rights to information at different stages of these procedures, they would help create more open decision making – and this is one of the main ways in which the power of the citizen/customer is enhanced.

There are at least two other strategies associated with the 'rights approach' which could help to empower citizens in macrolevel decisions. One would be to set up procedures, possibly in the form of statutory codes, to apply the principles of judicial fairness to specific planning processes. Thus, decision making would be required to be open and to follow explicit guidelines. It would have to be unbiased and aim to ensure the equal and consistent treatment of individuals. Reasons for decisions would have to be given, and there could be rights of appeal against some decisions. Procedures could be set out in statutory codes. The main virtues of this would be to create clear and transparent decision making, to encourage good communications, and to provide safeguards for individuals who feel they have been treated unfairly.

A second strategy would be to strengthen group rights. In some circumstances the liberties and abilities of citizens are more effectively protected by groups than by individuals on their own. The rights of appropriate associations to be consulted in policy formation, to participate in decisions and to pursue complaints and appeals could be promoted through legislation as well as through codes of practice. Public policy should in any case recognize the importance of group activity in the process of empowering individuals. Where appropriate, groups should be encouraged to inform, advise, represent and act as advocates for their members. They should also be supported with resources (space, shared expertise, equipment, etc.). All this deserves further exploration – and it will be necessary for any such work to address the problem of how far groups can be genuinely representative.

A danger inherent in the 'rights' approach to empowerment is that it may lead to a proliferation of rules and regulations. Too many decisions will end up in the courts and no one will benefit except the lawyers. It would therefore be important to develop routes for enforcing rights which do not inevitably fall into these traps. This might be achieved by strengthening complaints procedures, by giving more teeth to the local ombudsman and to health service commissioners, by resolving not to use courts where tribunals will do, and by beefing up advice and advocacy systems so that laywers are brought in only as a last resort. But in any case, rights should be seen as a complement to, rather than a substitute for, other routes to public empowerment. They are not a panacea, but one strategy which may be combined constructively with 'voice' and choice.

In Conclusion

I have suggested ways in which members of the public can be disempowered by the welfare state, and how an uneven distribution of power can cause public discontent and distort the effects of welfare strategies. I have indicated a range of options for involving members of the public – as customers and citizens – in decision making at different levels. IPPR's work on citizens' juries, described in the next chapter, arrives directly out of this analysis. There are benefits, for individuals and for communities, to be derived from greater public involvement in planning and providing services. There are also costs and complications. However, the fact that empowerment is a troublesome issue does not mean that it can be set aside from other deliberations about social justice. The distribution of power has a bearing not only upon the basic concept of social justice, but also upon its interpretation and implementation. We cannot contemplate a 'fair' society in which only a few decide what 'fairness' means and how it is to be achieved.

Reference

Coote, A. (ed.) (1992) *The Welfare of Citizens*. London: IPPR/Rivers Oram.

12

Citizens' Juries

ANNA COOTE AND JO LENAGHAN

This chapter describes a remarkable experiment in democratic practice. Between March and November 1996, the Institute for Public Policy Research conducted a series of five citizens' juries in a pilot project designed to test a new way of involving the public in decisions which affect their lives. These, together with a parallel series sponsored by the Local Government Management Board, were the first such juries to be conducted in the UK. We shall argue that the experiment has opened up new possibilities for democracy: it suggests that if we heed the lessons offered by the pilot juries, we might begin to transform what is now a rather sterile and immature relationship between citizens and policy makers into something more dynamic and constructive for the next millennium.

Dysfunctional Democracy

The citizens' jury experiment was inspired by a critique of representative democracy as practised in the UK and elsewhere. It is widely acknowledged that, although democracy is highly prized as an ideal, its implications for the modern world are problematic. In mass society, direct democracy is not a serious option. Instead, the people consent to elect representatives to govern on their behalf (Held, 1993, pp. 18–21). But what constitutes and sustains a consensual relationship between electors and elected? What makes for a flourishing or moribund relationship? And how much does the quality of the relationship matter?

These are substantial questions which can only be dealt with briefly here. In our view the main problems with the relationship at the centre of representative democracy can be summarized as follows.

Distance

In a large and complex society, the distances between the electorate and their elected representatives can be very great. The distance is perceived both horizontally (the geographical distance between localities and increasingly centralized government) and vertically (multiple layers of decision making, reinforced by a culture of secrecy, through which information and consent must be filtered).

Distorted representations

The structures of representative democracy pre-date modern communications technologies. The two do not synchronize easily and adjustment is clumsy and painful. Citizens and their representatives must learn to understand each other (and themselves) as reflected in mirrors held up to them by the mass media. They cannot control the undulations of the glass, however subtle or sensational. Much grotesque posturing results. Can they find ways of looking directly at each other, or can they only hope to refine their skills of interpretation and manipulation?

Mistaken identity

Successive Conservative governments in the 1980s and 1990s . . . sought to redefine the citizen as customer. Political behaviour, which involves thinking and acting collectively to negotiate and change the conditions in which we live, is thus reduced to consumerism, which involves thinking and acting individually and passively, and which is contingent upon the individual's resources (see Bynoe, 1996). Accordingly, members of the public should be content to choose from products or services provided by others, and have no role in determining what these should be or how they should be delivered. The quasi-market relationship between customer and supplier of public services is real and important. But it is atomized and reactive, and only one part of the picture (Prior et al., 1995). It can neither substitute for, nor be allowed to pre-empt, the political relationship between citizen and government.

No dialogue

Elected representatives, in whom the public have vested responsibility to make decisions on their behalf, owe accountability to the public for those decisions. They render themselves accountable by standing for election every three to five years and, generally, this is where accountability begins and ends. But John Stewart (1995) has argued persuasively that account-ability is not guaranteed merely by democratic election; it is a two-way process. It involves *being held to account* and *giving an account*. This suggests that what is needed is, in effect, a continuing dialogue with the electorate in which the public has power to obtain and provide informa-tion, while the authority is open to scrutiny, listens and responds. If such a dialogue occurred, it would inform the authority's decision making between elections as well as voters' choices at election time. It would also help the public to exercise control, informing its choices about conferring or withholding consent. Without dialogue, the relationship between elected representatives and the public remains superficial, stilted and predomin-antly silent.

Denial

If, as seems apparent, democracy is disabled by distance, distorted rep-resentations, mistaken identity and lack of dialogue, it is sustained by an assumption that citizenship is a passive rather than active condition (O'Leary, 1996). This assumption rests on a mutual denial of worth and ability. On one side, there is a widely held view among decision makers that ordinary members of the public lack the capacity to grasp complex issues or to form views of any relevance, that they are too gullible and will believe anything they read in the popular press, that their views are inevitably shaped by narrow and selfish concerns, and that they are generally apathetic and will not take the time or trouble to consider anything which does not affect them directly and personally (Renn et al., 1993, p. 205). It is thus futile or hazardous to attempt to involve them in any kind of dialogue. On the other side, there is a widely held view among the voting (and non-voting) public that the decision-making process is hopelessly impenetrable and whatever they do or say will make no difference. Many believe their own contribution would be worthless – a fear compounded by their lack of experience; most believe politicians are selectively deaf and unscrupulous in pursuing their own interests. In these ways, the assumption of passive citizenship serves to deskill the people's democratic practice, justifies their continued exclusion and shores up their consent for a moribund relationship.

Bad Government

Passive citizenship and an immature relationship between electors and elected make for bad government as well as dysfunctional democracy. Without dialogue in politics there can be no understanding. Without understanding, there can be no trust. Without trust, there is no real consent. Political influence flows through channels which ought to be peripheral rather than central to the working of democracy: favours exchanged, deals finessed, elite networks, spin-doctoring, the foibles of media folk (Keane, 1988, p. 4). What can ordinary people do? Nothing, for the most part. But then there are sudden eruptions of popular protest which seem to stand for much more than the issue immediately at stake. Whether it be a blockade against the export of live animals or the construction of a by-pass, a demonstration against hospital closures, or a riot against the poll tax, such expressions of active citizenship take on a symbolic quality, carrying a weight of feeling which cannot be distributed elsewhere. Opinions tend to polarize, views are encoded and differences oversimplified. Options for negotiation and compromise are closed off and the experience can be profoundly frustrating for all sides (Stewart, 1996, p. 2).

Meanwhile, decision makers operate with severely limited understanding. They may (or may not) consult experts and interest groups, read the pollsters' tea leaves, rifle through their post-bags, lunch with lobbyists, heed their pick of media commentators or simply contemplate their navels. They do not bring to the process any substantial knowledge of the views and experience of most ordinary citizens whose lives will be affected by their decisions. Furthermore, they have no obvious means of forging a compromise building a consensus where difficult choices have to be made between options where there are strong interests and arguments on either side. Government is thus deprived of a vital resource, often with dismal results. Homes are designed that residents can never cherish. Roads are built in the teeth of popular revolt. New but unloved shopping malls and parks fall to vandals. Health authorities save redundant hospitals to appease local campaigners. Two-thirds of voters stay away from local elections. Politicians sink lower and lower in the public's esteem. Distrust, frustration and mounting insecurity pollute the democratic environment (Stewart, 1995, 1996).

Our experiment with citizens' juries was born of a conviction that the situation is not hopeless. First, we must be clear about what is likely to nurture a flourishing, rather than moribund, relationship between citizens and decision makers in a modern democracy. Then we must look for ways to make that come about.

Mutual Trust and Active Citizenship

As we noted earlier, trust is the key; not blind faith, but the kind of measured confidence that comes from informed understanding, forged in a mature, adult-to-adult relationship. If there were this kind of mutual trust, both sides could share responsibility for the difficult choices that have to be made in a 'runaway world' – where the risks associated with new technologies and global communications cannot be predicted or controlled.[1] In place of secrecy, passivity and mutual contempt, there needs to be openness, interaction and mutual respect. Then the relationship could have a chance to flourish.

How can we begin to change the democratic environment? Stewart et al. argued, in an earlier discussion of citizens' juries (1994), that the aim should be to build the 'habit of active citizenship'. Assumed passivity is the enemy of trust, offering no incentive to develop informed understanding on either side. But innovation should 'work with the grain of how citizens actually behave' and acknowledge that 'citizens are not the passive beings they are often assumed to be' – even if they never attend public meetings or demonstrations. They vote, if not in *sufficient*, often in *significant* numbers, not only in elections but in ballots on such issues as the opting out of schools and the transfer of housing estates. They do jury service – an obligation most take seriously. The process of responding to surveys could be seen as a form of participation, as could membership of a studio audience or a focus group used for research purposes. Innovations should build on such familiar forms to create a range of opportunities for active citizenship.

Citizens and Service Users

In considering ways of involving the public in decisions about services to the public, it is important to bear in mind that members of the public have a dual relationship with those responsible for commissioning and providing services. They are both service users and citizens. In each capacity they have different interests and these sometimes conflict. For example, in the National Health Service, individual patients have an immediate and personal interest in the service they receive. Citizens, meanwhile, have a broader and longer-term interest, as voters, tax payers and members of the community: they are interested in what happens not only to themselves, but also to their families, neighbours and fellow citizens both now and in the future. These two perspectives must always be taken into account, but it must be acknowledged that they may conflict, for example, where an individual requires an expensive treatment which would use up substantial resources so that others could not receive the help they needed.

Too often, public involvement exercises confuse the patient/user and the citizen. Consulting the public is taken to mean consulting relevant user groups, so that individuals and groups who are not current users, but who may use the service in the future, or who do not use it although they need it, are excluded from the process.

Once the citizen/user dichotomy is recognized, efforts can be made to involve the public in both capacities. It is relatively straightforward to identify users and to locate them: they are usually in direct contact with providers, or organized in special interest groups for the purposes of campaigning or mutual aid. Furthermore, users are often highly motivated to take part in decisions. Efforts to involve them are sometimes insensitive, off-putting and futile: there is undoubtedly much room for improvement in many of the methods employed (Renn et al., 1993). Nevertheless, it is relatively easy, if attention is paid to problems of language, literacy, mobility and small group dynamics, to establish a meaningful dialogue with service users – for example, by inviting them to meetings, by conducting surveys or by asking them to fill in questionnaires or comment on consultation documents. On the other hand, ordinary citizens who are not current users will either remain invisible, silent and excluded, or will turn, if provoked, to oppositional politics – where views become entrenched and negotiation futile. Different methods are required to draw them into the decision-making process.

Options for Citizen Involvement

A spectrum of possibilities exists for connecting the citizen to the decision-making process – from a simple transmission to a complex negotiation. Below, we set out briefly some examples to illustrate different points along the spectrum. How far different models encourage mutual trust and active citizenship depends on the extent to which views and information are exchanged, on the nature of that exchange, and on how power is distributed among the parties involved. Our list is not definitive and is merely intended to signal a range of generic approaches to public involvement.

Opinion polls can reach substantial numbers of individuals relatively cheaply and can be scientifically verified if the sample is large enough. But they are superficial and non-interactive, designed to elicit the *uninformed* views of the public through single- or multiple-choice questions. The organization commissioning the poll controls the agenda and decides how to interpret and deploy the results.

Focus groups are a feature of qualitative research. They are usually conducted in sets, each group comprising eight to ten individuals recruited to represent a section of the population, and lasting for about 90 minutes, during which time one or more topics are discussed. While some information is provided, this is strictly limited and the purpose is to probe uninformed opinion in more depth than can be achieved by opinion polls. As with the latter, the organization commissioning focus groups controls the agenda and decides how to interpret and deploy the results.

Referenda can include entire populations, resembling an election, but inviting votes on a single question (for example: should the UK join the European Monetary Union?). Depending on the nature of the campaign leading up to the referendum, there may be opportunities for the spread of relevant information and for public debate, although this may be minimal and there is nothing built into the process to ensure that views are developed through deliberation. The media are likely to play a substantial role which may be more or less illuminating. Since a referendum must enable large numbers to register a view, the issue at stake has to be distilled into a simple yes/no vote, and the model can therefore be likened to a blunt instrument rather than a precision tool. As a rule, power to determine what question should be put in a referendum remains with the government of the day, although in other countries there are arrangements for a people's referendum, where a sufficient number of signatures are collected in its favour. The results cannot easily be distorted or misrepresented to the public. If the referendum is binding, it confers considerable power on the voting public (McNulty, 1995).

Public meetings are the traditional means by which ordinary citizens are invited to participate in a decision-making process. Audiences are, of course, self-selected and, in general, meetings are attended only by seasoned local activists or people with a special interest in the agenda. At best they can provide an opportunity for the exchange of information and views and for an open debate over two to three hours or longer. At worst, they are poorly attended, dominated by narrow interests and given over to the futile rehearsal of fixed positions. Power to set the agenda and act on the results remains with the commissioning organization, but as the meetings are open and local media are often present, opportunities to (mis)interpret the event are restricted.

Citizens' forums or panels are gaining currency among local authorities and health authorities seeking ways of involving the public in their decisions. They come in several varieties. Broadly, they have a defined membership drawn from the local community and meet regularly for 90 minutes or more, to discuss a specified range of issues. Forums may be open to anyone living in a locality, or belonging to a particular range of interest groups. They have been used in some instances to negotiate a decision with the local authority (Thomson, 1992). Panels usually have a fixed membership, sometimes with a proportion replaced at intervals of one or more years. Members may be invited representatives of local organizations or ordinary citizens recruited to represent the local population. Because members meet over a period of time, they have a chance to become informed about the subjects they are asked to address, as well as to debate issues for a matter of hours. One danger is that panel members may develop an 'insider's' mentality, becoming less detached from the interests of the organizers. The commissioning body controls the agenda and decides what to do with the results. Its freedom to manipulate the proceedings or interpret the outcome depends on the degree of openness with which the sessions are conducted.

Deliberative polls are a way of involving statistically significant numbers of ordinary citizens in an extended, informed discussion leading to a vote or series of votes. A national sample of voters is brought to a single site, for one or two days, to interact with witnesses and debate the issue at stake. Their views are polled, usually before and after the event. Deliberative polls were developed in the United States by James Fishkin and have been introduced to the UK in a series organized by Social and Community Planning Research, which was televised on Channel Four. John Stewart has commented that 'deliberative opinion polls take as their starting point opinion polls and seek to correct their weaknesses' (1995). The organizers control the agenda but the process is open and the results are not easily manipulated. Deliberative polls have not yet been commissioned in the UK by any official organization but have been used by the mass media to explore public opinion in depth.

What Is a 'Citizens' Jury'?

The model described here is based on the IPPR pilot project, reported in Coote and Lenaghan (1997). Accordingly, a citizens' jury consists of between twelve and sixteen individuals who are recruited to be broadly representative of their community. Their task is to answer questions on a matter of national or local importance.

What distinguishes a citizens' jury from other models? This particular process aims to combine *information, time, scrutiny, deliberation, independence and authority*. Most other forms of opinion research and public involvement have some of these features. What is distinctive is the package: the model is designed to ensure that all features are present to a substantial degree.

The jurors are brought together for about four days. They are asked to address one or more specific questions and are given as much relevant information as possible. They have the chance to cross-examine the witnesses who present data and arguments to them, and to call for additional witnesses and information. They have time to deliberate – to discuss and debate the matter in hand, both with the witnesses and amongst themselves in small groups and in plenary sessions – before drawing conclusions. The jury is independent of the commissioning body and its verdict is expected to carry some authority, derived from an understanding that the jury is unbiased and the proceedings are fair and appropriate to the task of citizen participation.

Who convenes a citizens' jury?

Any organization may convene a citizens' jury. In the UK in 1996, they were commissioned by a range of health and local authorities. Voluntary and private-sector organizations, including the utilities and regulatory bodies, have also expressed interest. The juries in the IPPR pilot series were all commissioned by local health authorities with the exception of one which was commissioned directly by IPPR. All were asked to consider question/s relating to a policy or planning issue of some practical importance for the citizens represented by the jury.

How are jurors recruited?

The IPPR juries were recruited and moderated by the market research organization Opinion Leader Research. Different methods of recruitment were employed, but each case combined random selection with stratified sampling, to match a profile of the local population derived from census and other data. The jurors were ordinary citizens with no particular axe to grind. They were not self-selected, or chosen because they had a special interest or expertise relating to the question before the jury. They were paid up to £200 for their time.

How are the jury sessions organized?

The agenda for each jury was drawn up by IPPR, which also took responsibility for inviting and briefing most of the witnesses, and for compiling the jury's report. For three of the five juries, an advisory group was set up to involve a range of local organizations in the preparatory stages. The jurors heard from up to four witnesses a day. The witness sessions and plenary discussions were moderated by a team of two from OLR with experience in facilitating group work. Each jury was expected to reach clear conclusions by the end of the fourth day.

What happens to the jury's verdict?

The juries were not obliged to deliver a unanimous verdict. In each case, the jury's conclusions, including minority views, were compiled in a report. Once this was approved by the jurors, it was presented to the commissioning body. The jury's conclusions were not binding, but the commissioning body was asked to meet certain conditions. It was expected to publicize the fact that the jury had been convened and the question/s it had been asked to consider, and to respond publicly to the jury's report within a set time. Where the jury made clear recommendations, the commissioning body was expected either to abide by the recommendations or to explain publicly why it did not intend to do so.

How much does a citizens' jury cost?

The total cost of a jury can be hard to calculate. It varies according to the amount of time required for the preparatory stages and how this time is accounted for, how much the jurors are paid, witnesses' expenses, and whether accommodation and catering are charged at commercial rates. We estimate that a four-day jury is likely to cost between £16,000 and £20,000.

How Does a Citizens' Jury Compare with Other Models?

Citizens' juries are closest to focus groups in form and to deliberative polls in purpose and procedure. They are more intensely interactive, providing more information and more time for scrutiny of evidence and deliberation, than other models. They involve very small numbers and could make no claim to be statistically significant unless a series of juries were convened to consider the same question – this has not yet been attempted in the UK. Their status is independent, they can call their own witnesses and the jurors must approve the report of their conclusions before it is distributed. Whether or not their findings carry a weight of authority will depend on whether they are seen to be fairly recruited to represent the local population, and to be conducted openly and without bias or distortion.

Note

1 'Runaway World: People and Politics in the Late Modern World' was the title of a conference in January 1997 to coincide with the publication of Giddens (1997). The conference was organized by the Institute of Contemporary Arts in collaboration with Routledge, IPPR, Polity Press and King's College, Cambridge; see also Beck (1992).

References

Beck, U. (1992) *Risk Society: Towards a New Modernity*. London: Sage.

Bynoe, I. (1996) *Beyond the Citizen's Charter*. London: IPPR.

Coote, A. and Lenaghan, J. (1997) *Citizens' Juries: Theory into Practice*. London: IPPR.

Giddens, A. (1997) *Critical Assessments*. London: Routledge.

Held, D. (1993) *Prospects for Democracy*. Cambridge: Polity Press.

Keane, J. (1988) *Democracy and Civil Society*. London: Verso.

McNulty, D. (1995) *Referenda and Citizens' Ballots*. London: Commission for Local Democracy, University of Greenwich.

O'Leary, S. (1996) *European Citizenship: The Options for Reform*. London: IPPR.

Prior, D., Stewart, J. and Walsh, K. (1995) *Citizenship: Rights, Community and Participation*. London: Pitman.

Renn, O., Webler, T., Rakel, H., Dienal, P. and Johnson, B. (1993) Public participation in decision making: a three-step procedure. *Policy Sciences*, 26, 189–214.

Stewart, J. (1995) *Innovations in Democratic Practice*. Birmingham: Institute of Local Government Studies.

Stewart, J. (1996) *Further Innovations in Democratic Practice*. Birmingham: Institute of Local Government Studies.

Stewart, J., Kendall, E. and Coote, A. (1994) *Citizens' Juries*. London: IPPR.

Thomson, W. (1992) Realising rights through local service contracts. In A. Coote (ed.), *The Welfare of Citizens*, London: IPPR/Rivers Oram, pp. 129–52.

Part III

Service Design and Delivery

The Commission on Social Justice argues that 'everyone is entitled, as a right of citizenship, to be able to meet their basic needs for income, shelter and other necessities'. In the concluding part of this *Reader*, we ask how these needs should be met by focusing on the planning and delivery of welfare services. We ask how quality can be assured in the interests of citizens and service users, and who should provide those services.

Anna Coote (chapter 13) presents a critical analysis of quality assurance in health and welfare services, developed with Naomi Pfeffer in *Is Quality Good for You?* (IPPR, 1991). She describes the strengths and limitations of four approaches to quality – traditional, scientific, managerial and consumerist – and proposes an alternative *democratic* approach which combines the best of these and embodies strategies for making the public more powerful.

We then (chapter 14) consider the impact of the Citizen's Charter, in pursuit not just of efficiency, but of fairness and a commitment to social rights. Public services should respond to society's needs and be appropriate and effective for the individuals who use them. The Citizen's Charter claims to have improved services but it has been flawed in its approach and, in practice, often ineffective. Reforms are needed if public services are to meet public expectations while resources remain limited. Ian Bynoe proposes a new programme to take public services into the twenty-first century, which tackles the weaknesses of the Citizen's Charter and seeks to build on its strengths.

To illustrate the impact of this approach on policy development, Anna Coote and David Hunter (chapter 15) argue that, in a democracy, the means to health can be understood as an essential part of citizenship. Yet how can we promote health for all on an equitable basis with limited resources? Jo Lenaghan (chapter 16) argues that to reconcile citizen's rights to appropriate health care with the need to manage scarce resources, we need a new framework for decision making in the NHS. Since rationing decisions are not just made on the basis of clinical discretion, but also involve moral and political judgements, they should not be made by the doctor alone. She suggests that a framework of rights, set out in a code of practice, would ensure that each citizen has guaranteed access to a fair assessment procedure within the health service, based upon national principles open to public scrutiny and challenge.

13

Understanding Quality

ANNA COOTE

'Quality' is a word we see everywhere. We could be forgiven for thinking it is a simple concept. We're all in favour of quality, just as we're all against sin. In fact it means different things to different people and those differences can be controversial – perhaps especially when applied to public services. In this chapter, I shall describe four approaches to quality, and different ideas and strategies applied to achieve it. I shall summarize their strengths and limitations, and then outline briefly another approach which combines the best of these. The four main current approaches to quality can be described as traditional, scientific, managerial and consumerist.

The Traditional Approach

This is the most familiar and commonplace usage, most readily understood outside the world of 'quality' specialists. The traditional and still widespread assumption is that a quality product or service is superior to others and probably more highly priced. It speaks of high standards of production, delivery and presentation associated with exotic restaurants, French perfume, Rolls Royce cars. It is about 'no expense being spared' and delivering 'the best that money can buy'. It is luxury. It suggests perfection. It has class connotations: 'the Quality' is how working-class people used to refer to upper-class people – at least in some Victorian novels.

In the marketplace, this kind of quality confers status on the customer. If you buy a quality product you signal to others that you are someone special or superior, or richer than others. With public services which are delivered free on the basis of need, this meaning has no direct relevance. However, it has an important influence – because no matter how the word 'quality' is used, this is the meaning that sticks to it. Even when measures are introduced to camouflage a deterioration of services, if those measures are referred to as 'quality assurance', it will make them sound as though there is a striving for perfection. So this meaning has a public-relations function, because of its association, through the traditional usage of the word, with 'no expense being spared' or 'every effort being made' to ensure the best possible product or service.

The Scientific Approach

According to this approach to quality, experts define and prescribe standards of acceptability. It is associated with scientific management, a set of ideas about how to manage organizations which developed during the first quarter of this century and which has continued to dominate the public sector and much of the private sector until recently. It grew out of the era of mass production and assembly-line working methods, which have been described as Fordism and Taylorism.

The scientific approach is about measuring 'fitness for purpose'. The British Standards Institute refers to assessing 'the totality of features and characteristics of a product or service that bear upon its ability to satisfy a given need' (BS 4778: 4.1.1, 1990). Features and characteristics have to be specified to set standards and then performance is monitored to assess conformance to standards. The idea is that goods and services that fail to come up to scratch are rejected; the producers or providers may be punished by loss of contract or job, or by incurring a financial or other penalty.

This approach challenges the notion of professional autonomy in decision making, for instance the 'clinical freedom' of doctors to decide about treatment. It can improve information about outcomes; about what is expected and what is delivered, and establish shared standards of practice. These may be regarded as positive factors. On the negative side, the scientific approach tends to promote measures of quality which are unilateral and brook no dissent: they are laid down by 'experts', rather than by those who receive or use services; they have an aura of scientific authenticity and are not generally negotiable. Moreover, this approach is paternalistic. The experts are in control. They decide what is a 'given need'; they decide what is 'satisfaction'. They may or may not be guided by a public-service ethic.

They may or may not tailor standards to suit their own predilections. And while experts tend to focus on inputs, it is outputs which matter more for the users.

Examples of the scientific approach would include national standards set by the British Standards Institute, hospital accreditation schemes, 'QALYs' [quality adjusted life years] and most forms of performance measurement, audit and inspection. The Citizen's Charter Performance Indicators issued by the Audit Commission (1992) under the Local Government Act 1992 also come into this category.

The Managerial or 'Excellence' Approach

According to this approach quality is about satisfying the customer. Customer satisfaction is central to the management philosophy which is currently in the early 1990s fashionable and fast becoming dominant in the commercial world, and is also a force behind the restructuring of public services. It was developed in the US between the wars, and taken up enthusiastically by Japanese manufacturers and by innovative British retailers such as Sainsbury and Marks and Spencer. The key text is Peters and Waterman's *In Search of Excellence* (1982). This demonstrated that customer orientation was the key to commercial success, and made the pursuit of quality in this sense a managerial holy grail. While the scientific approach can be said to be Fordist, this is post-Fordist. Total quality management is the strategy which most thoroughly expresses the managerial approach to quality. However, TQM is only as good as the sum of measures invoked in its name – and these can vary almost infinitely.

The managerial approach promises managers a strategy for the survival of their organization in rapidly changing competitive environments. While more traditional strategies advocate the accumulation of tangible and intangible assets, as a hedge against hard times, the 'excellence' strategy is to 'get it right first time, on time and to cost'. Getting it right is about giving the customers what they want.

In place of control by bureaucratic procedures which prescribe how things are to be done, there are strategies which focus on results and aim at controlling output. Management by status is replaced by management by leadership. The issuing of mission statements is becoming a familiar feature of the 'excellence' landscape – to inspire and lead the workforce. According to this approach, everyone is responsible for output, not just the person at the top: the whole workforce is involved. Customer satisfaction is the key to success; all workers have a stake in the success of the organization and therefore are committed to satisfying the customer. Vertical organization may give way to horizontal structures, which help to spread responsibility. Large organizations may be broken down into smaller, semi-autonomous units, to get close to the customers, in order to improve understanding of how they will be satisfied, and to respond more effectively to their demands. Control by ownership is replaced by control by contract – both inside and outside the organization's boundaries. The aim is to be able to respond more flexibly to changing customer demand.

An obvious strength of the managerial approach is that it encourages an organization to focus on what the customer/user wants instead of what the expert thinks is best. It can help break down hide-bound bureaucratic structures, increase flexibility and transparency of decisions, and make for more responsive services. However, there is one fundamental aspect of this approach to quality which does not transfer easily from the commercial to the public sector. Where services are free and allocated on the basis of need (as in the public sector) and where resources are limited, there is no straightforward causal link between customer satisfaction and organizational success. Indeed, if customer satisfaction leads to increased demand, rather than adding to the success of the providing organization by boosting business and profits, it can merely add to its troubles, because all the extra demand must be met with the same, finite resources.

The managerial approach promotes, to a far greater extent than does the scientific approach, the idea of competition between alternative providers (to see who can satisfy the customer best). In the public sector, however, competition is not always appropriate, and where providers fail to satisfy their customers, it may sometimes be a more effective use of public funds to help them improve their service, rather than simply to force them to close down.

While the scientific approach challenges the autonomy of individual professionals by introducing standards against which their performance can be measured, this approach goes further, shifting power from professionals towards managers. (This makes it popular with managers.) There has been a vast influx into the public sector, especially the Health Service, of managers whose job it is to manage, not to provide. A wide range of decisions has passed into the domain of managerial discretion. Management as a science is supposed to be value free and above politics but in fact it can be highly political, especially when it operates in the public sector. It is not regulated in the way that professional practices are through the self-regulating codes of professional bodies. Nor are managers in the public sector directly accountable for their political actions to the democratic representatives who are responsible for political decisions. This points to a need for a new management discipline, and a new structuring of managerial discretion, which is geared towards the goals and values of the public sector.

Furthermore, the managerial approach, by focusing on the customer, side-steps an issue of central importance in the public sector. The customers (in the sense of service users) are not the only ones who matter. The interests of the general public must be taken into account. Some services have more than one customer. Take schools, for example: whose interests are paramount? The children who are currently at the school or their parents, or local employers, or the community at large? And what about tomorrow's parents and pupils? Surely all of these are important.

The Consumerist Approach

While the excellence approach expresses the desire of producers to satisfy customers, the consumerist approach expresses the desire of customers to be satisfied. It casts customers in an active role and seeks to increase their power.

An important dimension of this approach is the encouragement of customer choice through enhanced competition. The idea is that customers reject shoddy goods and shop elsewhere, so that providers either mend their ways or go out of business. How readily providers respond depends on the selling power of the provider and the purchasing power of the customer. A monopoly supplier can afford to worry less about satisfying customers. A monopoly buyer has considerable clout.

In the commercial sector, consumers may be individual buyers or large and powerful purchasers (an example would be a large motor company like Ford or Nissan: when they buy components from suppliers they are extremely powerful in their position as customer). An equivalent in the public sector is the new institutional consumer, such as a fund-holding GP, a health authority, or a local authority when it puts services out to tender. Individuals have far less muscle, but their consumer power can be increased in two ways. One way is by joining forces with other individuals in consumer groups and movements, such as the Consumers' Association or (in a more institutional mode) bodies like Passenger Transport Authorities. Another way is through the development of enforceable consumers' rights.

The Citizen's Charter, issued by John Major's government in 1991 (HMSO, 1991), encapsulates the consumerist approach to quality. It is based on the premise that individuals can be 'empowered' by means of specified (though not enforceable) guarantees about the nature and content of services.

It is committed to increasing competition and choice, so that individuals can exercise power by 'shopping around' for alternatives. And it endorses strong and clear procedures for complaint and redress if what is provided fails to tally with the specifications.

The consumerist approach shares many of the strengths of the managerial approach to quality. It focuses on the user rather than on the provider and places great emphasis on the importance of the user's satisfaction with goods or services. In addition, it seeks to increase the power of individual users to express satisfaction or dissatisfaction, and to put pressure on providers. It would be hard to overstate the value of measures to empower ordinary citizens in a modern democracy.

The main weakness of the consumerist approach (and the Citizen's Charter) is that, like the managerial approach, it can relate to individuals only in their capacity as customers or service users. Yet members of the public have a far more complex relationship with public services. They are both customers, interested in what happens to them today at the point where they use a service, and citizens, interested in what happens to their families and their neighbours, today, tomorrow and in the years to come.

Consumerism relies on individual choice as a means of empowerment. But choice may be illusory or irrelevant in the public sector. In some areas of provision, such as care for the mentally ill or accident and emergency treatment, alternative providers cannot be found, because services are not potentially profitable. In some cases, users may not want to 'take their custom elsewhere'. For example a young man with a broken leg just wants to get his bones set; an elderly woman in a residential home may not want to pack her bags and go elsewhere, preferring to stay in familiar, but improved surroundings.

Rights to complain or receive redress may amount to too little, too late. If a doctor or a social worker gets something wrong, the results may be fatal – and in general this kind of problem is likely to have more serious consequences than imperfect goods purchased in a high-street store. The consumerist approach does not embrace rights of appeal against decisions, or public participation in decision making. As far as consumer groups are concerned, those which deal with public services were mainly developed in the 1960s and 1970s, when service providers were different from the ones we know today. These groups were geared to challenge big bureaucracies and monopoly suppliers, not the fragmented, market-orientated structures of the 1990s. They have found it hard to adapt to new conditions and have had no help from the government to do so. The community health councils are one obvious example. The new institutional consumers of the public sector, shaped by the reforms of the 1980s and early 1990s, are supposed to represent the individual consumer and act on their behalf.

However, it is doubtful that they can ever be relied upon to do so, since they must also serve their own interests. A fund-holding GP, for example, may be influenced in her decision about which treatment to purchase for a patient not just by what the patient needs, but also by a desire to protect the financial viability of her practice.

It is also doubtful whether these fund-holding bodies should be expected to behave as consumers, shopping around among competing providers to find the best bargain. In some cases, it would be an unacceptable waste of public money to create a choice – for example, in a rural area where one hospital serves the whole population. In other cases, it is possible to generate competition for a contract, but this can be hard to sustain between tenderings. If there is already a thriving private market (for example, in catering, cleaning or house repairs), organizations which fail to win a contract to supply public services may find business elsewhere to keep them going until the next tender. In areas of provision where there is no such market, failure will mean certain death for the unsuccessful companies. In many important health and social services, the break-up of monopoly supply and the creation of competition is either impossible or irrelevant to the pursuit of quality. For example, accident and emergency, most acute health services and child protection fall into this category.

Where the choice of institutional purchasers can be maintained, it may be no guarantee of quality from the user's point of view. This will depend on the criteria for choosing between competitors: If choice is driven chiefly by a desire to contain costs, then quality will probably suffer. Where resources are scarce, there is bound to be a tension between cost containment and quality assurance. How that problem is resolved depends on who takes part in decision making, whose interests have priority, how quality is defined, how resources are allocated. The main political battles over the future of welfare revolve, to a large extent, around these questions.

A 'Democratic' Approach to Quality

In this final section of the chapter, I shall outline an alternative approach to the pursuit of quality in public services. This acknowledges the differences between commerce and welfare, and recognizes that the public has a complex set of relationships with welfare services, as citizens, customers and providers; it is concerned with planning and delivery. It draws upon other approaches to quality and adapts them accordingly. The traditional approach (conveying prestige and positional advantage) is clearly inappropriate. The remaining three all have something to offer. Thus, *fitness for purpose* is derived from the scientific approach. *Responsiveness* is derived from the managerial approach. *Empowerment* is derived from the consumerist approach.

This approach to quality starts from the premise that the primary purpose of a modern welfare system, for which services must be 'fit', is *equity*. This does not mean giving everyone the same, but giving everyone an equal chance in life, so that every citizen can participate in society, enjoy its fruits and fulfil their own potential. If this is the purpose, then we must take account of the fact that people do not start out as equals. Some have disadvantages, which may be avoidable or unavoidable. It is part of the purpose of a welfare system to eliminate avoidable disadvantages and compensate for those that cannot be overcome. It is also necessary to recognize that individuals have diverse and varying needs and that people want and need more control over their own lives. The goal of equity (or equal life chances) thus points to two further goals: *responsiveness* and *empowerment*.

The goal of equity may conflict with the goals of responsiveness and empowerment: as far as possible, these must be reconciled. The process of defining and assuring quality provides a bridge between them: a means by which that reconciliation can be negotiated.

Strategies for Making the Public More Powerful

Openness

An open system is one which makes relevant information easily accessible to the public, sustains transparent decision making, is open to information from the public, and is susceptible to ideas for change which come from the public.

Individuals have different information requirements as customers and citizens. As customers, people need to know: what services are available and how to apply for them; the bases on which decisions are taken about their own treatment and care; information which will help them participate in those decisions; how to complain about unsatisfactory services; and how to appeal. As citizens, people need to know: how welfare services are planned and delivered; how money is spent; who makes the relevant decisions; and where and when they are made. As citizens and customers, people need information about outcomes, for example: how different forms of treatment and care affect patients and clients; what patterns can be detected; what are the costs and benefits; criteria for rationing and targeting; how members of the public can influence decision making.

People need easy access to this information, in a form they can readily understand, in their own first language. Individuals may need someone to help them process the information and make appropriate use of it, especially where it involves technical knowledge. It is also important that everyone knows where to go to get information.

Openness is essential if the systems of planning and delivery are to be properly accountable to the public as citizens and customers. Information should be a right of citizenship, not a privilege conferred by politicians and providers. Furthermore, the system should be open to public participation in decision making and be ready to adapt and change.

Rights for customers and citizens

The case for a new framework of rights in health and social services is developed elsewhere in a volume produced by the Institute for Public Policy Research (Coote, 1992). Rights cannot be seen as any kind of panacea, but it can be argued that they are essential if power is to be shifted towards the citizen/user, and as such they are an important part of a democratic approach to the pursuit of quality.

Rights are not worth having unless the public understands they can be claimed and enforced – although this should not inevitably lead to a system over-run by lawyers. Particularly relevant to this discussion are proposals for *procedural* rights, which promote the fair treatment of individuals, by ensuring that they have access to information, advice and advocacy, as well as to a range of rights governing decision-making procedures (Galligan, 1992). Where resources are scarce, procedural rights may be easier to enforce than substantive rights (that is, rights to stated benefits or services).

An important new dimension to the idea of welfare rights can be found in recent local experiments with *service agreements* (Thomson, 1992). Briefly, these are the product of negotiation between local authorities and local communities – about what services should be provided and to what specifications. They incorporate a guarantee that services should be provided as agreed, and specify channels of complaint and modes of redress for individual users, should things go wrong.

Public participation in decision making

A democratic approach to the pursuit of quality depends on members of the public participating actively in decisions about what constitutes a quality service, and whether such services are actually being delivered. Individuals can participate collectively as citizens and individually as customers. The impediments to public participation are manifold: for example, the time and place at which meetings are held, the language in which they are conducted, and the difficulty of balancing paid employment with the demands of unpaid work. Where sufficient numbers do not turn up regularly, the process is easily dismissed as 'unrepresentative' and therefore worthless.

Individual 'representatives' of the public who sit on decision-making bodies are often ill informed, isolated and without any firm sense of purpose in being there; they may be overwhelmed by impenetrable documentation, or thrown into confusion when committee papers arrive late. There may be no effective channels for reporting back to the people they are supposed to represent. Many people in this position burn out quickly and drop out – or else the job falls to those who are rendered unsuitable by their relish for unrepresentative committee work. Many individuals do not want to participate, because they have been led to believe by long experience that their voice will not be heard. In order to take a more active role, people need to believe it will produce some positive results; they must feel they have the power to make a difference. They must also feel they will not be tyrannized over by a few who are 'expert' at public participation.

What all this points to is the need for a strong infrastructure supporting different forms of public participation. Relevant information should be made accessible – not simply available to people who come in search of it, but taken to people who would not otherwise know it existed. Individuals should have clear rights to participate at different stages of decision making. There should be proper support for representatives, and effective channels for them to communicate with the public they are representing, as well as adequate space and resources to hold public meetings and advertise them widely. Furthermore, strategies should be developed to ensure that the views and experience of those who cannot participate are taken fully into account. Data about decisions that are taken and how they affect the public should be collected and publicized on a regular basis. But perhaps the greatest spur to public participation is likely to be provided by clear signs from public authorities that they want to enter into dialogue with the public, and that they will listen to their views and be guided by them.

In general, communication between individuals and public authorities can be aided by *intermediate bodies* – for example, user groups and community groups. These can be a source of information, advice and advocacy, a catalyst for individual involvement, a forum for discussion and decision making, and a means of representation. Public policy can be aimed at supporting these intermediary bodies, recognizing the vital part they can play. However, intermediate bodies should not themselves escape the quality process: they too must be open, responsive and subject to audit.

Choice

Choice has a useful but limited part to play in the pursuit of quality. The scope for collective choice can be enhanced through service agreements, and generally by opening up decision making to public participation. The scope for individual choice can be widened too. It depends on alternatives being available and on people having access to the information necessary to make choices which will benefit them. Where choices – large or small – can be provided without undermining the common goals of a welfare system, they should be supported and sustained.

Strategies for Building a Responsive System

Most people would favour the idea of a welfare system which responds to individual needs. However, a system whose primary goal is to give everyone an equal chance in life, and whose resources are limited, cannot hope to respond equally to all individual needs. Some are more urgent than others; some have been unjustly overlooked in the past. If these differences are to be accommodated, some individuals must get more and others less. Responsiveness involves deploying information about needs and resources, and negotiating with the public about how resources are allocated. That process of negotiation should take place within a framework of nationally agreed goals, set down by Parliament, and should attempt to develop agreements with local communities about how those goals are reached.

Involving the workforce

A key factor in the pursuit of quality in welfare is the motivation of the workforce – especially those in direct contact with the public. Resources are scarce and, as we have noted, productivity is not linked to profitability in welfare as it is in commerce: financial incentives cannot be regarded as a major way of motivating staff. Even in the commercial world it is now widely recognized that success depends on gaining the commitment of all workers at all levels to the pursuit of an organization's goals. It is also understood that commitment is not bought by money alone, but by training, security and involvement in developing products (Peters and Waterman, 1982).

However, a sense of commitment cannot survive the continuous punishment of low wages and poor working conditions, without prospect of improvement. A combination of factors is needed to harness the commitment of public-sector workers and maximize the contribution they can make, both individually and in groups. These factors would include training and career development, flexible working arrangements and employment-protection measures – especially for those with family commitments. They would also include involvement in planning and organizing services by employees at all levels: 'front-line' workers who are closest to the public often know more about how to meet their needs than managers, senior professionals and other more senior personnel. For this to happen, there would need to be substantial changes in the rules governing competitive tendering, since these currently insist that value for money is the determining factor. Purchasing bodies are not allowed to specify any organizational arrangements or working conditions which may interfere with competition on this basis.

The horizontal structures associated with the 'excellence' approach, in which workers at all levels are supposed to be responsible for quality, would seem to demand this kind of development. Moreover, a genuine commitment by the organization as a whole, which reaches all levels of staffing, to fulfil the purpose of the welfare system (a change in the 'culture' of the organization) could strengthen workers' sense of doing a worthwhile job; it should also provide a sound justification for decent employment policies. Employees of the welfare services are citizens and customers too. You cannot build a system which aims to give everyone an equal chance in life on a disadvantaged and exploited workforce.

Changing management and professional cultures

The concept of *public service orientation* represents an attempt to translate the 'excellence' approach into the language of the public sector. In their pioneering work for the Local Government Training Board, Michael Clarke and John Stewart (1990) have argued that it is possible to develop a rigorous and distinctive form of management that does not simply reproduce the patterns of commercial management, but is geared to the special requirements and conditions of public service, and able to manage for equity as well as for efficiency. Furthermore, there is scope for extending these ideas to begin to change the ethos of the 'caring' professions to one marked more strongly by an outward focus, continuing development and strong communication.

Strategies for Ensuring 'Fitness for Purpose'

All the strategies listed so far should help to ensure that welfare services are fit for their purpose – which is to give everyone an equal chance in life. Last but not least, it is important to stress the value of systematic auditing, built into the system, based on specifications negotiated with the public and using methods of review which take full account of users' needs and experience.

Is It Worth It? The Question of Cost

It will be clear by now that the pursuit of quality will incur costs – to provide information, advisors, advocates; to set up and run systems for enforcing individual rights and for negotiating service agreements; to provide public meeting spaces and publicity; to train staff and to measure performance. Is it worth spending money on quality when the whole system is so hard pressed for cash? Some would say that it is better to spend the money on the services themselves – more home helps, more hip replacements, more holidays for carers – and that line of argument is certainly compelling. However, there is far more at stake than providing more of the same.

There is no shortage of evidence that the public is concerned about what kind of services they are getting, not just the quantity. Indeed, it is this concern, no less than the problem of resources, which has prompted politicians on all sides to look for ways of reorganizing the 'welfare state'. The whole system needs to be redesigned and redirected, in order to cultivate and sustain the active support of the public it is there to serve. That support becomes more, rather than less, crucial in times of scarcity – because it is the public who must pay.

Note

These arguments are developed more fully in Pfeffer and Coote (1991).

References

Audit Commission (1992) *Citizen's Charter Performance Indicators*. London: Audit Commission.

BS 4778: 4.1.1 (1990) quoted in Trades Union Congress, *Quality in Public Services: Quality Assurance in a Trade Union Perspective*, London: TUC.

Clarke, M. and Stewart, J. (1990) *Developing Effective Public Service Management*. London: Local Government Training Board.

Coote, A. (ed.) (1992) *The Welfare of Citizens*. London: IPPR/Rivers Oram.

Galligan, D. (1992) Procedural rights in social welfare. In A. Coote (ed.), *The Welfare of Citizens*, London: IPPR/Rivers Oram, pp. 55–68.

HMSO (1991) *Citizen's Charter*. London: HMSO.

Peters, T.J. and Waterman, R.H. (1982) *In Search of Excellence: Lessons from America's Best-Run Companies*. New York: Harper & Row.

Pfeffer, N. and Coote, A. (1991) *Is Quality Good for You?* London: IPPR.

Thomson, W. (1992) Realising rights through local service contracts. In A. Coote (ed.), *The Welfare of Citizens*, London: IPPR/Rivers Oram, pp. 129–51.

14

Beyond the Citizen's Charter

IAN BYNOE

It is tempting to ridicule the Citizen's Charter. Before it ended as a separate service, the ludicrous 'Cones Hotline' was part of the programme. After a total of £120,000 had been spent on set-up and running costs, it received 11,500 phone calls leading to the removal of only five sets of traffic cones (Guardian, 1994). Former Whitehall mandarin Sir Kenneth Stowe, in evidence to the Treasury and Civil Service Committee, termed the Charter 'the latest management toy', amongst those which 'tend to be marketed, usually at high cost with unproven claims about their efficacy' (quoted in Treasury and Civil Service Committee, 1994). The policy and its impact are often wrapped up in language amounting to little more than political hyperbole, and there is no systematic programme of independent research to evaluate the effects of the policy.

All governments need good news stories. The Conservative government in the mid-1990s is keen to attribute any positive development in services to its charter. The 1994 summary report stated that London Underground's new charter had introduced 'a new right of unrestricted access for wheelchair users' (Citizen's Charter Unit, 1994). One cannot imagine just how this new entitlement was meant to be enjoyed by those needing to negotiate a wheelchair through the narrow and crowded passageways found in most stations on the system. It is no surprise to discover that the whole programme is regarded by so many as a public-relations exercise.[1] Does it add up to anything more than this?

The policy touches subjects of widespread public concern which politicians ignore at their peril. Not the least of these is how valued public services can become more responsive to the wishes and expectations of those who use them (Prior et al., 1995). No less important is the need to find ways of improving poor services and eliminating waste or duplication, whilst available resources remain constrained. The charter philosophy and programme have experimented with measures to tackle both these questions and should be neither dismissed nor underestimated (Deakin, 1994; Lewis, 1993; Pollitt, 1994). The Treasury and Civil Service Committee and Select Committee on the Parliamentary Commissioner have approved aspects of the policy. The critique most often levelled at the programme is not that it is wholly misconceived or plainly wrong; rather that it is incomplete, unbalanced or simply ineffectual (Prior et al., 1995).

Although the Treasury's hand is clearly seen in those aspects of the policy designed to drive down costs (Deakin, 1994), one aim of the programme is improving standards in public management and administration. In parallel, we can see a vital stress on consumer perceptions of current standards and on the need for future improvements. Such objectives may have been only poorly accomplished by present policy, but this does not detract from their importance. If the aim is a robust, popular and long-lasting public sector, able to offer services of high quality and also to respond to contemporary needs and expectations, they need to be recognized and pursued.

Information means power

Elements of charter policy aim to render the service user both more informed and more active in their relationship with services, and providers more responsive in their attitudes and expectations. One way is by simply defining what it is that public organizations offer the citizen. There are many problems with this approach, not least the difficulty many people have in adopting the role of 'active' consumer, particularly where services are provided because of ill health or vulnerability or in coercive conditions (Beale and Pollitt, 1994; Barnes and Prior, 1995). Despite this, the aim clearly meets a widely held belief that people should know the broad features or minimum standards of available services and how to go about securing them. Pursuing such an aim has to be a priority for any open organization.

The programme has required providers of complex services to see the importance of agreed and publicized descriptions of their services. Although their efforts have often produced brief, incomplete or vague statements, to abandon the process now would benefit neither those who have to use services, nor the public at large. The former need the information in order to secure an appropriate and responsive service; the latter to render it accountable. If organizations cannot agree upon the scope, coverage and planned effectiveness of what they do and present these attributes in clear and intelligible ways to the public, one must wonder how they are to be held accountable in any way at all for the resources which are voted to them in the public's name. Without information, the public are robbed of any opportunity to participate in even the most rudimentary way.

Diagnosing difference: tackling inequities

As well as needing information, citizens and public service users are entitled to justice. Inevitably, there are considerable variations in the ways in which different services are experienced. Recent reports have illustrated such differences – for example, in health care, social services, policing and education.[2] The scope, level and quality of services may differ as a result of decisions by those managers to determine different priorities, based on locally assessed needs. Where the decisions are down to democratic choice, they will depend on politically determined preferences.

However, such factors will not account for all geographical variations. If the service delivered to some users is of lower quality or effectiveness than that enjoyed by others in a similar position and the reason for this cannot be justified, how can such a publicly funded service be regarded as equitable, or its administration seen as fair?

The charter programme focuses on the measurement of performance, on comparison between similar providers and on the importance of independent inspection and audit. These are all relevant to the pursuit of equity in public-services provision. This aim may not be one which commands high priority within government but the information now becoming available may force ministers to give it greater attention when deciding on their policies.

The publication of local education authority comparative performance figures in March 1995 (Audit Commission, 1995) for the first time highlighted wide variations in provision for nursery education and other spending on schools. For children aged 3 and 4, the average provision represented 62 per cent of this age group, whilst the highest was 95 per cent and the lowest just over 20 per cent. Spending per pupil on schooling also varied considerably.

Some of the Citizen's Charter changes have begun a process which will enable these and many other variations to be unravelled, with consequences for politicians which they may not welcome. The charter approach may not provide answers but it does help to identify problems. Initial attempts at enabling comparison have often proved crude and inaccurate. If such early experimentation has shown the need for greater fairness and sophistication when analysing the reasons for difference, now is the time to work towards achieving those objectives. Performance measurement may have created perverse incentives, distorted performance or reinforced mediocrity (Audit Commission, 1996), but rather than abandoning such tools of analysis altogether it is worth investigating the defects and trying to eliminate them.

Rewarding quality

The Charter Mark award scheme has proved popular amongst many provider organizations. It has highlighted evidence of quality in public services, signposting for the whole public sector how this might be achieved. Such awards cannot, of themselves, protect and preserve standards. Recent experience with water and gas utilities has shown this. However, they can help to capture the defining characteristics of responsive and innovatory services and demonstrate how changes can be made to work. If the scheme continues under a new government, it should be further developed. It is also worth examining the value of extending this award scheme, or a similar one, to privately supplied services. Changes are needed which render far more public the system of nomination, assessment and award. Harden (1992, pp. 72–3) has usefully proposed a formal 'notice and comment' procedure.

Complaints and redress

The Citizen's Charter highlights the need for improvements in the handling of complaints and provision of redress to service users when things have gone wrong. The record which many services have in this field is lamentable and the case for fundamental reform is undeniable. The task force on complaints, together with the parallel inquiry by the select committee and reports on particular services, such as the NHS, have certainly made progress in setting out the minimum requirements for a fair and effective system. Future policy should build on the advances which have been made.

Lay involvement in inspection and adjudication

Besides stressing the importance of independent inspection, the charter has highlighted the need for lay involvement in the scrutiny of public services, such as prisons, courts, social services and schools, and the desirability of lay adjudication of complaints. This principle is essential if accountability is to be vigorous with consumer and citizen perceptions able to influence the running of services.

The lay adjudication of complaints within public services, currently found in the Inland Revenue, is likely to become more prominent in the future. The changes to the NHS complaints procedures will introduce a panel with lay membership to adjudicate a complaint before it may be considered by the health service commissioner. The new NHS panels to hear and consider appeals against a refusal of continuing health care will also have lay representation. These new institutions will provide a model for other services wishing to improve procedural justice for people seeking or using a service. The reports of the Complaints Task Force and the select committee also point to the benefits of intermediate adjudication and each may give this some impetus.

There has been progress with lay involvement in inspection, though the trend has been towards consumer not citizen participation. This may result from confusion as to what is really expected. 'Lay' involvement suggests something other than mere independence from the body inspected, hinting that the wider public's interest needs to be represented. The First Charter Report defined the role thus: 'people who are not professionally connected either with the Inspectorate or with the service itself should take part in inspections to represent the views and concerns of the general public' (Citizen's Charter Unit, 1992).

Taking social services as an example, guidance issued to local social services authorities in 1994 (Department of Health, 1994b) stressed the importance of 'lay assessors' in inspecting social care and children's services and the value which should be given to their views. Authorities were told that those appointed could include 'present and former users, their relatives and friends' (ibid., para. 12). With only a limited pool of people willing and suitable to help with the inspection of any service on an entirely voluntary basis, past and present users of a service, or their relatives, are bound to figure prominently amongst them. Again, these changes have begun to open up inspectorates formerly closed to public involvement. These are some positive features of the policy and its potential impact. They provide a basis for further development and experimentation. However, they do not reflect the sum of charter policy, or its full effects.

The Citizen's Charter: Limits of Current Policy and Philosophy

When the charter is judged as a whole we have doubts, which are widely shared (Deakin, 1994; D. Cooper, 1993; Lewis, 1993; Barron and Scott, 1992; Prior et al., 1995; Rhodes, 1995; Tritter, 1994; McKibbin, 1993).

- There is ambiguity and confusion around the terminology which the charter uses – charter, rights, standards, expectations, etc.
- The charter makes no provision for or lacks effective sanctions for non-performance of public service duties including the withdrawal of a service or a reduction in its overall standards.
- The prominence accorded to consumer interests, rather than those of citizens, has reduced accountability and diminished the notion of citizenship, when the aim of policy should be to enlarge these ideas.
- Though the charter claims to bring decision making closer to people and their concerns, much of the programme's content and direction derive from a managerial, 'top-down' approach at odds with the commitment to reflect citizen or user priorities and preferences.
- The charter's reliance on standard setting, conventional measurement of 'performance' and publication of selected information on 'results' is inappropriate for important characteristics of public services.
- Although the charter has been given a high profile at substantial public cost, its practical policies frequently appear marginal to other government programmes or priorities.

The Citizen's Charter: Lessons after Five Years

Before proposing what policy should replace the charter we should assess the lessons that five years of experience have given us.

A single policy or programme intended to reach every part of the public sector must be based on a full understanding that public services are hugely diverse.[3] Arrangements for providing them have many distinguishing characteristics, for example:

- some are universal, whilst others are selective;
- some are elective, whilst others are involuntary;
- some are needs-based, whilst others are available without proof of need;
- some are highly personal, whilst others are wholly impersonal;
- some are free, whilst for others user charges are collected for the whole or part of the cost;
- some are still delivered by public authorities whilst others are now provided independently, many by private limited liability companies.

Thus, there are services which nearly everyone uses (highways); services people choose to use or not to use (railways, BBC broadcasting); services which are needs-based such as health care or community care; services only used by narrow and identifiable social groups, often with no choice whether to do so or not (income support, social services, public housing); and there are services only used when the law compels a person to do so (prisons, secure psychiatric treatment, residential childcare). Some organizations will be run from remote, impersonal and inaccessible bureaucracies (Inland Revenue, DSS Contributions Agency). Others will be familiar and have face-to-face contact with service users often on a regular basis (GP, class teacher, legal aid solicitor or local beat police constable).

Not only are these provider/user relationships widely varied, but the aims of the services themselves differ as much. They range from measures to combat poverty and inequality to the resurfacing of motorways, from the preservation for public view of prehistoric dinosaurs to the deportation of illegal immigrants. Some contacts involve only a discrete and uncomplicated provision of service whilst others, such as education, depend for their effectiveness on a continuing 'partnership' between provider and user, the quality of which will influence the level of benefit obtained from state provision. While some services operate within tiny margins of uncertainty, the outcomes for others are wholly unpredictable. How can any policy maker attempt to work on so vast a canvas without the necessary messages becoming diluted and confused in the process?

The charter offers a broad approach to public administration whose appeal lies in its simplicity and apparent adaptability. To step beyond it, new policy would have to propose principles or ideas, adaptable without being anodyne or ineffectual, yet creative enough to offer real and practical benefits which capture the public's imagination and win and maintain its confidence. Public services are mainly provided by large and complex organizations which are difficult to manage and which have their own histories and individual cultures. Any principles we propose must be relevant and useful to managers and others needing to change attitudes and ways of working. They need to offer opportunities for those already working for public-service improvements. Below, we propose a set of principles which meets these requirements.

The need for real transfers of power

The charter claims to have increased the power of those who use services. We assume that this means the power to be listened to; the power to contribute to decisions about services; the power to secure redress for failed or poor-quality services. We have outlined some of the progress which has been made but the reality is that, when compared with the demands facing most services, such changes have been marginal at best and counterproductive at worst. Furthermore, the background is one in which many services have been withdrawn or curtailed rather than expanded, and many have been removed from directly elected democratic control. There is no evidence that those whose situation renders them especially powerless – the poor, the sick, the ill educated, the vulnerable or those whose race or culture otherwise excludes them – have been given greater influence and priority because of changes related to the Citizen's Charter.[4] Indeed, the reverse may be true.

If the charter has done little or nothing to redress the inequalities all too often seen in citizens' experience of services then what should this suggest for future policy? It must be prepared to back rhetorical talk of 'rights' with defined and enforceable duties on service providers. Although the rhetoric of the policy promises more power for the citizen, charterism has not transferred influence from those who control the level and scope of provision to those whose well-being or opportunities are inextricably linked to such choices.

Recognizing the 'public' in public services: the limits of choice

The charter promises choice and adequacy to public-service consumers as though in some way these are their entitlements. The *realpolitik* surrounding cash-limited services, and wider public-interest considerations, frequently limit the capacity of any service to acknowledge these as true 'entitlements'. New policy must affirm the political foundations on which publicly funded and provided services are based. It must recognize the difference between market customers and public-service users, and the choices which each may be able to exercise. Policy needs to reinterpret the 'public interest', that is, the purpose for which services exist and against which they will be judged, and acknowledge public responsibility for the hard choices which are necessary.

New policy must also prevent the exclusion of legitimate user and citizen expectations by political, professional or provider interests. The Citizen's Charter does not offer such an assurance since at its heart it simply wants to encourage individual consumerism. Its approach leads to a form of reductionist customer relations, attempting to drive the politics from the governance of services, particularly when it is combined with privatization.

What Next?

What then should follow the Citizen's Charter? A future government would seem to have three options:

- a retreat from public-service consumerism;
- the Citizen's Charter (Mark II);
- the social rights perspective.

The first option attempts to put the clock back to the time when public-service consumers as consumers had little or no recognition and even less influence on the shape or quality of services. Not just five years of the charter, but other social changes, have raised public expectations to such an extent that this option is simply not available to any administration expecting to win support for its public-services policies.

The second choice would take current charter policy further in the direction in which it is currently moving. We could expect more of the same, couched in the terminology we have described and realized by those methods we have also outlined. Even were this to be a political option, such a choice would reinforce and repeat the very faults in current policy and practice which we have identified. It would continue the trend towards a dilution of citizenship to mere consumerism. It would miss the chance of linking reform in public-service policy to opportunities for wider political and social renewal.

Our third option calls for an altered course and a number of new and distinctive themes. Aspects of the charter programme, tested and known to have merit, could be combined with ideas based on different assumptions about the public sector and about citizenship. We argue this last alternative offers the best framework for future action and a sound basis for change.

Social rights: fresh principles for a balanced programme

New policy must be based on clear and coherent principles. Clarity is essential if the principles are to form the foundations for many different administrative structures and legal relationships and to be useful across the full range of public-sector activities.

The huge variety of services and the different provider/user relationships by which they are delivered may make it hard for any single set of principles to apply in each setting. Should the new policy reach to every corner of the public services? The answer will depend upon the aim of the policy. If, for example, it is simply to raise standards of general public administration by ensuring that the phone is answered or letters written promptly, it will be generally applicable. If, on the other hand, the aim of policy is to grant new legal rights – for example, to a guaranteed level of service or to consultation – then it may be possible only to introduce such changes in a few services.

Some social groups will be intended to gain more than others from the changes, for overall commitments to equality and opportunity to be achieved. But such differences are bound to flow from a policy rooted more in the notion of citizenship – where citizens recognize a plurality not uniformity of needs and differences – than in one based on the dictates of individual consumption.

New social rights: real or rhetorical?

Should policy promise to deliver a new system of formal rights to parallel the civil and political rights obtained by constitutional reform? The public can be sceptical when politicians talk of rights and 'charters' which are bound up with ideas about rights, or at least expectations. Published principles alone have never determined the level of public funding which is provided to services and, as we have already outlined, there has been enormous reluctance to place obligations owed to citizens by central or local government on any formal, enforceable footing. Yet the level of funding can be crucial to the experience of anyone using a service.

This is the . . . difficulty with the Citizen's Charter. To many of the public its homilies on good standards of public administration count for little when social security entitlement is cut, class sizes rise beyond tolerable limits or prisons experience inhuman levels of overcrowding (Guardian, 1995b).[5] If politicians describe the public's claim on such services in the language and concepts of 'rights', many may sense that they are being conned. No wonder the charter is widely perceived as a public-relations exercise.[6]

On the other hand, public trust in government will increase with initiatives that not only bind politicians to fund a defined scope and level of services but also hold those providing them to account when such standards are not reached. We outline below some possible approaches which could achieve this result without producing costly and unnecessary work for lawyers.

The appeal of a new programme

A fresh initiative could help to define the characteristics of public services in contrast to independent or commercial ones. It could clarify the framework of rights and duties within which services are provided and help to encourage uptake by those who are entitled. New policy could also identify how the 'public interest' is represented in this framework, providing an opportunity to refine and reassert public-service values of integrity, equity, impartiality and inclusiveness.

Six Principles for New Policy

We propose six principles as starting points from which policy should develop as it seeks to redefine and clarify the nature of social rights and, by this, important elements of citizenship. We have not rejected the six 'Principles of Public Service' found in the Citizen's Charter programme or its themes of quality, standards, value for money and choice. Our approach regards these ideas as useful where they are consistent with it. However, they cannot be sufficient for the task of reforming and renewing public service. A more robust and resourceful set of values is needed to underpin that process.

- *The principle of fair treatment.* People seeking access to or awaiting decisions on services are often treated in ways which fail to meet standards of fairness and just dealing. Policy should guarantee fair treatment for all those seeking or using services.
- *The principle of entitlement.* Policy should, so far as possible, secure and reinforce clear entitlements to services so those who provide and those who use them know what the latter should receive. Where appropriate, entitlements should be independently enforceable, not merely open to internal complaint.
- *The principle of participation.* Public services only exist because the public need and use them. Policy should ensure that the voices of the citizen and the consumer are heard and acted on in planning services, while also valuing the participation of those who work in the service.
- *The principle of openness.* Public services should be planned and operated in an accessible way. Information about services should be easily available to those with consumer or citizen interests in them.
- *The principle of public accountability.* Citizens and users are unable, on their own, to judge the overall performance or adequacy of public services. They need robust and resourceful proxies to help them to do this. Here, we focus on the functions of audit and inspection.
- *The principle of co-operation.* Many services require a partnership with their users for the greatest benefit to be obtained. The service is not simply a 'product' to be acquired. Collaborative relationships need to be built around notions of trust, co-operation, candour and responsibility.

Policy needs to encourage such mutual working and engagement and remind providers and users of the obligations they have toward each other.

The Principle of Fair Treatment

The Citizen's Charter promises those who use public services courtesy and helpfulness (Bynoe, 1996, p. 9). Important though these are they do not amount to a guarantee of fair treatment (Galligan, 1992). In our view, future policy should both elaborate the meaning of this term and propose robust measures which can make it effective. Fair treatment is uniquely important in the delivery of publicly financed services to citizens, and is of major significance within health, income maintenance, criminal justice, social welfare and educational services. It is also highly relevant to the manner in which privatized utilities are regulated (Baldwin et al., 1995). Someone using a service, particularly one provided following an assessment of their 'need' for it, will find themselves drawn into a process. It is the fairness of that process with which this principle is concerned. It can apply as much to coercive services (tax assessment, imprisonment, child-support assessment and collection) as to elective ones – indeed, some would argue that with the former there is even more call for it.

The thinking behind it is derived not just from public administration but from law. There is now being developed in the common law or introduced in legislation a class of procedural 'rights'. These are associated with ideas of natural justice, procedural propriety, and the responsibility of authorities possessing public powers to exercise these reasonably. Such ideas are far from fully recognized in current jurisprudence – for example, there is no universal duty on a public authority to give reasons for its decisions – but they offer a coherent body of possible fair-treatment rights to be considered in this context. They can be summarized as follows:

- 'a right to be heard': a right for someone to be consulted by a person or body adjudicating on their entitlement or making a decision which affects their circumstances;[7]
- 'a right to consistency' in decision making: a right to treatment which is consistent with any established practice or promise;[8]
- 'a right to relevance' in decision making: a duty on those making decisions to take into account all relevant factors and to disregard irrelevant ones;[9]

- 'a right to unbiased decisions': a duty on those making decisions to act without bias;[10]
- 'a right to reasons': openness in decision making, expressed as a requirement for the decision maker to give reasons to those affected by decisions concerning them;[11]
- 'a right to review': the right to have the refusal of a service, or a complaint about one, independently reviewed, sometimes by a body able to substitute its decision for that complained about.[12]

When applied to the allocation of public services, not one of these principles, by itself, will provide any right to a service such as housing accommodation, surgical treatment in a hospital, a state-school place or a social security payment. They focus, instead, on the ways in which it is decided who should or should not obtain such social benefits, on how people will get access to a service or benefit. They control how much the person affected is involved in that process, how much they will learn of the reasons for those decisions or of their opportunity to seek a review, if aggrieved by its outcome. They help ensure that decisions will exclude unfair bias or discrimination and will be consistent.

Why is 'fair treatment' an important principle?

If entitlement to many services is to remain a matter largely for the exercise of discretion, not the application of detailed regulation, then measures designed to 'structure' the use of that discretion and guarantee its fair application will become all the more important if principles of equity and equal treatment are to be respected. As efforts to improve opportunities for choice and user involvement become more effective, so such professional judgements are rendered ever more complex – and contentious. What will increase with this trend is the risk that a person's expressed wants may often diverge from the needs assessed by professional 'gatekeepers'. This tension has been seen recently where decisions have been made to refuse the funding of NHS treatment or local authority community-care services to those who want them.

Guaranteeing that the public are treated fairly in their dealings with a service may be just as important a mark of its quality as ensuring that telephones are answered promptly or assessment targets met. Indeed, such an aim should not be seen as just a 'quality' issue, for it is of far greater importance. It is a factor affecting the long-term future of the public's relationship with services which they vote and pay for, since people will trust and value services they judge to be fairly administered.

Fair treatment in practice

The procedural rights we describe are by no means consistently applied, but can be seen, at least partly, in some areas of public administration, and in a few settings they have been highly developed. Some are mentioned in charter documents.[13] Since they relate to the actions of all public authorities or bodies, they may apply to situations far more varied than the simple provision of a public service. They feature to some extent in advice on 'good administrative practice' issued to local authorities by the Commission for Local Administration in England (Commission for Local Administration in England, 1993). Breaches of the standards with which we are concerned are found in a recent summary list of examples of maladministration published by the Parliamentary Commissioner for Administration (1994, para. 7). See box 14.1 below.

Rudeness (though that is a matter of degree)
Unwillingness to treat the complainant as a person with rights
Refusal to answer reasonable questions
Neglecting to inform a complainant on request of his or her rights or
    entitlement
Knowingly giving advice which is misleading or inadequate
Ignoring valid advice or over-ruling considerations which would produce
    an uncomfortable result for the over-ruler
Offering no redress or manifestly disproportionate redress
Showing bias whether because of colour, sex, or any other grounds
Omission to notify those who thereby lose a right of appeal
Refusal to inform adequately of the right of appeal
Faulty procedures
Failure by management to monitor compliance with adequate procedures
Cavalier disregard of guidance which is intended to be followed in the
    interest of equitable treatment of those who use a service
Partiality
Failure to mitigate the effects of rigid adherence to the letter of the law
    where that produces manifestly inequitable treatment

Source: Select Committee on the Parliamentary Commissioner for Administration (1994)

Box 14.1 The parliamentary commissioner's 'examples of maladministration'

Being heard

This involves ensuring that someone has an opportunity to provide all relevant and necessary information to the person or body making a decision which affects their obtaining a service or continuing to receive one already provided to them. It may be a right held individually or one held by a group of people similarly affected, such as the residents of a care home or parents whose children attend a day nursery. The system of administration by which a person applies for or obtains a service, or the manner in which that service is modified, needs to ensure that those who are affected will have a chance of being effectively heard. Many people will already be able to engage in the oral, written or face-to-face processes by which they can be heard, but practical measures can make these more accessible to them. Others, without assistance, may find it is difficult or impossible to do so. The principle must therefore include, where appropriate, guaranteeing that assistance is readily available. In some situations what may be needed is an advice or advocacy service provided to those needing to participate in the decision-making 'process'. Furthermore, some public services are used by the small but significant minority of people who are unable to make valid decisions for themselves (Law Commission, 1995). Respecting this right will require changes that give such citizens opportunities to have their interests fully recognized and represented.

Consistent treatment and unbiased decisions

Ensuring fair treatment will make decision makers conscious of how they make their decisions and the factors which influence this process. Those who have to adjudicate claims which are highly regulated by law (such as some social security claims)[14] may be given extensive guidance on relevant and irrelevant issues. Many decisions, though, will be made without such clear direction. Local policy or guidelines may then be desirable or essential. It is clear that such means of ensuring that discretion is 'structured' (Galligan, 1992) are now being proposed and adopted to resolve current problems. It could be a doctor listing a patient for treatment, a head teacher refusing a child admission to a school, a social worker assessing a disabled person's need for personal assistance at home, a teenage care leaver refused financial help from the authority which once looked after her. Each is entitled to know that their circumstances have been fully and accurately assessed. Often, it is likely that this can only be done when some written procedure or protocol is produced for this purpose and information provided to the person on the basis of its contents.

As well as offering a means to encourage greater fairness and consistency, agreeing and introducing local written policy or procedures will often be crucial to achieving the aims of primary legislation. We see this with recent law concerning community care, child protection or services for 'children in need', state-school policy on admissions or on special education.

Central and local government has a clear role to play in encouraging measures which will protect citizens from biased, inconsistent or otherwise unfair decisions. New policy will need to assess what further protections are needed for those using public services to ensure that the principle is fully recognized and respected in practice.

Reasons for decisions

For someone to be treated fairly, they will expect to learn the reasons for a decision which affects their interests or needs. However, there is no general rule that public authorities supply reasons for decisions, and even where recent administrative codes have sought to change this, the onus is often placed on the person affected to seek out the reason rather than find it recorded and supplied to them. Anyone adversely affected by any decision of a public authority stands a better chance of being treated fairly when given its reasons. Only then will they have any means of comparing how they have been treated with published standards, or other guidelines or criteria. The requirement is poorly respected by many public-service organizations, unless the law specifies it. For example, people assessed for community-care services are not legally entitled to receive a written record of their assessment and plan of care, and compliance with this administrative expectation has been highly variable. GPs have no obligation to provide their patients with any reason for striking them off their list (Perry, 1995). In the field of utility regulation, regulators are currently under no legal obligation to give reasons for the decisions which they take despite the clear public interest in their responsibilities being fairly and thoroughly discharged (Baldwin et al., 1995).

Reviewing decisions

No system of decision making is infallible, least of all one involving the exercise of discretion. Pursuing fair treatment as a principle of public administration will highlight the need to provide an avenue for review which is independent and accessible, affordable and effective. Current attempts at providing review systems often have only limited success (see, for example,

Dean, 1995; Dalley and Berthoud, 1992; Department of Health, 1994a). A series of widely respected reports has highlighted the need for fundamental change and their impact is being felt, particularly in the field of health services. However, change is likely to be limited unless the principle is firmly applied in every setting where it is needed. A review is to examine the role of the Commission for Local Administration – the 'local ombudsman' – and the continued need for it. If the recommendations of an earlier 'prior options assessment' are accepted, then its current role and powers are in jeopardy (Legal Action, 1996a, 1996b). If these are curtailed, this would greatly limit the citizen's ability to challenge the actions or omissions of their local authority.

Why is it difficult to introduce fair treatment?

It will be said that procedures are bureaucratic and time consuming, distracting hard-pressed staff resources from the main task of providing substantive services. It may also be argued that such approaches are inconsistent with the professional or organizational freedom enjoyed by those expected to comply with new requirements. A different problem may be the low level of administrative competence or motivation for such measures within many services. These may present a significant challenge for organizational cultures. Lastly, the impact of fair-treatment practice on levels of professional or service accountability may make it unwelcome where decisions have been conventionally made in secret and service users have not been allowed to learn the reasons for them.

None of these factors poses an insuperable barrier, though some may affect how procedural rights are to be introduced in practice and the time scale for doing so. The perception of being treated unfairly creates the urge to complain, or, at the very least, a negative experience of a service and those who provide it. The former may cost that service a significant amount in time and resources. The latter will lessen the chance of maintaining a consensus about public services. There is therefore a strong public interest in fair treatment being an essential foundation for a modern public service . . .

The Principle of Entitlement

The Citizen's Charter has required the formulation and publication of service standards. At the same time it has highlighted rights to redress. In doing this, it has clearly raised expectations of entitlement. However, there has been ambiguity about what is or is not an enforceable standard, and charter policy has generally refrained from pursuing the principle that service providers should be subject to legal duties to provide specified services.

There are, of course, overt political considerations which underlie such an approach. Should the principle of entitlement be built into the provision of services? Is the public interest served by pursuing in this way the logic of 'charterism' to its conclusion? Given the difficulties with guaranteeing levels of substantive services, is it easier and more appropriate to guarantee procedural rights and standards of fair treatment rather than substantive entitlements?

In our view there is scope for the concept to be used with imagination and effect and it is time for new approaches to be explored. These should affect both procedural and, where appropriate, substantive entitlements. Some social rights are already provided within a detailed legal framework and some are more closely aligned to the civil court system than others. However, if entitlement is to be further extended it does not follow that the same methods must be adopted. What are the options for interpreting the principle of entitlement in the context of public-service provision?

Social rights: meanings and effects

'Rights' here is a term weighed down with differing meanings, firstly because it has a powerful attraction to those seeking or introducing social change and secondly because the concept has to work within a highly political context. For every 'right' there has to be some kind of 'duty' – a word as potent and as ambiguous . . .

Binding entitlement or mere aspiration?

Sometimes, 'rights' are described in ways that are meant to denote mere aspirations, nothing more. They may be targets for which service providers are to aim – with no guarantee that performance will achieve them – or a set of medium- or long-term goals, more or less a wish-list. The aim of policy or planning is to pursue them, not guarantee to provide them. There is no prospect, or intention, that current levels of service or their standard will be influenced by any notion of the provider having any enforceable duty to fulfil the specific aspiration. The concept of the 'target duty' – non-enforceable by the individual citizen – is now recognized in public law.[15] The Citizen's Charter provides ample examples of such aspirational 'rights' as the national and local standards included in the Patient's Charter or the

Department for Education and Employment's National Targets for educational attainment. However, the charter is not at all clear about the status of the 'rights' it advertises.

By way of complete contrast, a right may be set up in such a way as to be absolutely binding or enforceable in relation to an individual. If it is, then those who qualify are truly 'entitled'. Providers will then have to be conscious of the need in every case to meet the defined expectation; service users who can demonstrate non-performance will be able to challenge this and obtain redress – with either performance being ordered or compensation provided. Apart from certain social security benefits, this latter approach is rarely encountered in public-service provision. However, some elements of it can be seen in the laws now governing provision for special educational needs,[16] to a lesser extent in the law on accommodation for the homeless[17] and in the legal framework within which GPs' services are provided.[18]

Numerous duties have been created and imposed on public bodies without any corresponding substantive rights being given – a plethora of 'target' not 'absolute' duties. This is especially so with the broad statutory duties that apply to housing, education, health and community care. Social rights are most often seen framed in this way rather than as clearly enforceable entitlements. Here, the obligations imposed on public bodies are to further community aims, not those of identifiable individuals able to enforce them. Statutory duties, and public law in general, may influence the ways in which those public bodies order their priorities, allocate resources and respond to criticism. But unless a legal duty is made highly explicit and absolute, the authority's room for manoeuvre is considerable. If it claims that resources are not available to meet its 'duty' this may render the obligation virtually unenforceable.[19] For new policy to develop ideas of entitlement, it must be clear as to the true nature of any duties which are created and honest with the public as to their enforceability.

Entitlement can be provisional . . . or permanent

Public-service rights more than others have their origins in manifestos, policy statements, and the commitments of political parties. Though we may find them elaborately described in declarations of human rights or other international instruments, these rarely guarantee entitlement or curb the powers of politicians to dismantle them. They are provisional.

Service entitlement is not always illusory but it rarely acquires any quality of permanence on a par, say, with rights to equal treatment under the Treaty of Rome or to freedom from arbitrary arrest under European human rights law. However, there are ways by which entitlements can be rendered more permanent. For instance, clearly specifying entitlement in an Act of Parliament can make it harder for rights, once granted, to be taken back. To pursue the principle of entitlement will mean finding the most appropriate means of expressing the value given to the aims of policy and to the public interest in ensuring those aims are met. For some measures this will mean that entitlement must be written into law; for others, the means chosen may be less fixed and entitlement may then rely on the terms of an administrative document such as a 'charter' or code.

Rights declared unilaterally or negotiated to agreement

In the field of public services and benefits, some rights are granted 'unilaterally', without negotiation and without any process leading to agreement with those intended to benefit. The public-service provider declares what the criteria are for eligibility, and what are the standards and guarantees. A different approach is based on a consensual or contractual type of relationship. Here those seeking the service are able to bargain for certain terms or standards. This method is not always practicable, but some highly localized or discrete services – environmental services, for example, or some features of hospital services – could be provided within a framework genuinely negotiated and agreed with local groups. Non-performance or a lowering of standards should then amount to a breach of agreement.

What determines eligibility and entitlement: national or local policy?

Deciding who determines the criteria for entitlement to a public service will crucially affect financing and accountability. Should the centre set minimum standards or should these be determined by the service provider, particularly where the latter is democratically accountable to a local electorate? Traditionally, many local-service providers have been given considerable freedom to resource and plan their own levels and standards of service, taking account of local needs and, where applicable, politically agreed priorities. The current system of financing local authority services – by calculating standard spending assessments and funding according to these – does not represent any attempt by government to determine and cost levels of performance.[20] Indeed, this is the case even where a statutory duty obliges local authorities to provide a service and the secretary of state has issued directions specifying its core elements.[21] Together with the freedom to determine the level of service goes the right to decide who should benefit. Examples include nursery education, community-care services provided by local authorities, public housing accommodation, and resources for young people who have left the care of a social services authority. In such examples, levels of service may be highly variable, with local criteria for entitlement or locally determined priorities correspondingly variable.

The NHS can demonstrate similar variations, though in the case of this national service paid from central tax revenue the justification for locally determined eligibility is less obvious. If new policy is to incorporate our ideas about entitlement then greater clarity must be shown as to the relative importance of national or local standards. Where local providers deliver services on behalf of government and with resources largely provided from national tax revenue, there may be a place for a new legal and financing framework which better reflects this relationship and government's expectations as to the services which are to be provided within it. Below, we propose a new policy which may form part of such a framework (Bynoe, 1996, pp. 122–7).

The discretion barrier

Public services are often delivered not according to clearly defined and acknowledged criteria of need and entitlement but after professionals or administrators judge that the service should be offered. We see this in decisions as varied as DSS Social Fund claims, diagnosis and treatment by an NHS doctor, decisions to grant or refuse legal aid, or to treat a homeless person as in 'priority need'. In other situations, the room for discretion is greatly restricted. Claims for some social security benefits (such as retirement pension) based on national insurance contributions, or simple applications for a driving licence, a passport or a local library ticket, should not involve discretion.

Where there is a 'discretion barrier', entitlement may be difficult or impossible to pursue. Without clear boundaries, service users' experience may continue to be highly varied. Such differences will often be justified on the basis of professional autonomy. However, it is possible to 'structure' the way in which discretion is used and render those who exercise it more accountable. Measures can ensure that discretion is exercised within clearly agreed and understood guidelines or criteria, limiting the range of decisions which are possible and the circumstances in which the person affected may experience an adverse outcome. Although the aim of these is to guarantee fair treatment for the service user, in practice they will also support the principle of entitlement by helping to ensure that those who are entitled in fact receive the service due to them.

Individual or collective entitlements: how to enforce the collective duty?

Sometimes, duties are owed to the community as a whole rather than to identifiable individuals who are given rights to enforce. Within the UK, measures which would enable the enforcement of rights by an identifiable group or class of citizens have hardly begun to be developed. There are few avenues for the positive enforcement of duties or standards by any others than those personally affected, and these may have neither the capacity, resources nor motivation to take enforcement action. Responsibility for collective enforcement largely rests with inspection and regulatory bodies. Clearly there is a role for such bodies acting as proxies for the public. However, new policies could also develop ways of accommodating collective social rights into systems of representation and enforcement.

Barriers to entitlement

Any new policy which attempts to set standards and accountability for performance on more formal foundations will undoubtedly meet resistance.[22] The following objections are commonly raised:

- *Cost and the open-ended financial commitment.* The difficulty of predicting the likely demand for services combined with limited resources will render it impossible to guarantee that for each and every citizen entitled to a service, one will be available when they need it.
- *The distorting impact of enforcement measures.* Enforcement of entitlements adds unduly to the costs of public-service providers, diverting already scarce resources away from direct provision into compensation, penalties, legal or administration expenses.
- *Some services cannot be clearly specified.* Unless duties are described clearly and specifically, it would be wrong to expose any public-service provider to the risk of enforcement. Many services are considered complex and beyond easy specification. If only those services which can be easily specified are rendered enforceable this distorts the overall shape of the service, skewing resources towards a limited range of services.
- *Entitlement restricts political choice and reduces the capacity for priorities to be set locally.* Public services are ultimately the creation of a political system which demands flexibility, prioritization and rationing for the public interest to be advanced. Formal entitlements will compromise and weaken the necessary political controls.

- *Entitlement only benefits active consumers.* Consumers who will be active in pursuit of their rights, in general, already have many social advantages and are not those upon whom the state should concentrate its assistance.
- *Entitlement threatens co-operation.* Encouraging 'entitlement' will create adversarial and confrontational relationships between service providers and users . . .

Public interest and entitlement

The public sector is not unfamiliar with having to work to absolute standards. Annual budgets for social security benefits must meet sometimes unprecedented demands it would be impossible to predict with accuracy. This does not preclude the provision, for example, of cold-weather payments on the basis of an entitlement. The independent ombudsmen routinely investigate and rule on standards of administration and the consequences of delayed or underprioritized action. The Health Service commissioner can even recommend the provision of an NHS service when this has been refused, and does so. Many consumers of particular services are owed a general legal duty of care which, when it is broken, can trigger substantial compensation. However, the system within which most services are delivered is an administrative one and the standards set for them are neither legally defined nor enforceable. In view of the concerns which we have identified, it is essential to consider whether there are clear policy gains which can outweigh these difficulties or make them worth overcoming.

To provide much-needed services on the basis of an entitlement rather than a mere privilege will correspond with broadly held views about social justice and fairness. Short-term political advantage, avoidable administrative failure, or poor financial planning can often compromise social objectives which are widely approved. The policy would have especial importance for services for vulnerable groups such as those who have a severe mental illness or disability, poor children, prisoners or homeless people. The creation of entitlements may encourage the take-up of services by those who may otherwise be discouraged by their unwillingness to be seen as the objects of 'charity'. Accountability and efficiency may be aided where entitlement requires clarity about scope and quality . . .

The Principle of Participation

It is necessary to make public services more responsive to the needs and wishes of those who use them. It is also essential that the perceptions and priorities of a wider group – citizens – are incorporated into the planning and shaping of services. This applies not just to operational standards and procedures but also to the setting of overall policy aims and the shape of government programmes. There is a third dimension to participation[23] – the voice of those who work within the services themselves. It will be as important to enable employees to express their views freely to those in charge without fear of detriment.

Public services have been created to advance wider notions of 'fairness' and 'social justice'. They depend for their existence as well as for their effectiveness on citizens sharing responsibility and pooling resources. The public interest requires participation in order to ensure that what is considered fair and just is determined, not by a managerial or political elite, but by a wider constituency, particularly one which is sensitive to what is wanted by those who use the service. If public confidence in traditional forms of 'representative' democracy – national or local – continues to decline, participation will be all the more necessary.

Benefits of participation

Encouraging participation can provide information of value to service organizations on the design, performance and desirable staffing make-up of the service; can help to legitimize decisions which shape how they develop; can improve the effectiveness of service delivery and build up public confidence in the service and in its capacity to meet social needs. The Citizen's Charter already refers to a principle of 'consultation'. This, we would argue, is one method of participation, though in practice it can be limited. Policy which seeks to achieve real transfers of power will need to step beyond merely consultative processes, important though these are.

The public should be involved – as citizens – more closely in decisions about priorities and the distribution of the scarce resources available to the public sector. Another aim should be to strengthen the user voice, drawing on the expertise of those with an intimate knowledge of receiving the service in question. For both, greater participation should not only reveal important insights about the service and how it should develop. It should also encourage public support for services and promote responsibility in their use.

Participation by public-service employees also brings many benefits. Front-line experience sharpens staff perceptions on quality issues and the pressures of meeting rising public expectations. Such employees have to deliver change when this is introduced: encouraging their participation, and respecting it when it is given, are essential to the process of monitoring and raising standards.

Making participation a mainstream service issue

Where service planners and providers already want to listen to users and involve them in setting standards and running services, little is there to stop them. Many examples over recent years demonstrate how this can be done and the benefits which result (Consumer Congress and National Consumer Council, 1994; National Consumer Council, 1996; Beresford and Croft, 1993). There is clear evidence that effective and valuable ways of gathering views have been developed.[24] There are also examples of citizen participation, though these are rarer since the thrust of charter policy has been to equate citizens with consumers, leading providers to treat their interests as the same.[25] Now, the challenge is to render the good practice which the few enjoy into universal practice which all can benefit from. Sceptics may argue that barriers to effective participation make efforts of only marginal benefit. It will be the task of new policy to seek to overcome these difficulties and provide new impetus to a principle which is rarely applied with rigour and imagination.

Why is participation difficult?

Users of services are often at a severe disadvantage when offering observations and opinions on services. To do this they may need information which is denied to them; communication skills in which they are neither trained nor assisted; and the reassurance of being listened to when they have often met with indifference in the past. Citizens are at an even greater disadvantage. Policy will need to examine ways in which users and citizens can help to set the agenda or shape the parameters of consultation and participation, as well as practical measures which will cover the incidental costs and effects of doing so . . .

The Principle of Openness

Public-service provision can be distinguished from private commercial activity by the importance it should give to the principle of open dealing with those seeking or using services and with citizens generally.[26] 'Transparency' offers a prospect of government without disguise or dissembling. In operation, it has two principal components:

- Telling the public, unambiguously, what a service is and how to obtain it, and the standard of performance which they should expect. We may term this 'customer' openness. Examples include: the corporate agreement and publication of standards of service, criteria for entitlement etc., publicizing how to apply for the service, complain about its poor quality or failure, etc.

- Providing facts, figures or documents, etc., about the policies, costs, operations and performance of the service to those with any interest (from a user or citizen perspective) in discovering them. We may term this 'accountability' openness. Examples include: publishing regular reports on performance, responding to requests for information from the public, admitting the public to board or council meetings, etc.

Why is openness important?

Firstly, openness will assist the public to obtain the service or services to which they are entitled or which they need. Applying for a service, exercising choice, pursuing redress – all of these depend on clear and full information. Secondly, unless service organizations are frank with the public about their policies and standards, about how they perform and their costs, then failures in service quality or waste will never be discovered and the need for improvements or changes will not be recognized and acted upon. Without openness, there can be little participation, less responsiveness and no accountability. This is why the public interest demands that the principle be reflected at every level of service activity.

Customer openness

The principle is particularly important where a service can only be obtained after some assessment or professional judgement of a person's need for it. Unlike using a public road or switching to a BBC TV channel, these benefits are guarded to a greater or lesser extent by a professional and/or administrative bureaucracy. Most housing, social services and social security benefits are allocated on this basis. Health-care services, though far less legally regulated, are offered only on the basis of a professional judgement of clinical need, which can amount to much the same type of hurdle.

Attempting to obtain such a service then can resemble a tortuous journey through a jungle of complex and impenetrable rules and procedures. The deliberate pursuit of openness can lower such barriers, encourage access and increase uptake by those who are entitled. In operation it will therefore encourage the fairer distribution of services, and, where this is a problem, may help to reduce the stigma associated with receiving them.

Though opportunities may be limited, some services may be able to offer choice, and users and citizens may wish them to do so. In community care, for example, disabled people may shortly be able to purchase their own services with direct payments of local authority cash provided for this purpose.[27] For choices to be genuine, those making them need to be informed. Openness on the part of service providers will help to ensure that the necessary information is received and understood before important decisions or choices are made.

Accountability openness

To be effective, accountability requires openness. Decisions should ideally be made or accounted for in public with the reasons for them being known. Public participation will be severely compromised unless deliberate steps are taken to open up the ways in which decisions are taken on strategic and operational policy. Non-disclosure may be justified only on narrow and strictly defined grounds where an identifiable public interest is served by such restrictions. Only in this way will citizens be able to judge whether services reflect the public interests relevant to their task and are meeting the needs for which they are designed.

The 'open organization': why is this so rare?

Why do many public-service organizations remain poor at being open? There are likely to be many reasons – we offer a number of possible explanations which suggest future directions for policy:

- *Uncertainty or disagreement on information to be disclosed.* Services with a high level of professional discretion (health care, education, social services) may exhibit limited consensus amongst staff on the specifics of the service on offer. Where experience of the service is highly varied, those providing it will find it very difficult to give clear and useful information.
- *Fear of opening the floodgates.* Many public services do not need to advertise for custom since they are not in a competitive market. With limited budgets to deploy, managers may fear an uncontrolled rise in demand which could result from effective strategies for promoting information on eligibility and entitlement. This may be so particularly if policy decisions have led to any 'guarantees' being given.
- *Cost of information.* Spending to provide high-quality, accurate information may be hard to justify when budgets are falling and services are being restricted. Many organizations may consider the resources required are better devoted to providing the services themselves.

- *Flexible and uncertain services.* The complexity of a public service may partly derive from its need for flexibility. This renders all the more difficult the task of informing the public with clarity and certainty.
- *Accountability openness – who needs it?* Reluctance to provide general information to citizens has been justified on the grounds that other means of accountability to the public (such as via elected or appointed representatives) suffice, that to be effective management needs to be conducted in relative secrecy, or, worse still, that the public cannot be trusted with information.
- *Accountability openness – having to buck the trend.* It has been government's aim, over many years, to transfer responsibility for many services away from local authorities, whose culture is better disposed to openness and disclosure (due to the electoral mandate and the legal framework within which they have to operate).[28]
- *Professional discretion.* Many services are provided by professional staff exercising discretion in ways that have not traditionally been open to scrutiny by users or the public.
- *Commercial secrecy.* Many public services are now provided by commercial organizations and public providers are often expected to operate commercially. Such organizations can justify secrecy on grounds of commercial confidentiality and the over-riding need to retain competitive advantage.

The Principle of Public Accountability

The next principle is concerned with improving accountability. Stewart (1995) has described the concept as having two elements: giving an account, and being held to account. There is also a distinction between political accountability, which centres on the policy and broad objectives set for the organization (usually the responsibility of authorities or boards), and performance accountability, which will focus on the day-to-day delivery of the service (the province of executive managers and staff).

Clearly, the principle is compromised whenever citizens are unable to choose who runs their services. Responsibility over vast areas of public-sector activity in education, training and health has been transferred from directly elected authorities to appointed quangos. The case for restoring the democratic dimension to the public sector has been cogently argued and need not be repeated here (Stewart et al., 1995; Democratic Audit, 1994; L. Cooper et al., 1995). To rely on the ballot box, however, would offer an unsatisfactory level of public accountability. Citizens need procedures and institutions which, in the public interest, provide more regular and informed scrutiny. These act with or on behalf of citizens and service users, improving the standard, quality and value for money achieved within the public sector, as well as ensuring probity. In this section we focus on the relevant institutions listed in box 14.2.

Central government and Next Steps agencies
National Audit Office

Local authorities
District Audit Service and Audit Commission for England and Wales
Scottish Accounts Commission

Local authority social services
Social Services Inspectorate
Audit Commission
Scottish Accounts Commission
Local authority inspection

Primary and secondary education
Audit Commission
Scottish Accounts Commission
Office for Standards in Education (OFSTED)

Health
Audit Commission
Scottish Accounts Commission
Mental Health Act Commission (England and Wales)
Mental Welfare Commission (Scotland)
National Development Team (England and Wales)
Health Advisory Service

Independent health or social care accommodation
Local social services authority inspectors (private residential care homes)
Local health authority inspectors (private nursing homes)

Criminal justice
Audit Commission
HM Inspectorate of Constabulary
HM Inspectorates of Prisons (England and Wales/Scotland)
HM Inspectorate of Probation
HM Magistrates Courts Service Inspectorate

Box 14.2 Principal inspection and audit bodies (UK except Northern Ireland)

Public interest and audit and inspection

What should be the role of organizations such as these? Since they report publicly, one of their most important functions is to provide information about services from behind doors literally or metaphorically closed to citizens and consumers. Many regard their relationship with services partly as a collaborative one, helping the process of development and improvement as much as observing and reporting on standards from a distance. A range of concerns might constitute the proper province of audit and/or inspection bodies:

- *Probity*. Are public resources being spent lawfully?
- *Compliance with legal standards*. Where legal duties define a minimum level or range of service to be provided, are these being respected?
- *Efficiency*. Are the public resources devoted to services being employed in ways which obtain the best possible benefit from them?
- *Economy*. Can savings be made by reducing waste or duplication or improving co-ordination?
- *Effectiveness*. Does the performance of the organization achieve the policy aims and objectives set for it, reflected for example in the standards of service to be provided?
- *Scope*. Is the organization able to deliver an adequate service taking account of the estimated or identified needs for it, or are there needs remaining unmet which call for higher levels of resources or modifications to policy?
- *Appropriateness*. Are the services in question relevant and appropriate for the needs of citizens requiring them?
- *Access*. Are services accessible to all those who need them or are there barriers which exclude potential consumers and discourage take-up of services?
- *Responsiveness*. Are services able to respond to the priorities which citizens and users set for them, and are they doing so?

The past development of audit and inspection bodies has not encouraged a rational or consistent approach since it has been piecemeal and haphazard, leading to numerous separate bodies often with very similar aims but different ways of working, different profiles and different cultures (Day and Klein, 1990). Although the Citizen's Charter programme has highlighted the need for public reporting and the involvement of lay people in inspection, this has been an administrative measure prescribed for a diverse and highly variable group of organizations. It should be the role of future policy to seek to achieve greater coherence and rationality within this system with clear principles for audit, inspection and regulation.

Bodies responsible for these roles must be clearly independent from the services which they monitor and from politicians who can influence service effectiveness or efficiency. Some inspectorates lack such independence; audit or inspection of service quality is sometimes undertaken without any external verification. To work effectively, audit and inspection bodies must balance two separate roles: they must apply pressure for change when this is needed but at the same time provide support. Without ignoring this balance, the independence principle should in future be applied more rigorously to the constitution, organization and practice of inspection and audit.

Services and spending in the public sector are often so closely interlinked that investigations and reports which simply take a service-based focus may miss the true extent of public resources committed to particular social needs and the options for reallocating them. The public needs reliable information on which to judge the wisdom or priority of spending decisions. For example, in order to reduce crime does the prudent citizen sanction more prison building or higher spending on preventative measures? Which represents the better use of public resources? The work of public audit bodies must provide insights to help resolve such controversies. Their work should adopt a 'whole picture' approach where this is useful or necessary.[29]

The public and service users often know little of the role or importance of audit and inspection bodies, which should be more widely publicized and promoted. More formal links with lay citizens and with service users should be developed in both their national and local work. Local publicity for the assessments – good and less so – resulting from audit or inspection should be the norm, particularly whenever the public are supplied with spending or budget details. The principle of lay involvement in inspection needs to be widely and imaginatively employed throughout the public sector and where services have been contracted out.[30]

The Principle of Co-operation

Many public services are provided in ways which require some degree of reciprocal responsibility, commitment or motivation from anyone wishing to receive them. A service may need to encourage a high level of responsibility in those who intend to use it in order to prevent abuse or misuse of the service, or to enable it to be effective. Thus, a GP will not want her patient to call her out in the middle of the night for a trivial problem which she cannot resolve and that could await a consultation on the following morning. A housing authority will expect an applicant for public-housing accommodation to be honest when describing the reason for seeking it, in order that priority can be fairly determined.

Sometimes those who provide and those who receive a service are drawn into a partnership requiring, on the latter's part, a significant investment of time, attitude and application in order for the most to be gained from the state service. Education is an obvious example. School pupils are expected to undertake homework in the evening: their parents to provide the space and encouragement in which this can be done, and demonstrate interest in their children's progress in school. Sometimes the contribution which is needed may involve public duty rather than the chance of any personal gain. The police service needs information and co-operation from members of the public – whether crime victim or witness – before it can begin to provide an effective service.

Why co-operation?

Receiving such public services cannot be compared with acquiring a simple consumable product. Almost by definition, public services are rarely provided under any formal contractual relationship with recipients. The law will have a limited role to play in defining what an individual is to get and how. The public interest is meant to be reflected in this unregulated and informal relationship. This administrative and flexible quality has allowed provider/user relationships to develop which involve reciprocity, mutuality, trust, confidence and candour.

Such co-operation is clearly at one with the public interest in having services which are efficient, economical and effective. Collective as well as individual expectations must be reflected in the ways they are distributed. If services are scarce and their inappropriate use may deprive others of opportunities to use them or will limit the chances for improvement or expansion, the public should surely be informed – or reminded – of their responsibilities as well as of their rights.

Where does it lead?

The principle will figure more prominently in some services than in others. If it is recognized and acted on then it must encourage greater participation along the lines outlined above. It should make the idea of openness less threatening to providers if users have responsibilities and are 'co-operators' instead of merely consumers. If providers are reassured that policy aims to encourage responsibility and collaborative approaches, they may be more able and willing to deliver guaranteed standards of fair treatment and service and increase opportunities for choice and the space for personal decision making. In short, a 'high-trust' rather than 'low-trust' environment would enhance the quality of public service.

Notes

1 Two-thirds of a poll of 1,000 people by NOP for the TUC in 1994 described the charter as a 'public relations exercise' (*Financial Times*, 17 October 1994).

2 See, for health, Clinical Standards Advisory Group (1995); for education, Audit Commission (1994); for social services, Social Services Inspectorate (1995); and for policing, Audit Commission (1993).

3 This fact is illuminated by an interesting 'taxonomy' of services in Beale and Pollitt (1994).

4 The introduction of charges for services previously free will have compounded the disadvantages faced by those needing to obtain them (Guardian, 1995a).

5 Surprisingly for a distinct group depending on a public service, there is no Prisoner's Charter, simply a very brief statement of 'Standards of Service', which refer to standards owed to others, such as the non-imprisoned public, reliant on the Prisons Agency for certain functions. The inhuman conditions in HMP Holloway revealed by HM Inspector of Prisons during December 1995 arose in a system apparently unaffected by minimum environmental standards.

6 See n. 1 above.

7 This does not imply any right to a literal 'hearing'. Generally, see *R*. v. *Gloucestershire County Council, ex parte Mahfood and others*; *R*. v. *Islington London Borough Council, ex parte MacMillan* (*Independent*, 20 June 1995); *Council of Civil Service Unions* v. *Minister for the Civil Service* [1985] AC 374; *Ridge* v. *Baldwin* [1964] AC 40; *R*. v. *Devon CC ex parte Baker* and *R*. v. *Durham CC ex parte Curtis* [1995] 1 All ER 73; see also 'consultation' duties recently framed in Children Act 1989, and in Mental Health (Patients in the Community) Act 1995.

8 *R*. v. *Devon CC, ex parte Baker* [1995] 1 All ER 73. This is called by lawyers the doctrine of 'legitimate expectation'. It refers to a person's right to assert that a procedure should apply because of a public body's promise or past practice.

9 *Bromley LBC* v. *GLC* [1983] 1 AC 768; *R*. v. *Secretary of State ex parte Bugdaycay* [1987] AC 514.

10 *R*. v. *Gough* [1993] AC 646.

11 *Doody* v. *Secretary of State for the Home Department* [1994] AC 531; *R*. v. *Higher Education Funding Council, ex parte Institute of Dental Surgery* [1994] 1 WLR 421; Cragg and Ashiagbor (1994).

12 See, for example, statutory duties to compel social services authorities to provide complaints and representations procedures found in Children Act 1989, NHS and Community Care Act 1990.

13 For example, Patient's Charter and Parent's Charter.
14 Though see criticisms of inconsistency and unjustified variations in Social Fund decisions (Committee of Public Accounts, 1991).
15 See McCowan, LJ in the recent case *R. v. Gloucestershire County Council, ex parte Mahfood and others* [1995] 3 All ER 353.
16 Education Act, 1993 and Code of Practice made under this.
17 Part III, Housing Act, 1985 and Code of Practice made under it. Government proposals, currently before Parliament, will significantly reduce such rights.
18 The National Health Service (General Medical Services) Regulations 1992. The jurisdiction of the Health Service Commissioner to determine a failure to provide an NHS service is also comparable and will be vastly enlarged when he or she is able to investigate the clinical basis for such decisions. See Health Service Commissioner (Amendment) Act 1996.
19 A result graphically demonstrated in the recent 'Child B' and Gloucestershire cases: *R. v. Cambridge Health Authority ex parte B* [1995] 3 All ER 129.
20 For recent inquiry into SSAs [standard spending assessments] see Environment Committee (1994).
21 The Department of Health's main circular to local social services authorities on community care includes directions from the Secretary of State as to the services which should be arranged. See LAC (93) 10.
22 For an interesting illustration of Whitehall resistance to creating legally enforceable obligations, see the arguments unsuccessfully used by the Prison Service against the Woolf Inquiry's proposal to create a code of legally enforceable minimum standards for prisons (Woolf and Tumim, 1991).
23 For a full discussion of participation in the NHS see L. Cooper et al. (1995).
24 Research on patient attitudes to the NHS conducted jointly by St Mary's Hospital, Paddington and Social and Community Planning Research (Bruster et al., 1994; Tate et al., 1995).
25 See examples of public consultation described in L. Cooper et al. (1995), pp. 53–9.
26 This principle, together with accountability, were included by the Nolan Committee in their list of principles of public life (Committee on Standards in Public Life, 1995).
27 See Community Care (Direct Payments) Bill.
28 See the Local Government (Access to Information) Act 1985 and evaluation of its effectiveness, viz. Steele (1995).
29 For an example of how this approach might be undertaken see Shapland et al. (1995).
30 For example, in the inspection of local policing services (Police Foundation and Policy Studies Institute, 1996, para. 7.12).

References

Audit Commission (1993) *Helping with Enquiries: Tackling Crime Effectively*. London: HMSO.
Audit Commission (1994) *The Act Moves On: Progress in Special Educational Needs*. London: HMSO.

Audit Commission (1995) *Local Authority Performance Indicators*. Vols I and II. London: HMSO.

Audit Commission (1996) *By Accident or Design: Improving A & E Services in England and Wales*. London: HMSO.

Baldwin, R., Abel-Smith, B., Cave, M., Fenn, P., Hodges, M., Marsden, C., Mossialos, E., Scott, C. and Woolcock, S. (1995) Regulation in question: the growing agenda. Unpublished report with recommendations on policy and law concerning regulation of utilities, etc.

Barnes, M. and Prior, D. (1995) Spoilt for choice? How consumerism ca 1 disempower public service users. *Public Money and Management*, 15 (3), July–September, 55–8.

Barron, A. and Scott, C. (1992) The Citizen's Charter programme. *Modern Law Review*, 55, 526–46.

Beale, V. and Pollitt, C. (1994) Charters at the grass roots: a first report. *Local Government Studies*, 20 (2), 202–25.

Beresford, P. and Croft, S. (1993) *Citizen Involvement: A Practical Guide for Change*. Basingstoke: Macmillan.

Bruster, S.J., Jarman, B., Bosanquet, N., Weston, D., Erens, R. and Delbanco, T.L. (1994) National survey of hospital patients. *British Medical Journal*, 309, 1542–9.

Bynoe, I. (1996) *Beyond the Citizen's Charter*. London: IPPR.

Citizen's Charter Unit (1992) *The Citizen's Charter: First Report*. Cm 2101. London: HMSO.

Citizen's Charter Unit (1994) *The Citizen's Charter: Report Back 1994*. Cm 2540. London: HMSO.

Clinical Standards Advisory Group (1995) *Urgent and Emergency Admissions to Hospital*. London: HMSO.

Commission for Local Administration in England (Local Government Ombudsman) (1993) Good administrative practice. Guidance on Good Practice Note 2. London: Commission for Local Administration in England.

Committee of Public Accounts (1991) The Social Fund. Twenty-fourth report, House of Commons session 1990–1. London: HMSO.

Committee on Standards in Public Life (1995) *First Report of the Committee on Standards in Public Life*. London: HMSO.

Consumer Congress and National Consumer Council (1994) *Consumer Representation in the Public Sector*. London: National Consumer Council.

Cooper, D. (1993) The Citizen's Charter and radical democracy: empowerment and exclusions within citizenship discourse. *Social and Legal Studies*, II, 149–71.

Cooper, L., Coote, A., Davies, A. and Jackson, C. (1995) *Voices Off: Tackling the Democratic Deficit in Health*. London: IPPR.

Cragg, S. and Ashiagbor, D. (1994) A duty to give reasons? *New Law Journal*, 25 February, 291–3.

Dalley, G. and Berthoud, R. (1992) *Challenging Discretion: The Social Fund Review Procedure*. London: PSI.

Day, P. and Klein, R. (1990) *Inspecting the Inspectorates*. York: Joseph Rowntree Memorial Trust.

Deakin, N. (1994) Accentuating the apostrophe: the Citizen's Charter. *Policy Studies*, 15 (3), Autumn, 48–57.

Dean, H. (1995) Social care provision: problems of redress. *Legal Action*, December, 8.

Democratic Audit (1994) EGO trip: extragovernmental organisations in the United Kingdom and their accountability. London: Charter 88 Trust.

Department of Health (1994a) *Being Heard: The Report of a Review Committee on NHS Complaints Procedures.* London: Department of Health.

Department of Health (1994b) *Inspecting Social Services.* LAC (94)16. Unpublished departmental guidance.

Environment Committee (1994) Standard spending assessments. House of Commons session 1993–4, first report. London: HMSO.

Galligan, D. (1992) Procedural rights in social welfare. In A. Coote (ed.), *The Welfare of Citizens,* London: IPPR/Rivers Oram.

Guardian (1994) Cones Hotline relaunched despite initial flop. *Guardian,* 30 December.

Guardian (1995a) Council services 'too expensive' for a fifth of disabled people. *Guardian,* 23 August.

Guardian (1995b) Prisons reduce services as cuts loom. *Guardian,* 28 November.

Harden, I. (1992) *The Contracting State.* Milton Keynes: Open University Press.

Law Commission (1995) Mental incapacity. Law Com 231. London: HMSO.

Legal Action (1996a) Local ombudsmen under threat of closure. *Legal Action,* January, 4.

Legal Action (1996b) Ombudsmen welcome next review. *Legal Action,* March, 4, 5.

Lewis, N. (1993) The Citizen's Charter and Next Steps: a new way of governing? *Political Quarterly,* 64 (3), 316–26.

McKibbin, R. (1993) Customers of the state. *London Review of Books,* 9 September.

National Consumer Council (1996) *Consumer Representation in the Public Utilities.* London: National Consumer Council.

Parliamentary Commissioner for Administration (1994) *Parliamentary Commissioner for Administration Annual Report for 1994.* London: HMSO.

Perry, J. (1995) Removed from care: a report of patients removed from GP lists at the doctor's request. Unpublished paper in local circulation.

Police Foundation and Policy Studies Institute (1996) *The Report of the Independent Inquiry into the Role and Responsibilities of the Police.* London: Police Foundation/PSI.

Pollitt, C. (1994) The Citizen's Charter: a preliminary analysis. *Public Money and Management,* April–June, 9–13.

Prior, D., Stewart, J. and Walsh, K. (1995) *Citizenship: Rights, Community and Participation.* London: Pitman.

Rhodes, R. (1995) The new governance. Lecture in ESRC/RSA series, 'The State of Britain', 24 January.

Select Committee on the Parliamentary Commissioner for Administration (1994) Maladministration and redress. London: HMSO.

Shapland, J., Hibbert, J., l'Anson, J., Sorsby, A. and Wild, R. (1995) *Milton Keynes: Criminal Justice Audit.* Sheffield: Institute for the Study of the Legal Profession.

Social Services Inspectorate (1995) *Caring for People at Home.* London: Department of Health.

Steele, J. (1995) *Public Access to Information: An Evaluation of the Local Government (Access to Information) Act 1985.* London: PSI.

Stewart, J. (1995) *Innovation in Democratic Practice.* Birmingham: Institute of Local Government Studies.

Stewart, J., Greer, A. and Hoggett, P. (1995) The quango state: an alternative approach. CLD Research Report No. 10. London: CLD.

Tate, C. Wedderburn, Bruster, S., Broadley, K., Maxwell, E. and Stevens, E. (1995) What do patients really think? *Health Service Journal*, 12 January, 18–20.

Treasury and Civil Service Committee (1994) *Treasury and Civil Service Committee Inquiry. Fifth Report. Vol. II: Session 1993–1994*. London: HMSO, p. 116.

Tritter, J. (1994) The Citizen's Charter: opportunities for users' perspectives? *Political Quarterly*, 65, 397–414.

Woolf, H., and Tumim, S. (1991) *Prison Disturbances April 1990*. Report of an inquiry by the Rt Hon. Lord Justice Woolf and HH Judge Stephen Tumim. Cm 1456. London: HMSO.

15

Better Health for All

ANNA COOTE AND DAVID J. HUNTER

Health and autonomy have been defined as the two basic needs which are shared by all human beings (Doyal and Gough, 1993). The first goal of any government should be to ensure that these needs are met. In a democracy, the means to health, as well as to autonomy, can be understood as an essential component of citizenship. The Commission on Social Justice (1994) observed that the foundation of a free society is the equal worth of all citizens; everyone should be entitled, as a right of citizenship, to be able to meet their basic needs, as well as to enjoy opportunities and life chances; and since all citizens are of equal worth 'unjust inequalities should be reduced and where possible eliminated'.

If we accept these principles, the first goal of health policy should be to promote health for all on an equitable basis, to give everyone the opportunity to enjoy as much good health as possible ... [T]his is a lot easier said than done, not least because the means to health go far beyond the remit of the NHS and the Department of Health. The goals set out below follow from the first but are concerned primarily with health care rather than simply with health.

- *Appropriate health services.* Effective treatment and care.
- *Equity: no unfair discrimination.* Everyone should have equal access to health services which are appropriate to their needs.
- *Autonomy.* Respect for the individual, full and fair exchange of information, and the means for citizens and patients to participate in decisions which affect their lives.

- *Social solidarity.* Strategies which are inclusive, and which build and maintain a shared sense of ownership and mutual benefit.
- *Democratic legitimacy.* Key decisions about health care must earn the support of the public through open and accountable governance.
- *Value for money.* Efficient use of public resources.

There is a strong case, in our view, for an explicit set of goals, expressed approximately in these terms, to guide health-policy makers through the next decade. We have not ranked them in order of importance. Each has a valid claim and policy makers must work with the tensions between them. The claim of the individual to appropriate treatment may conflict with the goal of social solidarity, if a single treatment is very expensive and funds are limited, so that others' needs cannot be met. National standards or protocols may help to promote equality of access, but could also infringe local autonomy, which in turn may (or may not) promote greater equality of outcomes. Such claims are not easily reconciled, but open and participative decision making can help to build public support and understanding for difficult political decisions for which there is no 'right' answer.

Our framework rejects a paternalistic system which claims to protect and provide, but fails to consult or involve the public in decisions. The goals of autonomy and democratic legitimacy imply the need for *mature relationships* between patients and doctors, and between citizens and policy makers – based on informed understanding, a caring ethos and mutual trust, rather than on the current mid-1990s mixture of blind faith, fear and contempt. But significant changes would be required in the organization of the NHS and in the culture of the health professions to develop a service capable of sustaining such relationships.

Our framework also supports an NHS which is there for everyone, not merely a residual service for those unable to purchase private health care. We may accept that people with different levels of income drive different cars, or live in homes of different sizes, or eat different foods – because of what they can afford. But we cannot, within this framework, accept that the *quality* of health care should vary according to the patient's means. The idea that, in times of scarcity, the NHS can be 'saved' by targeting resources on needier groups carries the seeds of its own destruction. If queuing systems or hospital conditions encourage the middle classes to opt out in significant numbers, the political base for an inclusive service will soon erode. Those who 'go private' will be less and less content to pay for an NHS they think they can do without. Starved of funds, the service will deteriorate further, lose more support and spiral into decline. One only has to look across the Atlantic to see where this path leads: a service for the poor becomes a poor service. It is essential to sustain the firm commitment of all social groups – in the interests of appropriate health services, equity and social solidarity.

It could be said that the current absence of clear public-interest goals is a lot more surprising and controversial than the case for introducing them. Of course, there are countless ways in which goals can be pursued and what matters ultimately is how they are implemented. But at the very least we need an extensive public debate about whether explicit goals are desirable and, if so, what they should be. The goals themselves, if they can be shown to command broad support among ordinary members of the public as well as specific interest groups, would provide a principled framework for shaping policies and assessing performance . . .

Public Health

Concern about public health has probably never been higher. In almost every sphere of policy there are signs that politicians are putting the people's health at risk. Dramatically in 1996, the BSE crisis raised fears about the effects of 'agribusiness' on health. But this was just one health scare among many. People have had cause to worry about the quality and availability of water in the new era of privatized utilities, about the link between traffic density, air pollution and the rising numbers of asthma sufferers, about the impact on mental health of increasing fears about crime, about the effects of homelessness on vulnerable families and individuals, and about the links between poverty and ill health as the income gap widens between sections of the population. In each case, the threat to public health can be seen as a consequence of government policy, which has either exacerbated the problem or failed to mitigate its effects.

We cannot afford to underestimate the obstacles which lie in the way of achieving better health for all. Powerful commercial and professional interests will have to be tackled. The NHS is weak and muddled in its approach. Since public health departments were moved from local government to the NHS in 1974, they have arguably lost their way, as they have been drawn into the narrow managerialist agenda of the NHS, which is chiefly about delivering health services. The British beef fiasco demonstrated all too clearly how we need and lack strong political leadership in public health to drive intersectoral action. It also revealed a lamentable absence of clout and purpose on the part of the NHS, which prevented it from playing an effective role. If there is any cause for optimism it must lie in the mounting scepticism of the public about the government's claims to be protecting and promoting public health. We can only hope that an increasingly canny and distrustful electorate will force the politicians to abandon glossy platitudes and commit themselves to change. A radical overhaul of public health policy and practice is long overdue.

Few would disagree that the over-riding goal of health policy should be to improve the health status of the nation as a whole and to promote health for all on an equitable basis. Successive governments have acknowledged the importance of promoting public health. Yet the implications are profound. It means ensuring that risk and opportunity are distributed as evenly as possible across the population and that every individual enjoys equitable access to appropriate services and to the means by which they can live a healthy life. It means recognizing that the National Health Service plays a small, though significant, role in promoting better health for all, and that policy makers who are serious about health gain cannot focus simply – or even primarily – on the treatment of illness and injury. In this chapter we consider the causes of inequalities in health, barriers to achieving better health for all and strategies for turning good intentions into practical outcomes.

Inequalities in Health

The causes of ill health are familiar and well documented. Strategies for promoting better health and tackling inequalities in health have been widely discussed and there is a considerable degree of consensus among experts about what ought to be done. The arguments can be summarized as follows:

- People who are poor and/or socially isolated are likely to be ill more often and more seriously than those who are not, and to die younger. Inequalities in mortality and morbidity between social classes in the UK have grown in recent years.
- Income, education, employment, working conditions, housing and environment, diet and social relationships are important determinants of health. Health status and gender are linked, with men dying younger than women.
- An integrated approach is required, linking local, regional and national policies, and crossing traditional departmental boundaries to combine resources and co-operate in policy implementation.
- Policies for better health must aim:

- to strengthen individuals;
- to strengthen communities;
- to improve access to appropriate facilities and services;
- to encourage macroeconomic and cultural change.

- Ideas about what could be done at each level are well developed, notably by the King's Fund (Benzeval at al., 1995) and the Association for Public Health (1996). Action at any one level is unlikely to make a sufficient impact unless there is also action at the others.
- There are impressive examples of successful practical initiatives, but these tend to be confined to particular localities.
- The importance of promoting better health for all has been clearly endorsed by government as well as by the opposition parties.
- Strong and sustained political will is required to bring about a fundamental shift in how health policy is conceived and pursued.

Health Gain and Equity

The term 'health gain' has become current in recent years. It provides a useful focus on the need for improvements in health status rather than simply in health care, and directs attention to health outcomes and away from an obsession with inputs to health services. We take 'health gain' to mean improvements in the health of groups and populations, rather than an individual's capacity to benefit from a particular treatment. Health gain as a framing policy objective must be understood and measured in this way: not simply for the individual or for the few, but for all on a fair and equal basis.

The government has acknowledged the importance of health gain as a policy objective in its *Health of the Nation* White Paper published in 1993, and has set up a special Cabinet committee to co-ordinate policy. The challenge is to turn rhetoric into sustained action and demonstrable outcomes. Growing inequalities in health have been reported by the government's own working group (Department of Health, 1995). And according to a National Audit Office (1996) report on the *Health of the Nation* strategy, progress towards achieving the twenty-seven targets is proving generally slow and uneven. While, on present trends, good progress is being made towards many of the targets, trends are moving in the wrong direction in three key areas: obesity in men and women, drinking by women and smoking by young people. For seven other targets, progress cannot currently be monitored due to data limitations. The NAO concludes that it is too soon to say how far the initiative will succeed.

What Are the Barriers?

Economic and political trends

There are continuing and growing gaps between income levels and risks incurred by different social groups. Economic recession and rising unemployment have restricted opportunities, with successive generations trapped in poverty and deprivation. Reversing these trends has become an increasingly complex and intractable problem. Structural adjustments to reduce the size of the public sector and the development of a 'low-tax' culture have diminished resources available to promote health gain. And the ideology of four Conservative governments has resisted acknowledging links between poverty and ill health, preferring to attribute the causes to individual behaviour, genetic predisposition or bad luck.

Entrenched interests

The public health agenda is regarded as marginal to the concerns of the Department of Health which, in spite of its recent restructuring, remains almost entirely preoccupied by the National Health Service. Government departments tend to focus their energies on areas of responsibility where most of their money is spent, whether or not this is ultimately in the public interest or even in accordance with government policy. Anyone who wants to shift the balance between health care and health gain would have to contend with the entrenched traditions and culture of the Department of Health as well as with the considerable power of professional groups with vested interests in the NHS.

Short-termism

In any event, pursuing health gain is a long-term project. Political parties prefer to focus on short-term measures which are popular with the electorate, rather than on policies aimed at longer-term gains. Public perceptions shore up these distortions. The public understands health policy in terms of the NHS and the NHS in terms of hospitals, 'white coats' and acute interventions. Efforts to shift resources from acute care towards preventative and public health goals tend to encounter strong resistance from voters.

Lack of direction

There are no effective mechanisms to co-ordinate policy making or implementation at national, regional and local levels or between government departments. Opportunities to learn from insights and experience in different parts of the UK and in other countries are wasted. There is little co-ordination or dissemination of good ideas or of best practice. A central problem has been observed by a group of local authority chief executives (Society of Local Authorities Chief Executives, 1995): 'One of the key characteristics of government policy over the past 15 years has been a tendency to tackle complex social and economic issues by simplifying them into problems and tasks which can be more easily managed.'

The new 'contract culture' encourages disaggregation of policies and services into a series of discrete programme areas without much overlap. Indeed, overlap is actively discouraged in order not to complicate further the tasks of objective setting, targeting and monitoring for results. Yet issues like poverty, environmental deterioration, transport policy, drug dependency and an ageing population do not fit neatly within this kind of simplified framework.

What Can Be Done?

It is always easier to diagnose a problem and offer a prescription than to ensure effective treatment. Why have so many good intentions, shared by successive governments, come to so little? Does the problem lie with the policies put forward or with strategies for implementation, or with the sincerity or commitment of the governments involved? Whatever the reasons, we shall have to identify and confront them. As Long and Eskin remind us: 'resistance to change, vested interests in maintaining the status quo, financial implications and the enormous collaborative and altruistic efforts which are required to make the appropriate changes create daunting barriers which need to be taken into account' (1995, p. 174).

A new understanding of health

To begin with, we may need to reassess our ways of understanding the public's health and the public-health function of government. Until now, the focus has been more on disease than on health, more on immediate than on underlying causes, more on easily measurable than on hard-to-measure factors – all tending towards a reductionist approach to what is, in fact, a broad and multifarious issue. The health status of an individual and of a population is the product of a complex interplay between human beings and their environment which we do not understand very well. Our focus continues to be on ill health not on health.

What is needed is an epidemiology of *health*, drawing on lay experience, in order to understand better why people remain healthy, to complement our knowledge of how some people become ill. Studies in this area attach importance to such factors as a sense of meaning, purpose and self – implying a paradigm shift for public policy at all levels.

Strong political leadership

What is required above all is a clear direction from government and a designated secretary of state who will champion, as a matter of priority, the pursuit of equitable health gain for the nation as a whole. Both should be concerned with questions of health as much as with questions about the NHS. A senior minister of state should have day-to-day responsibility for the development and implementation of policy on health gain. This concurs with the Labour Party's proposal for a minister for public health.

Build from the local level

Strong political leadership must be combined with a community-based approach to implementation, so that measures are geared to local needs and conditions. Of course, this is easier said than done, but there is no irreconcilable conflict between a national policy framework which seeks equity in health, and local variations to suit local needs and circumstances. Strong, self-sufficient and cohesive families and communities are the best foundation for a healthy society. Measures which help to build local autonomy and competence as well as understanding and co-operation between and within social groups are a vital part of a strategy to promote better health for all. They are consistent with our commitment to an epidemiology of health.

Integrated planning

The designated secretary of state should be responsible for leading and co-ordinating at Cabinet level the health-related work of the Department of Health and other government departments, including environment, education and employment. There must be a clear understanding of the way in which different functions contribute to health gain and how these relate to each other. The principal components of the new health agenda can be summarized as follows:

- co-ordinated planning of public functions and services which affect the key determinants of health, at national and local levels;
- environmental health, including hazards such as hygiene in public buildings, restaurants but also air pollution and noise levels;
- occupational health (dealing with hazards, minimizing the effects of unhealthy working conditions, alleviating stress, etc.);
- health education (information and advice about healthy living and health hazards);
- support and encouragement of self-help and mutual aid;
- clinical prevention (screening, vaccines, etc.);
- clinical practice (for example, early intervention to prevent deterioration, standards which minimize problems of infection, recurrence);
- effective care and support for long-term care groups to avoid unnecessary dependency.

A lead government department is required to make a genuinely intersectoral approach effective. Although it is reasonable to assume that the Department of Health (DoH) would take on this role, other options might be considered, especially in the light of the DoH's traditional preoccupation with health care rather than health. A radical alternative would be to give the lead role on health policy to the Department of the Environment, which is responsible for a number of policy sectors which impact critically on health. A new minister for public health, as proposed by Labour, might thus be located in the Department of the Environment, heading up health, as distinct from health care, policy, and supported by arrangements dedicated to the task . . .

Whichever department assumes a leadership role, there remain strong barriers within Whitehall which will continue to inhibit progress. The Cabinet's Special Health Committee, set up under the Conservative government's *Health of the Nation* initiative, is charged with putting health explicitly on the whole government agenda. While its rhetoric is impeccable and gives all the right signals about ensuring that all of Whitehall plays its part, it needs to be given far greater prominence and to be seen to achieve success, with departments other than the DoH making significant contributions to creating a healthier nation. As it stands, the Special Cabinet Committee's profile is too low. Its purpose, membership and work programme are hidden among Whitehall's many mysteries. It may pursue worthy initiatives, but there is no evidence that it is succeeding in its overall aims of a health-driven agenda.

It is over twenty years since central government last attempted to grapple with these difficulties. In the early 1970s, the 'think tank', the Central Policy Review Staff, launched its joint approach to social policy which became known as JASP (Central Policy Review Staff, 1975). This was based on a number of concerns: the government's inability to see people or problems 'in the round'; a failure to exploit research effectively; a poor relationship between central and local government, especially over the implementation of national policy. JASP aimed to improve co-ordination between services, to provide better analysis of complex problems and to develop collective views on priorities between different programmes. It sought to apply analysis to the process of working out governmental priorities, to ensure that individual developments reflected these priorities, to counteract fragmentation of policies among competing agencies, and to pursue a more deliberate relationship between different decisions, taken at different times about different issues.

Blackstone and Plowden (1988) describe JASP as 'an ambitious, schematic, and completely unsuccessful attempt to devise a comprehensive system' for rational and co-ordinated policy-making. One reason why JASP failed was that few ministers remained committed to it or understood its relevance for the long term. It became a technical concern of interest principally to senior civil servants. It was seen, especially in its early phase, as too rational and apolitical and therefore doomed (Challis et al., 1988, p. 100).

It has been argued with hindsight that more attention should have been given to involving ministers directly and in identifying issues in which they themselves had a particular interest, so that JASP could be seen to contribute directly to the ministers' own objectives. Only in this way could the dangers of 'departmentalitis' be overcome, since JASP did represent a potential threat to ministers' empires and budgets. Co-ordination as an abstract notion held little appeal. It invariably created more work with no obvious or quick return. After a strong start, JASP appeared to lose its sense of direction, with the initial vision getting lost in details and with a tendency to run too many projects simultaneously. Another major weakness was that it had no clear relationship with the resource allocation process (known as PESC). Isolated working groups not connected to central policy-making and budgetary machinery could serve little purpose. JASP concentrated on strategic thinking, taking too little account of the inertia in the system and of the power of vested interests. It was also at odds with ministers' preoccupation with the short term.

After its initial phase JASP gave way to a more modest attempt to encourage joint action in a limited number of contexts. The second phase was more political in that it accepted the need for allies and stratagems; it went 'with the grain', was more incremental and less ambitious. At the time, this approach was widely viewed as more appropriate, as Challis and others have observed: JASP in its first phase 'had wrongly tried to influence the detailed aims and methods of departments, whereas it should have concentrated on getting ministers to identify broad priorities in the social field' (in Klein et al., 1988, p. 100). However, phase two came too late to save the day. Separate financing to lubricate joint approaches may also have been necessary, because departmental budgets were not seen as a legitimate source of funds for such activities.

There are lessons to be learned from the experience of JASP. One is the supreme importance of *sustained* political leadership. Another is that good will and altruism are not enough to ensure that departments collaborate: incentives are needed so that all parties involved stand to win something from a collaborative approach. Joint approaches to policy making must be political, not merely rational, and appeal directly to the interests of ministers, aiming to sustain their commitment in the long term. They must be selective and incremental, not attempting to proceed on too many fronts at once. They should be well integrated with the central policy-making machinery, and there should be separate financing to prime the process.

We can also learn from a new initiative by the Department of the Environment, which has produced a National Environmental Health Action Plan (NEHAP) (Department of the Environment, 1996). The UK is the first European country to produce such a plan and it is to be used as a pilot for others. NEHAP notes the contribution other government departments will have on its outcome. It also points to the *Health of the Nation* strategy and to the importance of environmental health services in achieving its targets. It is vital that initiatives such as this are built upon and used to secure action across policy sectors.

Stronger institutional support

There may be a case for a new organization, dedicated to health promotion, whose job it would be to gather, analyse and disseminate information about health and to advise the government on policy formation and implementation. The Health Education Authority does not fit the bill as it stands. One option would be to change the status and role of the chief medical officer from an employee of the Department of Health to an independent ombudsman, although some critics argue that the CMO can be more influential as an 'insider' than an 'outsider' . . . A third option, which we favour, would be to develop the HEA into a new Health Promotion

Authority or Commission. This would have to be accountable to the secretary of state or minister responsible for public health, but might enjoy the same degree of independence as the Audit Commission, which rarely pulls its punches in appraising government policy. It would have the task of devising and monitoring performance indicators for health and publishing results for each locality. A fourth option would be to give this job to the Audit Commission itself. An essential part of any reorganization would be to separate responsibility for nutritional standards from the producer interests which predominate within the Ministry for Agriculture, Fisheries and Foods.

Arguably, the best combination would be a strong and semi-autonomous Health Promotion Authority working closely with an 'insider' chief medical officer, both accountable to a senior minister responsible for public health. In any event, it will be essential to avoid duplication and unnecessary costs, and to ensure that any new or reformed organization is as slim, agile and assertive as possible, as well as being properly accountable.

Tackle inequalities in health

It must be understood that efforts to promote health gain should aim to bring the health status of relatively poor and disadvantaged sections of society into line with that of the better off. This will involve directing resources at improving the quality of life in areas where there are high levels of economic and social deprivation, through improvements in education and housing, through local economic regeneration and community development, and through outreach work with isolated social groups. Poverty is a key determinant of ill health and so ways must be found, through employment programmes and income-support arrangements, to ensure that all individuals have sufficient income to enable them to provide for themselves. The impact of the social environment on health must be confronted. Communities lacking social cohesion lose health advantages.

Integrated goals for better health

National policies to promote equitable health gain should be expressed in terms of explicit goals and strategies, with performance measured and publicized at regular intervals. As mentioned above, this could be undertaken by the proposed Health Promotion Authority. Ideally, it would involve publishing public health goals (such as diminishing mortality and morbidity rates; reduced consumption of tobacco, alcohol and drugs) alongside and *explicitly related to* goals for educational attainment, employment, income distribution, housing, recreation and environment. Measures of progress towards these goals – which might be published as health league tables – would be co-ordinated by gender, age, ethnicity, socio-economic back-ground and region, so that absolute and relative achievements could be charted. The purpose would not be to lay blame at the door of authorities in less healthy localities, but to focus public attention on the relationship between health and other factors and on the need for targeted policies to boost the health status of low-scoring communities.

Health impact statements

As a parallel exercise, but not as a substitute for the above, government departments could be required to demonstrate, where possible, the impact of their policies on health, developing a new system of audit with the results published as health impact statements. If this idea were implemented, close attention would need to be given to monitoring and evaluation, to ensure that departments took the exercise seriously.

More relevant and better co-ordinated research

Research and development within the NHS has been largely devoted to biomedical health care services, at the expense of public health. The gold standard of evaluation in biomedical research is the randomized control trial, but this has limited relevance to public health, as such trials cannot measure the effectiveness of most public health interventions. Different methodologies are required and these must be brought into the mainstream of health-related research activities (Hunter and Long, 1993). In addition, more could be made of the annual reports of locally based directors of public health (DPHs). These show how DPHs approach their work, their priorities and methods, and how each one views activities and perform-ance on their own patch. Yet the reports are not pooled, so that each can learn from the others, and their findings are not compared or published nationally. The freedom of DPHs to produce reports on their own terms is jealously guarded, but this should not rule out a degree of consistency, with each report including a range of findings in terms which allow com-parative analysis. They are potentially a rich resource, which should be properly co-ordinated, analysed and disseminated.

Close collaboration between health and local authorities

Effective local action depends on this. At present, degrees of co-operation vary greatly from one locality to another. Health and local authorities are now obliged to draw up joint plans for community care, which are supposed to be based on local consultations and which must be published. There is no such obligation to co-operate over the pursuit of health gain: the production of joint five-year health strategies is purely voluntary, although several examples exist. Local government reform introducing unitary local authorities is likely to make collaborative working more difficult in some localities.

The achievements and failures to date of the Healthy Cities projects have a lot to teach us about what is required for effective collaboration. For example:

- Joint operations must be central, not marginal to the work of both local authorities and local health agencies.
- The quality of local leadership and the relationships between key individuals can make a huge impact on the success of collaborative projects.
- Measures must be designed for local needs and conditions, although opportunities to spread and adapt good ideas from one locality to another must not be wasted.
- There must be real and sustained participation by local people in decisions about what strategies are best suited to the locality and how they are to be put into practice.
- Local initiatives, however successful they are in the short term, will not survive unless they are backed by strategies and resources to sustain them in the longer term.
- Government policies to reduce public spending, the capping of local authority budgets, the market ethos fostered by the NHS reforms and by the introduction of compulsory competitive tendering into local public services – all tend to discourage productive collaboration between health and local authorities, and to foster distrust. Innovations and efficiency drives encouraged by these changes must be critically assessed for their impact on health gain.

Pilot local authority commissioning for health

Many of the problems associated with collaboration between health and local authorities stem from the fact that the two institutions are separate and quite differently constituted . . . [T]here is a case for pilot schemes to test the viability of local authorities becoming commissioners for health services.

Foster self-help and mutual aid

In a separate study (Wann, 1995) IPPR has identified self-help and mutual aid as activities which are central to the development of health and well-being . . .

Renew and strengthen the commitment of primary health care to health gain and equity

Primary health care practitioners should participate in collaborative working with other local agencies in the pursuit of equitable health gain. A health policy which puts health, not illness, first, should inspire and shape primary health care and strengthen the case for giving the lead within the NHS to the primary health care sector . . .

Improve training of clinical staff

Doctors and (to a lesser extent) nurses are trained to treat illness rather than to promote good health. Understanding health determinants and the importance of collaborative working for health gain should be a major element in the training of all clinical staff. Public health training programmes should stress the importance of working as advocates and agents for change, as well as working across organizational and professional boundaries.

A new approach to planning and management

A report from the Society of Local Authority Chief Executives (1995) has observed that 'The time is now right to seek greater sophistication in the mechanisms of government, to recognise that complex problems need something more than single-issue, centrally-determined approaches.' In a similar vein, the chief medical officer's report on health variations recommended that inequalities must be tackled not through yet another new initiative isolated from mainstream work, but through more explicit targeting of the issue within existing policies and activities. A paradigm shift is required from a simple approach to problem solving, to one which acknowledges the complexity of health problems, as set out in box 15.1.

Simple	Complex
Top-down Centralized policy formulation and resource allocation, inflexible rules	*Bottom-up* The flexibility to react to local needs and opportunities
Spotlight vision Failing to focus on either the links between issues or the environment they exist in	*Broad vision* Recognizing interlinkages, tackling root causes not just symptoms
Fragmented Many agencies, all pursuing their own policy agendas, no overview of whole community	*Holistic* Seeing the community in the round, seeking synergy from co-operation
Uniformity Local application of national solutions	*Context-sensitive* Opportunistic, reacting to local circumstances

Box 15.1 Policy frameworks

Making progress will require a long haul as well as commitment and steady nerves on the part of our political leaders. Above all, the approach must be flexible, adaptive and dynamic. . . . [T]he health policy landscape is subject to continuing and unpredictable change. We need, therefore, to be constantly alert to shifts in context and circumstance, and to modify policy accordingly. Our recommendations which follow should be viewed in this light.

Recommendations

- The first goal of health policy is to improve the health of the nation as a whole and promote health for all on an equitable basis.
- Concerted efforts must be made to bring the health status of poor and disadvantaged sectors of society into line with that of the better off, by ensuring a fair distribution of opportunity and income between social groups, and other appropriate strategies.
- There must be strong political leadership at the highest level of government, with a designated minister of state for public health, and active investment in integrated planning to involve all departments whose policies influence health.

- An integrated agenda for health must include: co-ordinated planning of all public functions and services which affect health; environmental health, nutritional health, occupational health, health education, self-help and mutual aid, clinical prevention, clinical practice, care and support for older people to prevent unnecessary dependency.
- Stronger institutional support is needed. This could be achieved by transforming the Health Education Authority into a new Health Promotion Authority, with the task of devising and monitoring new public health performance indicators. Another option worth considering is to transform the role of the chief medical officer into that of an independent ombudsman.
- Health league tables, showing progress towards public health goals, should be published at regular intervals. These should be explicitly related to performance on education, employment, income, housing, recreation and environment. Government departments should be required to publish health impact statements.
- Clear national goals and political leadership must be combined with a community-based approach to implementation, and measures to build local autonomy and competence.
- More effective collaboration must be developed between health and local authorities, applying the lessons learned from the achievements and failures of the Healthy Cities and Healthy Alliances initiatives, as well as from other experiences of joint planning.
- There should be more investment in, and better co-ordination of, relevant research, developing appropriate methodologies and drawing public health research and evaluation into the centre of NHS concerns. The annual reports of local directors of public health should be co-ordinated, analysed and published nationally.
- A new epidemiology of health should be developed, to understand better why people remain healthy, complementing knowledge about why people become ill.

References

Association for Public Health (1996) Draft Manifesto Statement. APH.

Benzeval, M., Judge, K. and Whithead, M. (1995) *Tackling Inequalities in Health: An Agenda for Action*. London: King's Fund.

Blackstone, T. and Plowden, W. (1988) *Inside the Think Tank: Advising the Cabinet 1971–1983*. London: Heinemann.

Central Policy Review Staff (1975) *A Joint Framework for Social Policy*. London: HMSO.

Commission on Social Justice (1994) *Social Justice: Strategies for National Renewal*. London: Verso.

Department of the Environment (1996) *The United Kingdom National Environmental Health Action Plan: Overview*. London: HMSO.

Department of Health (1995) *Variations in Health: What Can the Department of Health and the NHS Do?* London: Variations sub-Group of the Chief Medical Officer's Health of the Nation Working Group, DoH.

Doyal, L. and Gough, I. (1993) *A Theory of Human Need*. Basingstoke and London: Macmillan.

Hunter, D. and Long, A. (1993) Health research. In W. Sykes, M. Bulmer and M. Schwerzel (eds), *Directory of Social Research Organisations in the UK*, London: DSRO.

Klein, R., Plowden, W. and Webb, A. (1988) *Joint Approaches to Social Policy*. Cambridge: Cambridge University Press.

Long, A.F. and Eskin, F. (1995) The new public health: changing attitudes and practice. *Medical Principles and Practice*, 4.

National Audit Office (1996) *Health of the Nation: A Progress Report*. HC656 Session 1995–6. London: HMSO.

Society of Local Authority Chief Executives (1995) *Lighthouses not Spotlights*. Birmingham: SOLACE.

Wann, M. (1995) *Building Social Capital*. London: IPPR.

16

Rationing and Rights in Health Care

JO LENAGHAN

There has always been rationing in the National Health Service, but recent reforms in the mid-1990s have made it more explicit. Different treatments have been excluded in different localities, so that UK citizens do not have equal access. We recommend a new rights-based framework for decision making in the NHS, aimed at reconciling citizens' rights to appropriate health care with the need to manage scarce resources. This would comprise:

- national guidelines – a code of practice setting out criteria and procedures for rationing decisions in health care;
- a National Health Commission, to involve stakeholders in advising Parliament on the code of practice;
- a *prima facie* right to appropriate health care on the basis of clinical need, with a right of appeal;
- procedural rights to ensure fair dealing between patients and providers;
- citizens' juries to involve the public in decisions.

Is Rationing Necessary?

Some claim that the gap between demand and supply will grow ever wider, leaving the NHS unable to meet health-care needs in the future, and services drastically reduced. There is insufficient evidence to support this view. But while there may not be a 'crisis' looming, there will always be a need to ensure the fair distribution of finite resources...

Rationing decisions in the NHS have largely been controlled by the medical profession, and have tended to be implicit in nature, with little reference to agreed systems or criteria (New and Le Grand, 1996). Central government is responsible for deciding how resources for health care are distributed around Britain and sets the legal context, but should it do more and develop a national framework for rationing health care? A recent spate of reports and articles revealing variations in the provision of and access to health-care services highlights the urgent need to address this question.

The House of Commons Select Committee on Health (1995) surveyed the priority-setting practices of forty-nine health authorities, noting: 'We have been struck by the seemingly enormous variation in access across the country.' A study by Sharon Redmayne (1995) has revealed that one in six health authorities are now excluding treatments from public provision, whilst a recent survey on IVF has shown that couples in Scotland are seven times more likely to get NHS *in vitro* fertilization (IVF) than a couple in the South and West region (National Institute for Assisted Conception, 1995).

Variations in health-care provision are nothing new, but the purchaser–provider split has made rationing more explicit, and, more importantly, revealed variations in the criteria used to justify these decisions. For example, in Humberside, fertility treatment is provided to women up until the age of 40, whereas in Liverpool, the guidelines favour women under the age of 35 (House of Commons Health Committee, 1995). As New and Le Grand have observed, explicit rationing has not been accompanied by an explicit or shared understanding of how such decisions should be made (1996, pp. 16, 21).

It has been argued that if the UK government increased the amount of resources available to the NHS, then this would remove the need to ration. However, this ignores the fact that decisions about whether to provide a treatment are not always determined by financial considerations alone. For instance, the new genetic technologies may not just cause us to question whether we can afford to fund particular types of screening, but may provoke debates about whether or not it is appropriate or relevant for the NHS to provide certain services (McLean, 1996). Such issues raise fundamental questions about the nature and purpose of our health service, the rights of citizens and the responsibilities of professionals, and are too important to be left to individual health authorities and medical practitioners to resolve alone . . .

It is not the need to ration which causes difficulties, but how it is done and by whom, whether it is seen to be done in the public interest, and whether it can command the confidence of the public.

Why Are Rights Important?

Health is an essential component of citizenship. Citizenship implies entitlement, which in turn implies enforceability: citizens claiming and obtaining what is theirs by right. Health cannot be an enforceable 'right' but health services, as a means of achieving health, and the manner in which they are distributed may be.

The concept of citizenship, as opposed to consumerism, is central to our analysis. Rights arising from citizen status are not contingent on other factors, such as income, age or location. Tensions between the claims of individuals and those of the community as a whole are inevitable. There is a political task of negotiating between competing claims, and deciding what can and cannot be an enforceable right.

Increasing awareness of rationing in the NHS has coincided with rising anxiety about what patients can expect. This has led to a symbolic confrontation in the health-policy field between those calling for more explicit patients' rights and those urging more explicit rationing. This chapter represents a radical attempt to reconcile these apparently contradictory aims, and develop a rights-based approach to rationing. If rights to health services are realistically defined, consensually based, broadly understood and consistently enforced, then they can help to mitigate uncertainty, build trust and promote equitable distribution of resources.

What Kind of Rights?

A distinction is made between substantive rights to actual benefits and services, and procedural rights which guarantee fair treatment (in the non-clinical sense) of individuals by service providers and purchasers.

Substantive rights, if rendered enforceable by individuals, can introduce rigidities into the health-care system as well as committing governments to open-ended expenditure (Lenaghan, 1996). Procedural rights are more flexible and cost less to enforce. This chapter recommends that a rights-based approach to rationing should concentrate on process, underpinned by national guidelines . . . [T]he provision of health-care services is increasingly subject to geographical variation. This is a result of the fact that responsibility for rationing decisions has been devolved to individual health authorities, who have been left to set their own priorities and define their own criteria for doing so. This raises important questions not just of legitimacy, but of competence. In the field of health-care provision, who should have responsibility for taking what kind of decision?

Who Decides?

In *Treat Me Right*, Kennedy poses the question, 'What decisions are within the specific competence of a doctor to make?' (1988, p. 20) It may be argued that it is up to doctors to decide about issues of 'health and ill health' but, as he points out, the problem of definition of these terms is 'virtually unmanageable'. For instance, whereas homosexuality was once considered an illness, it is now considered a matter of lifestyle. Depression or unhappiness was once merely seen as bad luck, whereas now it is the subject of sophisticated medicine and therapy. Definitions of illness and therefore treatment are thus subject to socio-historical forces.

Kennedy suggests that 'the normalising of abnormality' has become the job of the doctor. He argues that there are many non-medical decisions being taken by doctors, and that responsibility for many areas of human concern has been improperly shifted onto the medical profession:

> There are a large number of decisions being made by doctors which I would not categorise as being medical or wholly medical. And, that being so, they are not for doctors alone to make ... although doctors may have to take them in the sense that they are 'in the field', as it were, decisions taken in the field must conform with standards set by others. (ibid., p. 22)

Kennedy goes on to quote the case of whether an elderly lady should receive expensive treatment:

> Whether her life will be worth living subsequently and who is to judge are moral issues. Whether the NHS should spend money on her, and thereby not spend it on another, and who is to judge are issues calling for economic analysis, political judgements and moral theory. All are involved in the medical decision, but our question is whether they are for the doctor alone to assess. (ibid., p. 24)

This suggests a need to set the boundaries within which doctors can be free to exercise their clinical judgement, as well as a principled framework within which health authorities and managers should make their decisions. This would require us to develop a shared understanding of the nature and purpose of the National Health Service, which would be a matter for the government and society as a whole to decide. The BMA have called for wider public debate and involvement in these issues:

> The medical profession has in the past called for a national debate about rationing and priority setting because as resource considerations become more

explicit, it wants the public and individual patients to continue to trust that doctors are taking clinical decisions based on what is best for an individual patient. At the same time, the expertise of the doctors should be available to advise on wider health priorities. (BMA, 1995)

In trying to define the boundaries of the NHS, our objective should not be primarily to save money, but to develop a consensus about the aims and values of the National Health Service. For instance, infertility was considered a curse fifty years ago, now it is an 'illness', primarily because we can 'treat' it. As we have seen, whether infertility treatment is available on the NHS very often depends upon the policies of individual health authorities. This is an example of the government devolving responsibility for these difficult issues down to a local level. Klein critically observes that:

the fact that no patient under the NHS system has a legal right to any specific kind of treatment – that it is the clinician who determines what the patient 'needs' – means that it is possible to fragment and dissolve national policy issues into a series of local clinical decisions. Political problems are, in effect, converted into clinical problems. (1995, p. 78)

As more high-tech and high-cost treatments are developed, these issues will become increasingly urgent. For example, health authorities were recently under pressure from users and the media to provide the drug beta-interferon for multiple sclerosis (MS). A recent publication by the Cambridge and Huntingdon Health Authority (1995) argues that this drug is of limited clinical efficacy, as it only delays the onset of some types of MS but does not cure it. It is estimated that the cost to the nation could be £190m, and to the Anglia and Oxford region £16m. 'In this instance the opportunity cost may be just too high for the responsible purchasers to contemplate.' On whose criteria are such decisions to be made? Surely all sufferers of MS should have the right of access to appropriate treatment, regardless of where they live? There are probably no right answers, which is why it may be more appropriate to focus instead on getting the process of deciding right.

These are moral, ethical and political decisions, which health authorities and doctors should not be left to resolve unaided. In order to increase the coherence and clarity of decision making in the NHS, it is necessary to redefine what kind of decisions are appropriate to be taken at which level. What is within the competence of the various professionals and institutions involved in health-care provision and distribution?

Kennedy defines a medical decision by identifying where a doctor's special competence lies:

the knowledge which allows him to make a diagnosis and prognosis of what is generally accepted as being ill health; second, the knowledge of what therapies, if any, are available in the context of a particular condition of ill health; third, the judgement of which therapy or response to adopt so as to produce, to the best of his ability, an end result deemed appropriate not by him but by the patient, one approved by society at large. No more, no less. (1988, p. 30)

Responsibilities may be distributed as follows:

- The government should decide *what services* the NHS should provide.
- Health authorities should decide on the *level of services* to be provided.
- Clinicians should decide *which individuals* to give priority to, according to the framework set by government.
- The public should be *involved in debates* about what services should be provided, and should have the opportunity to *challenge unfair decisions*.

Education and training within the different health-related professional groups would encourage more competent and legitimate decision making at all these levels. In addition we propose the creation of a national body to develop appropriate guidelines within which the different groups can exercise their particular skills and judgement. Although at the end of the day doctors must actually take the decisions in the field, the criteria which they use should conform to standards which are seen to be consensual, legitimate and consistently applied. We need to develop a framework within which professional discretion and judgement can be appropriately exercised.

A Framework for Decision Making

If rights are to be used to improve health services, ways must be found to establish a set of values to clarify health-care decision making and to promote good practice. A framework of rights can provide positive statements of values that professionals and patients can aspire to respect, a consistent foundation for good practice, a means to prevent and redress wrongs, and a flexible framework for ethical judgement. Such a framework would not supersede the skills of health-care professionals, but would define the context in which care is offered (Montgomery, 1992). The challenge is to create a consensual but flexible mechanism for creating such a framework, which promotes, rather than constrains, good practice.

There are growing calls from practitioners and policy makers to create, at national level, some kind of forum for resolving rationing dilemmas.

Ian Kennedy called for a standing commission as far back as 1977, but recently the all-party House of Commons Select Committee on Health also recommended something along similar lines:

> It is questionable whether the current national framework for priority setting provides adequate support to purchasers in taking decisions about the limits of local health services . . . We recommend that the Department set out clearly the framework within which purchasers will be expected to define the local package of services, and set out the criteria by which these decisions may be debated, scrutinised, and if necessary, challenged by individuals. (1995, p. xxxv)

More recently, the Royal College of Physicians (1995) has called for a National Council for Health Care Priorities. They recommend an expert membership, made up of epidemiologists, economists, ethicists and social scientists, and suggest that the council would advise on a framework for making decisions on priorities and develop educational and consultation strategies with the public, as well as monitoring decisions taken.

We broadly support these proposals, and indeed, IPPR recently put these issues to the public, as part of our pilot project on citizens' juries. Citizens' juries represent a radical attempt to involve the public in decisions which affect them in their own communities. Approximately sixteen people sit for four days, to hear evidence and deliberate upon a policy question. When we asked a citizens' jury who should set priorities in health care, all sixteen members voted for a national body to set guidelines for priority setting . . .

The recent NHS reforms have exposed an absence of a clear, shared understanding of how choices should be made fairly and equitably in the NHS (New and Le Grand, 1996, p. 34). The reforms have also revealed how few rights citizens have to health care in the UK. Citizens have a limited right of access to the NHS (for example, through GPs or accident and emergency units), but they have no right to be involved in determining exactly what the NHS provides, and they have no guarantee that they will be fairly assessed for treatment purely on the basis of their clinical need. In the case of IVF, for example, it is often non-needs-based characteristics which determine whether a woman gains access to treatment. It may depend upon where she lives, whether she is married, or how old she is. In effect, we do not have equal rights as citizens of the UK to the National Health Service.

Local flexibility is important, but the boundaries between local and central decision making are blurred and it is increasingly unclear where responsibility, and therefore accountability, lies. The relationship between the centre and the localities needs to be redefined, so that power and responsibility can reside at the appropriate level. In order to allow local flexibility to operate effectively, the limits to this freedom must be established. As Bynoe has suggested:

> Where local providers deliver services on behalf of Government and with resources largely provided from national tax revenue there may be a place for a new legal and financing framework which better reflects this relationship and Government's expectations as to the services which are to be provided within it. (1996)

We therefore propose a code of practice for health-care rights, to be established under an Act of Parliament. The code of practice would have two main functions. Firstly, it should redefine and clearly state the principles and purpose of the National Health Service. Secondly, it should set out the procedures and criteria by which decisions about rationing and resource allocation should be made at both a micro- and macrolevel. In the following section, we suggest the creation of a National Health Commission, whose role would be to develop the code of practice, before discussing the advantages and disadvantages of such an approach. This policy has many critics and it is important that we address their legitimate concerns.

The Role of a National Health Commission

In a letter to the *British Medical Journal*, the Royal College of Physicians clarified what they thought should be the role of a National Council for Priority setting:

> The council that the college proposes would be charged with considering and developing the principles that should guide both national and local health authorities in setting priorities. It would be advisory, not prescriptive, and would have a monitoring role, but it would not provide a forum for considering individual services or specific local decisions. (Turnberg et al., 1996)

IPPR broadly supports the above objectives, but feels that there is a need for a national body to address not just what services the NHS provides, but how these finite resources are distributed fairly amongst the population. We therefore suggest that the National Health Commission should carry out its work in two stages: first setting out basic principles for defining the purpose and scope of the NHS; second considering ways of distributing resources fairly.

Stage one: what is the NHS for?

The commission would be asked to:

- build a broad consensus about the aims and values of the NHS;
- develop national guidelines for defining health care;
- review existing areas of uncertainty;
- define what ordinarily the NHS will not provide at a national level.

We now consider each of these in more detail.

To build a broad consensus about the aims and values of the NHS   The work of the commission would be informed by an analysis of the status quo, and the experience of other countries. It would redefine what the NHS is for, providing an opportunity for government to recommit itself to the best of the NHS's traditional principles, whilst also clarifying and strengthening its role for the future.

All of the stakeholders, including the public, need to be involved in resolving these issues to ensure that, wherever possible, genuine consensus is achieved ... It is important to remember that the commission or the public may disagree with the recommendations of this chapter, which represent our attempt to contribute to the debate about rationing. We are aware that, while the notion of citizenship has strong intellectual appeal and consistency, the consequences of this analysis may not always be in tune with popular opinion. Any mechanism for public involvement should provide enough time and information for an informed and meaningful debate before decisions are reached.

To develop national guidelines for defining health care   The commission should attempt to agree a broad but national definition of what constitutes health care as opposed to social care (Kennedy, 1988, p. 22).[1] Secondly, it would need to define what principles distinguish those treatments considered to be a matter for individual responsibility from those which qualify for public funding. The purpose of this aspect of the commission's work would be to provide strong and practical principles to help assess the appropriateness of new technologies in the future.

To review existing areas of uncertainty   A review of all the current services provided, we would suggest, is both unnecessary and undesirable. It is unnecessary because it is not worth reviewing the 95 per cent of treatments which have always and will always be provided. The bulk of purchasers' contracts stay the same from year to year, and changes tend to occur at the margins. It is these grey areas which the NHC would help to clarify. Why waste time and money considering the provision of treatments which are not contentious? The experience of New Zealand reveals how futile such an exercise can be.

In New Zealand the government set up a Core Services Committee, which was asked to define a core package of health-care services which should be available out of public funds. However, after much work, it was felt that the development of a detailed list along the lines of the Oregon initiative would be complex, time consuming, costly and divisive. More importantly, the committee found a lack of data on clinical effectiveness and a lack of public support, which would make implementation difficult. Instead, it took a cautious approach to defining the core, starting from the premise that the services which already existed were necessary and suitable, representing the values and priorities of past generations, but that changes may be made in the way in which resources are allocated. It also embarked on a public consultation exercise, in order to develop a broad ethical framework for health-care provision (Honnigsbaum et al., 1995).

This would appear to offer a pragmatic and achievable approach to rationing which might usefully be adopted in the UK. Thus, services currently available on the NHS would continue to be provided until there were sufficient proof of their ineffectiveness. In effect, all treatments currently provided would be considered innocent until proven guilty. Our concern is that the National Health Commission should attempt to resolve existing problems, not create new ones. If it reviewed all existing procedures, it might increase public suspicion and be perceived as a means to reduce rather than improve citizens' rights to health care. Our objective is not just to restore clarity and accountability to the NHS, but also to rebuild public confidence.

The commission would review those services which have been subject to exclusions or limitations and consider whether or not there are legitimate grounds for excluding them, and if so, on what basis. Such a review could result in some services being brought back into NHS provision, such as aspects of long-term care. The Royal College of Nursing has recommended that the costs of long-term care for the elderly should be divided into hotel costs (which should be the responsibility of the individual and means-tested) and health costs (which should qualify for NHS funding).[2]

To define what ordinarily the NHS will not provide at a national level As we noted, there is a very strong case against blanket exclusions in health care. We would therefore recommend that the commission should state what *ordinarily* the NHS will not provide and define the criteria by which exceptions would be justified. This would be a clarification of current practice: a recent study found that most exclusions by health authorities were not total, and that 'they contained provisos that individual cases of clinical need would be considered' (Moore, 1996). It would also ensure greater consistency in decision making.

Priority setting at the local level is taking place at the margins, and the issue has been not so much about whether the NHS should purchase a service or not, but whether it should buy more or a little less of a certain service; that is, marginal analysis (Wordsworth et al., 1996, p. 26). Ideally the commission would create a framework within which marginal analysis could take place, rather than define blanket exclusions.

Principles need to be established to guide the assessment of new techniques and procedures, and to promote evidence-based medicine and deal with evidence of ineffectiveness as it arises. This is the approach which is being followed in Spain, where a kind of guaranteed entitlement to health care was introduced in January 1995 (Cabasés, 1996). We should however observe closely how this approach works in practice before making assumptions about its potential for the UK.

Stage two: how can we distribute resources fairly?

The commission would be asked to:

- develop a code of practice that sets out criteria and procedures for how decisions about resource allocation should be made in the NHS, and by whom;
- explore the feasibility of creating prima facie rights to treatment;
- consider the wider issues of procedural rights in health care;
- suggest mechanisms for evaluation and appeal.

Code of practice   The code of practice would set out the fundamental principles of the NHS, and the criteria and procedures which should guide decisions about resource allocation, at both a macro- and a microlevel. The rest of the code would then be interpreted in the light of these principles.

Kennedy called for a code of practice to be developed back in 1977. He also suggested that this might form the basis of a prima facie right to health care, in the following manner:

> Once the Code of Practice was published, it would serve as the guide for conduct. If a doctor were challenged as to the propriety of a particular practice, he could say that he had complied with the Code. Compliance should, in my view, be regarded as prima facie evidence of lawfulness. If a court subsequently decided that something in the Code was unlawful, the doctor who had complied would not be subject to sanction. Conversely, non-compliance would be prima facie evidence of unlawfulness, and the doctor who had deviated from the Code would have the onus of proving that he had, in the event, behaved lawfully. (Kennedy, 1988, p. 410)

This would require a legal presumption that all citizens are entitled to receive NHS treatment and care if they have a clinical need for it. Departure from the code would not automatically amount to negligence, nor be proof of unsatisfactory care. The need for flexibility and clinical judgement means that health professionals would have to have the opportunity to offer a justification for their actions, and explain why they had not followed the code of practice. This approach would ensure the flexibility necessary in the field of health-care decision making, whilst shifting the balance of power in the direction of the citizen. Instead of a patient having to prove that a professional had acted unreasonably, the professional or authority would have to justify departing from the code. This would result in a significant shift of power, and greater transparency of the decision-making process.[3]

The code of practice would define what is and is not a legitimate reason to refuse to offer the desired treatment. We suggest that non-needs-based criteria would not be a legitimate reason for refusal to provide treatment for a patient. For example, under our proposals, infertility treatment could lawfully be refused if it were judged to be neither clinically effective, nor clinically necessary, nor cost effective. Refusal on the basis of social characteristics alone, such as the mother's marital status, or other non-needs-based criteria, or on the grounds of cost alone would give rise to a *prima facie* case of maladministration, and the professional or authority would have to justify their departure from the code. This would ensure that rights to health care arose from an individual's citizenship, and were not contingent on other factors. As Plant has argued:

> Rights do not arise out of a particular feature of a person's life, but rather are based upon the basic interests which we all share . . . Because basic rights arise out of our common interests, they are categorical in the sense that they are held on the basis of common humanity or citizenship and do not arise out of specific contracts. (1989, p. 3)

As with the Mental Health Act 1983, a code of practice can supplement statutory provision in positive and flexible ways. A framework of rights, set out in a code of practice, would ensure that each citizen has guaranteed access to a fair assessment procedure within the health service, based upon national principles which are open to public scrutiny and challenge. The idea of a *prima facie* right to health care is an exciting and radical one, which we feel merits serious consideration. However, it will be important to test the idea carefully before applying it in practice.

The commission would also have to find ways of resolving conflicting rights and claims. Kennedy has argued that, when utility and pragmatism collide with human rights, it is the former which must give way, otherwise 'the game is lost' (1988, p. 413). Clearly, this is an area which requires a wide and informed debate, involving all the stakeholders. It highlights the importance of creating a consensual basis for the code of practice. As with the Mental Health Act's Code of Practice, this code would be revised as good practice developed and difficulties were identified and resolved.

Mechanisms for evaluation and appeal   Mechanisms for monitoring, regulating and implementing the decisions made by health authorities would need to be created in order for the code of practice to make an impact. There is a range of options which the commission could explore:

- extending the powers of the health service commissioner;
- a tribunal system of appeal and review;
- a new Public Administration Commission.[4]

Any new rights in the field of health-care provision should be dealt with by a local, fast-track review system. A rights-based approach is intended to benefit patients, not lawyers. Only in the last resort should there be an appeal to the courts. Alderson and Montgomery have observed in their report on making decisions with young people: 'Legal action can be avoided if there is a clear framework for decision making, set out in a manner accessible to professionals, parents and young people. It is they who will implement good practice, not the lawyers who pick up the pieces if things go wrong' (1996, p. 65). The same applies to decisions involving adults. Arrangements between NHS purchasers and the providers of services could specify compliance with the code of practice as a contractual term. This already happens with services for the mentally ill (Code of practice, 1983). The new framework must be flexible, be open to review, and allow proper scope for professional judgement.

Wider issues of procedural rights in health care   Our approach to citizens' rights outlined above builds upon other work carried out by IPPR. Although this chapter is mainly concerned with creating fair procedures for rationing finite resources, this must be situated within a general framework of procedural fairness, including:

- a right to be heard;
- a right to consistency;
- a right to relevance;
- a right to unbiased decisions;
- a right to have reasons for decisions;
- rights of appeal and complaint.

What Could a National Health Commission Achieve?

A National Health Commission could aid the development of a fair and transparent decision-making process in the NHS which is open to public scrutiny and challenge. It will clarify areas of responsibility, and therefore accountability. It will also signify a new relationship between citizens and the public services which they pay for, transforming grateful but silent recipients of care into active and interested participants in deciding what that care should consist of. The decisions which are taken in the future may not always be perfect, but the proposals outlined above are aimed at making these decisions, and the people who take them, more legitimate in the eyes of the public. A clear code of practice is intended to strengthen public confidence and trust in the National Health Service, as a result of the clarity which it provides, and the consensual process by which it is designed.

In *Beyond the Citizen's Charter*, Ian Bynoe has developed a programme for public services based upon six principles (1996. p. v). These are:

- to guarantee fair treatment to those seeking or using public services;
- to meet the public's informed expectations of entitlement;
- to ensure that services are responsive to users and to encourage greater public involvement in planning services and holding them accountable;
- to render public service organizations more open in their dealings with users and the public;
- to improve public accountability by making audit and inspection more effective;
- to stress to citizens and users their respective responsibilities and the value of a co-operative approach.

It is hoped that the development of a code of practice by a broadly based National Health Commission would help to achieve these objectives.

What a National Health Commission would not do

- It would not attempt to define specifically a package of services which would be available on the NHS.
- It would not replace ministerial responsibility or accountability.
- It would not be prescriptive, or unduly inhibit local flexibility or appropriate clinical judgement and discretion.
- It would not solve all the problems of the NHS.

How the Proposals Might Work in Practice

In order to clarify how we envisage the code of practice working and with what effect, we have sketched out the following hypothesis.

Stage one

The commission redefines the purpose and role of the NHS, and concludes that existing services should continue to be provided. Following a review of services currently excluded by some health authorities, they recommend that some of these treatments should be generally available within the National Health Service, but define certain treatments which would not ordinarily be paid for out of public funds.

Stage two

The commission is then required to define how finite resources for health care should be distributed amongst the population, and develop the appropriate criteria by which such decisions should be made. The commission then defines the categories which would be acceptable reasons for refusal. These might include that the treatment was considered to be:

- not clinically effective;
- not cost effective;
- not appropriate to the objectives of the NHS.

Unacceptable reasons for refusal might include any non-needs-based characteristics, such as:

- social characteristics; for example, marital status, geography, age;
- cost alone;
- quality of life.

The above examples are not meant to be definitive, but are an indication of the kind of criteria the National Health Commission may develop. The consequences of this approach can only be assessed through the use of pilots, but for now, let us consider the likely impact of a code of practice by means of the following examples (see box 16.1).

Sarah, a child with Down's syndrome, requires a heart and lung transplant if she is to survive into adulthood. Although her parents feel that she has a clinical need for this treatment, Sarah has been refused even a clinical assessment for a transplant. Her family suspect that this decision has been made on the grounds that she is suffering from Down's syndrome, and that therefore her quality of life has been judged to be less than that of a 'normal' child. Under our proposed polices, Sarah and her family would be entitled to a reason for the decision by the relevant authority or clinician. The decision makers would have to demonstrate that they had complied with the code of practice. If it were found that the decision had been based not upon Sarah's clinical need, and that a judgement about her quality of life had been made, then this decision would constitute a *prima facie* case of maladministration. It would then be up to the clinician or authority to provide compelling reasons for departing from the code. If the defence failed, Sarah would then be entitled to a full clinical assessment and, if appropriate on clinical grounds, treatment and care for her condition.

Miss B has been refused NHS funding for fertility treatment by her health authority. (We are assuming that the National Health Commission does not identify fertility treatment as being one of the services not ordinarily provided by the NHS.) Miss B suspects that the decision in her case was made because she and her partner are not married, and therefore challenges the authority's decision. If it were found that the health authority ignored the code and refused treatment purely on the basis of Miss B's marital status, this would then constitute a *prima facie* case of maladministration. The onus would then be on the health authority to justify its departure from the code of practice. If it were unable to do so, then Miss B would be entitled to a clinical assessment of her need for fertility treatment.

Mr C is going bald at the age of 30. He has heard of a new treatment to alleviate the symptoms of baldness, and wishes his GP to prescribe it for him. When his GP refuses, Mr C challenges the decision. The treatment in question has been identified as one which is not ordinarily provided by the NHS, so the GP may be found to have complied with the code of practice. In this instance, it would therefore be up to Mr C to demonstrate that his case should be treated as an exception to the code.

Box 16.1 Examples

As these cases suggest, it is intended that the code be flexible, allowing doctors and managers to take account of individual needs, within a consensual framework which requires decision makers to be open about their reasons for refusing treatment. It is not about defining blanket exclusions, but about taking account of individuals and their clinical needs. It aims to provide all citizens with equal access to appropriate treatment. It is an attempt to encourage transparency and accountability in a meaningful way. Citizens will not only be able question the judgement of doctors and health authorities, but will also be entitled to answers and, if appropriate, the service which they have been denied.

The creation of a legal presumption that all citizens are entitled to receive appropriate treatment and care results in a significant shift in the balance of power. Instead of patients struggling to assert their right to treatment, the onus is placed on the decision maker to prove that they acted in accordance with the code of practice. This approach is currently being developed in EU law, where Commissioner Padraig Flynn has suggested that it be used in sexual discrimination cases (EC, 1988).

As Bynoe (1996) has pointed out, public-service provision can be distinguished from private commercial activity by the importance it attaches (or should attach) to the principle of open dealing with service users. Transparency offers a prospect of government without disguise or dissembling. Openness will assist the public to obtain the services to which they are entitled or which they need. The ability to exercise a right or a choice is dependent upon open and honest information.

Possible Objections to a Code of Practice

It is hoped that a National Health Commission would help to improve the quality and the legitimacy of decisions about resource allocation in the NHS. However, as New and Le Grand observe, a systematic process should have modest aims, as any attempt to 'solve' the grand problem of allocating resources in the NHS is likely to fall foul of one of the competing aims of the NHS (1996, p. 25). Below, we briefly consider issues and arguments which must be taken into account if the report's proposals are pursued.

'Eroding public confidence in the NHS'

Whether public confidence would be restored or eroded by the measures we recommend would depend heavily upon who implemented them, what their objectives were and, more importantly, how their objectives were perceived by the public. Nigel Lawson has admitted that Conservatives may be seen by the public as non-believers in the NHS (Dickson, 1996).

The work of the National Health Commission could be presented as a welcome reassertion of faith in the NHS, and provide government with an opportunity to recommit itself to the very best traditions of the National Health Service, whilst clarifying its role for the future. The code of practice could encourage open and accountable decision making in the health service, address public fear and suspicion about the reasons behind many medical decisions, and help to rebuild trust.

Conversely, the establishment of a commission, with a high-profile remit to look at what the NHS does and does not provide, could undermine public confidence in the NHS. New and Le Grand point out that any attempt to introduce rational rationing is fraught with danger because, although rationing has always occurred, the public do not perceive this to be the case (1996, p. 16).

To assess the validity of this concern, we must compare the risks of doing something against the risks of doing nothing. Public confidence in the NHS already appears to be ebbing. The development of new technologies is likely to raise new challenges and confusions in the future. Unchecked, health authorities are bound to continue to exclude various treatments; the media and the opposition parties are well aware of the publicity to be gained from such incidence, whether reporting is accurate or otherwise. The private health-care sector is likely to benefit from the increasing uncertainty about what the public can expect from the NHS.

Some have argued that if the lack of rationality and certainty inherent in most medical decisions is exposed, the public will lose confidence and trust in the NHS and its decision makers (Hunter, 1995). This argument tacitly approves continuing public ignorance and blind faith in the wisdom and omnipotence of doctors. Yet the public are more informed than ever about health and health care. Information is increasingly available through conventional media, new communications technologies and user groups. The genie is out of the bottle and this can only be a good thing.

The policy proposals outlined here are built on the premise that a mature democracy requires honesty and openness. Politicians and experts must enlist the support of the public in sharing the burden of difficult choices. That means restoring clarity about the purpose of the NHS, involving the public in these debates, and creating open and accountable decision-making mechanisms.

'A Trojan horse for cuts'

Although the aim of a National Health Commission would not be to define a discrete package of services available on the NHS, concerns have been expressed that this might be a consequence of the policy. If, over time, ineffective treatments were weeded out and new interventions were assessed according to national criteria, there might evolve a generic definition of what the NHS does and does not do. Some commentators, including Philip Hunt, Director of NAHAT [National Association of Health Authorities and Trusts], have argued that setting up a National Health Commission could be the 'thin end of the wedge' (Hunt, 1996).

Again, concerns about new policy proposals must be measured against concerns about current policy trends. If health authorities continue to exclude or limit services from their purchasing plans, a variety of packages of care will emerge by default. They will be on offer in different areas according to different criteria. National guidelines to govern the process would help to ensure transparency, consistency and a consensual basis for decisions.

'Rational rationing is impossible'

Some critics have insisted that any attempt at rational rationing is futile and that it would be impossible for a National Health Commission to reach a consensus on the difficult issues it would be asked to resolve (Hunt, 1996). Notably, David Hunter (1995) has argued that the best policy is to 'muddle through elegantly'. Much will depend upon the selection and remit of the commission, discussed below. The experience of West Glamorgan health authority is encouraging. It set up a local ethics committee, with members drawn from a number of different backgrounds including the local community, to subject its purchasing plans to ethical review (House of Commons Health Committee, 1995). The model is not dissimilar to that of the National Health Commission and is thought to have worked well.

Rationing can never be reduced to a precise mathematical formula such as QALYs. It will certainly not become rational overnight. But it should be possible to develop rationing policies that are socially acceptable and conform to standards of common justice. This is what a code of practice would attempt to do, by concentrating on how decisions are made, rather than just on outcomes, by opening up the process, and by requiring those invested with public money and trust to explain the reasons for their decisions.

'Increasing costs'

There would be costs associated with establishing and running a National Health Commission and an appeals procedure. However, there would also be savings. Resources are currently wasted as individual health authorities attempt to define what they should and should not purchase each year and on what grounds. The commission would absorb some of these functions and prevent costly replication.

A code of practice might help to reduce or manage costs in the future, as new technologies and therapies were subjected to more rational scrutiny. If clinically ineffective treatments were gradually removed from NHS provision, then savings could be substantial.

The costs of allowing people to challenge refusals to treat would be unknown until implemented, which is why it is important to move cautiously in this direction. We recommend piloting the process in order to assess the volume of appeals and cost implications. The pilots should be confined initially to local health authorities, before being extended to other decision makers, such as GP fundholders.

'Increasing bureaucracy'

Would the commission be just another layer of red tape? This would depend on how it was set up and with what objectives, on levels of public involvement and support, and on how much professional confidence the code of practice could command . . .

'Politically unattractive'

As we have noted, any attempt to grasp the rationing nettle is likely to be seen as an attack on the NHS. The strength of a rights-based approach to rationing is that it offers a positive approach to a contentious issue, and a way of building public, and therefore political, support. As Klein has observed, politicians will only act when the cost of doing nothing is greater than the cost of doing something. If health authorities continue to exclude different treatments according to different criteria, then pressures will mount for the government to act.

'Inhibiting clinical freedom'

Doctors are likely to reject anything that threatens to restrict their professional autonomy and judgement. Yet they do not want to be left alone to make difficult rationing decisions. A code of practice offers a way to balance these competing needs. It would define the limits to professional discretion, and provide clear principles and flexible criteria to guide the allocation of resources.

A role for local government?

IPPR has long argued that the role of purchasing health care should be passed to local authorities, who have a greater understanding of local needs, and possess powers over services necessary to the pursuit of health gain.[5] Others have argued that such a policy would lead to the fragmentation of the NHS, and to different levels and types of treatment between authorities. 'The universality and the principle of equity would be lost' (BMA, 1994).[6]

These criticisms cannot be dismissed lightly. However, a code of practice would provide a framework for local decision making and set limits on local diversity. A code of practice could therefore be part of a wider reform of local and regional government. It is beyond the scope of this chapter to assess the merits of local authority purchasing, but changes in the political and constitutional context are bound to affect citizens' and users' relationships with public services (Bynoe, 1996, p. 108).

The role of the private sector

Although the number of people with private health-care insurance has risen during the 1980s, the level of take-up in the UK is still low compared to that of other countries (Alton and Frydag, 1995). Would these proposals lead to an increased role for private health care and, if so, how would it affect the NHS?

One of the consequences of the recent NHS reforms has been the blurring of private and public roles, which has made it difficult for the private sector to market its services effectively. If it became clear what the NHS would not ordinarily provide, private health-care companies could then compete to provide these services. If, as we propose, the commission reviewed only those interventions which were new or had already been excluded by some health authorities, the impact on the NHS would be marginal. If the range of services available on the NHS gradually decreased and the private sector offered all the extras which the NHS excluded, this could result in a two-tier health service – which is one of the reasons why we caution against blanket exclusions.

As Bynoe has suggested, in the future the private health-care sector may find it necessary or desirable to adopt principles and procedural rights similar to those proposed here. A new form of 'public service contract' may be needed if public-service principles are to be reflected in private-sector provision, and the public interest protected (Bynoe, 1996, p. ix).

Summary

A code of practice, developed by a National Health Commission, has the potential to provide all citizens with greater clarity about what they can expect from the National Health Service, and greater transparency and consistency in the decision-making process. Throughout Europe health services are in a constant state of flux, and this points to the need to ensure that they are governed by strong and clear principles, and that finite resources are distributed through fair and accountable decision-making processes. The code of practice offers a map for navigation in an uncertain future.

As this approach focuses on the processes of decision making, rather than listing the specific services provided or excluded, it avoids problems of rigidity. It should be more capable of responding to developments in medical technology than a system based on substantive rights. The code should be kept under review, so that it remains appropriate and practicable.

It is neither possible nor desirable to control the future flow of information to citizens about their health status and the options available to them, but citizens can be empowered to make informed choices. It may be unnecessary to restrict the health-care menu except at the margins, but in any event the process of decision making can be opened up, providing opportunities for people to participate, both as individual patients in decisions about their own treatment and care, and as citizens in local and national decisions about how services can be distributed fairly.

Notes

1 The House of Commons Health Committee (1996) also called for a national definition of what constitutes health care as opposed to social care.
2 See evidence to House of Commons Health Committee (1996).
3 This idea was first suggeted to me during a conversation with Jonathan Montgomery, Lecturer in Law at Southampton University, and has since been developed in Alderson and Montgomery (1996), pp. 64–84.
4 As recommended by Bynoe (1996).
5 For a fuller discussion, see Harrison et al. (1991).
6 NAHAT have also argued strongly against these proposals, as has the Royal College of Nursing.

References

Alderson, P. and Montgomery, J. (1996) *Health Care Choices*. London: IPPR.

Alton, P. and Frydag, J. (1995) *UK Health Care: The Facts*. London: Petrol Press.

BMA (1994) Accountability in the NHS: a discussion paper. London: BMA.

BMA (1995) Rationing revisited. British Medical Association discussion paper. London: BMA.

Bynoe, I. (1996) *Beyond the Citizen's Charter*. London: IPPR.

Cabases, J. (1996) Guaranteed health care in Spain. In J. Lenaghan (ed.), *Hard Choices in Health Care*, London: BMJ.

Cambridge and Huntingdon Health Authority (1995) Challenging choices. 2nd annual report of the director of health policy and public health. Cambridge: CHHA.

Code of practice (1983) Code of practice issued under the Mental Health Act 1983. London: HMSO.

Dickson, N. (1996) Blood, sweat and tears. *Guardian*, 12 September.

EC (1988) Proposed directive on burden of proof in relation to equal pay and equal treatment of men and women. EC Directive.

Harrison, S., Hunter, D.J., Johnston, I., Nicholson, N., Thunhurst, C. and Wistow, G. (1991) *Health before Health Care*. London: IPPR.

Honnigsbaum, F., Calltrop, J., Ham, C. and Holmstrom, S. (1995) *Priority Setting Processes for Healthcare*. Oxford: Radcliffe Medical Press.

House of Commons Health Committee (1995) Priority setting in the NHS. *Purchasing*, vol. 1, annex 1. London: HMSO.

House of Commons Health Committee (1996) *House of Commons Health Committee Report on Long Term Care*. London: HMSO.

Hunt, P. (1996) The problem with guarantees in health care. In J. Lenaghan (ed.), *Hard Choices in Health Care*, London: BMJ.

Hunter, D.J. (1995) Rationing health care: the political perspective. *British Medical Bulletin*, 51(4), 876–84.

Kennedy, I. (1988) *Treat Me Right: Essays in Medical Law and Ethics*. Oxford: Clarendon Press.

Klein, R. (1995) *The New Politics of the NHS*. 3rd edn. London: Longman.

Lenaghan, J. (1996) *Rationing and Rights in Health Care*. London: IPPR.

McLean, S.M.A. (1996) Mapping the human genome: friend or foe. *Social Science and Medicine*, 39, 1221–7.

Montgomery, J. (1992) Rights to health and health care. In A. Coote (ed.), *The Welfare of Citizens*, London: IPPR/Rivers Oram.

Moore, W. (1996) *Hard Choices: Priority Setting in the NHS*. Birmingham: National Association of Health Authorities and Trusts.

National Institute for Assisted Conception (1995) *Report of Fourth National Survey of NHS Funding of Infertility Services*. London: National Institute for Assisted Conception.

New, B. and Le Grand, J. (1996) *Rationing in the NHS: Principles and Pragmatism*. London: King's Fund.

Plant, R. (1989) Can there be a right to health care? Occasional paper. University of Southampton. Institute for Health Policy Studies.

Redmayne, S. (1995) *Reshaping the NHS: Strategies and Priorities Amid Resource Allocation*. Birmingham: National Association of Health Authorities and Trusts.

Royal College of Physicians (1995) *Setting Priorities in the NHS: A Framework for Decision Making.* London: RCP.

Turnberg, L., Lessof, M. and Watkins, L. (1996) Physicians clarify their proposal for a national council for health care priorities. *British Medical Journal,* 312, 1609–10.

Wordsworth, S., Donaldson, C. and Scott, S. (1996) *Can We Afford the NHS?* London: IPPR.

Index